GW00357760

ALIEN DAYS

A Science Fiction Short Story Collection

THE DAYS SERIES, Vol II

Alexander Harrington
Andrew Myers
Anthony Regolino
Beth Frost
Charles E. Gannon
D. B. Crelia
David M. Hoenig
Dennis Mombauer
J.R. Handley & Corey Truax
Jason J. McCuiston
Juleigh Howard-Hobson
Killian Carter
Leigh Saunders
Lisa Fox
Mark Lynch
Mickey Ferron
Mitch Goth
PP Corcoran
Quincy J. Allen
S. K. Gregory
Vivian Kasley

Cover design & Interior formatting by The Gilded Quill
www.TheGildedQuill.co.uk

www.CastrumPress.com

Printed in the United Kingdom

First Printing: May 2019
Copyright ©2019 Castrum Press

ISBN-13 978-1-9123273-6-2

CONTENTS

THE SHANTI HEIST
by Killian Carter

– Reflections in the Rain –

Worry clawed at Eline's shoulders as her eyes swept over the empty restaurant. She had known Kibble most of her two decades on Claracia. He was the only person still alive she would trust with her life. The old hustler was too much of a loose cannon for Eline to consider him a father. He was a little too fond of Claracian firebrandy, but he had always acted as a mentor of sorts when she was growing up. The streets of Claracia were rarely kind to a kid, and one had to accept what help one could get.

Despite Kibble's vices, the old war veteran had always been quite the renaissance man. If one was to believe his often-outrageous stories, he had traveled most of the known galaxy, and he knew something about almost everything. He could strap together a bomb with nothing but a length of string and a handful of nails—the kind of guy accustomed to fixing things with elbow grease and spit.

As a jack of all trades, Kibble was many things, but despite his ever-inebriated state, he was never late. He's probably caught in traffic, she told herself, noting the clogged road outside the broad restaurant window. The storm had picked up, causing people to favor their ground vehicles. A Shanti male and Terran female holding hands hurried past the window, the rain soaking their expensive clothes in defiance of the large umbrella they shared.

Eline checked the serial interface gate strapped to her left arm for the time. She swiped the SIG's interface and scrolled through her messages until she found the one Kibble had sent earlier that evening.

Meet me at Olley's restaurant right away.

It wasn't like Kibble to be so short with his instructions either. He usually rambled and provided a list of unnecessary details, but Eline figured he was in a hurry. Kibble always seemed to have more plates spinning than any normal person could manage.

"Can I get you something else to drink while you wait for your friend, ma'am?" The new waiter appeared at Eline's side without so much as a sound, startling her. She stopped her hand halfway to the blaster on her hip, and shifted in her chair, pretending she was merely getting comfortable.

The half-melted ice cubes sloshed and clinked as he removed her otherwise empty glass from the table.

Eline hadn't realized she'd finished the beverage. It seemed she was becoming more like old Kibble than she cared to admit.

"Have you got anything sweeter?" She figured something a little more exciting would lighten her mood.

"The young ladies usually go for a sex on fire," he pointed to the drink on the cocktail menu.

"Is that an offer?" she joked.

"I didn't mean...I...ah," the waiter said, stumbling over his words. "I'll return with your drink in just a moment."

He scuttled away, his furry, black tail coiled nervously behind his back and his fluffy, pointed ears twitching.

The new guy was cute. He dressed well and had a nice ass, but he was too slight and skittish for Eline's tastes. Then again, it's been a while. She purred at the thought and considered asking him for his SIG number, but she quickly decided against it. Her way of life didn't leave much room for messing around.

Lightening flashed outside, drawing her attention back to the window, the rain pelting the pane like pebbles.

She regarded her semi-reflection in the glass, and a sharp pain stabbed at her heart as thunder rolled overhead. That was the problem with being an identical twin: When your counterpart died, you still saw her everywhere you looked.

Vale's face was a little narrower and she didn't have a scar under her fringe. As children, they had played tricks on their street-kin, one pretending to be the other, but as they grew into adolescence, their appearances deviated. Eline ended up a little heavier set, which was just as well since she ended up becoming something of a fighter. Vale, on the other hand, never needed to fight. She had a way with words—a way of wrapping everyone around her fingers. Well...almost everyone. Vale's wily words hadn't worked on Malek.

The heist had been going smoothly...too smooth in hindsight. It turned out to be a set up, and on the night they were to finish the job, Eline had watched in horror from a distance as Malek's golden-cloaked figure sliced Vale's legs off using some kinds of shimmering plasma blade. Kibble had to drag Eline away when she tried to get to her sister. That had happened over two years ago, and Vale's screams still haunted Eline most nights.

The knife in her heart twisted in response to the memory, and another fork of lightening momentarily lit the sky.

Eline had vowed to hunt Malek down, but the crime boss was well beyond her reach, at least for the time being.

Eline watched the seething, black clouds above the city. She and Vale had always dreamed of leaving Claracia, but the planet had crushed those hopes and then some.

She sighed and some of the pain evacuated with her breath, but a dull ache remained. It always did. She had just learned to mask the worst of it, at least until she caught a glimpse of herself—or Vale rather—in a mirror or window.

The new guy needs to hurry it up with that fucking drink.

Blue lights flashed in her reflection's eye, plucking her from her reverie. Her focus shifted to a scene across the street outside. A medicar had mounted the curb and a medic in a high-visibility raincoat started erecting a barrier.

She stood up too fast and the room spun. She grabbed the edge of the table and steadied herself, cursing her foolishness.

I shouldn't have drunk so much so quickly on an empty stomach.

Someone in Eline's position had to stay sharp. There was no telling when one needed to think fast or act faster.

She shook her head, bringing her mind back to the present and stumbled toward the restaurant entrance.

The door slammed behind her; the waiter's objections inaudible in the howling wind.

She kept low as relentless gusts whipped her hair and cloak about her face.

She shouldered her way through the raging maelstrom, dodging puddles as she skipped between traffic.

By the time she reached the other side of the road, a flickering holocast wall had been erected next to the medicar. The shimmering holocast blocked the view of whatever lay beyond, its blue strobe lights cutting a warning about an accident into the air. Ignoring the message, Eline stepped through the light-barrier, emerging on the other side to find two yellow-clad medics going about their jobs amidst a grizzly scene.

***

– Processing The Property –

Up close, Eline realized they weren't medics at all. They were city organ harvesters. The harvest chip inside whoever lay on the wet pavement had alerted the harvest organization to which he'd sold his body. Or the harvesters had been dispatched to call in a debt. Either way, Kibble fit the profile. If it really was him, he was dead for sure.

Both collectors had their backs turned to her as they worked, their slick, yellow rain cloaks flapping wildly in the wind and rattling with the rain.

The nearest harvester attended the corpse while the other wrestled in vain with an uncooperative sheet of tarpaulin that was probably meant to act as cover for the scene.

The harvester working on the body crouched over the subject, blocking the dead person's face, but the length of the body suggested that it could be Kibble. There was no way of telling for sure without getting a closer look.

Even just a little closer...She decided to go for it.

Rain hammered the concrete and the tarpaulin snapped and crackled in the wind.

Hopefully all this noise will mask me, she thought, taking a tentative step closer. One of the body's hands had something resembling a piece of torn fabric clutched in a tight fist. Could belong to the attacker.

One more step would have given Eline the view she needed, but the alcohol got the better of her, and she stumbled forward, sidestepping into a puddle while trying to regain purchase.

Shit! How many glasses did I have?

The nearest medic twisted onto his feet and pulled a mean-looking baton free from the folds of his cloak.

Eline caught a quick glance of a tranquilizer gun on his hip.

"I'm going to have to ask you to stand back, lady," his voice grumbled.

He bore down on Eline like a brick wall. Crouched over, the harvester had seemed so short and stubby, but standing upright, he loomed a head and a half taller than her and was built twice as wide. He stepped around a lamppost, allowing Eline a glimpse of the body. She gasped as the pain from earlier stabbed her in the heart again. It drove twice as deep as it had in the restaurant and felt thrice as cold.

The harvester waved his baton as a warning.

Eline lifted her open palms to show that she meant no harm, her head spinning with shock or brandy—or both. "I haven't touched anything. I just want to know what happened."

"Our job isn't to know what happened," the harvester spat, bearing his long canines. "Our job is to process the property."

"Can I see your I.D. at least?" she pressed, trying to look over his shoulder.

"Back through the barrier," he growled undeterred. "This body is Medexia property, hear?"

Eline took another step back toward the holo-barrier. She wasn't surprised that Kibble had flogged his parts. Organs were big business and Medexia were one of the biggest in the game.

The second harvester—a gangly male—finally untangled himself from the plastic and joined his colleague. "Need a hand, Butch?"

"No," Butch grinned. "Just caught this bitch snooping around. I got it under control."

Eline was certain she could take them both, but that would have risked drawing unwanted attention.

"Okay, I'm going," she said, stepping back into the blue light. The light shifted and shimmered before settling back into an opaque wall.

"Bother us again, and we'll harvest you instead!" Butch called after her.

"Asshole," she muttered. Waiting in the rain wasn't ideal, but it was better than getting nabbed by law enforcement in the middle of a fight. She leaned against the medicar, her ear twitching as she listened for any snippets of conversation between the harvesters.

"Leave the cover," Butch said. Eline could barely make him out over the howling wind and rain. "Help me process this bastard before the cops arrive."

Distant sirens rang out as if in answer.

"Fuck!" Butch shouted. Eline heard that part loud and clear. "This happens every damn time. Come on. If the cops get here before we're done, you're doing the paperwork."

Eline's head snapped around, her ears straining to work out the direction of the sirens. If the cops arrived before the harvesters left, she'd never know what Kibble had been holding as he died. She'd lose any clue to what had happened to the old-timer.

She slipped around the other side of the harvesting vehicle, taking care not to make too much noise in the water pooled around its wheels. She leaned out slowly, sneaking a peek at the harvesters as they worked. Both were crouched over the body now. One fished organs out of Kibble's cavity while the other sealed them in black and yellow boxes.

Maybe they'll leave in time for me to check Kibble over before the cops arrive.

The growing wail of sirens told her that was unlikely. The cops would be here in no time, and as frantically as the harvesters worked, it looked like they weren't going anywhere in a hurry.

Eline was about to pull back behind the vehicle when a strong gust snatched the plastic sheet from under a box. It whipped and crackled as the wind tossed it at Butch and his colleague, tangling them in a mess.

"Didn't I tell you to put it away!" Butch screamed from inside the tangle. "Get the damn thing off me!"

Before Eline knew what she had done, she was kneeling at Kibble's body while the dynamic duo tossed and turned under the yellow tarpaulin. She pried the fabric from Kibble's cold, stiff fingers. He'd been dead for a while.

"Hey!" Butch shouted. "What the hell did I tell you?"

Eline turned in time to see the harvester bring up his tranquilizer gun. She darted for an alleyway. A pop rang out behind and something bit the inside of her right thigh. She bounced of the alley wall and pushed herself onward.

"After her. She's fresh!" Butch ordered.

Eline drew her blaster and fired two shots at the harvesters, hoping it would deter them, before running through the darkness, slinking through shadows. She bounded over fences and took random turns in an effort to shake her pursuers. The energy quickly drained from her joints, and she leaned against a concrete wall concealed in the shadows of an overhanging fire-escape.

The tranquilizer is taking effect.

She checked where Butch had shot her and found a mere graze wound.

No dart. But how much of the drug made it into my system?

Judging by how heavy her legs were starting to feel, Eline guessed it was more than enough to do its job.

She quickly checked her SIG and found her vitals were all over the place.

Her numb fingers dipped into her utility belt pouch and fumbled several items, looking for her anti-sedative cocktail. Anyone with an ounce of sense always carried one. Organ theft was no rarity on Claracia, after all.

Eline forced her unresponsive fingers to wrap around the syringe and plunged it into the side of her neck, the injector hissing as it dispensed the medicine.

Within seconds, her head stopped spinning and feeling seeped back into her muscles. Her SIG showed her vital signs gradually returning to normal. She steadied her breath and took a moment to gather herself. She took the opportunity to check the piece of fabric she'd taken from Kibble's corpse.

She unfurled the sopping material, looking for some clue as to what it might be. It was thick and grey and frayed at the edges, like it had been torn from a uniform. She flipped it over and found part of a word: three characters that read 'orp'.

She swore under her breath. It didn't make any sense. She stuffed it into her pouch anyway with a mind to think more on it later.

Shouting rang out back the way she'd come. She vaguely recognized the voice as belonging to Butch.

First, I need to lose these suckers.

She tested her legs and they felt able to carry her weight once more. She pressed against the wall and forced her body back into a run, telling herself not to stop again, for if she did, she likely wouldn't start again.

***

– Always in an Alley –

Eline leaned against a dumpster, breathing heavily, the vile stench of rotting waste a tether to reality. The pain helped too. She focused on the burning in her thigh. Her legs rubbing together as she ran had upset the projectile wound, spreading a violent rash up her leg, but she was thankful for the pain, given that it was helping her stay conscious.

Somewhere along the way, she had lost sense of time and direction. Much to her relief, she had also lost Butch and his friend—or so Eline figured. They wouldn't have chased her so far, leaving their quarry unattended with the cops so close.

She hadn't even noticed the storm had passed. The rain had stopped, and the wind had died down, leaving a humid feel in the atmosphere.

Other than the background city drones and the sharp slush of water falling from overflowing pipes, the alleyway had a quiet quality to it...that still quietness that rushed in to fill the void left behind every storm.

Eline licked her dry lips and reached for the water canister on her belt. It was gone.

Shit! I must have knocked it off when I was trying to get away.

The sound of falling water drew her attention again. Her ears flicked as she traced the sound back to its source: a broken gutter running above a narrow side alley.

She sidestepped into the crevice and stood under the cracked half-pipe, allowing the crisp water to shower her sweat-matted hair and face. She drank as the cold liquid ran under her cloak collar, soaking her under-armor and shocking a little more awareness back into her body.

Eline finally shook her head, feeling more alert, but the beginnings of a headache pounded at the base of her skull.

Whatever the harvesters were slinging these days was strong. She walked back to the main alley and listened for any sign of the harvesters one more time before making her way back toward the streets.

She turned a sharp corner and a silver smear cut across her vision.

She barely evaded the blade, and only because she was already fighting to keep herself steady.

The cloaked attacker came at her again, moving with incredible speed. He swung his long knife in a wide arch.

Eline feigned a move to the right—the wound shooting pain through her right leg—and twisted left at the last second.

The knife struck the wall, jarring the wielder, and Eline drove her shoulder into his pelvis with what strength she had left. The attacker was much heavier than he appeared, but he stumbled back several steps, dropping his knife.

Eline lost her balance and rolled sideways into a small mound of trash.

The attacker reached down for his knife as Eline pulled her blaster from its holster.

The assassin darted toward her.

Eline pulled the trigger, taking him in the shoulder. The shot barely slowed his advance.

In a panic, she aimed for the head and repeatedly pulled the trigger until her power cell ran dry.

The cloaked foe lay inches away, smoke rising from what little remained of his head.

He must be wearing a tactical exoframe kit under that cloak. If that's the case, he's got to be a hired assassin, but who the hell would go to the trouble of paying someone to kill me?

Eline drew a deep breath and braced before climbing onto unsteady feet. She kept her blaster handy, just in case. Not that the weapon would be any use without time to recharge.

She tapped him with the tip of her boot to make sure he was dead. Satisfied, she kicked part of the cloak away and found that he was wearing a TEK, and quite an expensive looking one too. She noticed that the cloak had been torn on the inside. A row of black letters stared back at her and her heart leapt. She removed the fabric Kibble had been holding and threw it onto the attacker's cloak. It fit like a missing puzzle piece. Together the letters spelt Autonocorp. It took Eline a second to remember that Autonocorp was the umbrella organization that owned the company Vale and Kibble had tried to scam two years before—Malek's company.

Eline moved to the steaming mess that used to be a face. She kneeled down and pulled the tattered bits of hood out of the way with her free hand. She stifled a gasp. The assassin wasn't a Shanti or even a Terran. It was some kind of advanced attack bot. She touched the melted skin on its face. The flesh felt real, but the frame underneath was solid metal. She looked into a hole she'd blasted through its forehead. Looks like I got it in the primary processing unit.

She ran a quick scan to make sure the unit didn't have a backup processor, but her readings indicated that it was dead.

She had never encountered a machine that looked and moved so much like a person. Development of such technology had been forbidden by the Galactic Council after the robot uprising on Tlalox Prime half a century before. Malek and his company were waist deep in some serious shit. It explained a lot, but it didn't explain why the android had attacked her.

Maybe it was hiding in here after killing Kibble, and I stumbled on it by accident. Something told her that was wishful thinking. It was too much of a coincidence, and it didn't explain why it had killed Kibble.

Eline gave it some thought. She didn't know why, but it seemed like Malek wanted everyone who knew anything about the heist killed. He had already killed Vale, and now Kibble. Eline knew it was only a matter of time before they got her too.

Her ears twitched and her nose flared as footsteps approached from behind. She spun on her heel and brought up her blaster. The rifle butt snapped her head back and cast her consciousness into oblivion.

***
– Bars and Guards –

Eline came to, her face pressed against a cold, hard surface. She peeled herself from the floor, her brain slushing around inside her skull like a lump of meat in a bowl of soup.

She tentatively felt her broken nose as her eyes took time to adjust to the sudden light. It had set at an awkward angle and dried blood covered her nostril and mouth. She licked her lips and tasted the sharp tang of iron.

The haze gradually cleared, and Eline found herself sitting on the floor of a small barred cell. A concrete bed with no blankets lined one wall and a rusted bucket sat in a corner. Otherwise, the cell was empty, the walls bare.

She rocked forward onto her knees and fought down a wave of nausea as an icepick drove through the back of her skull. She controlled her breathing and waited for the agony to pass.

Eventually, she crawled to the bars. She used the metal rods to pull herself onto her feet, ignoring the objections in her joints and bones.

She looked through the gaps but couldn't see anything bar a dull concrete wall with a security camera pointed at her cell.

She was about to make her way back down to the floor when a bleep echoed in the hallway and a door slid open out of view to her right.

A heavy-set Shanti in a TEK appeared before the bars with a smug look on his face.

"So, the sweet angel is finally awake," he said grinning. "You should be thankful the boss warned me to keep my hands off you. A bit of a pity, really."

He licked his lips and blew her a kiss.

"What the hell do you want?" Eline spat.

"Hey now angel. That's no way to speak to a gent," he said with mock hurt. "I just thought we could get to know each other a little is all. Sorry about the nose, by the way. Nothing personal."

"What does Malek want with me?" she pressed.

The guard's eyes lit up and he quickly made a poor attempt to conceal his surprise before giving up. "You're a smart cookie, aren't you? No one's supposed to know Malek's here. What gave it away?"

"Answer my question first and I'll answer yours. What am I doing here?"

The guard shrugged. "Like I said, Malek wants to see you. That's all I know."

"Bah," she spat. "You expect me to believe that?"

"I honestly don't know. But I think it has something to do with missing that pretty sister of yours. He really liked that one, you know."

"What are you talking about?"

"Malek's a man of...principles," he said in an attempt to sound clever. "He treats his women well, but if they ever cross the line, he has to...take care of business. I reckon Malek regrets what happened, so he went after you. I could be wrong, but if I'm right, I wouldn't blame him."

The guard winked with a cocky grin and went back the way he came.

"Wait, I haven't finished with you," Eline croaked.

"No funny business!" he called back down the hallway, ignoring her. "I'll be watching you on the camera."

***

Eline was dozing off when she heard a clank and the sound of a lock scraping. A second later, a bleep registered in the hallway.

She immediately moved to the bars and found that the cell had been unlocked. She looked down at her feet and found a cardboard box sitting on a food tray.

Am I dreaming? she wondered.

She opened the box's lid, and her eyes lit up. Her clothes were folded inside next to her SIG and a piece of paper. She felt around inside the box and found her utility belt, holster, and blaster buried under her clothing. She set the box aside and read the note.

You have one chance to get out of here. Run and never come back. You'll find a map loaded onto your SIG. It'll show you the way out of the building. The guards will be distracted, but not for long, so don't delay. You'll also find enough credits in your pouch to leave Claracia and live a comfortable life until you figure something out. Go, and never look back.

Eline cocked her eyebrow and looked toward the open cell again. She suspected it was some kind of trick—a game to entertain Malek or perhaps the guard who had mocked her earlier in the day.

She regarded the box again with curiosity and figured she had nothing to lose. Eline fitted her under-armor and clothing and equipped her gear before cautiously making her way out of the cell, pulling the bars as gently as she could. She gritted her teeth hard when they shrieked regardless.

She looked both ways and was more than a little surprised when no one tried to stop her. Giving the security camera one last glance, she moved toward the exit. The door at the end of the hall was open. Eline poked her head into the adjoining corridor, expecting to find the guard, and she did. He sat against the far wall, a deep gash across his throat. Blood had pooled around him.

She followed the map until she reached the first T-junction. The sounds of distant gunfire popped off the corridor walls to her left. The map told her that the exit lay to the right. The fighting in the other direction sounded intense.

Who the hell let me out? And what kind of distraction were they talking about?

Eline looked to her right again. According to the map on her SIG, freedom was no more than three doors away. Eline took a step that way but hesitated. The guard had claimed that Malek was in the building. For some reason, the crime boss wanted to see her in person.

No, she thought, changing direction. I'm going to give Malek exactly what he wants. He's going to meet me in person. And I'll be the last person he ever sees.

***

– Mass Madness –

She sneaked into the loading bay, staying low so as not to be seen, and holding her blaster tight. The fighting seemed heaviest near the loading bay doors which were no more than thirty yards away.

Eline ran to a stack of crates and peeked between the cracks. Among the guards defending the loading bay, with his back against her, stood the person she was looking for.

Eline would have noticed that golden cloak anywhere. Malek!

He was still too far away. She sprinted from behind the crates and sidled up to a broad support beam, edging her way closer to the man who killed her sister.

She ran from the support toward a piece of machinery resembling a generator. A bolt of plasma sailed overhead, missing her by inches. She rolled to cover and leaned against the generator's metal plating.

Malek was less than a dozen yards away now. Eline took a deep breath and leaned out, ready to fire.

He was no longer there.

"Looking for me?"

Eline turned and jerked her head sideways as a meat cleaver struck the generator's control panel. Malek caught her right wrist with an off-hand strike using the blade's flat edge, knocking the blaster from her hand.

The golden-cloaked Malek wore a deep hood, masking his features in shadow, but Eline could feel him peering into her eyes.

"I've been looking forward to meeting you, Eline," the crime boss hissed with unconcealed excitement. "You know, Vale told me you were a much better fighter that she was, and I'm glad to see the lying bitch told the truth some of the time."

He swiped at Eline's shoulder and she rushed him head on, grappling his chest and limiting his reach. They tumbled to the ground and wrestled for a time before Malek got the upper hand. His strength was impressive. Even if Eline had been at her best, she knew he still would have beaten her.

What was I thinking? Her heart beat furiously in panic.

Worry must have flashed across her face, for Malek released a howl of delight.

Eline thought she could see his canines flash in a wild grin, but she couldn't be certain.

Malek had one of her arms pinned with his knee and the sleeve of the other arm held with his hand. Eline knew that she could free her hand with a quick jerk.

And then what?

The idea occurred to her suddenly. It seemed desperate, but it also felt right. If she was going to die, she was going to look her killer in the eyes as he performed the deed. She pulled with all her might and her sleeve slid free. Her hand snapped up and pulled away Malek's hood.

Eline almost choked, for the waiter from Olly's restaurant stared back at her. He pinned her arm back down with ease and giggled.

"You're Malek?" She could barely form the question.

"Surprise!" he exclaimed with a crazed shriek.

"I thought you didn't let people see your face," Eline muttered, trying to buy herself time. For what, she didn't know.

Malek chuckled again. "I don't mind people seeing my face just before I kill them. In fact, I prefer it!"

"What do you want with me?" Eline cried out. "Why couldn't you just let me be?"

"You know too much." His eyes took on a crazed look. "And those who know too much must die!"

Malek lifted the cleaver into the air and the blade came down.

A bolt of plasma smashed into Malek's head, forcing him off Eline and onto the floor. He screamed and writhed as flames engulfed his black hair. Someone in a TEK stepped over Eline and moved toward Malek, firing at him several more times.

Eline climbed onto wobbly knees, and her savior spun to face her. Eline almost passed out.

"What the hell are you doing here, Eline? You never listen!"

Eline was so stunned, she couldn't speak, let alone move. Her ears rang and her head spun. As much as she moved her mouth, words refused to form.

"You were supposed to go, dammit!"

An endless flood of questions saturated Eline's brain. So many tried to escape at once that she only managed to squeak one word. "Vale?"

A shot fired behind Vale and a hole exploded in her breastplate.

Vale looked down at the gaping wound in disbelief and crumbled to the floor.

Malek stood behind her laughing, a plasma rifle in his arms.

"No!" Eline screamed as she ran for Vale.

A second blast of plasma struck Eline's left shoulder, the force throwing her to the ground. She choked on the stench of burning flesh as acrid smoke stung her eyes. The pain threatened to engulf her soul entirely, but Eline caught sight of Vale's twitching fingers. The burning plasma wound paled in comparison to the resulting anger swelling within her.

Fury, hatred, and spite combined and lent Eline the strength to roll onto her side. Her blaster lay on the ground, just out of reach.

Malek stood with one foot on Vale's neck, his warped eyeballs—baked into his half-melted face—staring from odd angles. He aimed the plasma rifle at Vale's head, his teeth somehow still managing to grin without a mouth.

Eline kicked her legs out, and her hand gripped her blaster. She emptied the battery into Malek, and he fell on top of Vale, a gaping maw where his face should have been.

Eline cast her spent blaster aside and pulled herself toward Vale with her only working arm.

She reached out for her sister with little regard for Malek and what threat he might still pose. The world could have burned for all Eline cared, if only she could look into Vale's eyes one more time.

She pulled her sister's head around to face hers and was relieved to find life still shining in them.

"It's okay, Vale," Eline said desperately, tears clouding her vision. She wiped them away, not wanting to miss one more second with her sister. "Malek's dead, sis. Help will be here soon."

Vale's lips moved but barely made a sound. Eline had to lean closer to hear her words.

"Go be free, Eline," Vale whispered.

"But I can't be free without you, sis."

"Yes...you can." Vale's words came in gurgles and rasps. "Leave...this place. Be...free. For me."

The life in Vales eyes waned and Eline cried out, leaning her forehead against her sister's cheek and inhaled the scent she so dearly missed...the smell of home. "Don't you dare leave me again, Vale."

"I never...left," Vales words were barely audible. "I watched you...from...the shadows."

Vale closed her eyes.

"Open your eyes, Vale! Don't go to sleep! Help is on its way!" Something deep inside told Eline it was pointless.

Vale's eyes suddenly opened wide and for an instant they were full of recognition and life. "I love you...Eline."

"I love you too."

The light suddenly fluttered out as the last dregs of life left Vale.

Eline huddled closer, sobbing into her sister's chest, just as she'd done so many times when growing up. Vale had protected her from the brutality of Claracia, and

Eline couldn't even return the favor. She had a second chance to save her sister, and instead her sister had saved her.

As Eline's fingers brushed Vale's hair aside, something pulled at her ankle, snatching her away.

"No!" she screamed. "Vale!"

Eline repeatedly screamed her sister's name, the words drowned out by the gunfire as she was dragged toward the hangar doors.

She looked back to find that she was being dragged by an Aegis warrior. The Aegis dragged Eline with one hand while fighting her way through the throng with the other. All the while, Eline struggled in vain to break free.

The Aegis dragged Eline up a ramp and into the back of an assault vehicle.

Eline kicked the armored warrior, but it carried on without so much as a glance in her direction, its vice-like grip holding tight.

The Aegis finally dropped her on the deck and stepped away.

"Relax, child," a female Shanti voice demanded in sultry tones. The Aegis pulled a lever on her neck, and her helmet retracted into the TEK's collar, revealing one of the most beautiful Shanti Eline had ever seen.

"To hell with relaxing," Eline objected, wincing in pain. "That bastard just killed my sister."

"There's nothing you can do about that now," the Shanti snapped.

"Who do you think—"

"Stay here," the Shanti ordered, as if Eline had a choice.

The Aegis snapped her helmet back into place and charged back down the ramp, closing the vehicle bay doors behind her so Eline couldn't leave. Not that Eline could have gone anywhere even if she'd a mind to. She had spent every remaining ounce of her strength to get to Vale, and it still wasn't enough. It never was.

✳✳✳

– X. Clariacia Farewell –

Eline held onto the rail as she watched Vale's face through the suspension chamber's glass cover. Aegis Inx had returned to the loading bay to retrieve Vale's body.

Their dream had come true, after all. They had left Claracia together, but one of them had left as a corpse.

"We were supposed to leave Claracia together," she muttered under her breath. "But not like this."

Eline tried to force a smile to match the one on Vale's face—on her true reflection. At least she's at peace now.

Eline cocked her eyebrow. She realized that Vale wasn't just smiling. She wore that knowing half-smirk that told everyone she got her way. Vale had seen to it that Eline was free, but Eline knew that it was Vale who had achieved true freedom.

The suspension room door hissed and Eline turned her head to see Inx enter.

"I don't mean to disturb you, child," Aegis Inx said. "However, we're getting ready to enter the G-Gate and need to lock this suspension room down."

"Of course," Eline said, wincing as she let go of the rails.

"Is everything okay with your wound?" Inx asked, walking toward her.

"The ship doctor said I'll need another round of regen therapy, but my next session is tomorrow."

"I see," Inx said, joining Eline at the rail. "Your sister was very special, you know."

"I know," Eline whispered. "I know it was for my own good, but I can't believe Kibble lied to me like that."

"They had to make you believe Vale was dead. It was the only way she could protect you. Otherwise you would try to return to her."

"I understand that, but it still hurts."

"Most wounds heal in time," Inx explained like an old sage.

"I spent the last two years believing she'd died because of something I'd done, and I got her killed in the end anyway."

"Something tells me that Vale wouldn't see it that way," Inx said with a smile— the first Eline had seen from the Aegis since meeting her.

"And to think I believed Vale and Kibble about it being a heist."

"It was part of their cover," Inx explained. "Though I suppose you could call the operation a kind of prolonged heist. Kibble and Vale lasted all this time under cover and they stole the most valuable thing in the galaxy. Information."

"I guess you're right." Eline sighed. "I just can't believe that she stuck with the operation the entire time, even after Malek cut off her legs. I know he gave her robotics, but still...What a psychopath."

"Like I said, Vale was special." Inx looked back at the only other suspension chamber in the room and Eline followed her gaze. "I'm sorry that they have to share the same suspension room, but this rig is low on space." She gestured to the Aegi ship.

"That's okay." Eline limped to the opposite rail and ran her eyes over Malek's remains. "I'm just sorry you didn't manage to get the real Malek. It's incredible how real the android looked."

"We'll track him down in time. Thanks to Vale, we uncovered his operation and closed down several of his factories. We also have evidence that he has broken several major laws. That'll give the Galactic Council the power they need to take him down. Your sister didn't just save your life, she saved the lives of millions."

"I know," Eline muttered. "I'd hate to know what would happen if he'd succeeded in building his android army."

"That's what the Aegi Order is for...to stop things like that from happening."

"What happens now?" Eline asked.

"Well, I was going to save it for later, but since you've brought it up...part of the deal was getting you safe passage off Claracia and enough money to have a decent life elsewhere. She knew you would never be safe as long as you were together. We're still happy to honor that arrangement. However, Vale was going to join the Aegi Order at the close of the operation." Inx swallowed. It was the first time Eline had seen her so uncomfortable. "I understand it might appear insensitive at this time, but the position is yours if you want it."

Eline's eyes went wide. "You want me to join the Aegi order?" She had to stifle a nervous giggle.

"Don't underestimate yourself, child," Inx said with a sense of pride. "You're a Shanti and we Shanti are strong. You've survived on Claracia all these years, and you've often done so on your own. You're a survivor. And the Order values that above all else because it is an Aegis's job to survive."

Eline was stunned to silence.

Inx offered her a curt nod. "Give it some thought."

"I'll do it," Eline said without hesitation.

Inx furrowed her brow. "Are you certain?"

"I couldn't be more certain." More than anything else in the universe, Eline wanted to hunt down and kill Malek. Becoming an Aegis seemed like the quickest route to achieving that goal.

"Very well then. We'll make preparations as soon as it is appropriate." Inx gestured to the doors. "Shall we?"

Eline hesitated. "Can I have one more minute?"

"Of course," Inx said. "One more minute."

The suspension room doors hissed again as the Aegis left Eline alone. She limped back to Vale's suspension chamber to speak with her sister one last time.

"See you again one day, sis." She turned away and hobbled toward the exit, thinking about Kibble, and Vale, and what they had achieved. Eline was beyond sad to lose the two people she'd cared about most, but she liked to think that she would swap stories with them again one day. When that day came, they could laugh about how they had pulled off one hell of a Shanti Heist.

###

About Killian Carter

KILLIAN CARTER WAS BORN WITH a blaster in his hand (it was a complicated delivery) and grew up hunting cyborg aliens and extra-dimensional beings. He specializes in tracking and capturing space-ware-vampire-ninjas aka the TRAPPIST-1e leprechaun. Killian is well versed in the use of advanced photon weaponry, intergalactic quantum spacecraft, and a wide range of technology the government doesn't want you to know about. On weekends, Killian likes to kick back with a space-beer and a top-secret data crystal he stole from the REDACTED archives. Killian is rarely seen without his automaton chihuahua, Tequilabot.

Warning: Killian will not hunt endangered Centauri unicorns or nebula pixies for you, so please don't ask. If you insist on asking anyway, he will set his robot chihuahua on you.

Killian is an active member of SFWA

Connect with Killian here:
www.castrumpress.com/authors/killian-carter

ANTITHESIS
By Mitch Goth

The wind of the Maltese summer whipped at Doctor Jonah Edwin's straw sunhat, carrying the salty aroma of the Mediterranean with it. Despite the leisure his hat suggested, he was all business from the neck down. He donned a navy suit and tie that hadn't seen daylight since the last wedding he attended. Although he knew little about his mission, the brief stated, 'dress appropriately.' He tried.

As if the beaming sun wasn't bad enough, his directions stuck him on a baking, black tarmac, awaiting instruction. Every so often, a jet liner belched wind his way, offering minor reprieve. And, he killed time watching those rainbow-colored vacation planes disappear into the cloudless sky.

"Doctor Edwin," a familiar voice called. Colonel Arthur Wilberforce, Jonah's tall and physically foreboding chaperone appeared behind him. His simple military fatigues served as a stark contrast to Jonah's tailored suit. "We're ready to go."

"Right, yes." Jonah nodded, and followed the Colonel in his brisk walk toward a line of unassuming hangars at the airport's edge. "You know, you have yet to explain where we're going." Jonah scratched at his stubby short hair beneath his hat.

Colonel Wilberforce glanced back; his bald scalp resplendent against the sunshine. "Our rendezvous has a debrief scheduled on the flight. Be patient, Doctor."

Jonah just nodded and hurried along. Confusion wasn't new to him. As a psychoanalyst, it was pivotal to his job. Of course, remedying said confusion was just as pivotal. To him, that part wasn't going so well.

It wasn't unheard of for the government to seek psychologists for contract work, so Jonah began more flattered than flustered. But Wilberforce wasn't much of a talker, and they'd had a long journey from New York City. Supposedly, they needed him for something top secret. Apparently, too secret even for him to know.

Wilberforce led him to the last hangar in the cluster, which housed just one airplane. Placed dead center inside, a near-windowless, olive-toned jet with an oblong fuselage faced out into the sunlight. Its sleek, wing-embedded engines hummed, ready to move.

Several stone-faced MPs ushered them to a mobile staircase at the front of the aircraft. Jonah searched their uniforms for any patch or insignia. They didn't look like Maltese forces, although he didn't know what Maltese forces looked like. To Jonah, it was odd enough to even have government work take him international, much less this international.

On his first step into the aircraft, Doctor Edwin stopped short. It looked like some kind of sonar jet, filled with computers almost as old as him. Every metal surfaced was scratched and tattered. The lights above had gone yellow with decades of age, and a few had died out.

"Doctor Edwin," Wilberforce called to him again. "Our debrief is in the back."

"Right." Jonah meandered along. "So, um, how old is this airplane?"

"You're asking the wrong person."

"Figures." Jonah sighed. "You're not concerned about this?" he glanced a few active monitors. They beamed the neon green lettering that came with the earliest of computer designs.

"If this plane weren't safe to fly, it wouldn't have made the flight to this airport." Wilberforce reached a small seating area in the tail and greeted a lively voice. He sat down in the nearest seat available, revealing Jonah to the wide, bright grin in the aisle.

"And you must be Doctor Jonah Edwin, no?" a short man in simplistic military fatigues approached Jonah, an unmistakable Australian accent cascading from his lips. A warm grin widened across his tanned face. His long, blonde curls were undone and untouched, far from any military leader Jonah had ever seen.

"Y-yes, that's me." Jonah nodded, giving another nervous glance around the plane. "Can tell me how old this plane is?"

The man nodded. "Why, yes, I can." He extended a hand. "Former Wing Commander Rupert Roundy, pleasure to meet ya."

Jonah removed his hat shook the man's hand. "Former Wing Commander?"

Rupert led him to a pair of seats at the very back, facing each other. "Yes, yes." He sat down and gestured to the empty seat. "I understand you have lots of questions."

"Plenty," Wilberforce commented.

"Well, I'm excited to hear them. Our flight isn't long, though, so spit 'em out while you can."

"Okay." Jonah sat down across from Roundy, beside one of the few tiny windows. "So, what's this plane's story? If you don't mind starting there."

"Ah, yes, they commissioned her back in the seventies and she served well for maritime reconnaissance until a few years ago, when my firm scooped her up." Roundy knocked against the wall. "She's seen a lot, but she's a trooper."

"She's a trooper that's pushing fifty." Jonah stirred in his seat.

"Don't sweat the design, my friend. This jet design has seen, and since subverted its share of failures, leaving only the timeless innovations."

"Failures?" Jonah felt sweat form on his forehead as the plane lurched forward.

"Don't scare the doctor, Roundy," Wilberforce said. "And you said it yourself, this flight is short. Stick to specifics."

Roundy snickered. "Come now, Arthur, I'm only answering the man's questions. You know, being a gracious host." He eyed Jonah with a straight, unblinking stare. "Yes, failures."

Jonah watched the lines on the tarmac drift by as the jet eased its way to the runway. "Care to share the story? Before we take off would be great. I need decide if I want to jump out beforehand."

"You wouldn't make it to the door," Wilberforce said, not peering up from his version of an in-flight magazine, a computer manual that looked as old as the plane.

Roundy's intense gaze drew Jonah's attention back in, and he began his story, "When they first manufactured these old birds, they were commercial liners. But, not just any commercial liner. These were the first anyone made." He touched a finger to his ear. "Relatively quiet jet engines, and the first passenger planes to have pressurized cabins. Hypoxia? Never heard of it." Roundy smirked.

"Uh-huh." Jonah's eyes turned out the window again, watching the plane slow to a stop at the end of the runway. His gut sunk as the jets roared.

"Now, this was in the fifties," Roundy explained. "To folks back then, these were game-changers. Alas, they didn't yet understand the science behind what they were doing." He clicked his tongue. "How could they, right? Perils of being the first to do anything. The Marie Curie effect, we may say.

"They never fully grasped the effects pressurizing and depressurizing a plane of that era would have. And, not long after they hit the skies..." he made an explosive gesture with his hands, followed by a toothy smile as the heave of departure hit. Roundy let the moment sit while the plane bolted down the runway and lifted. "They called it the Comet. And, sure enough, they went through the sky in flames."

Jonah couldn't hide the terror on his face. Although, it probably helped that he glued himself to the window, watching for any sign they may careen into the Mediterranean. This guy needed to debrief him on his government contract, but all he did was scare Jonah shitless. "So, uh, why are we flying on a Comet, then?"

"Oh, this isn't a Comet," Roundy said. "This is a Nimrod."

"A what?" Jonah stifled a snicker. "A Nimrod?"

"Yes?" Roundy showed a bemused look before craning around to Wilberforce. "Where d'you find this gent?"

Wilberforce glanced up from his light reading. "The States, where nimrod means dumbass."

Roundy shrugged and turned back around. "Well, I can see the humor now."

"Let me see if I got this," Jonah said. "The 'airplane of the future' burns into oblivion and kills a bunch of people. Then, they give the rest to the military to soup up and name after a moron. Now, we're flying in one of those souped up morons, going somewhere you have yet to tell me anything about. Is that right?"

"I mean, that's a wee bit of a simplification, but yeah." Roundy nodded. "And we did far more than 'soup up' these jets. They're damned near unrecognizable now, much safer. And, if that 'airplane of the future' had never burst into bits, it would've been another somewhere else. Sometimes tragedy is needed to make a little progress."

Jonah sighed. "Is that your way of telling me I'm flying to my death for the sake of progress?"

"Heavens, no." Roundy chortled. "Don't be so gloomy, you serve an important purpose here. Though, I'm afraid there have been no authorized briefs regarding this project. I can say that what we're taking you to is of the utmost secrecy."

"Come on, the feds back home already gave me the 'if you talk, we'll make you disappear' lecture," Jonah tried his best to speed things along. His curiosity beat at him harder the further the plane took them out to sea. "I already know I shouldn't be talking, but I have yet to hear anything about what I shouldn't be talking about. Feel free to skip to that part." The plane lurched under turbulence and Jonah nearly leapt out of his skin.

Roundy leaned in, an ear-to-ear grin on his face. "Aliens."

For a moment, Jonah just observed the strange Australian's expression. Humorous, a little silly, but not without seriousness. Jonah scoffed. "Okay, now I am upset I didn't leap out before takeoff."

"Come now, Doctor Edwin. If anyone would ever tell the truth about alien life, would it not be some international government officials and contractors? We are the people most invested in keeping crazy sounding shit like that behind a long, heavy curtain. Welcome to the other side of the curtain, mate."

Jonah shook his head. "For me to believe that, I'd have to believe I would serve a purpose in it. I'm a psychologist, Mr. Roundy."

"You're a psychoanalyst," Roundy corrected. "Beyond that, you're a specialist in abnormal psychology, neurodivergent psychology, psychology outside all perceived normality. What awaits you at the end of this plane ride is the pure opposite of normality. But you have a purpose, I promise."

The plane lurched again, and a voice came over a raspy, crackling speaker, "We're beginning final descent, belts fastened please."

Wilberforce tossed his computer manual aside. "I said you should have started the debrief sooner, Roundy."

Roundy rolled his eyes. "Descent has only just begun; I've got some minutes to clear it up. I've done a lot more with a lot less, I assure you."

Back to staring out the window, Jonah searched the sapphire seas for any sign of where they were landing. Nothing but open water, although his view was far from expansive.

"Penny for your thoughts, doctor?" Roundy inquired.

"Aliens." Jonah shot a glance to Roundy. He had a point before. Everyone he'd met seemed like exactly the kinds of people who would have the job of keeping aliens secret, keeping everything behind the curtain. But, why did he need to be behind it too? "How long have you all known?"

"Not long. An unknown vessel landed in the waters north of Norway five months ago. Ever since then, it's just been a whirlwind of information, trial and error, discovery, problems, the whole lot. I've been on this for three months; things are moving quick. But there remains a lot of aspects lagging behind, issues that require specialists like you."

"I hope you know I'm not a translator," Jonah replied.

"We're beyond the need for translators, my friend."

"You found a way to communicate with alien life already?"

Roundy shook his head. "They did."

Jonah wasn't sure why that answer bothered him so much, but it did. He wanted to ask one of the million more questions swirling in his mind, but couldn't find the words. Roundy appeared to notice his unease, smile fading and bright eyes turning cold and analytical.

"Don't sweat your purpose here, mate," Roundy said. "You are pivotal, and you 're no interpreter or linguist. We just need you to do what you do."

"You need me to do what I do?" Jonah took the first moment in ages to think critically about what he did. The titles were obvious, but they only led so far. He excelled in getting the non-verbal to verbalize, the liars to speak truth, and the secretive to show all. But bringing aliens into the mix threw off everything. How could he even take the concept seriously? "I'm...I'm lost."

"Understatement of the year," Wilberforce chimed in.

"They can speak," Roundy said. "But, they're not. We're not sure why, but they seem rather...perturbed."

Jonah couldn't help but chuckle. "Wouldn't you be? I mean, this could be the equivalent of rebellious teenagers stealing their dad's UFO and crashing it into a tree. Except, the tree is this planet, and the tree has now taken them hostage. Sounds perturbing to me."

A wide grin returned to Roundy's face. "See? You'll do just fine." He peered out the window. "And you've found your voice none too soon."

Even though from the window it seemed like the plane was setting down straight into the sea, the familiar jolt of dry land came through. Tires squeaked across runway, bringing momentary ease to Jonah's uncertain soul. He craned his neck to see what they'd landed on. From any window, they'd stopped in the middle of the water.

"Off we go then." Roundy hopped from his seat. Wilberforce was at his heels, albeit with less enthusiasm.

"You can't sit back there forever, Doctor Edwin," Wilberforce called back.

With a strange mix of hesitance and eager curiosity inside him, Jonah pulled himself up and made his way down to the door. As soon as it opened, and fresh daylight came in, a new pit opened in his stomach. There was a strange, new world waiting for him, and supposedly it had aliens in it.

In the end, curiosity about where they'd landed drove him through his nerves and to the edge of the plane door. The view on the outside nearly made him jump back, as he'd walked into a surreal dream. Something was there, but not anything he'd seen before. Roundy and Wilberforce stood at the bottom of the mobile steps, tapping their shoes against a runway made of translucent asphalt.

Descending the steps, the peculiar surface showed its true self. Rather than translucence, the substance appeared to mimic the color of the surrounding waters, even revealing light lines flowing across in kind with the waves. Jonah stepped down onto the watery runway, only to land on a surface as hard as steel. And yet, the false waves kept flowing beneath his feet.

Further down the camouflaged runway stood large, blocky buildings, all made of the same ocean-mimicking material. This whole complex, whatever it was, blended in perfectly with the water until they were right there in front of it.

"Can we go?" Wilberforce asked. Roundy gave a shrug and gestured for Jonah to follow.

The two led the way toward the master complex. Before they reached the first building off the runway, two doors swung open from the blue illusion, and lines of stomping military uniforms spilled out.

After first noticing their large guns, Jonah eyed the bright flag patches on all their uniforms. All were red, white, and blue, but they weren't all the same. He took a moment to piece it together, and when he did, he wasn't sure he believed it. "Are these, French and Russian soldiers?" he studied them as they stood like statues beside the door. The strangest welcoming party he'd ever seen.

"Indeed." Roundy nodded. "Did you think this wasn't an international affair?" he gestured to everything around them. "Everyone who is everyone has their hand in this pie. Who do you think built this place?"

Jonah furrowed his brow. "Aliens?"

Roundy pointed to a soldier with a Russian flag patch. The solider didn't so much as glance at them.

"Great, I guess." Jonah sighed. This new world threw a lot at him and gave him no time to process.

True to that form, a long, white lab coat appeared at the doorway. A tall, slim, dark-skinned man with sweat on his brow and a tired expression greeted them with a weak smile. "I'm happy to see you all made it," the man spoke with a slow accent Jonah couldn't pinpoint. Unfortunately, he didn't have a flag patch to go off. "Doctor Jonah Edwin, we're happy that you are here." He extended a hand. "I am Doctor Femi Nagobi, the director."

After a puzzled moment, Jonah shook his hand and tried to return the smile. "Hi. What is happening?"

Doctor Nagobi shot a look to Roundy. "I told you to debrief him on the flight, Rupert."

"He only got halfway," Wilberforce said.

"I gave him the gist." Roundy shrugged.

"Follow me then, all of you." Doctor Nagobi moved into the watery building. Jonah wanted to hesitate, but he had no time before Roundy and Wilberforce nudged him on. The lines of soldiers followed them in and maintained post by the doors as they shut.

Despite how unreal the whole complex appeared on the outside, everything inside was normal. White tile floors, whitewashed walls, and white paneled ceilings. It was like walking through a hospital, a militarily camouflaged hospital in the middle of the sea, that housed aliens.

"How long did this place take to build?" Jonah asked, recalling the short timeline Roundy explained.

"Much of it came pre-built," Nagobi explained, only peering back for a moment. "It is a mobile base, can move in pieces almost anywhere."

"God bless those Russians." Jonah laughed.

"I don't know if they ever expected to use it for this purpose. But it serves us well here."

"So...you guys house aliens here? Like, Area 51?"

Nagobi spun on his heels, facing Jonah in an instant. "I'm not certain I understand the reference, but we house the extraterrestrial life that made itself known to us several months ago. From here, we study them. And they, we believe, study us. You are here, Doctor Edwin, to make that process more efficient, for both parties."

"Efficient?" Jonah eyed Roundy, who hadn't explained nearly enough. "Why don't you take me through my role here, baseline, because I'm a little confused."

"Yes, efficient." Nagobi sighed. "They found a way to communicate with us, but they're not communicating. We need someone to speak with them, to get through to them, bridge whatever divide we're missing. That's your role here, Doctor Edwin."

Jonah nodded. That was a lot easier than gleaning anything out of Roundy, but it did nothing to calm his nerves. He understood where his niche was but doubted he could fill it. Communicational divides with humans were one thing, but he had yet to learn anything about this interplanetary species other than they could talk to him if they wanted. "Okay." He put on a brave face. "I can work with that."

"Good." Nagobi spun back and continued, everyone close behind. "We will begin introductions now." He made a sharp turn down a stairwell. "Please know, they can't hurt you. A pane of Plexiglas separates our environment from theirs."

"Are they violent?" Jonah asked.

"No, no. The separation is for their safety more than yours. Their needs aren't anything like ours, so they need a controlled environment, like the one on their vessel."

"They sure look intimidating though." Roundy gave Jonah a hearty pat on the back. "Don't let 'em scare you though, mate."

With another sharp turn, Nagobi rounded a corner at the bottom of the steps, down a dimmer hall. Jonah glanced around, wondering how far below sea-level they'd descended. After another corner, they found a set of doors guarded by two more soldiers, these with German flags.

In unison, both guards reached out and grabbed a door handle, pulling them open with seamless symmetry. They all piled into a tight room with a wide window on one end, and a slim door beside it. Jonah couldn't make much out through the dark beyond the glass, but his gaze stayed fixed. He was just feet away from alien life and still feeling entirely out of his element.

"So, their environment, what's it like?" Jonah wondered.

"They breathe ammonia," Roundy was the first to chime in.

"That's not true," Wilberforce corrected.

Nagobi let out another sigh. "A portion of their preferred atmosphere is ammonia, but there are other compounds that must be present for them to breathe properly. In addition, they like things a little cooler than we do. We keep their side of the room at around negative thirty Celsius, but don't worry, very little of that chill leaks over." He approached a small control panel below the window and flipped a switch, bringing a wash of light to the room beyond the glass.

All that was there was a long metal table with three metal chairs, all aimed toward the flat, dark pane of Plexiglas cutting the room in half. Unfortunately for Jonah's curiosity, nothing was visible through the shadows beyond the pane.

"So, how does this start?" Jonah asked.

"We're hoping you could tell us that," Roundy said.

"They will approach," Nagobi elaborated. "Just enough to be seen, and they will activate their translator, but don't expect to hear anything. Like we said, they communicate little. If they do speak, we placed microphones on their side to feed into speakers in the room and in here. We'll all be able to hear whatever they say."

"If you can get them to talk," Wilberforce noted. "You're only the first professional to try. Could be a lot of trial and error involved."

"Right." Jonah nodded; eyes transfixed on the dark pane. "Do I...go in?"

"Take your time, doctor. Whenever you are ready," Nagobi said.

Jonah stood for a long time, just staring through the window, trying to collect his thoughts. He flipped through his memories, searching for a good game plan for two interstellar curiosities. After a minute of thought, he had nothing to show. Rather than keep stalling, he forced himself around to the door, but paused with his hand hovering over the handle.

"You do not have to go in alone," Doctor Nagobi said. "They are used to others; they may approach faster if they see familiar faces."

After another moment, Jonah nodded. "Yeah, that might be good."

With Doctor Nagobi right behind him, Jonah moved into that compact room of wall-to-wall cement. Before he could even sit down, a sudden whine startled him out of his skin.

"We'll be right back here," Roundy's voice came over the intercom speakers in the ceiling, constructed right into the poured foundation. Jonah gave him an uneasy glance through the window, but he just showed off his same old smile.

Jonah took the middle chair and just stared ahead into the darkness, waiting for any movement. He'd never even thought to ask what these beings looked like, and now he was moments from seeing one. A little too late to ask, he figured.

Right then, something stirred in the shadows. From the darkness, two stick-thin figures approached the glass, at first just silhouettes. But the closer they got, the more unmistakably real they became.

These beings were humanoid only in the most basic sense. Bipedal, with the classic arms/legs/torso/head configuration, but that was where most every similarity ended. When they reached the edge of the pane, they loomed over the humans at the table. Jonah figured they had to be at least ten feet tall. Their skin appeared to be a deft mix of scales and epidermis. With every movement, scale-shaped patterns raised and shifted against a dark outer layer of skin. Once movement ceased, the scale pattern faded back into the body.

Long arms extended down to about knee level, although they didn't seem to have those. Rather than form into a hand or claw, these beings' arms coned outward like the muzzle of a bullhorn. Dozens of thin, seaweed-like tentacles dangled from the cone, swaying with every lumbering movement.

Their heads were almost devoid of feature. No hair, no mouth, and mere slits where a nose ought to have been, so thin Jonah wasn't certain they were even there. All that stood out were the eyes. Wide, unblinking, and so silver Jonah could see a small reflection of himself in them. Although they never blinked, their eyes constantly moved with a certain liquidity.

For a moment, Jonah just stared. He had no idea what else to do but quietly study them. And, he was certain they were studying him right back through those shining, mercuric eyes.

"Don't worry," Doctor Nagobi spoke up, shattering the tension. "This is normal."

"How do they communicate?" Jonah asked, staring up at their smooth faces.

"We don't know, biologically anyway. There would need to be a dissectible specimen to determine that. They do, however, possess the technology required to speak with us." He gestured forward just as the beings moved.

Both reached one arm back into the dark. Rather than their thin tentacles coiling around anything, they retracted into dense tufts near the edge of their coned arms. Then, out of the shadows, a small, metallic box floated forward.

Jonah stirred in his seat, watching the box slide up to the glass with the movement of the aliens' cones. Their tendrils loosened up, and the box eased down to the cement. Now that it was in more light, Jonah marveled at its simplicity. As silver as their eyes, and just as featureless as their faces. Literally, it was just a metal box, not much more substantial than the average mail package.

"That's their communicator?" Jonah asked.

Nagobi nodded. "Yes. And no, we don't know how it works. Nor do we yet understand how they use it."

"I'm guessing this is all stuff I'm gonna have to figure out?"

"Yes, Doctor Edwin. If you can get through to them."

At that, Jonah began as best he could. Leaning back in his seat and trying his hardest to focus, he considered what little he knew about these two strange figures before him. He watched them breathe their ammonia-stricken air, their stomach regions rather than chests expanding, scale patterns fluttering every time.

Only humanoid in the most basic of ways, and beyond that entirely different. However, Jonah felt they were just as humanoid psychologically as they were anatomically. That is, enough for a frame of reference.

He considered what he said on the plane, that perhaps this wasn't purposeful of them, that they were bored teenagers who'd crashed into a tree. Bored teenagers wouldn't have brought a translator device with them. But, if they came to make contact, why weren't they?

"Can I speak to them?" Jonah peered to Doctor Nagobi.

"Yes," a swift, mechanical voice came through the intercom system.

Jonah looked up with a start to the alien beings. They hadn't moved an inch, but they'd made contact. "You can hear me okay?"

"Yes."

"Can you tell me why you're here?"

No response.

"Do you know who we are?"

No response.

After a moment of pause, Jonah leaned to Doctor Nagobi. "Are you sure the translator works right?"

"Yes," the voice responded again, almost instantaneously.

"Can you say anything other than 'yes?'" Jonah asked.

"No."

Jonah scoffed, and couldn't help but chuckle. Perhaps these were two smart-ass teenagers after all.

"You may notice our issue," Nagobi said. "They affirm understanding but will not communicate."

Through another quiet pause, Jonah looked them over again, hunting for anything he missed. It took about a dozen goes, but Jonah noticed something off. They weren't speaking, but every living thing had body language.

Even though they loomed over him like trees, they seemed to slouch ever so slightly. Although, for all he knew, slouching was their natural state. Still, that wasn't the only sign. Despite being devoid of most features, their faces still held a subtle form of recognizable expression, and it wasn't positive.

It wasn't sadness; it wasn't that heavy. No, this was a vaguer melancholy. These beings were entirely foreign to Jonah's world, but there was something familiar in the feelings their postures exuded. A deep, primal depression.

"Why are you sad?" Jonah asked, so soft he wasn't sure they'd pick it up.

"Life," the mechanical voice replied. Both Jonah and Nagobi perked up. Jonah looked to the doctor to ensure this was new ground. Off Nagobi's wide gaze alone, Jonah knew he'd asked the right question.

Roundy's voice suddenly intruded over the intercom. "We've all been there, mate."

Nagobi spun around in his seat. "Please keep the audio system clear, Mr. Roundy."

A momentary glance back gave Jonah the opportunity to watch Wilberforce take over the intercom system. With a slight smirk, Jonah returned his focus to the melancholic aliens. They were sad, now he had to pinpoint why, and get them to discuss it.

"Life." Jonah repeated their word. "Do you think life is inherently sad?"

They took time to respond, "In...her-ent...ly?"

"I'm afraid their technology is not perfect, Doctor Edwin." Nagobi grumbled.

"Okay then." Jonah rested his elbows on the table and pondered for a while. "Do you think all life is sad? Do you think that is in life's nature?"

"No," the beings said. A straight-forward, yet still puzzling response.

"Why did you come here?" Jonah inquired.

No response.

THE DAYS ANTHOLOGY, BOOK 2

He sat back in his seat again and sighed. In another tangent of thought, he peered over their bodies again. All the makings of organic life. Jonah turned to Nagobi. "Do they eat, or anything?"

Doctor Nagobi shook his head. "They rarely do much more than stand still, walking only when necessary, levitating only what is necessary. No eating, no sleeping, no expelling waste. Nothing."

That couldn't be possible. Jonah aimed his attention back to the statuesque aliens. Their bodies had to be organic and there had to be something they required to sustain their life. He showed a soft smile. "We're a lot alike, I think."

"No," the beings responded. Afterwards, a low feedback still hummed through the speaker system. "We...are...antithesis."

"You know antithesis, but you don't know inherently?"

No response.

Figuring he was doing more harm than good; Jonah shelved that digression for later. He spoke slow, picking words carefully, "We sure share a lot of features."

"All life...advanced life...carry these features. They are most...productive for life."

"Efficient," Nagobi interpreted. "Our features are efficient, most conducive to maintaining advanced life. So, they are universal features."

"Yes," the beings agreed.

Before continuing, Jonah glanced to the observation window. Roundy and Wilberforce were still there, both obviously enamored. Although Roundy showed it far more, nearly sticking himself to the surface of the glass, Wilberforce couldn't hide the astonishment in his otherwise stony expression.

After some time picking his words, Jonah posed his next question, "How many other species of life have you seen? Are we not your first experience?"

For a moment, only more feedback came through. Jonah worried maybe he'd asked another wrong question. The last thing he wanted to do was be on the bad side of mysterious extraterrestrials.

"You are not," their mechanical voice responded finally. "You are...one of many."

"And what do you do when you encounter these other advanced life forms?"

"Watch."

"Watch?" Jonah shot a concerned looked to Nagobi, who could only send it right back to him. "Do you not usually interact this directly?"

"No."

Jonah couldn't help but smile at that. Even he knew that that was great progress. He gave another look to the window, showing off his newly found confidence. However, a glance to Nagobi killed his brightened mood. He seemed far more disturbed by this revelation, a certain darkness overcoming his gaze.

"So, we are a special case?" Nagobi wondered.

"Yes."

The curiosity of Nagobi's thought process set into Jonah's mind. "Why?"

"Advanced life on your...planet...required a closer look."

"Is this close enough?" Jonah asked in all seriousness.

"Yes."

Jonah scratched his head. Supposedly, these aliens encountered countless other intelligent life forms throughout the whole universe. And, out of all of them, humanity warranted closer inspection. "Being those close, what do you see?"

"Flowers."

"Flowers?" Jonah furrowed his brow. Was it a mistranslation, or were they saying exactly what they meant?

"Your...forms...decay. Like flowers."

This time, it was Jonah's turn to be disturbed and Nagobi's time to smile. "They recognize plant life," he spoke with a joyful exhale. "You're teaching us a lot, Doctor Edwin."

Decay. That was the word that stuck in Jonah's mind. Decay. He looked over their bodily forms again. Two different beings, two different lives, yet they looked identical. And, Jonah had a hunch this wasn't just a case of twins, just like it wasn't a case of stranded teenagers. Their bodies were flawless, devoid of scar, impervious to age. "How old are you?" Jonah asked.

"That...is...our antithesis," the beings explained. "We have watched...from distance...your kind decay...expire. This is our antithesis."

Even though none of the humans were speaking, a hush fell over them. Jonah, mostly just to take his eyes off the aliens and to have time to swallow the lump in his throat, turned back to the observation window. Wilberforce and Roundy looked roughly how he felt; confused, and deeply concerned.

Jonah addressed Nagobi, "So, I have some thoughts."

"Keep questioning. Please." Nagobi's eyes stared straight ahead, transfixed on the aliens. He looked starved for more information, and Jonah didn't blame him. He only wished the information was a little brighter.

"Are you saying you don't die?"

"What is 'die?'"

Silence hung over everyone again after that. To Jonah, the conversation's trajectory was clear, but he wasn't sure if he was ready to have it. Humanity had a lot to learn from this conversation, but Jonah couldn't find words to move it along.

"I'd like to ask a question," Wilberforce's stern, steady voice came over the intercom.

"Go for it." Jonah nodded.

"Were you born?" he asked.

"Born?" the beings wondered after some contemplative feedback.

"How did your existence begin?" Wilberforce rephrased.

Another stretch of silence crept through. It was a good question, Jonah thought, but the longer it went unanswered, the more he worried they'd never respond. Their interspecies relationship was brand new, and fragile as glass.

With a gush of feedback, the beings finally spoke, "We begin...together...in an instant. After...no new creation...no loss."

Jonah let out a breath. "We are very different."

"Yes," they agreed.

Doctor Nagobi chimed in, "Has every other intelligent life form you encountered come into being this way?"

"Yes. All together. No new creation, no loss."

Roundy's voice came over the speaker system again. "Let me see if I've got this straight: no other intelligent life form in the universe dies? Every other species gets to live forever, and humans get screwed?" the audio cut out.

Watching the silent act play out, Jonah witnessed Roundy and Wilberforce bickering over the intercom controls. Roundy moved toward the door to the hall, mouthing something like 'bullshit.' He stormed out, and Wilberforce let him leave.

"Yes," the beings replied after a long pause. The response opened a pit in Jonah's stomach. It couldn't be true; it couldn't be possible.

"Flowers." Jonah smiled. "You recognize plant life?"

"Yes."

"Is that not life? Plant life decays and expires, many things experience that cycle, right?"

"Not all life...is advanced life. Advanced life requires...longevity."

"Why does longevity require eternal life?" Nagobi asked. "Humanity builds on the progress of past generations. Living beings who expired long ago built the base of everything we know today."

"Yes," the beings replied. "We recognize this. However...your existence...complicates ours."

Jonah let out a dead laugh. "And we're understanding that all too well. Do you want to talk about your concerns?"

"We...do not have enough concept. Until the exploration of your life...we did not see advanced existence as...finite."

"Can you explain your definition of advanced existence?" Nagobi asked. "Where is the line between the two sorts of life you describe?"

Another drawn out pause of feedback came through before they spoke, "Life...that realizes it exists...is advanced life. Advanced life can understand existence...as its existence has no end."

Jonah chewed on this for a while. Their line for advanced was comprehending one's own existence, and the existence of the universe. "So, what do you think of us, advanced life that recognizes its own existence, and also recognizes that it ends?"

"You...do not seem to recognize that it ends," the beings retorted.

"How do you mean?"

"Over time...we have watched your kind...come together from expiration, find peace...community."

"Well, of course," Nagobi spoke with some exasperation in his tone. "Death is not the end, it is..." he trailed off. "It is the beginning of new life, new existence. An afterlife."

"Afterlife?" the beings wondered. Not even the mechanical tones could hide their confusion. "Do you...believe flowers have afterlife? Does...every plant have afterlife?"

Nagobi paused. "Well, no."

"But...you say it is life. Do they worry...over existence? Do they...find peace in others' expiration...like you?"

Nagobi fumbled over a few words before giving up. "No."

"Only those who realize...but do not recognize, existence's expiration...create concepts of afterlife. Do you...recognize your existence ends...truly?"

Jonah knew a jab when he heard one. And they were right. Humans never accepted existential end, and it was no doubt how religion took its hold in all facets of human development. Now, knowing they were the outliers in a universe full of immortal intelligence, what even was religious faith at all?

That's when he realized the gravity of the discussion. Humans built society around the idea of life after death. Now, reality came to light: death wasn't even a concept for other intelligent beings. Humanity was an outlier, a tragedy. A race of beings that spent most of their lifetimes and energy focused on prettying up the void that came after their existences' end.

How horrible that surely looked from the outside.

Peering to the observation window, Jonah found the room empty. Wherever Wilberforce had gone to, he figured it couldn't have been for any good reason. Most likely, he stormed out like Roundy, too frustrated to comprehend the realities that were arising. Jonah didn't blame them. He glanced to Doctor Nagobi, noticing the beads of sweat forming on his brow.

"What are you thinking?" he questioned the weary doctor.

"I..." Nagobi took a breath. "This is not something that humanity needs to know," he muttered, a suspicious eye stuck on the aliens. "It would not be an easy comprehension. It would be destructive."

"You can live an untruth," the beings replied. "Your existence will expire...and it will have meant only...progression of that untruth."

Nagobi appeared to stifle a sneer. "Watching us does not teach you anything. You do not know of our intricacies, our needs. Humanity...needs their faith, their beliefs."

"Their faith...leads them astray. You are advanced life...but you advance in a cycle...in a circle. This is our antithesis."

At that, Nagobi rose from his seat, the metal chair squeaking sharply against the floor. "Excuse me, I must take a moment. I'm sorry." He headed for the door before Jonah could breathe a word of protest. In no time, Jonah was alone in the chamber with the extraterrestrials he feared encountering mere minutes before. Somehow, it felt like he'd been speaking to them for years.

"So," Jonah hummed, "I understand why your existence is troubling to ours. But I don't think I understand it the other way around. Why are we so troubling to you?"

The feedback came through in ebbs and flows. Experiencing it alone, Jonah found it a little unsettling, like something that would play in a horror movie to puzzle the audience before a big scare. He stirred in his seat as the beings continued pondering.

"Considering existence...finite...is new to us. It was...never anticipated," they let another stretch of silence hang. "When we return this information...to our home...what will we say?"

Jonah could only shrug. "That we're existentially different from you?"

"Not acceptable."

"Why? Why can't we accept that we're...fundamentally different," Jonah trailed off. The more he considered what this information meant, the more he knew they were right. An equal and opposite reaction was likely to rip through every other species in the universe. So many existential crises happening simultaneously wouldn't result in any positivity.

Reality was harsh, but no one could fight it. Science taught Jonah that whenever it found the opportunity, and this was a moment ripe for the taking. While he'd never found a need for religion, he knew many people who thought otherwise. To know death as a universal anomaly, and human belief structures as just dissociations from the pain of reality, would be a crushing blow.

There was more to it than that though, Jonah knew. Human beings were more than willing to hand their existence off to causes that would long outlive them, and often not pay societal dividends for generations to come. But, they did so with the promise of afterlife, with the expectation of continued existence on some other universal plane. If they learned it was a lie of their own creation, would they still work toward progress? Would society fall back into selfish subsistence?

"Do you have to tell them?" Jonah wondered.

"No," the beings replied. "There are...ways to avoid. Do you...have to tell your world?"

Jonah shook his head. "No. As a matter of fact, it'd be far better if we didn't. They don't know about any of this. I only learned a few seconds before I got here. And they never have to."

"We feel...similar."

One more long, intense silence drifted through. Jonah considered the ethics of hiding the truth, and the ethics of revealing it. It would require humanity to make massive, sudden life changes, mostly despite themselves. Humans had come a long way from the days of cavemen, but Jonah figured they'd need thousands more years to reach that level of acceptance and understanding. But maybe he was too cynical.

Regardless of his thoughts, it wasn't up to him. He wasn't sure if he had any say in the decision at all. Although, based on how everyone else had cleared the room, he doubted that they would oppose the idea of closing the lid on it.

"I would have to discuss it with the others," Jonah said. "The people who left. But I think those are agreeable terms."

"Good."

Jonah nodded. "I hope we still have a lot to learn from you."

"Yes," they concurred.

With shaky, adrenaline-drenched movements, Jonah rose and headed for the door. He looked over his shoulder and gave the looming beings a wave. They remained still, not so much as fluttering a tentacle at him.

Once back into the hall, Jonah wasn't sure where to go. He had a basic understanding of the building, at best, and no real idea where everyone else went. The best he could do was retrace his steps and hope they turned up. Crossing through those basement halls to find a stairwell allowed him more time to stew in his thoughts, and it only heightened the anxiety. No one else had sat through the whole conversation. Maybe they were thinking of revealing the truth to the world. What a disaster that would be, he thought.

After he found a staircase and headed up, things became familiar again. Despite the wall-to-wall white halls and little variation, he found his way to the set of doors from before. The lines of statuesque soldiers stood exactly where he left them, standing at attention, awaiting instruction.

While he moved by, the thought returned to his head. Humans gave their individual existences to something greater, hoping for afterlife. Afterlife that would never come. In the image of those soldiers, loyal and dedicated to the defense and safety of their home nations, Jonah saw no better personification of that existential tragedy.

The moment Jonah stepped out; the harsh rays of Mediterranean midday blinded him. Once he'd rubbed the spots out of his vision, he saw that'd his search had concluded. Roundy, Wilberforce, and Nagobi leaned against the water-textured building side-by-side, staring out into the sea. Both Roundy and Wilberforce puffed on cigarettes, while Nagobi only chewed at his nails.

"How'd it go, mate?" Roundy asked, not taking his eyes off the horizon.

"No one can find out," Jonah said. "Humanity isn't ready for this."

Wilberforce nodded. "We know. If we weren't ready for it, why would the public be?"

"So, what happens now?" Jonah asked. Although it seemed like he had a great first day on the job, it also seemed like his job might not last.

"Keep learning," Nagobi answered. "We cannot turn away from such opportunity. But we also must realize the impact of what we may learn...and what we have already learned."

"They sound like they intend to leave here at some point," Jonah figured.

Nagobi nodded. "And we will let them. More reason to continue working now." He let out a sigh. "But, perhaps not today. I have thinking to do...notes to take. We have recordings of everything spoken. When we are ready, we will listen to what we missed of your communication, Doctor Edwin."

"They're not gonna tell anyone else about us," Jonah said. "They figure...it's in the best interest of the universe to keep us a secret."

"Lovely." Roundy flicked his cigarette butt. "Let's go back to Malta, gents, I need a drink."

All three of them pushed off from the wall, but Nagobi headed back for the door. "I have work here, I will catch the night flight." He looked to Jonah. "We will see you here tomorrow, Doctor Edwin." Jonah nodded and waved him off.

No one said anything the entire walk down the runway. Jonah could see deep thought still entranced his companions, and he didn't blame them. It'd take more than a few hours, and few drinks, to digest what they'd just learned about the universe. And, that wasn't likely to be the only disturbing realization they'd have. A sobering moment for every living thing who heard it.

The familiar roar of jet engines filled the air as they approached their antique ride. Even though the other two stayed stoic, the sight of the plane made Jonah perk up. As he ascended the stairs to climb on board, he paused and looked it over, remembering what Roundy had said about it.

It was the first commercial plane to use jets and pressurized cabins, two things on every plane Jonah had ever seen. And yet, as Roundy so eloquently explained, 'they went through the sky in flames.' But Roundy had also noted that it would have happened to some airplane sometime.

Mistakes cost lives sometimes, ended finite existences. Humanity had written so much progress in blood and tragedy. Jonah swirled that thought in his mind with everything else he learned that day, still staring at the exterior of the old plane. He couldn't help but smile a little, when he thought about it.

Humanity, and their uniquely finite lives, may have been the universe's saddest tale. But their sacrifices were noble to their society. That airplane, and all others like it, became safer and more well understood by human sacrifice. Jonah peered beyond, to the watery facility, and considered the multinational guards keeping watch. He couldn't imagine how many soldiers died over the decades for that level of peace and interrelation.

To other life forms, humans may have seemed like an unimaginable tragedy, beings given intelligent life only to have it snatched away after a few decades. But Jonah saw it a little differently. Heading to the top of the steps and entering the plane, one more of Roundy's earlier quips came into his mind: 'Sometimes tragedy is needed to make a little progress.'

###

About Mitch Goth

A PROLIFIC WRITER AND AVID DAYDREAMER, Mitch Goth wrote his first novel at age fourteen in his free time between high school classes. Since then, he has written twenty-five books across a variety of genres, from pulse-pounding thrillers to thought-provoking sci-fi stories. In 2017, he graduated cum laude from Antioch College, where his final thesis was a novel based on the US military's LSD experiments.

When not getting lost in his own daydreams, Mitch is a seasoned paranormal researcher, having investigated dozens of hauntings across the midwestern United States. Surprisingly, his writing backlist doesn't include any ghost stories...yet.

Connect with Mitch here:
www.castrumpress.com/authors/mitch-goth

A SERIES OF ANOMALOUS PHENOMENA
by D. B. Crelia

"Is this really necessary, Captain? Our cells are full of candidates for the Butaka. This just seems . . . reckless."

Captain Rilga swiveled his chair to face Humm, his shape shifting first officer. Rilga's irritation at being questioned deepening as he was confronted by Humm configured as an Olek female. "Do you have to do that?"

"What?" answered Humm innocently.

"Make yourself look like one of my women."

Humm's hand drifted up, as if to confirm the captain's observation. "Sorry . . . it's a subconscious thing." His face and hands transformed into something almost, but not quite identical to an Olek male.

Rilga regarded the shape shifter's new incarnation for a moment. "What is that?"

Humm's new face contorted into a grimace. "A human. They are the predominant sentient species on this planet you insist upon visiting. Somewhat akin to an Olek, don't you think, Captain?"

Rilga glared at him through narrowed eyes for a moment then spun his chair to face the console again, continuing to speak over his shoulder. "The Butaka pay very well for these specialty items. We have coordinates. It's in a sparsely populated area. We're in. We're out. No problem."

"It's rarely 'No problem' for us, Captain," said Humm, the edge of sarcasm blatantly obvious.

"They're pre-emergent. They don't even have any satellites in orbit," countered Rilga.

"Radio waves pour out from that planet like light from a star!" Humm argued. "They have industry and motorized transport. And if all the data we've collected can be believed, practically the entire planet has been very recently embroiled in war! I've even detected evidence of nuclear detonations! Fusion as well as fission mind you!

Fission! You know what that kind of dirty radiation will do to our more sensitive systems!"

"Calm down Humm. If it's bad, we'll call it off," Rilga said in an attempt to placate his subordinate. "And our holding cells aren't exactly full, now are they?"

Humm fidgeted nervously but didn't answer.

"Did any of the Pleems survive?"

Humm released a soft, resigned sigh before answering. "One still lingers. The other two have perished."

"Tell me one more time what happened?" asked Rilga, spinning his chair around again.

Humm contorted his human face in an odd way. "The crew was blowing off some steam. The Pleems look so damned funny. Those big heads and tiny bodies. You should have seen them running from the Saurgs. We didn't realize how fragile they were though. Kordon's tail swept all three into the bulkhead, and well . . . the medic suite couldn't get a read on their vitals and they just died, except for the one."

Rilga ground his teeth in exasperation then took a deep calming breath. "I suppose, if they were that fragile, the Butaka wouldn't find much use for them in the fighting pits anyway. Remind me to space them, when we leave this back water. Now get the crew ready, we're going in."

In a quiet and slightly mocking voice Humm said, "Yes, Captain." Exiting the bridge, Humm walked down the corridor toward the crew quarters attempting to transform into a Saurg as he did so, but he simply didn't have the mass to pull it off. He knew that if he showed up as a miniature version of the massive, lizard-like Saurgs that made up the majority of the crew, they'd rib him incessantly and want him to do it all the time.

Settling once more into human form, Humm stepped into the crew's open bay. Moist heat and reptilian stench assaulted his senses as he approached the sleeping heap of tails and limbs. Snoring vibrated the walls.

"Mmm hmmm!" Humm loudly cleared his throat.

Eyes opened here and there in the pile of reddish lizard skin. "Are you trying to look like the captain again?" asked a voice.

Humm stiffened at yet another instance of the Suarg's borderline insubordination. "No, this is what humans look like. We are visiting their planet for a little snatch and grab mission."

"Haven't we collected enough slaves for the Butaka arenas?" demanded a different voice from the yet-to-move mass of bodies.

"We are not here for slaves. Humans are pre-emergent, which, as you know, makes them off limits for slaving. We are here for a DNA capture."

"That just seems greedy," came yet another voice.

Humm examined his new fingers. "Well, if someone hadn't smashed our Pleems . . ."

Snickers coursed through the pile of lizards as they began to untangle. The crew started to stretch and flex and Humm affected what he thought was a human smile, spun on his heels calling over his shoulder, "Stations in thirty!"

An hour later they were beginning their descent. Captain Rilga piloted the ship while Humm monitored a bank of sensors and Gozh, one of the Saurg crew members, operated the various shields, including a cloak, and the weapons array if it was needed.

"Are you sure broad daylight is the best choice, Captain?" asked Humm.

"They have extremely limited detection capabilities," replied Rilga confidently. "With the cloak deployed, they won't even know we're here. If we came in at night, we'd burn atmosphere and light up the whole area."

"Their primitive active systems could show us as an anomaly which they might choose to investigate," persisted Humm.

"And if they investigate, what will they see? With the cloak in operation we are invisible to the naked eye. Furthermore, we'll see them coming long before they get close. Now close your face and let me pilot."

Humm stopped talking.

The normally smooth-running ship rumbled and groaned as they encountered the steadily increasing air pressure of the planet's stratosphere. On reaching sufficiently thick atmosphere, Rilga activated the atmospheric maneuvering system and the ship settled down to a steady vibration.

Humm experienced a brief moment of vertigo as the gravity generator switched off and the ambient gravity of the planet took over. Rilga seemed unaffected. Gozh vomited noisily into the chute beside his station, installed for just that purpose.

"Cloak status, Gozh?" Rilga's voice was full of irritation, as if the Saurg were distracted by some dalliance.

Gozh belched, spat and croaked, "One hundred percent, full spectrum."

"Coordinates acquired, Captain," said Humm.

A few minutes later Rilga ordered, "Alert the crew, touch down in five."

Humm activated the ship-wide comm and relayed the order.

When the ship had made a jarring landing, Rilga spun his chair around. "All right Humm, put on your human face and go get that nugget."

Humm looked at the captain as if he didn't quite understand. "With no escort?"

"I don't think big red lizards will fit in here," half joked Rilga. "We're already skirting the pre-emergent contact protocols. It's fine, you'll be done before you know it." He spun his chair back to the console, effectively dismissing Humm.

"Okay," Humm mumbled quietly, straightening his uniform before moving to the door.

Waves of heat rolled up the ramp as it lowered to the dusty surface. Humm reflected that the Saurgs may have enjoyed the heat however, they likely would have complained about having to wear respirators. Humm could tolerate almost any atmosphere if it had enough oxygen content. The Saurgs, on the other hand, for all their size, were more susceptible to atmospheric variances.

Carrying a bag containing the requisite equipment, Humm set out walking for the small building in the distance. During lulls in the hot wind, he could hear water running off to his left, where, according to the maps, a river ran through a shallow gully.

As he walked, Humm looked around him at the vicious spikes and spines of the local vegetation and concentrated hard on where he stepped. At one point he veered wide around a long slender creature that coiled itself and made a menacing rattling noise.

"Humm," Rilga's voice in his implant startled him.

"Yes, Captain?" he sub-vocalized.

"Your target is inside the fenced area to the right of the structure."

Humm was now close enough to see the area Rilga indicated but was shocked to see two humans standing inside the fenced area.

"There are humans here!" he said with as much emphasis as sub-vocalization allowed.

"It's okay, the computer will translate for you," Rilga replied with an odd tone in his voice.

Humm followed the fence around to where a gate opened into the area. The two humans watched him with deep curiosity as he approached. The gate latch took a few seconds to negotiate. When he stepped inside, the larger of the two humans spoke, the alien sounds meant nothing to him.

"This one is a male. He is greeting you, respond with 'Good day'," supplied Rilga.

Humm cleared his throat and attempted to repeat the words. The humans looked at him suspiciously, then the smaller of the two spoke.

"The smaller one is female. She asks where you came from. Answer 'walking'."

When Humm repeated Rilga's suggestion, the humans' expressions became even more puzzled. After a tense silence, Rilga said, "Say this to them, 'Where is the grave of William H. Bonny?'"

Humm didn't think his attempt to enunciate the question was anywhere close to correct, but the human male pointed to the stone marker in front of him. "Say, 'Thank you'," Rilga's voice said in his ear.

When Humm had complied, Rilga said, "Now move around like you're interested in everything but that stone until they depart."

The two humans watched warily as Humm ambled around examining the various stones.

"Humans bury their dead in the ground and commemorate them with these carved stones," Rilga said after a few minutes had passed.

Humm took in all the stones around him. The heat was intense, and a wave of disgust washed over him as he realized he was standing upon the decomposing corpses of dozens of humans.

When the couple left by the same gate through which Humm had entered, Rilga said, "Now move it! Let's not push our luck!"

Humm wasted no time in making his way over to the stone indicated by the human male. Letters cut into the stone matched the ones he had seen on the ship. From his bag he extracted a device. When it had booted up, Humm pointed it at the ground in front of the stone.

"Balls of shit!" he exclaimed after a few seconds.

"What?" demanded Rilga in his ear.

"There are DNA strands for at least eighteen humans here!"

"Calm down, Humm. Broaden your parameters."

Humm complied. The results seemed odd, so he ran the scan again.

"What have you come up with, Humm?"

"Eighteen humans and - one Olek male."

"That's our boy," said Rilga triumphantly. "Get him and let's get off this rock."

"Anything you'd like to explain, Captain?"

"It's better if you don't know."

Humm blew out a long breath, extracted a burrower and dropped it to the ground. As it disappeared into the loose, sandy soil, Humm monitored its progress on the other device. When it had acquired the appropriate DNA, he recalled it, collecting it as it emerged from the ground. Pleased with himself, he replaced the equipment into his bag. Turning to the gate, he stopped dead in his tracks as he faced a small crowd gathered in front of the gate. A human male in a uniform spoke forcefully to him.

"Uh oh," said Rilga in his ear.

"What do I do?"

"Run."

"Huh?" Humm said aloud as the uniformed male walked through the gate toward him.

"RUN!!" Rilga shouted in his ear.

Humm turned and ran toward the rickety fence standing between him and the ship. The human male yelled at his back, but Humm vaulted the fence and kept on running. The shouting behind him stopped, but he kept up his pace. Keeping the river on his right, he dodged the dangerous looking plants, keeping a wary eye out for animals.

As Humm approached the spot where he hoped the ship lay cloaked, he became aware of another noise. Off to his left a wheeled vehicle with a big red flashing light on top sped down what appeared to be a paved surface. As it got even with Humm, it left the pavement and bounced across the dusty ground toward him.

"Do something!" pleaded Humm aloud.

"On it," Rilga's voice said calmly.

The ship blinked into view for a fraction of a second and then the human vehicle's engine died, rolling to a stop amidst a cloud of billowing dust.

Now sure of his ship's location, Humm made a minor adjustment in his course. Through heaving breaths, he said aloud, "Please tell me you didn't just fire off a pulse."

"The machine used rudimentary electronics, the pulse has rendered them inactive," said Rilga dismissively.

"And fried all the equipment in my bag!" cried Humm.

"The DNA is still viable."

Humm wasn't sure if it was a question or a statement, but he answered as if it were a question. "It should be. But of course, we have no way to know until we reach a civilized port and spend a small fortune to purchase new equipment!"

His legs were getting fatigued. Just when he wondered if it was safe to slow to a walk, the male in the uniform emerged from the dust raised by the vehicle pointing what seemed to be a weapon.

"He is pointing a weapon at me!" Humm wheezed.

"He won't fire. And even if he does, that primitive thing can't be very accurate."

The ramp of the ship blinked out of cloak as it opened a short distance away. Humm called up his last reserves of energy and sprinted for it. As his feet pounded on the metal ramp, a projectile pinged off the side of the cloaked ship inches from Humm's head, followed immediately by a report from the human's weapon.

Armed Saurg guards hauled him inside as the ramp began to rise. Before it closed into position, Humm caught sight of another vehicle approaching at speed along the paved road.

"Get to your station, Humm!" Rilga shouted over the ship comm.

Humm gulped air and leaned on the bulkhead as he pushed himself toward the bridge. The captain was beginning pre-flight by the time he strapped into his station. Shortly thereafter, the ship lifted off more steeply and faster than usual, pushing Humm and the rest of the crew back into their seats.

Humm's breathing had almost returned to normal, when an angry red light began flashing on his panel accompanied by a blaring alarm.

"What is that?" demanded Rilga.

"Remember those nuclear detonations I told you about? We just flew over one!" Humm answered.

"I'm losing visuals and the cloak, Captain," said Gosz impassively, as if commenting on the paint.

"Dammit to Hell!" seethed Rilga.

"I would advise gaining altitude quickly, Captain," offered Humm.

"You think?" retorted Rilga.

"It's not like they have anything in orbit for us to hit," replied Humm, ignoring the captain's sarcasm.

Suddenly the ship shuddered lightly as if it had impacted something small. A second alarm joined the first.

"The engine intake is blocked! We're losing altitude! Brace for impact!" Rilga shouted.

Humm relayed the message on the ship comm. The ship's atmospheric maneuvering system screamed in protest. Without the ship's gravity to compensate, the free fall churned Humm's guts. Gosz vomited into his chute once again.

"Fire the main thruster, Captain," Humm yelled to be heard over the screaming engine.

Rilga turned, eyes wide. "We'll be visible to the whole hemisphere and we'll scorch everything below us. Then we'll be firmly in violation of the protocols. I've still got some stick; I think we can land."

Humm kept his thoughts to himself. The ship and the captain were one and the same. Rilga would destroy the ship and kill all of them, before he would risk having it taken from him for violating contact protocols. With his knees pulled up to his chin, seat restraints so tight they cut into his flesh beneath his clothing, Humm waited for fate to take its course.

Rilga vectored the ship tangent to the planet's terrain. After one jarring impact, the ship slid to a rough and noisy, but survivable stop. Almost before the momentum ceased, Rilga had unstrapped. "The cloak is out, we're vulnerable here. Let's get moving!"

Humm remained strapped in but began issuing orders. "Maintenance team one, get outside and see what damage we've incurred!"

When he had received confirmation on that order, Humm turned to Gosz. "Monitor local radio waves and see what the computer can translate."

Turning his attention to the interior of the ship, Humm called, "Maintenance team two, damage report!"

"Stand by," came the lackadaisical reply.

"Holding, how is our cargo?"

"Everyone lives. One of the Voots' cranial membranes popped, but its mate is secreting a new one for it," answered the guard, his voice full of disgust.

Humm wondered where Rilga had gone. "Captain?" he ventured over the ship comm.

"I'm outside. We hit what appears to be a balloon."

"A . . . balloon?" asked Humm, incredulous.

"It's packed with instrumentation, but it's still a balloon. Likely used for some type of monitoring," came Rilga's voice over sounds of the Saurg technicians grunting as they removed debris from the blocked intake.

"Is the damage repairable?" asked Humm.

"Some broken and bent fins. Maybe a few hours will do it. What about interior damage?"

Humm depressed the comm. "Team two, status?"

"Structural supports have ripped loose and caused a minor hull breach on deck alpha. We can affect repairs here, but more extensive repairs will be required when we next make port."

Gosz cut in on the ship comm, "Captain, we were seen by the human military. They are dispatching units to our location."

"What kind of units?" demanded Humm over the ship comm, even though Gosz was a scant few feet away.

"Ground only, so far."

"How long until they arrive?" asked Rilga apprehensively.

Gosz checked his display before answering. "A couple of hours, maybe longer."

Rilga began issuing orders. "Priority one, get that cloak up! Humm, meet me in the cargo bay."

Humm unstrapped and sprinted to the bay, skidding to a halt as he met the captain racing up the ramp.

"Get the Pleems," ordered Rilga as he ran past.

"What?"

Without stopping or turning, Rilga repeated, "Get the Pleems!"

Humm was barely bigger than any one of the Pleems, he couldn't hope to carry them all in any kind of hurry. Over the ship-wide comm, he ordered, "Team two! Two members, meet me in the infirmary!" Not waiting for a reply, Humm set off for the ship's infirmary.

The two Saurg crewmen were waiting for him when he reached the infirmary. "Bring the Pleems to the cargo bay," he wasted no time in ordering.

If the crewmen thought the command was as odd as Humm did, they didn't react. One crewman carried the two dead Pleems under his thickly muscled arms, while the other carried the still living one cradled in both arms.

When they arrived back at the cargo bay Rilga was hauling pieces of metal and useless scrap out of storage compartments and loading them onto a hover sled already loaded with the remains of the balloon recovered from the intake. Humm and the Saurg crewmen stood by and watched until the captain stepped back, assessed his collection and the Pleems, then nodded in satisfaction. "All right, let's go."

"Go where?"

"To throw the human military units off our trail," Rilga called over his shoulder as he began moving the sled down the ramp.

Humm glanced at the Suargs who appeared as confused as he was. Shrugging his diminutive shoulders, he set off after Rilga with the two Suargs in tow, pausing at the bay doors to allow Rilga and the Suargs to don small breathers. Rilga nodded to each member of the hastily assembled team before pushing the hover sled out into the desert-like landscape.

The ship had cut a wide gouge across the ground, skipped a short distance, then come to a landing. Rilga moved toward the first gouge. When he reached the torn-up ground, he stopped and surveyed the area.

"All right spread everything around randomly," he commanded.

"And the Pleems?" asked Humm.

"Them too," said Rilga as he began slinging the metal and scrap as far as he could across the hill side.

Humm took the living Pleem from the Suarg, surprised at how light the small being was. It remained unconscious as Humm gently laid it upon the ground. He didn't often let himself feel empathy for the slaves they gathered, but he found it oddly disquieting to walk away from the Pleem. Words of apology threatened to spill from his mouth. Shaking them off, he quickly joined the others in littering the hillside with miscellaneous junk and one mangled human balloon.

When Rilga was satisfied with the scene, they moved to the second gouge caused by the ship's landing. "Cover this up as much as possible before the military get here," he ordered as he headed back to the ship.

Humm and the Saurgs spread the sandy soil around and replaced shredded plants with others collected from nearby. The Suargs cursed vehemently each time they got wicked little spines stuck in their thick fingers.

When the sun was touching the horizon, Humm decided to call a halt, "That's as good as we can make it. Back to the ship."

Rilga was at Humm's station on the bridge when he returned. "What is our status, Captain?"

Rilga did not turn from the station, fingers continuing to work furiously, as he answered. "Repairs are under way. The cloak should be up soon, but the military vehicles are approaching rapidly. The light from the star will be gone momentarily. I hope darkness will cover us until the cloak comes up." He turned abruptly to Humm. "Did we bring the hover sled back from the first site?"

"I'll send a crew member to see."

Rilga turned back to Humm's console. "Everyone's busy making repairs. You go."

A few minutes later, Humm stood on the open cargo bay ramp, eyes searching the barren landscape beyond for the hover sled by the waning evening light, reflecting on the universal beauty of sunsets across the galaxy. The dim blue glow of the sled's energy field stood out starkly in the fading light.

"Shit!" he hissed to himself as he set out at a run, hoping the light held long enough for him to make his way back.

Reaching the hilltop they had littered with junk, he caught sight of the dust plumes of several approaching vehicles in the distance. Wheeling the sled around Humm stopped dead in his tracks. The ship was gone! The cloak must have come up while he was out. The ramp rising automatically as the cloak came back online.

Desperately, he ran behind the sled to the area where he had left the ship, disappointed his cover up didn't seem to be as good as he had at first thought.

"Captain?"

He received no response. That was odd. Captain Rilga was the only one with access to Humm's implant through his own implant. It was impossible for him to not hear his call. A wave of panic washed over him as the details of his conundrum became clear.

Even if he could see the ship's hull, the ramp could only be lowered from the inside. Furthermore, touching the cloak field would most likely kill him or stun him unconscious at the very least. On a whim, he backed up the hover sled and shoved it as hard as he could at the ship. It merely bounced off after making a slight ripple in the cloak field. Contact with the field shorted out the sled's energy and it dropped to the ground.

Through a break in the wind, came the sound of multiple engines approaching.

"Captain!" Humm called urgently. "I am trapped outside the ship! The humans are almost here!"

No answer came over his implants. Plumes of dust raised by the approaching vehicles were back lit as they topped the last ridge before the improvised vignette of Pleems and debris.

"Captain, let me in! Please!"

Rilga's answer startled Humm. "Sorry Humm. You've become a liability."

Humm was stunned. When he found his voice he asked, "Because of the DNA?"

"No one can know about that."

"I won't tell anyone!" Humm pleaded.

When Rilga didn't respond, Humm asked, "What am I supposed to do?"

"Look human and try to blend in."

Humm brought his hands up to touch his face. "But I don't know their language."

"I've downloaded it into your implant chip."

"When?"

After a few seconds with no answer, realization slowly dawned on Humm. "You planned to leave me here all along! You fired the pulse intentionally to fry the instruments."

"I needed that DNA. And like I said, you've become a liability. I had planned to space you along with the Pleems. But the opportunity arose . . . and I felt like I owed you a chance . . . at least, to survive."

Shouting voices caused Humm to turn back to where the vehicles had stopped and were disgorging armed human soldiers. Activating his translation files he found one called "English."

"You bastard," said Humm through gritted teeth.

"I know. But, uh . . . if those soldiers find this ship, I'll have no reason not to burn off with the main thrusters. So, if you don't mind?"

Humm wasn't happy about being marooned on a strange planet, but he had no desire whatsoever to be incinerated by a burst of super-heated plasma. Knowing the cloaked ship would block the soldiers' view, he used it as cover and ran, stripping off his uniform as he did so. Heading toward a small rock formation not too far away, he transformed himself to look like one of the rocks as much as possible. While he could drastically change the shape, color and texture of his skin, he couldn't do very much about his bone structure. Humm settled himself in for a long, uncomfortable night.

The soldiers remained intent on the other hill for several hours. As the planet's moon set, the night became very dark. Humm could only see where the ship rested when it blocked the small lights carried by the soldiers. Without warning, the ship's atmospheric maneuvering system revved up and it lifted off, the faint wavering of its cloak disappearing quickly into the night sky.

"Good luck, Humm," Captain Rilga's voice said into his implant as the sound of the ship faded.

"Eat shit, Captain," Humm sub-vocalized.

The sound of the ship's engines departing had caught the attention of the humans. As the noise faded, Humm heard their shouts followed by several vehicles converging upon the spot recently vacated by the ship. He closed his eyes and made like a rock for all he was worth.

The soldiers searched the area until sunrise. They found the hover sled, the depression where the ship had rested and his own hasty cover up of the gouge left by the ship's crash landing. However, they never came close enough to discover one slightly odd rock that managed to stay warm throughout the cool night.

The Pleems and other debris had been loaded and taken away some time in the night. Finally, they cordoned off the area with ropes, posted a handful of guards on the first hill and everyone else departed.

When the sun rose high and the heat began to climb, the posted guards sheltered in the shade of the sole remaining vehicle. Their backs were to Humm, so he stealthily crept out of his hiding spot and slipped behind the next low hill. With his uniform on and back in human form, he began walking.

When he was safely away from the soldiers, he scanned in all directions. Seeing nothing, he pressed on away from the soldiers across the desert the rest of that day, through the night and into the next day.

Humm wondered how humans could survive here despite their obvious dependence on water. He had always taken for granted his specie's independence from water when all others couldn't live without it. Maybe this place wouldn't be so bad after all. Laughing at an image of himself as a god among these primitive beings, he topped another hill and spotted a vehicle raising dust on a distant road.

After several more hours of trudging across the dry land, he found himself beside the empty road. He had only been following it for a short while before a vehicle stopped beside him and a human female asked through an open window, "You need a ride, sugar?"

While a furry creature in the back of the vehicle yelled angrily at him in a language unknown to his translator, Humm fumbled with the door handle. After watching for a moment, the driver leaned across the seat and opened it for him. Wearing what he hoped was a sheepish smile, Humm got in and held on tightly as the vehicle sped down the dusty road.

"You got a name?" she asked after a few minutes.

Humm thought back to the stone over William H. Bonny's grave. It had other names on it. Accessing his implants, he recalled them and used his newly acquired ability to translate English. Rejecting Billy the Kid, and Tom O'Folliard, he said, "Charlie Bowdre." The words seemed to come easier than when Rilga had supplied them.

"So, where you from, Charlie?" the female asked casually.

Humm searched the data banks in his implants, until he found the name of a community near the site of his abandonment. "Roswell."

###

About D. B. Crelia

D. B. CRELIA SPENT TEN YEARS traveling the world as a Security Policeman in the US Air Force, followed by twenty going nowhere in the US Postal Service, until one day, he up and quit.

For a while he tended horses and watched his already questionable social skills erode. He built outdoor furniture, most of which he gave to family and friends. He went to work in the oil fields in the Alaskan arctic and came home sick every time.

He worked as a county jailer for only a short while, but recommends it to everyone to put their lives into perspective. And all the while he was writing. Writing, writing, writing.

Finally, at age fifty, his passion for writing aligned with his hard-earned life experience and he, at long last, completed a novel. *Realmswood: Caleb's Mist* is the first book in a Sci-Fi/fantasy trilogy. Book two, *Better the Devil You Know* continues the story that will conclude with book three, which will probably be called *A Chasm of Realms*, or something close. He has also completed a psychological thriller entitled *Finger*, which takes place in the very familiar setting of small-town Texas.

In 2018, he and his wife sold their rural Texas home and almost everything in it, bought a very long recreational vehicle and hit the road, towing a Smart Car. Now he writes on beaches, in mountain forests and even on the snowy Northern plains. With his wife and their puggle named Berkley, he will travel until he's done, then settle somewhere . . . that isn't Texas.

Connect with D. B. here:
www.castrumpress.com/authors/db-crelia

AM I ALONE? AN ODERA CHRONICLES SHORT STORY
By J.R. Handley & Corey D. Truax

The pounding in Sergeant Alexis Monroe's head was matched by the sound of boots marching across the tarmac of Homey Airport. The outside world called the place Area 51, but to Alexis, it's where the military sent her to disappear. Shifting her duty belt, which was digging into her hips, Alexis trudged through another day at her new command. On loan from the Army, she felt detached from the sea of Air Force personnel.

Alexis was proud of her service in the Army. A pioneer, she was one of the first women through the elite Army Infantry School. She'd idealistically enlisted into the Army after graduating college, seeking to strike a blow for female empowerment. Her quest for glory hadn't turned out how she expected.

Every phase of Alexis's journey was marred by political correctness and cries of sexual bias from her peers. She believed, beyond doubt, that when she graduated at the top of her class, she would garner an assignment that would bring her validation. Alexis had been sent to jump school, then to the Non-Commissioned Officer Academy. Her next step should have been orders to lead from the front. Instead, she was given duty as a rent-a-cop guarding a sprawling warehouse complex.

Alexis swallowed her disappointment at night and chased it with whiskey. Every morning, hung over, she swore to go dry. She couldn't seem to keep that promise. Her sunglasses became an unofficial part of her uniform, and none of her superiors cared enough to object.

First, she'd been tasked with checking IDs at the dining facility. Then, she checked IDs at the gate. Now, she was assigned to check IDs at an old hangar that was turned into a warehouse. She'd been told not to look inside the warehouse, not to ask questions, and simply keep the stuff inside, inside, and those outside, outside.

Her domain was the guard shack. Two doors, a tiny desk, an uncomfortable chair, an old rotary dial phone, and a legal pad were her only companions. The phone never rang, and she never had to log a name in the legal pad. In the month she had stood this watch station, no one had ever stopped by her post to gain entry. While boring, this did allow Alexis to covertly sneak a drink from the flask in her cargo pocket.

Alexis had become bolder. Usually, she only took a sip or two once her twelve-hour watch was starting to wind a close. Today, she had started early. The more swigs she swallowed, the more interesting the forbidden door became.

"No entry. Authorized personnel only," said Alexis.

She'd never actually said it to a living person. This time, she was saying it aloud to herself. With a chuckle, she locked the door leading into the guard shack and turned to the entry door into the warehouse.

"Sergeant Alexis Monroe, respectfully requesting permission to enter this stupid warehouse," she said aloud. With a quick pivoting action, she responded to her own request. "Permission granted!"

The worn, brass colored doorknob she expected to be locked turned freely in her hand. As soon as the door pushed open just a crack, the doorknob ripped from her hand as the door sucked open. The sound of the door slamming against the metal warehouse wall was muffled by the many wooden objects inside of the sprawling expanse in front of her. Stacks of boxes, creating walls and aisles, stretched as far as she could see.

Scared the guard on the other side of the warehouse may have heard the door slamming, Alexis pulled the door shut and stepped back into her guard shack. Her shaking hand pulled the flask from her leg and she took another long swig. The warmth of the fluid gripping her from the inside calmed her nerves. Looking to the phone, she flipped to the front of the legal pad. There were three handwritten phone numbers: base security, her guard shack phone number, and the other guard shack phone number.

Alexis dialed the other guard shack. It took forever with the antiquated rotary dial phone. When she was finished dialing, she waited. It rang seven times before someone answered.

"Good evening sir or ma'am," — the person on the other line let out a long yawn — "this is Sergeant Owens at Guard Shack Sierra Two."

"This is Sergeant Monroe at Guard Shack Sierra One, did you hear a loud crash?" said Alexis.

"Monroe, seriously, don't wake me up again," said Owens. "I've been standing this post for six months and nothing ever happens. No one ever comes here. There are never any noises. Just relax and catch up on your girlie magazines."

Owens hung up before Alexis could respond.

What a dick, Alexis fumed.

Turning back to the door, Alexis tightly held onto the doorknob as she turned it this time. When the door cracked open, air began to hiss before the pressure equalized.

She gingerly let the door go and stepped into the dimly lit warehouse. The smell of musty wood filled her nose as she scanned the expanse in front of her.

The mountains of crates in front of her varied in size and shape. Some were larger than cars, others were the size of shoeboxes. While the potential for an endless Christmas was piled in front of her, Alexis decided she would do some exploratory searching first. Shifting her M4 rifle onto her back and pulling her flask out to drink, she walked down an aisle.

The deeper she walked the darker it became. The walls of wood boxes blocked the waning, yellow light shining from far above. Fortunately, the aisle she had chosen didn't branch off. It would be simple to find her way back. A glance upward gave her an idea.

If I can get up there, I can scout the whole place, thought Alexis. This place sure looked smaller from the outside.

Tucking her black, metal flask into her cargo pocket, Alexis began scaling the mountain of crates. She chose a spot that looked like the world's largest staircase. Some of the steps were waist high, but the one she struggled with was at chin level. Channeling her experience running Army obstacle courses, she pulled up, swung a leg onto the lip of the box, and rolled onto the top of the crate.

Sweat beaded her forehead as she sat and regained her breath. Alexis figured she was about sixty feet above the ground. Boxes surrounded her, creating a childlike fortress. Between the exertion and the whiskey in her blood, she felt strangely euphoric about this adventure. Her heart thumped happily as she dangled her legs over the side and took another long pull from the flask.

Warmth pooled under her left hand as she sat. Not thinking much of it, Alexis looked down to see she had sliced her palm open on a nail.

I must be drunker than I realized, she thought as she looked at the gash.

Observing her bloody palm print on the box she sat on, Alexis watched the crimson imprint get smaller. It didn't register as odd, at first. Panic rose in her stomach as droplets of blood began to float above the wood. Jumping to her feet, she looked down at the hovering drops. In an instant, the floating blood veered through the air and slipped through the cracks of a box sitting to her right.

Alexis felt something pulling at her cut hand. Holding her hand out, palm up, blood began to raise up out of the wound and float into the box next to her. She closed her fist tight and fell to her butt as the cracks of the box began to emit blue light. The panic in her stomach turned to nausea. Before she could swallow, Alexis threw up.

The vomit floated in front of her as if in zero-gravity. When the floating alcohol and bile comprising her vomit sucked into the crate, the blue light from within intensified. Not wanted to stick around and see what would happen, Alexis started scampering back down the side of the crates toward the floor. In her hurry, she missed a handhold and fell backwards.

The air pushed out of her lungs as she impacted a wooden box below her. The smack to the back of her head caused the light around her to dim for a moment. Above her, the glowing, vibrating box exploded into splinters. Alexis closed her eyes.

Drunk on duty, thought Alexis. Unauthorized access to a secured location. You've just lost your career.

Opening her eyes back up, the glowing blue from the inside the box bathed her area of the warehouse. An object, perfectly spherical and sky blue, hovered above her. She could hear Owens screaming something from below. It was muted as she stared at the object. It spun faster and faster. As it continued to whirl, the air around her began to whip and whistle. Holding her hands up to shield herself, she screamed as her arms started to shred apart and get sucked into the sphere.

The spinning projectile backed away and floated high above her. For a moment, she thought she would be fine. A thunderclap, louder than anything she had ever heard, obliterated the crates around her. Falling through the air in a shower of splinters, Alexis screamed. Before she could reach the ground, the object streaked like a meteor and impacted her chest.

***

Alexis awoke to darkness. Her head rested against metal, but it wasn't cold. Warmth radiated from the hard, smooth floor. Without the ability to visually check herself for injuries, she began patting herself down hoping there were none. Her fingers traced her chest and felt for where the object had blasted her. There was nothing. In fact, there was no pain at all.

Sitting up, Alexis blinked. Unsure if her eyes were open or closed, she poked an eye with a finger. The pain and surprise of her own finger smashing her eyeball let her know she wasn't dreaming. The silence was frightening. It was mute to the point where she couldn't tell if her mind was creating those ringing and dinging noises or not. Mostly, she heard her own panicked breathing.

Alexis began crawling. It was obvious she wasn't in the warehouse anymore. The floor felt metallic, not the cracked concrete she remembered. It was cool to the touch but would quickly warm up if she left her hand in place.

Is it reacting to me?

When she heard the low clank of metal on metal, slowly moving closer to her, she softly spoke out.

"Hello? Anyone out there?"

Alexis was met with only silence, and the continued shambling of metallic clicks getting louder and louder. Screaming, as frustration got the better of her, Alexis realized the noise could be danger. Her infantry training began to kick in.

Find a wall. Find cover. Find something, anything.

Alexis crawled as fast as she could. When her forehead impacted a wall, she let out a sigh of relief. She was starting to worry she was crawling in an endless expanse.

Standing, she began pacing out the room trying to determine the size and shape. Everything was metal. Like a prison cell or holding facility.

I've been thrown into some sort of brig. They found me. They found my flask. Abandoning your post. Drunk on duty. Destruction of government property. They are going to throw the book at me.

Before Alexis could figure out exactly how large the cell holding her was, she heard different noises, sounds she couldn't quite place. They seemed to exist just below her consciousness, making her wonder if she truly heard or sensed them, or if she was imagining it all. Time seemed to pass, though she had no clue how long.

"Hello, is anyone out there? Am I alone?"

Sitting on her butt, hysteria started to worm into her mind as she wrapped her arms around her knees. Still, she was greeted by metallic scraping, with only darkness to comfort her.

***

Alexis didn't know she'd fallen asleep, but she woke up curled in the fetal position on the metallic floor. She was glad that the strange material seemed to warm on contact with her skin. Standing, she stretched the stiffness out of her bones and tried to ignore the pounding in her head. The alcohol was sweating its way out of her pores, and the smell was sickly sweet.

I'd kill for a nip, she thought as she groaned at the growing pain behind her eyes.

She started talking to fight back the darkness and fear of the unknown.

"Why couldn't this thing have windows? I'd happily murder my own mother for some light."

The moment the words left her lips, the black surrounding Alexis gave way to light. Her head snapped around as she took in the octagonal room. Small, spherical balls spaced evenly at eye level emitted bright, white light.

Each of the eight walls had alcoves built into them. Planks, roughly the length of a person, were centered in each alcove. There was no exit, no doors, no way in or out. Looking at the planks, Alexis realized they appeared to be bunks. Her mind flashed to childhood tours of the naval ships her father served on in the Navy.

For once, something good came from Dad's service in bellbottoms, she thought. Here I was beginning to think the only thing I inherited was his taste for liquor.

She continued muttering to herself as she paced the room and tried to think. There weren't any cameras. The room had the Spartan feel of a brig, but how could there be no door? Clearly the lights responded to her spoken command, but would other commands give the same results?

"Let there be dark!"

The room fell to darkness. She tested the verbal commands in repetition, until the novelty wore off. Before she could get too comfortable, hunger pains hit in earnest. Months of an alcoholic liquid diet was catching up to her.

"Food and drink."

One of the depressions in the wall, which she'd thought was a sleeping alcove for her cell, opened. A mechanical arm, like a tiny version of one that assembled cars in factories, placed a tray on the plank. The silver, metallic arm disappeared momentarily into the wall and returned holding a cup. With a clink, the cup hit the plank and the arm retracted.

Alexis walked over to the tray and cup in a defensive stance. Taking a knee, she looked at where the arm had come from, only to see a smooth surface. Looking at the food, Army field survival training popped into her head. There were steps in determining if something was poisonous or not.

Alexis unbuttoned the cuffs of her sleeves and rolled them up to her elbows. Dipping a finger into the warm mush she rubbed some of it on the inside of her left arm. She did the same with the drink on her other arm.

Wait fifteen minutes...I think? If there is no reaction, rub some on your lips. Then the inside of the lip. Finally, swallow a small quantity.

Moving her hand instinctively to her watch, Alexis realized it was gone. Grasping at the many pockets spread out over her uniform, she realized everything was gone. Including her duty belt and rifle. Perhaps most importantly, her flask was missing.

"I need my watch!"

The room flashed red in response.

"Time. I need to be able to keep track of time."

The room flashed red again.

"Can't you just speak to me? What is this? Where am I?"

Alexis slammed her hands over her ears as sound bombarded her body. It was a deafening mixture of static and garbled electronic beeps. The room glowed bright blue then the sound ceased.

Allowing her fingers to unclench her ears, Alexis figured there were a few possible explanations for the current situation. One, she was part of some odd Army experiment. Likely a result of her negligence on watch leading to her being delegated to a lab rat. Two, she was experiencing alcohol poisoning leading to a bizarre lucid dream. Or three, she had died from the fall and was in some sort of strange purgatory.

None of those options indicated she would die from food poisoning. Taking a breath, she began shoveling the mush into her mouth with her fingers. The taste wasn't horrible, but it wasn't great either. The consistency was thick, and she could feel it working its way down into her stomach. Needing to wash it down, Alexis brought the cup to her lips. Her heart skipped as she took a whiff of the drink.

It smells like whiskey.

The comforting burn of the fluid as it wormed down her throat felt like a hug. Alexis closed her eyes as she swallowed, and for a moment, she was back at home sitting in her worn out recliner. The cup was empty in an instant. Alexis placed the cup back on the plank and stepped back.

"Another drink."

The panel in front of her opened as the robotic arm sprouted from the newly formed void. A mechanical, riveted finger pivoted above the cup and fluid dispensed from the tip. Once the cup was full, the arm snatched the tray and retreated into the wall.

Finishing the second cup and feeling less shaky, Alexis realized she needed to pee before trying to find a way out of the room. She attempted every variation of the word "toilet" she knew. With only red flashes of light as response, she unfastened her pants and peed in a corner. Finishing her business, and frowning at having splashed her boots, Alexis started pacing again.

I need to find a button or switch. Maybe try some more verbal commands while I'm at it?

After the fifth lap around the room and feeling under each of the planks in the alcoves, Alexis let out a sigh. The room vibrated as one of the walls opened abruptly with a grinding noise. A small, boxy robot buzzed into the room through the newly formed door. Emitting high pitched beeping, the shoebox sized robot drove into the puddle of urine Alexis had left behind and stopped.

With a quick rotation, the robot turned toward her. Two circular lenses, that appeared to be eyes, looked at her as the boxy automation began to hum and make sucking sounds.

"Well, this is awkward. Sorry about that little guy. You the janitor?"

The robot beeped in response and turned away from her after the question was asked. In a few moments, the puddle of urine was gone. The robot faced toward Alexis, who had taken a few steps toward the bathroom mishap, and glided toward her.

"I think I'm going to call you Jan the janitor," Alexis announced.

In response, a square panel opened on the robots' front underneath its eyes. Alexis hunkered over to look when black fluid belched from the hole all over her boots. The robot beeped loudly and rolled away toward the door.

Shocked, but not wanting the chance to leave the room to disappear, Alexis hurried after Jan. The moment she passed through the opening after the robot, the wall closed behind her. Alexis could hear beeping ahead of her, but she was standing in darkness. Taking her time, she noted she was traveling in a clockwise manner.

"Light," said Alexis.

Blue orbs along the walls revealed a grated floor with paneled walls. The panels appeared to be storage of some kind and rapping the metal with her knuckles offered hollow thuds. She couldn't see any buttons, latches, keyholes, or scanners to open the wall compartments. Continuing her slow walk, the easy bend of the passageway revealed a new path to the left. She figured if she kept walking straight, she would make a large circle. The passageway to the left would take her somewhere new. Taking the passageway left, there was a different hue of light at the end.

Don't walk into the light, she half-mused.

Beeping from ahead indicated Jan was waiting for her. Keeping her hand to the wall she approached the large, lit room. Alexis squinted as she stepped into the windowed space. The glass of the windows appeared to be convex and bubbled outward. Mentally dubbing the room the fishbowl, she walked up to a window and looked outside.

She choked on her own spit and began coughing as her eyes met the landscape. Brilliant, reddish-orange grass and a gray-blue sky felt wrong. Double moons sat next to each other and a blazing sun hovered to their right. Running from one window to the next, she observed that everything was off. Sure, there were trees and bushes and grass, but everything was the wrong color and size. Blades of grass wider than her body stabbed at the sky and made trees look tiny. Tucked between patches of growth were brick huts that reminded her of third world living conditions. There must have been hundreds of them.

"Is this a ship? Am I on a ship? I'm drunk or dreaming — maybe both. What was in that drink?"

Beeping sounds from behind Alexis caught her attention. Looking over her shoulder, there was nothing there. A bump to her boot caused her to jump, and she looked down to see Jan. A glass of fluid sat on his back.

Snatching the glass from Jan's back, Alexis swallowed the contents in three gulps. The burn in her throat was familiar, everything else was nonsense. Putting the empty cup back on Jan's back, she started looking around. Jan hurried off to a doggy door sized hole near the wall and disappeared. For the first time, Alexis took in the room. In her rush to the windows, she hadn't bothered to look around.

Computer terminals lined the walls and chairs sat empty in front of them. Odd rune-like writing appeared on the screens of the devices. The same writing was scrawled on the walls. One chair was centered in the room and all manner of strange buttons and dials covered the armrests. The chair was a welcome sight. The hard metal floor she had slept on hadn't been forgiving. Walking over and plopping down into it, Alexis smiled.

"Sergeant — no — Captain Alexis Monroe, here. I'll be commandeering this vessel for use in galactic piracy. First mate, fire up the engines for departure!"

Laughing out loud at the absurdity of her situation, Alexis screamed as black straps sprouted from the armrests and wrapped around her wrists and forearms. Kicking hard to try to stand up, something stabbed her in the back. Her strength began to wane as she felt the straps restrict her arms completely. Her entire body jerked as another object pierced her back. Unable to scream, she mumbled as searing heat radiated through her. The burning continued until her eyes closed.

***

Alexis stretched her legs out. Her hand instinctively went to the side handle of her treasured blue recliner and lowered the leg rest. Taking a deep breath in through her nose, she could smell the sweet scent of the candles she burned to hide the odor of booze prevalent in her apartment.

What a strange friggin' dream. I need to cut back on my drinking, she thought as she let out a yawn.

Opening her eyes, she choked down vomit.

"No! What is this? It was a dream!"

Alexis jumped from her recliner and spun in circles. The windowed room, the fishbowl, she was still there. It was just...different. Like pieces of her memory, of her life, were transposed into the room around her. Merged together into a sort of a waking nightmare.

Though the writing was still runic looking, she could read it all. There was the engineering station, the pilot console, the weapons station, and the recessed spot for the ship's executive officer. While the equipment looked mostly the same, the accoutrements were different. The kitten calendar that was on her refrigerator hung on the bulkhead above the engineering station. The wall clock from her bedroom, the giant one that looked like it came from a train station, was inset into the wall directly over the engineering station.

"What's going on here? What is this?"

A sharp, sudden jolt at the top of her spine pushed the air from her lungs. Her fingers grasped at the pain to find a small, hard lump under her skin. Falling back into the recliner, her head snapped right as a small door opened. A four-legged robot walked in that resembled a cat in shape and size. Before Alexis could cough out a word, the mechanical cat looked up at her and spoke.

"Hello, Ship's Mother. While you slept, I worked with the ship's repair robots to make this place feel more like your home."

Alexis stared at the cat. Unable to summon words, she pinched her arm.

"Yes, this is your species' attempt at determining whether you are in a dream state or not. I assure you, Ship's Mother, you are awake. Welcome to the Odera."

"Odera? What's going on and what are you?"

Two curved pieces of metal that resembled ears lowered as the cat heard her question. Perking again, the two circular lenses serving as eyes looked up to her.

"I am Jan. A name given to me after you marked the living space with your scent via fluid excretion. I returned the gesture in respect. This ship, Odera, is your new home. Your unbreakable oath was sworn the moment you sat down in the captain's chair. You are now the chosen dignitary for your species."

The moment Jan stopped speaking, Alexis thought of the name Odera. Something about the word pulled at her memories.

Odera means the tiny bird. It's a Yura Class Super Corvette that was retrofitted with cruiser class weapons and an overcharged engine. How do I know this?

Jan stalked over to Alexis and jumped into her lap. Mechanical purring began to sound as the robot vibrated softly.

"You know this because you were linked to this ship while you slept," said Jan. "Tiny machines, your species refers to them as nanobots, have linked the many synapses of your brain to the larger computerized brain of Odera."

If that's true, I need a drink.

"I expected you to say that," said Jan. "It's on the side table already."

Alexis looked to her right. The side table from her living room sat there. A bottle of Virginia Gentleman, her favorite whiskey, sat on top. Grabbing the bottle and turning it over in her hands, Alexis sighed. Her fingers trembled as she spun the black and silver, metal lid from the top of the bottle and took a long pull.

"So, now what? We going to get drunk and fly this thing, or what? Take me home."

"Ship's Mother, I recommend we —"

"Enough with the 'Ship's Mother' bullshit! Call me Alexis."

Jan jumped on top of one of the computer terminals, walked in three circles, and sat down.

"Alexis, I recommend you wake the crew if you want to fly. Just say, 'initiate milvus protocol.'"

"The crew? Where the hell have they been this whole time? You have them packed away in storage somewhere?" said Alexis.

"Yes. They must be assembled to resemble your species and merged with your biological blueprint."

Alexis looked over at Jan who stretched out in a box of light cast through the window. Two panels opened on its side and pointed toward the light.

"What do you mean by assembled and merged with my biological blueprint? What are they, cyborgs or something?" said Alexis.

"Define cyborg," Jan replied.

"Half machine and half human."

"Yes, cyborgs! I did not see this memory in your scans. You will want to initiate cyborg protocol," said Jan.

Alexis looked over at Jan who was still absorbing the sun's rays.

"On my planet, in stories at least, cyborgs usually end up trying to kill everyone," said Alexis. "They start off friendly, then start plotting, and before you know it, they end up trying to eradicate humans to save them or some nonsense. Will these cyborg crewmembers be under my control?"

The panels on Jan's side retracted as the robotic cat jumped to its feet.

"Your crewmates would never do that, Alexis! You are the Ship's Mother, and they are bound to your command. Their personalities will be imprints of humans from your memory, and Odera formats the master obedience command override."

I guess it's better than only having a robotic cat to talk to while I get drunk, thought Alexis.

"I thought taking the form of a cat would be pleasing to you," said Jan. The metal felines head hung low. "If we could find biological matter from one of these cat creatures, I could fully look like one."

Alexis let out a heavy sigh, having forgot her thoughts were being read by the ship, and by proxy, Jan.

"We'll cross that bridge when we get home, Jan. Go ahead and initiate cyborg protocol. If any of these cyborgs have an Austrian accent, we're going to have problems."

Expecting something momentous to happen, Alexis scratched her head when nothing, but silence followed the command.

"Um, Jan? Did the ship receive my command?"

A computerized voice, eerily like her own, responded.

Command has been accepted, Alexis. Assembly of crew will take approximately twenty-four of your hours. I recommend you rest in the meantime. Merging with me took a toll on your body.

Alexis wasn't sure what her future held as she pulled the wooden handle of her recliner and let her feet raise up. At least she had booze and a position of authority. A great combination by her estimation.

###

About J.R. Handley

J.R. HANDLEY IS A PSEUDONYM for a husband and wife writing team. He is a veteran infantry sergeant with the 101st Airborne Division and the 28th Infantry Division. She is the kind of crazy that interprets his insanity into cogent English. He writes the sci-fi while she proofreads it.

The sergeant is a two-time combat veteran of the late unpleasantness in Mesopotamia where he was wounded, likely doing something stupid. He started writing military science fiction as part of a therapy program suggested by his doctor, and hopes to entertain you while he attempts to excise his demons through these creative endeavors. In addition to being just another dysfunctional veteran, he is a stay at home wife, avid reader and all-around nerd. Luckily for him, his Queen joins him in his fandom nerdalitry.

Connect with JR here:
www.castrumpress.com/authors/jr-handley

About Corey Truax

COREY TRUAX IS A WRITER, editor, blogger, stay-at-home dad, and a husband. A veteran Navy combat cameraman and journalist, he has dropped his anchor on the shore of civilian life. His wife, on the other hand, keeps them moving around the world as an active-duty Navy nuclear engineer.

When he's not using a handheld dosimeter to scan his baby boy for radiation, he is dutifully creating new stories and worlds. Corey works to continuously improve and share his knowledge of the craft by offering writing tips to fellow scribblers on his author website.

Connect with Corey here:
www.castrumpress.com/authors/corey-truax

ALIEN DAYS

DEAD RECKONING
By Anthony Regolino

"Bennett! I can't move!" were the last words spoken by my Special Task Force partner. I turned around, pointed my pistol at his head, and fired.

I left his body there in the ventilation shaft of the alien vessel we had infiltrated. But only after first making sure that it was lifeless.

He had almost made it with me to our destination. Almost. Just ahead of me I could see the grating which should lead into the Prisoner of War detainment cell. I trudged onward, furiously shuffling on my worn elbows and knees, and cursing the fact that I couldn't rise even to a crouch in this cramped shaft. Our layouts of the lair were correct. This was the cell I sought.

The POWs were lying slumped against the walls, sometimes on top of each other, motionless but not lifeless. I lay flattened atop the grating and found that it was possible for me to slip my arm through, at least up to the elbow. I knew that many beneath me could see my dangling appendage, while there would be those who would not suspect my presence. It did not matter. Their salvation would come. There— someone I recognized. A soldier from my previous unit. What was his name? Sachs, that was it! Hold on, Sachs, I'll rescue you.

I retracted my arm and adjusted my laser for the job it had to do on the grating. Then I set to work disintegrating the metal with as narrow a steady beam as the weapon could produce. I hoped that I would not have to drop down into the cell, but a quick glance at all the prisoners assured me that it would not be necessary.

I readjusted the laser, dropped my arm through the widened opening, and proceeded to blast the brains out of everybody in the room.

When I was certain that no life existed in the cell beneath me, I looked again at the carnage that remained and turned the barrel of the gun upon myself.

***

"WHY ME?"

Is that what everyone would say if they were in my shoes?

I thought back to how it all began. The beginning of the end. In the war. And as I thought back to the war, I looked with bitter hatred on my brother man. The human race. A race of inhumans.

Take any other rational race and ask them what they would do if a strange new alien race should come along and introduce itself. Do you think their answer would be "Start a war with them"? I don't.

At least I hope not. I hope that our race is the only one with so heartless an inclination, and I hope that all other life-forms stay clear of us. It's too late for the Progellics. They have met mankind (mankind, ha! —as if man were kind) and have suffered for it. We took their bodies and used them for food, took their fluids and used them for drugs—powerful, hallucinatory drugs, not even for medicinal purposes.

Ah, but maybe I'm being too hard on mankind. The majority of the population didn't know what the government and its military were doing to the Progellics. Some didn't even know about our contact with them until the war started!

It had been going on for a year (quite a long time for wars these days) before I was drafted. The battlefield was the Arctic. The Progellics were reptilian, but they hail from a planet far colder than ours and to them the Arctic Circle was paradise. I don't need to tell you how our 'heroes' felt, freezing their parkas off and struggling to maneuver on a ground that the Progellics' webbed feet took to easily.

So, it was no wonder that our boys were being taken out left and right. And we just kept sending them more to kill. Were there any alternatives? Missiles? You forget, we were dealing with an advanced race. They had some kind of protective shield blanketing their entire setup. Even planes and helicopters would experience interference when approaching the force field and would be grounded, often taking casualties. We had to go at them at ground zero. Which, fortunately, was how they came at us. Their massive spaceships were apparently not for fighting purposes and constituted their headquarter base. Five of them, linked by docking chutes, looking eerily like a misplaced Pentagon building, anchored up there on the ice of the North Pole.

As far as weapon technology was concerned, we seemed to be evenly matched. Seemed to be. We had the typical, standard laser rifles and pistols, and they had handheld (or rather claw-clutched) projectile weapons. In that regard it looked like we had the better technology. (It would figure—wouldn't it? —that the only technology we would excel in was in the weapons department!) However, better weapons or not, we still had trouble moving, breathing, standing, eating, ad infinitum, in a climate that the enemy felt at home in.

And I took my place in the ranks, just as all those before me. I took a projectile in the leg and fell to the ground amidst the snow-covered bodies that beat me to it. I squeezed my eyes shut against the searing pain, and in seconds I passed out.

***

When I regained consciousness, I underwent that understandable delirium that leads one to wonder where I was, how I had gotten there, and how much time had passed. Well it couldn't have been that long, or I would have been covered by more snow than I was. All it took was one glimpse around to know where I was and why. The dead bodies told me all I needed to know. But for some reason there didn't seem to be as many human bodies as there should be. And there were Progellic bodies not too far away. A lot closer than they were when I exited the battle. I concluded that they must have hit us suddenly during a body cleanup run. I wondered if they would try to retrieve their dead from the battlefield, or if that was only a human thing.

I moved slowly, not wanting to re-experience the shocking pain in my leg, but to my surprise I felt nothing. The cold must have numbed everything. In this temperature, the blood hardly even flows, which is convenient if blood loss is the only thing threatening to take your life. I stood and didn't even wobble. I felt like casting aside the parka, since I didn't feel the cold, but I figured that this was just a side-effect of lying in the numbing snow and ice and if I stripped naked I would not feel the cold but it would kill me just the same.

So, the question was: Could I make it to the nearest base without succumbing?

✳✳✳

The winds were blowing fiercely, practically carrying me along, making my progress easier, till finally the gate stood before me, and behind it a very surprised guard. He approached and scrutinized me, shielding his eyes from the gale. His hood flew back from his head, and I pulled mine back so he could see me better.

"Are you in need of medical assistance?" He screamed, his voice sounding like a distant whisper in the wind, as he pulled a key ring from his pocket and fished through them for the right one.

"Yes!"

He admitted me and pointed out an enclosed encampment. Once inside, I shrugged off my parka and collapsed into the nearest chair. I rose again quickly as a medic approached me with a chart in one hand and a pen in the other. Before he could open his mouth, I was already providing my information. "Bennett! Private Roger Peter! Serial number A-six-two-F..." Had I lost him already? He was staring down at my body, a nervous expression on his face.

"Y-You don't belong here," he stammered.

"I don't? Great, then send me home. I've had enough of this war anyway." Typical grunt response, but one I felt wholeheartedly, nonetheless.

"No, I mean, in this emergency ward." He was taking a few steps back, but I matched each with a step forward of my own.

"Whatta ya mean? I'm injured, right? Where else should I go, the kitchen? Bleed all over the rations?"

We were joined by an older man who wanted to help clear things up. He peered down at my body and his helpful expression disappeared, replaced by a look of annoyance. "Oh, you don't belong here," he said disgustedly. "Why didn't you tell us you were dead?"

That took a few moments to register. "Excuse me? Dead? Is that what you said?"

"Yes," the older man said, "dead, killed on the battlefield. He walked past me and pointed out the window at another encampment. "You gotta go over there."

"And then I'll be in heaven or something?" I said, not sure what kind of joke this was.

"You wish," the younger man replied with a snort.

"Now, Jeffrey," the older one said in rebuke. "That's no way to treat someone who gave his life defending our world. He turned back to me with a solemn expression on his face, as if in remorse for his previous attitude toward me. "Go there, son. It's where you belong." I had stooped to retrieve my parka, when he informed me that I wouldn't need it anymore.

Not understanding, I trudged over to where I was told to go and found a guard at the entrance. The wind had died down for the moment, making it easier to travel and speak. The guard stared at me without any expression, and so I asked him, "Are you Saint Peter?"

"Who are you here to see?" He said in a predictable monotone.

"No one. I was told I was dead and had to come here."

He then glanced down, and it was as if he was seeing me for the first time. "What are you doing out there?" He asked as he sprang forward to let me in. "You don't belong out there."

"So, I was told. I just wandered in from the battlefield."

"Where you were killed."

"No, where I was shot. But, as you see, I'm fine. I'm not even limping with the leg I was shot in." Then I remembered how everyone looked down at my body first before presuming me to be dead. "And just how does everyone come to the conclusion that I'm dead by looking at me?"

"One of your tags was removed."

I reached up, and sure enough only one dog tag dangled against my chest from the chain hanging around my neck. I thought back to the conditions I awoke to on the battlefield, and what I had perceived the situation to be prior to my regaining consciousness. "That doesn't mean anything!" I exploded. "They were in the process of retrieving our bodies when they were suddenly hit by a wave of attacking Progellics. Lizard skin was everywhere! They didn't get to check our bodies thoroughly. I wish I could get my hands on the bastard who did the half-assed job of checking me for life . . ." I thought of how my loved ones were already being informed of my alleged passing and the grief it would be putting them through, and all for nothing!

The guard lifted my tag, then turned and pressed a buzzer. "Mister Bennett, you are experiencing the shock that accompanies finding out that you are no longer alive. A trauma team will be here momentarily."

"Private Bennett! My rank is private second class!"

"Mister Bennett, once you died you became a civilian again. You have no further obligation to the military. In fact, the military considers itself obliged to help you.

I could hear the rushing feet of the trauma team and the squeaky wheels of the hospital gurney that they ran alongside. I turned and bolted through the exit, apparently had someone out there waiting. He swept my feet from under me and I fell hard, face first, into the packed snow. And you know, it didn't hurt at all.

***

As I was led around the grounds that were to be my new home, everything was explained to me carefully, twice, and to my eternal dismay. The Progellics may only have projectile weapons, but their ammo was unlike anything known to man. And if only it had stayed unknown to man. When the projectile enters the body it releases a poison into the bloodstream, a poison which kills the body but leaves the mind alive— preserved, in fact—so that the victim remains conscious, fully aware as the body rots and decays, a process which itself is slowed down for prolonged effect.

We rolled past a young soldier who'd been dead for a month. Beside him sat his wife, the young widow, trying to be strong and talking to him in a soothing voice that occasionally broke, followed by spells of silence. The soldier just stared ahead, seeming to all the world to be oblivious to her presence. But in his tortured mind there was no rest, no peace from the mental hell from which he could not escape.

You see, movement is the first to go. That's why they were carting me around in a wheelchair. The rigor mortis sets in at different times for different people, depending on God knows what: Metabolism, point of bullet entry, extent of damage outside of poisoning, age, hair color, who knows! For some, the stiffening is instantaneous; for others, it could take weeks. I would prove to be one of the lucky ones. However, as we passed the motionless stiffs, positioned in either sitting or lying poses depending on how they were when they lost the ability to move, I was convinced that my muscles were hardening right then and there. And fear gripped me. A fear unlike any I had ever known—and, facing reptilian aliens in a war we couldn't win, I was no stranger to fear.

Each blank stare seemed to lock onto me, to try to give me some ominous message, to warn me of what I would soon be going through, even though I understood that none of them had even the ability to focus their vision.

I was lifted and placed on a bed. Sure, I could have just up and lay down on my own, but I was momentarily paralyzed by all the information I had to assimilate. And, I guess, I was trying to prepare myself for my impending immobility.

My 'new home' was a bed in a tent surrounded by other beds with corpses on them. Only, I was beginning to think of them as more than just bodies. I mean, there was an intelligence still at work in each one of them. Although they sure would make for lousy neighbors. I was left alone with them and told that a social worker would be with me shortly to discuss my visiting privileges. Visitors? Were they serious? Do they really think I would want anyone to see me like this—or rather, like those around me? And yet, I could imagine the terrible boredom, the intense tedium they were experiencing. Imagine sitting in a room with no one to talk to, staying up day and night, just praying for a change in scenery. Not moving, not doing anything pleasurable like eating or making love, just sitting and staring. Hoping for a fly to come into view for some entertainment—only you wouldn't be able to focus on it or follow its movements. You could only pray that occasionally it or something else moves into your line of vision. With these as the conditions, would you want to live forever?

I peered over at the victims lying on either side of me (I didn't want to stiffen up without ever knowing who was next to me; the curiosity would drive me mad!), then suddenly felt a wave of guilt overcome me. Sure, I could still do that, but what about them? I felt the heat of all the consciousnesses in the tent focusing on me, with envy, hatred. I didn't want them to hate me. I wanted them to accept me. After all, I was one of them. I wanted to tell them this, stand up, move into everyone's line of sight, introduce myself to them and assure them that in no time I would be just like them! Sick, huh? And I might have done it, too, if my social worker hadn't suddenly leaned into view (must be a habit of theirs, or a precaution) and introduced herself.

My, was she pretty. I wondered if she'd give a dying man a last request, something to stay with me for the rest of eternity. Then I almost gagged at the thought of asking her to have sex with a dead body. And let's face it, that's exactly what mine was. I doubt I could even get it up for her. Did I say that movement is the first to go? My mistake. Feeling is. Any tactile sensation whatsoever.

"Hi, my name is Dorothy. It is my duty to inform you of all rights you retain after you have died. If you wish to have visitors, they must participate in our secrecy program . . ." Yeah, yeah. I got the gist of all this as they rolled me in. The government didn't want the whole world to know about this horrible predicament they had gotten us all into. As she restated all this in a more formalized manner, all I thought about was her hair. Strawberry blonde, and looking as if she had just washed it, I would've given anything to be able to smell its freshness and guess which fruity scent her shampoo was.

". . . which brings us to your right to end this all and simply die. If you wish, you can waive this right and leave it up to your family to decide . . ." What was that?

"Wait a minute. Are you saying that I can die for good? Not go through this hell-on-earth?"

"As I was saying, you have the right to end this now, or, if you feel that you haven't lived long enough, to set a date for the termination of your existence . . ."

"But how? I thought that the whole terribleness of this weapon was that you could not die."

"We . . . believe—we are not certain—that destroying the brain will do the trick. You see, there is a difference between a body being dead and being brain dead. If I hooked up an EEG to any of these bodies around you, they would still exhibit brain activity. That's how we know they're still conscious. Nevertheless, somehow, even though the brain is made useless by the poison in that it can't give or receive commands from the body, it is still active and alive. And putting a bullet through it or searing it with a laser kills it and puts an end to all mental activity, at least as far as we can tell from our machines. We can only hope that, for those we can't help, the misery ends when the body eventually decays and the brain crumbles to dust with it.

"There are some who have volunteered themselves for such experimentation, and it's something you should consider yourself, something to help give meaning to your death, by helping us learn more about this condition, so we can help assure others who have fallen victim to this horrible Progellic weapon . . ."

I could hear a sales pitch in the works and stopped her before she got her hopes up. She looked disappointed, but then reassumed her cheery countenance to tell me about how my death could still be made fulfilling through visits from loved ones. Of course, they would not be allowed to take me home, since their secrecy program was still in effect. Although, if more and more victims ask for their families to be informed of their condition so that they could come and visit, keeping this from the general public will become impossible. But for now, a relatively small percentage had been requesting this, and the families had been so disturbed and emotionally distraught that they couldn't bring themselves to tell anyone about it anyway and prefer to tell people that their spouse/child/parent was dead . . . which would be true, of course.

"Forget it. My parents are the real militant types who would be proud enough to declare that their son died in battle. As for loved ones . . . There's no one." I turned my head away as I said this. She probably thought I was upset about not having a wife or lover, but this wasn't the case. I lied. There was someone. Someone very special. So special that I couldn't bear for her to see me—Wait . . . that's not the reason, nothing so noble. My real reason was a selfish one. I didn't want to see her and not be able to put my arms around her, to tell her the things I didn't get the chance to before I left. In fact, there was a good possibility she forgot about me already. We had only been going out for a month when I received the call to serve. I don't know if I meant as much to her as she did to me, but I like to think back fondly on the expression on her face when I told her I'd been drafted. She was devastated. I must have meant something to her.

"Well, if you'd still like visitors, we have numerous volunteers who spend their days consoling and entertaining . . ."

"I'm sorry. I just want to be alone right now."

"Well all right, but . . . if you think that you're starting to stiffen up, press the button behind you and I'll be here to take your decision. Remember, don't take too long. And move around a lot so you know you still can. You don't want to lose the opportunity to express your wishes."

I rolled over on my side, ignoring what she said, and drew my legs up into a fetal position. My first impulse was to buzz her and tell her to kill me immediately. But that led me to wonder just what would happen to me then. I didn't much believe in an afterlife. I mean, I hoped and prayed, just like everyone else, that there would be one, but I had resigned myself to an acceptance that maybe there wasn't anything afterwards. My faith was not strong enough to provide comfort, and so I had to find something else to look forward to. But what?

I lay for a week, refusing to see or speak to anyone, just sorting and resorting things out in my head. I guess you could say I was doing some interior decorating to see if I could live there. At times I could feel eyes upon me, and I would spring around to catch Miss Strawberry Blonde Dorothy watching me. As soon as I'd turn to her, she'd make a note on her pad, an impressed expression on her face, and walk away. Why was she watching me, though? To make sure I don't harden before filling out her organ donor cards?

I knew I was running a risk by not telling them what I wanted done with myself. If I waited too long, the decision would no longer be mine. And maybe that's what I wanted. For someone else to decide. But who had the right to decide? That was what was bothering all the higher officials, doctors, and clergy involved. No one wanted to take the initiative, or the blame, and it was apparent that it would eventually be put before legislature, but that would have to wait until the secrecy program was scrapped.

So, all those poor souls who were already immobile when they were salvaged had to just sit and rot. Occasionally one would be put out of its misery. Periodically, machines were carted around to each body to determine its state of mental activity. And if the readings suggested that the person was in excruciating mental anguish, the brain of that person was destroyed. What got me was that every one of these victims probably went through periods of extreme anguish, alternately followed by periods of calm, and the doctors just happened to get them during a bad spell. It seemed normal to me; there was probably a cycle one went through. I would find out soon enough. And I grew determined that the decision—whatever it would be—would be mine.

I just needed more time to think it through.

***

As I approached the two-week mark, I began to feel invincible. I imagined that maybe I was different, maybe I would avoid losing my mobility, maybe I was the one exception to the rule. The scientists could study me and learn why I was immune to the rigor mortis. An antidote could be developed, and we could cure everyone who had ever been afflicted or ever will be!

Sure, and maybe the Progellics would forgive us, throw down their weapons, and provide the cure for us. Not likely. And I was still another two weeks short of setting any records.

When I was officially dead two weeks, I received my first visitor outside of my social worker. A major. He had a proposition for me. The major was putting together a special task force made up entirely of dead men to go on suicide runs. One objective might be to cause as much damage and take out as many Progellics as possible (after all, once they killed us, their weapons were useless against us); another mission might be to collect and send back data. A trial run had already provided a pathway that we could use to sneak into their base of linked ships. And it also sent back information that would disturb the world if it got out: they had POWs. Dead soldiers just heaped together in rooms, awaiting God-knows-what kind of mental torture. If the higher-ups had been divided in their views of whether or not to kill the helpless dead in our own camps, they were united in their views concerning the dead prisoners of war. They should be mercifully killed. It was unanimous. We would all rest better knowing that they didn't have our dead. Our imaginations cooked up all sorts of terrors that our boys must be going through, and we wanted it stopped. And yes, I mean we. That was how I felt, and upon hearing about them I knew what I wanted to do with myself. I wanted to go on a successful suicide run.

They approached me, as they approached anyone who retained movement after two weeks. Seems that if we made it this far, we'd probably last the whole month before freezing up. I would spend the next week in training, along with the rest of my task force, and then we'd be off on our assignment. We may have already had combat training, but this was different. We had to learn the art of espionage, to sneak around without being seen, to spy. Hell, we even had to learn how to move!

Since our bodies were devoid of feeling, we had to get used to using them to their fullest, now that we didn't have pain to worry about. We could work our legs harder, throw our bodies around more efficiently and give little care to how our heads got banged around—provided we still protect our eyes and ears, our only working sensors.

We practiced scrabbling about with bound appendages (any two picked at random) to simulate what it would be like if we were discovered and had some of our limbs shot off. We could train day and night without ever feeling fatigue. We would not feel compelled to eat or go to the bathroom. We were beginning to feel good about ourselves—the super soldiers! —as long as we didn't think about how temporary it all was.

We were assigned partners. This was so that if one of us got overzealous and ended up hardening before he could off himself, the other could do it for him. Pretty grim business. It was naturally agreed upon (an unspoken agreement, in fact) that we would not get to know our partners too well. All I knew about mine was that he was young and gung-ho about our mission. (But then I guess I gave off the same outward impression.) And that his name was Williams.

Normally you vow to protect your partner's life to the end; we vowed to take it.

Three weeks dead, we embarked on our mission. Ten Special Task Force units, each made up of six soldiers. The units were ordered according to their objectives and were sent out at hourly intervals. I was in Unit Three, and we were the rescue team, as were Units Four and Five. The first two had already left to secure positions for following units and provide them aid. The later units were each made up of three assassins paired with three demolition men.

Don't confuse the rescuers' mission with the assassins. We were going to kill our fellow fallen soldiers in order to save their souls (an assignment I insisted on), while the assassins were going to exterminate as many lizards as they could. They were being sent after us so as not to interfere with our work, which was given a higher priority. It was apparent that once they set to work killing and destroying things, our force would be discovered. That's why the earlier teams were to be more discreet, hiding the bodies they take out and only causing damage that could not be discovered at once. By the time Unit Ten arrived it would be a free-for-all, bombs going up and lasers going off in an attempt to blow the aliens right the hell back to Progell!

It would be glorious. But I wouldn't be there to see it. After our unit finishes its objective, it was to eliminate itself. Remember, the driving force behind this Task Force was to keep our captured dead from existing in some hell or limbo. That's why the later units had to make sure they didn't get shot up so badly they couldn't finish themselves off. Hence all that training. We all underwent the same training, naturally, since anything could go wrong at any point and we may all be called upon to fight our way in to do our job.

So as Unit Three was sent off, we didn't know what to expect. Units One and Two may have failed in their secure-and-hold missions, and we may already be expected. We all carried walkie-talkies—the old-fashioned kind, whose low-range weak frequencies were expected to go undetected by their high tech—and if we walked into a trap, we were supposed to send off an emergency signal. But that blanketing force field overhead even had a way of interrupting our ground communications once we were past its perimeter.

Our route was a tunnel beneath the ice, and since neither breathing nor freezing was a concern for us, we progressed easily. After twenty minutes we reached our hidden passage into the ship's hull and entered the framework of the Progellic Pentagon. We found every member of Units One and Two where they should be as we moved further into the enemy base. They pointed out which ventilation shafts passed over the rooms with the POWs in them and informed us that they had already removed the gratings that covered the entrances we were to use. We then split up into our teams of two and told the first units that we didn't need their help and to look out for the next team.

I jumped and pulled myself up into the overhead hatchway with ease and glanced back to see that Williams was having difficulty and fell back down. The hatchway was only nine feet up!

An older-looking soldier from the last unit helped Williams to his feet and steered him back beneath the opening. With a steadying hand at my partner's back, he peered up at me and a silent dialogue passed between us. I nodded and looked down, signifying my understanding. Williams wouldn't make it.

With the vet ready below in case Williams should slip again, I reached down and helped my partner up. I could see in his face how strenuous the effort was for him and how frustrated he was becoming. He avoided my eyes and I turned and trudged ahead on my elbows and knees, muttering an encouraging word on how the rest of the way should be easier and how he should make it without any problem.

I lied. Five minutes later he called out to me and you know the rest. Job is done and now what?

Yeah, I know what I'm supposed to do, but I am still as uncertain as I was in that tent, lying on my side on my bed, pondering the mysteries of the universe and all that shit. I still don't want it to end.

I stare down again at all the victims in the room below me. A voice next to me makes me practically leap out of my skin. "Clean job. Hell, we didn't have nearly as many bodies to mind-wipe in our cell. So, what are you waiting for? You want to live forever?" I turn and recognize another member of my unit.

"What if I do?" I ask innocently, a disarming smile on my face.

"Can't let ya do that," he says as he reaches for the laser pistol in the holster at his hip. Mine is still in my hands.

I turn it on him and fire at point blank range, searing the whole top of his head off.

Now what'd he go and make me do that for? Why was he wandering around after finishing his job? Looking for "just the right place" to die? Or maybe he took it upon himself to make sure everyone else was dead and not frozen in place in these ventilation shafts, unable to finish themselves off. I enlarge the hole I made in the grating and shove his body through. It now lies with the rest of the corpses.

Am I a murderer? He was dead anyway, just like the rest of us, ready to turn the trigger on himself at any moment. I regard what's left of his face. He would have to fall face up! I watch his eyes for some sign that maybe he's still alive. They did admit that this might not do the trick. They only believed that killing the brain would end our consciousness. They didn't know. I cannot pry my eyes away from his, hoping against all hope that his soul was freed from its earthly vessel when I splattered his brains all over this shaft.

It's funny. Whenever I refer to anyone else, I mention his soul as if I have no doubt that he has one. But when I think of myself, I'm not so sure. I'm afraid. Of not having a soul or any promise of an afterlife. Of living as a conscious corpse. Of our mission being for nothing if this doesn't work. Of everything at once.

Oh, why didn't I stay at the camp? Why didn't I request visitors? Would it have been so bad? To see Lonnie's face again . . .

Then Lonnie's face disappears, and I once again see the half-face of the man I killed. I hear a voice, drifting up the shaft from behind me, but the words are meaningless to me now. "Hey Rogers, where'd ya go?" it says.

That must be the name of the man I just shot. Rogers. I say a silent prayer to help his soul find its way, and the voice speaks again, closer this time, the words barely working their way into my distracted thoughts: "Hey, get a load of this poor sap. Let himself freeze solid right over his targets. Hang on, buddy, I'll be right with you. And then it'll all be over."

I had been wondering about this Rogers person wandering around these shafts . .

I had forgotten about his partner.

###

About Anthony Regolino

WITH OVER TWENTY YEARS' EXPERIENCE in the publishing industry, mostly as an editor, Anthony Regolino has acted as ghostwriter and contributing writer, as well as creating professional blogs for company websites.

While studying on scholarship in NYU's Dramatic Writing Program, he enjoyed seeing his first sketch performed before an audience—on Broadway, as he likes to say (which is technically correct)! Participation in local theater, both on and off stage, allowed him the opportunity to create an adaptation that was cleverly translated for the stage.

His novel, Canis Sapiens: The Dingo Factor, was released in 2016, while his short story "The Mystified Morpheus" was included in the 2018 horror anthology Fierce Tales: Shadow Realms.

In addition to the publication of his short story "Dead Reckoning," 2019 sees the addition of Anthony Regolino into the ranks of Arthurian scribes, as his story "Curse of Avalon" and his first published poem, "The Duty," offer two different takes on the same legendary event: the delivery of Excalibur to King Arthur by the hand of the Lady of the Lake. Perfect companion pieces to each other, these can be found in Left Hand Publishers' Classics Remixed and Dragon Soul Press's Organic Ink, Volume One, respectively. He is currently working on having more of his works brought before an audience, in the form of prose, screenplays, teleplays, and comic book scripts.

Connect with Anthony here:
www.castrumpress.com/authors/anthony-regolino

ALIEN DAYS

AFTER THE CRASH
By Jason J. McCuiston

Resnick opened the glovebox, grabbed his .45 and an extra magazine. One could never be too careful in "Bat City" after dark. The Noctu weren't the nastiest of the Guests, but they were pretty high on the list. Particularly those who had blended into the criminal underbelly of New Orleans.

"Why couldn't this be a Nolphid case?" Tossing a still smoking butt to the gutter, he stepped out of his old Packard and onto a dingy stretch of Alabo Street. Resnick didn't like any of the Guests, but at least the Nolphid weren't ugly. Their chattering voices could grate on the nerves, but they always seemed to be smiling. The Noctu, on the other hand, resembled giant bats about to take a bite out of you. And here he was, in the heart of Bat City looking for Jaxtifar M'Koth, a Noctu gunsel responsible for breaking a couple skulls while stealing something from his client, the wealthy philanthropist Archibald Perigeaux.

Skirting a trio of young Noctu hoods—their eyes glowing red in the streetlights—Resnick headed across the trash-lined street to the one place in all of New Orleans he wished to never see again. Lilly's Place. Despite being in the heart of the Lower Ninth Ward it remained a favorite hangout for the city's well-to-dos, Guest and human alike.

Resnick recognized the man at the door and hoped the familiarity was mutual. He had downed his fair share at Lilly's back in his bootlegging days. Before the Twenty-First Amendment forced him to turn the skills he'd learned in the Great War and Prohibition to legitimate ends; before he became 'respectable.'

"Big Jim." Resnick smiled and offered his hand to the towering black man. "Been a long time."

The bouncer narrowed his dark eyes, jaw clenched, before recognition washed over his rugged face. "Billy. Billy Resnick. It has been a long time, sure 'nuff. Not since I seen your picture in the paper for saving them Beaufort twins. Shaking hands with the mayor and everything. What brings you down here? You on a case?"

Resnick grinned, acknowledging the double-edged sword of fame. It opened doors, but it also hindered keeping a low profile. Not necessarily the best thing for a gumshoe. "Just wanted to make the rounds, see some of my old haunts, y'know?"

"Sure, sure." Big Jim replied. "Well you come right on in, Billy. Marquez will set ya up at the bar, and Miss Lilly'll be going onstage any minute now."

"Thanks." Resnick walked inside, pausing at the hatcheck to let his eyes adjust to the gloom. Relishing the scent of expensive booze and tobacco mingling with soft jazz on the heavy air; the flavor of money and decadence. From the outside, Lilly's Place appeared to be a rundown conglomeration of boarded-up storefronts. But inside, it could have been a swank Hollywood movie set. Resnick half expected to see William Powell and Myrna Loy dance through the crowd of tuxedoed gents, gowned ladies, scantily clad cigarette girls, and waiters in ties and tails.

It occurred to him how accustomed he'd grown to seeing Guests mingling in such settings: Noctu in tuxedoes styled to accommodate their arm-wings, curvy Nolphid women in expensive gowns that paled in comparison to the lustrous sheen of their own pearlescent skins. And, most alien of all, the bipedal, four-armed insectoid Anterix; their red and black exoskeletons "painted" to simulate modern fashion. There were others, he knew. But these three species made up the bulk of the Guests who had come down in the southern United States when their titanic colony ship had broken up in the atmosphere six years ago.

"Like 1929 didn't give us enough hungry mouths to feed..." He mumbled while pocketing the stub for his fedora as he made his way to the bar. "The stock-market tanks and then hell's rejects fall from the skies."

"Billy Resnick!" Marquez, the Creole bartender exclaimed. "I ain't seen you in a coon's age, brother. How ya been?"

"Fair to middling, my friend." Resnick leaned against the marble-topped bar and scanned the crowded main room. He spotted three city councilmen, two judges, and a senator among the night's patrons. "Looks like business is booming even with legal hooch."

"That's a fact," Marquez agreed. "Miss Lilly's got a head for business on those curvy shoulders for sure. You're usual still Glenmorangie?"

Resnick nodded, speechless as he caught sight of the lovely owner and songstress gracefully taking the stage. The lights went down. A gentle murmur, then silence replaced the boisterous carousing. All eyes turned on the beautiful mulatto in the red dress. The spotlight bathed her in shimmering silver light. Her opening notes were acapella, soft and husky yet powerful, reaching out and drawing her audience into the deep pools of her sparkling green eyes. The jazz band joined in, completing the audient delicacy.

Resnick took a sip of Scotch to break the spell before whispering to Marquez, "You had any trouble in this neighborhood? With the Guests? Any bat-boys?"

Marquez shook his head, eyes dropping away. "No, Billy. Nothing like that. Everybody here goes along and gets along, ya know?"

Yes, he knew. That was the party line these days, handed down from Washington, London, Paris, Berlin, Moscow, and every other damn capital on the planet. "Welcome our new neighbors. Make them feel at home, and we'll all get along just fine." Of course, the fantastic technology the Guests brought with them, even if most of it was scrapped during the crash, was the carrot dangled in front of these world powers. Resnick shuddered to think of Guest technology being used in another war. Things had been bad enough in the Argonne Forest without hoverships, particle bombs, and ray guns.

Marquez asked in a low, conspiratorial tone. "Why you ask, Billy? You on a case or something?"

Resnick shrugged. "Maybe. Just keep your eyes peeled and drop a dime if you see or hear anything about a character name o' M'Koth. Might be worth a couple bills to you."

Marquez nodded, but his dark eyes flashed around the bar. "Sure, Billy. Say, why don't you get yourself a table for the next number, huh?"

"Better yet," a raspy voice growled. "Why don't you join me in my office, Mr. Resnick? I'm afraid I must insist."

Resnick turned. Jaxtifar M'koth stood in the shadows mere inches away. Resnick was amazed that the alien had gotten the drop on him, despite the Noctu being synonymous with predatory stealth. "Mr. M'koth, I presume. I didn't realize you were an employee."

The Noctu showed his fangs in a smile, one hand in the pocket of his tuxedo; no doubt gripping a heater. At this range, it didn't matter if it was a .38 or a ray gun. Shot dead was still shot dead. "Please, call me Mack."

"Sorry, Billy," Marquez mumbled.

Resnick stepped away from the bar, hands spread. "Okay, Mack. Let's talk in your office." The Noctu directed him to one of the private rooms behind the saloon area. It wasn't a spacious office, but it was nicely furnished with thick red carpet. Silver-chased ceremonial blades and armor hung on the dark-paneled walls. M'Koth motioned him into one of a pair of leather chairs in front of a heavy mahogany desk. The alien took the plush, high backed chair on the opposite side of the desk, facing Resnick.

"Care for a smoke, Mr. Resnick? I've got Cubans, Dominicans, and Gelkindu."

Resnick scanned the room, trying to ignore the fact that being this close to the Noctu made him queasy. "I'm fine, thanks. I guess we should talk, huh?"

"I guess. I can tell by the look on your puss that you didn't come all the way down here just to gawk at me. And please keep your hands where I can see them. I smell the gun oil under your jacket. I'd hate for our conversation to end on an abruptly rude note."

Resnick shifted in the chair. He could try for the gun, but then he wasn't being paid to fight—only to deliver a message. "Okay then. My client wants to make a deal. He's authorized me to offer you twenty-thousand dollars in exchange for the item you took from his men."

The Noctu chuckled, revealing more fangs. "Let's see it. Slowly."

"I don't have the dough on me. He wants to set up a drop-off."

M'Koth scratched absently at the tuft of black fur beneath his elongated jaw. "Tell me, Mr. Resnick, what exactly do you know about your client? What do you know about the item?"

Resnick shrugged. "I know he's a very rich and influential man, especially in this part of the country. As for the item, I know it's a piece of Guest technology."

M'Koth reached into his pocket, extracting a shiny ray gun. He placed it on the desk between them and settled back in his chair. "Did you know that his real name is Albrecht Pohl? That he is also a Grand Wizard in the Ku Klux Klan, and secretly a high-ranking member of the Bund?"

Resnick didn't, and that bothered him. He hadn't done the legwork to find out. He'd simply looked at all those zeroes on the check—a check with the Perigeaux name on it might as well have been a bar of gold. "What difference does that make? He says you almost killed two of his employees when you stole his property."

M'Koth growled and his clawed fingers flexed. "His property? It was ours before his people—using the United States government as their muscle—stole it from us. I just stole it back. And they should be damn glad I didn't kill anybody. Malgrim knows I wanted to..."

The door opened behind Resnick. He tensed, sensing an ambush, but caught the scent of vanilla and jasmine instead. "Lilly..." He couldn't help but smile as he rose from the chair, M'Koth and the ray gun forgotten. He faced the tall, lovely woman gliding into the room. In that moment, Resnick was in his twenties again; a reckless rumrunner with pockets full of cash and eyes for only her, his Jazz Queen of the Crescent City.

"Hello, Bill." Lilly offered him a half smile. "Been a long time." She settled on the edge of the desk and opened a silver cigarette case.

"Too long," Resnick agreed, regretting the day he'd swore never to come back here. They had come to that point in every relationship where you have to take the plunge or move on. And he had made the wrong decision. "But I'm back now."

"On an errand for a racist and a fascist," M'Koth observed as he lit Lilly's cigarette. "Not to see you, my dear."

Lilly tilted her head back and exhaled a jet of perfumed smoke. "Looks like you're on the wrong side of the ball. But then..." She locked eyes with him. "It's not the first time... Is it, Bill?"

"No, I guess not." Resnick eased back into his chair. "So what's the score? What is this thing, and why all the fuss over it? I mean twenty-thousand bucks is a lot of dough." Not to mention the three grand Perigeaux was paying him.

"It's called a proto-nexus," Lilly explained. "If used right, it could make the entire generating capacity of the Tennessee Valley Authority look like a pot-bellied stove."

M'Koth growled. "And if used wrong, it could turn your planet into a scorched cinder."

Resnick inhaled and sat up straighter. "And you say Perigeaux is in with the Nazis?"

"Yes." M'Koth nodded. "You really want him packing this thing off to Berlin any time soon?"

Resnick rubbed the bridge of his nose. He had stepped in it good this time, and now he was stuck smack-dab between Guests and Nazis. He glanced at Lilly, saw her hooded green eyes studying him, and he knew what his play had to be. M'Koth was an alien, a crook and a thug, but at least he wasn't a fascist. "So what do we do now?"

The sounds of gunshots and screams came from outside.

M'Koth pushed a button under his desk. A ceremonial shield on the wall slid upward to reveal a bulbous mirror. Resnick blinked as the mirror's surface played a movie of men in white hoods and robes with shotguns and pistols storming the front rooms of Lilly's Place. Staff and patrons were returning fire, creating chaos as men and women went down in the haze of gun smoke.

"I guess twenty-thousand was too high a price to pay, after all," Resnick muttered.

"You led them here!" M'Koth snarled, snatching up the ray gun.

Resnick jumped to his feet. "Not intentionally! I didn't know anything about the Klan. They must have been tailing me all day." Though he wondered how. He could spot a shadow a mile away.

"We can work it out later." Lilly said as she pushed another button. M'Koth's desk slid across the carpet to expose a steel hatch in the floor. Lilly yanked this open, revealing a spiral staircase. "Come on, we've got to get out of here!"

"What about the nexus-thingy?" Resnick asked as he helped Lilly onto the first step.

The office door crashed open and M'Koth fired. The ray gun's bolt incinerated a pair of sheet-clad Klansmen. "Use that to light your next cross, boys!"

"It's not here," Lilly said as Resnick hastily followed her down. "Come on, Mack! We've got to go!"

Resnick heard the frenetic sounds of combat in the room above. "I'll hold 'em off, Lil," the Noctu shouted. "It's up to you to get it out of here!" The steel door slammed shut above them, plunging the stairwell into darkness.

Lilly flicked a switch and an array of lights came on, illuminating the old bootlegger tunnel. "I see you've made some improvements since my day," Resnick said as they bounded off the iron stair and headed down the cramped corridor.

"One thing about running a speakeasy, I already had the infrastructure in place to help the Guests when the locals turned against them."

"So how'd that happen?" Resnick wondered. "What made you become a champion for the batboys, the smoothies, and the buggers?"

Lilly turned and glared at him. "Buggers! You know that sounds an awful lot like the word your people use for mine, Bill."

Resnick blinked, mouth dropping open at her sudden rage. "I'd never—"

Lilly spun on her heel and kept going. "Doesn't matter," she said. "I guess when you're treated like a second-class citizen by the world you're born into, you notice when newcomers are treated even worse."

Resnick swallowed the bitter words. He deserved them. He wondered how fine a line separated him from the bastards in the hoods upstairs; from the goose-stepping jerks in Europe. Hell, he knew people still called him Pollack behind his back, so why did he look down his nose at the Guests? "Always gotta have somebody lower on the pole to kick, I reckon. Makes us feel better."

"What?" Lilly asked as they climbed a flight of stairs dug into the tunnel, ascending to an upper level.

"Nothing. I hear something behind us. You think it's Mack?"

Lilly flicked a wall mounted switch. "One way to tell."

The lights went out. Shouts and curses, the sounds of men falling echoed from the darkened tunnel's origin. "Not Mack..." Her voice was hard with emotion. "He doesn't—didn't need light to see."

"But we do." Resnick reached for the book of matches in his pocket.

"Wait." Lilly flicked the lights back on.

"What are you doing? I've got a pistol, but it sounds like a hell of a lot of guys coming this way. Pissed off and armed guys."

"Just wait." Lilly smiled. It was a hard, angry smile, the kind he hadn't seen in a long time, and one he didn't miss. He knew from personal experience that whoever was the reason for that smile was in for a great deal of trouble.

Shadows appeared on the tunnel floor below them. Resnick drew the .45 and worked the slide; stepped to put himself between Lilly and their pursuers. He figured it had to be at least a dozen men. "Have to make 'em count."

"You won't need to pull that trigger." Lilly pushed a button beside the light switch.

The rank stench of river water and the thunderous roar of thousands of gallons rushing through a breach in the walls filled the tunnel. The cries of the drowning Klansmen were choked off almost instantly. The water rose to the level of the bottom step, a single hood floating on its surface. A hood bearing the circled cross of a Grand Wizard.

Resnick safetied and holstered the pistol. "I guess I'd better cash that check soon."

"Come on." Lilly turned back up the tunnel. "We're not out of the woods just yet."

They hurried through the winding corridor which emerged into what resembled a cramped root cellar. A Noctu woman armed with a ray gun stepped out of the shadows. "Lilly! We heard there was trouble at the club."

"Mack's dead." Lilly placed her hand gently on the Noctu's shoulder. "But he bought us time to get the proto-nexus to safety."

The alien levelled her pistol at Resnick's face. "He's a spy!"

Resnick raised his hands. "What? No!"

"He's got a tracer on him!"

Lilly stepped between Resnick and the ray gun's muzzle. "Let me see."

The Noctu handed Lilly a device about the size of a cigarette lighter. It had a tiny movie-screen, and it beeped as she held it up to his hands. She looked up with a frown. "An Alphaeton gene-tag. That's how they tracked you to the club," Lilly explained. "You said Perigeaux gave you a check? The tag must have been in the ink."

"I'm sorry, Lil. I swear I didn't know."

Lilly turned to the Noctu woman. "It's okay. He's not a spy. But we have to hurry. They'll be coming soon."

The female Noctu reluctantly allowed Resnick to follow Lilly up the steps and out of the root cellar. Resnick blinked, overwhelmed at sight of what was on the other side of the flimsy-looking doors. They had emerged into a massive building bigger than any warehouse he had ever seen. Occupying most of that cavernous space was an immense shiny metallic sphere dotted with lights, antennae, windows, and other mechanical oddities. "What the hell...?"

"Another colony ship," Lilly said. "We've been building it for four years. But the proto-nexus is the only thing that can power it."

"So, you're trying to help the Guests leave?"

Lilly frowned. "I'm helping them escape. Hopefully they can find a world that will actually welcome them, instead of greeting them with hate, contempt, and exploitation."

Resnick shook his head. "That thing's enormous, but it ain't nearly big enough to hold all of 'em. The original was at least ten times that size."

"It doesn't matter," a little lizard man announced, scurrying over an open supply crate filled with ray guns, and up the side of a bank of machinery to look Lilly in the eye. "We don't have enough time to summon all the selected passengers, and the proto-nexus isn't at full charge."

"You're a Bh'inn," Resnick said recognizing the lizard man's race. "I thought all of you came down in Central Europe."

The Bh'inn licked one of his bulbous eyes, head cocking to the side. "Most of us did. Hitler and Stalin were not the most cordial of hosts, however. Not to us, at least. They preferred to buy into the propaganda espoused by the Alphaeton and their Ch'kath enforcers. Great minds may think alike, but so do evil ones, it seems."

"Doctor Ssilke is our chief engineer," Lilly explained. "This is his baby."

"One that is doomed to be stillborn, it would appear." The Bh'inn sighed.

"How much energy and time do you need?" Resnick asked.

Ssilke looked at him in thought. "The proto-nexus has barely enough power to get us out of Earth's orbit at present, and it'll take at least a week to summon everyone."

Lilly rubbed her eyes. "We don't have the time. Even if that was Perigeaux's hood in the tunnel, he certainly wasn't working alone. I'm sure the Bund will be coming next."

Resnick thought for a moment. "Can you reach the moon? Maybe you could set up a colony there until your nexus-thingy recharges."

Ssilke cocked his head. "Probably. But if we use the energy now, at less than full power, we could be there for thirty or forty of your years before it recharges. And we only have about ninety people here."

Gunshots sounded outside the building along with police sirens. "Perigeaux must have had political allies," Resnick said. "Looks like you've got a choice, Doc. Whether you get some of your people to the moon or not, we can't let the nexus fall into the hands of whoever's outside."

"I'll begin the launch countdown." With that, Ssilke scurried away.

"And I'll give you as much time as I can." Resnick snatched a ray gun from the opened crate.

"Wait." Lilly grabbed his shoulder. "Even with that, you can't fight them all. You'll be killed."

Resnick took her in his arms and kissed her the way he used to, the way he had wanted to for years. Letting her go, he looked into her eyes. "I've made a lot of mistakes in my life, Lil. Maybe this'll help to balance the scales."

Lilly picked up another ray gun and winked. "That's not what I meant, Romeo. I'm a better shot with these."

###

About Jason J. McCuiston

JASON J. MCCUISTON WAS BORN IN the wilds of southeast Tennessee, where he was raised on a carnivorous diet of old monster movies, westerns, comic books, horror magazines, sci-fi and fantasy novels, and, of course, Dungeons & Dragons. He attended the finest state school that would have him with the intention of becoming a comic-book artist. Following his matriculation and a whirlwind tour of spectacularly underpaid and uninspired career paths, he finally realized that he was meant to be a professional storyteller.

Jason has been a semi-finalist in L. Ron Hubbard's Writers of the Future contest, with stories published by Parsec Ink, Pole to Pole Publishing, Left Hand Publishers, Spring Song Press, StoryHack Magazine, Crimson Streets, Tell-Tale Press, and SERIAL Magazine. Other tales are forthcoming.

He lives in South Carolina, USA with his college-professor wife (making him a Doctor's Companion) and their two four-legged children. He can be found Facebook and he occasionally tweets about his dogs, his stories, his likes, and his gripes.

Connect with Jason here:
www.castrumpress.com/authors/jason-j-mccuiston

ALIEN DAYS

WHERE ALL MEMORIES ARE ONE
By Leigh Saunders

How to convey, so a human mind can understand, the memories of an entire warren that I hold in my own? Memories that are mine as much as if I had scuttled in fear every dark passage, felt every blow on my own carapace, writhed in the agony of the flames as my thorax blistered from the heat of the bounty hunters' weapons.

Memories that are my burden to bear, as a Queen of the Callibrini – for I am Y'reui, the Queen who sacrificed her warren to save her human friends, the Synths.

✳✳✳

I see through the eyes of Satish, my eyes whirring in and out of focus at the strange creatures I will later come to know as humans, crossing the field of ripening amaranth toward me for the first time. I am not alone in my observations – around us, the wedge-shaped heads of dozens of my warren-brothers, in shades of gold (like my own) and glossy black and speckled green and brown, have risen above the gently waving clusters of purple flowers, pairs of multifaceted eyes whirring as they follow the strangers' progress through the field.

Only the presence of the small, brown, warren-brother of the serving-caste guiding the humans toward me prevents us all from driving them immediately from our fields – we know not who the strangers are or why they have come, but the brown's chittering tells us that they have not come as intruders.

I watch them approach with great curiosity. They walk upright, as do I, but on two legs as opposed to my four, and the limbs of their upper body swing forward and back aimlessly as they move, and lack the hard-shell casing and sharp, spiny ridge that gives my own forelimbs strength. They emit strange sounds from their flat faces as they approach, though my own chittering is likely as unintelligible to them.

I see as they grow closer that the humans have wrapped their bodies in close-fitting fabrics in a deep shade of blue, not unlike the color of my warren's Senior Queen. They bear patterns on the chest and forearms that are like those I have seen other cloth-wrapping races use to indicate their status among their peers. I rise to my full height – the humans are easily twice my size, but the elaborate etchings on the golden, chitinous shell of my abdomen and thorax proclaim me also to be of high esteem in my warren. With a click of my mandibles, I could instantly summon a hundred of my warren-brothers to my side. I have no fear of the humans.

The brown skitters up to me, and I dip my head toward him and brush my slim, segmented antennae against his, an exchange of memory that conveys more than just the knowledge of his current task. He has brought the humans to my field at the behest of the Queens of our warren. The brown's knowledge and memories are now mine, and mine his; other interactions will share them with more of our brothers, strengthening the bonds of our warren.

The humans do not experience the chemical memory, keeping their thoughts bound tightly within their own skulls. As they have not understood my initial greeting, I address them in the language called "Standard" that is used to connect the races of the Hundred Worlds. The words come awkwardly to my mandibles but serve their purpose.

"I bid you greeting," I say.

The humans stop a short distance away, and one of them answers, also in the common speech. "We come in peace."

***

The memory of greeting the humans as Satish is mine, as is the memory of dozens of other first greetings – all new, yet old, meeting them for the first time and the fiftieth in the same thought. Such is the nature of a Callibrini's understanding, where all memories are one.

As myself, as Y'reui, I knew of the humans who were called "Synths" from the memories shared with me by the senior Queens, and they from memories shared by the Queens of other warrens who had shed their shells many times over.

But for the century's worth of memories I had of the Synths and their lonely sojourn amid the Hundred Worlds, exiled from their homeworld, I was a newly made Queen, the youngest of the five who governed our warren, when I first saw them with my own eyes.

They had come to our warren and been brought before the Queen's Council. The Great Cavern, where such audiences were held, was a vast hollow carved out of the earth hundreds of cycles before I was birthed, with massive stone pillars to support the labyrinth of the warren above. I loved this space, deep below the surface where only the phosphorescence of certain plants cast their light and the air was cool and moist.

A vast crowd of the warren-brothers had gathered to hear our judgment, a sea of shells in black and brown and gold and green filling the chamber. Their excited chittering echoed from the rocky formations suspended from the ceiling, for our warren was small and visitors were few, and these five Synths – two male and three females – had come bearing gifts.

As the Synths were led up onto the smooth stone of the dais where we received them, they placed large woven baskets of fruits and vegetables – delicacies from distant planets – on the floor in front of them. The sweet, heady smell of the ripe fruit wafting toward us from the baskets was intoxicating, and I found myself salivating in anticipation of biting into the luscious flesh and slurping down the syrupy juices.

"What do you seek in our warren?" asked Val'en, her voice reminding me that our duty was to address the larger matter at hand. She was the Senior Queen of our Council and towered above the rest of us – and above the Synths as well – tall and blue, the great, feathery fronds of her antennae folded over her back like wings.

"We wish to learn more about your people," said the leader of their group, a male who called himself Elliot Gar.

I felt a shiver of excitement at his words. I had many questions I wished to ask them.

Would I have encouraged my sister-Queens to allow the humans to stay with us, to study our ways and we theirs, had I known where it would lead? I cannot say for certain.

But given my part in the events that followed, I suspect I would have done no differently.

✳✳✳

For three full changes of the seasons, the Synths dwelt among us, making their nests aboveground in a small cluster of permashelter domes of their own construction, and spending their time scattered among the warren-brothers according to the interests of their research.

The male called Elliot Gar spent most of his time in the fields with the large, green-and-brown-shelled warren-brothers of the cultivator caste, learning from them about our agricultural crops and farming practices.

Two others, a male called Loren Kol and a female by the name of Kara Jem, were fascinated by our species' chemical memory. They hoped to discover the key to decoding the memory molecules by which we shared information with the touch of our antennae. A pack of the small, green, courier caste warren-brothers clustered around them, constantly running in and out of their permashelter dome, their chittering interspersed with whispery-soft Standard.

The two remaining females, Jessica Lim and Brianna Rei, wanted to learn more about our history and culture, and how they could, as they said, "interact more productively with us." They met often with Satish and other gold warren-brothers of the intellectual caste, first in the permashelter domes on the surface, but later coming into the upper levels of the warren more and more often.

I, of course, never ventured out of the warren, but received regular knowledge of the above-ground activities passed through the chemical memory from one warren-brother to another until they reached me and became my own. However, being still a young Queen, and small enough to move easily throughout the warren, unlike my older, larger, sister-Queens, I came frequently to the dwellings of the golds, and spent many cycles in conversation with Jessica and Brianna.

It was during these conversations, while we sat on large cushions and sipped at the clear water or sweet nectars provided by our gold-shelled hosts, that I came to consider these intriguing and curious Synth females my sister-friends.

"Why did you come to our warren?" I asked during one of these meetings. Satish had invited us to his warren and was a most gracious host, providing an abundance of phosphorescent plants to light the chamber for our human guests and dishes of freshly picked fruits and vegetables for us to nibble on.

"Surely a warren near one of the above-ground cities would have provided food and dwellings more suited to your species than your rations and permashelters," I continued. "There are many warrens that are well-accustomed to travelers of other races and do much commerce with them. Why come to us?"

"We were looking for a warren that was not heavily engaged with off-worlders," replied Brianna. "One that had not been influenced as greatly by other races and would offer us a better understanding of your peoples' true culture."

"And have you found what you sought."

"Yes," she replied, and Jessica nodded in agreement. "We are grateful for the welcome we have been given and the knowledge that you and the warren-brothers have shared with us."

My curiosity on that subject satisfied, I nodded, then ventured into a new topic, but one that had long intrigued me. "I know you were driven from your homeworld," I said, "but I do not know why."

"We are different from other humans," Jessica said simply, setting aside her empty cup and raising a hand to forestall Satish from refilling it. "They fear us."

I had come to recognize the shifts in skin coloring and temperature when the humans found themselves talking about difficult topics – sometime only a subtle warming, sometimes turning their pale skin an unusual, rosy hue – and saw none of this in Jessica. Nor was there any undercurrent of hesitation, of the need to choose her words carefully, in her straightforward reply. I turned my gaze on Brianna, and found that she, too, was nodding in silent agreement.

"In what ways are you different?" I asked. "Are you larger or stronger than the others, like the black-shelled warrior-caste brothers of the Callibrini? Or cleverer, like our gold-shelled brothers of the intellectual caste?"

Brianna laughed, a sound I had found jarring when I first heard it, until coming to understand that it was akin to the enthusiastic clicking of mandibles when the warren-brothers were amused by some turn of events.

"To outward appearances, a Synth is no different than any other human," she said. "And the castes humans create are divided less rigidly along differences in our gender or appearance and more often by our social standing or philosophical beliefs or choice of profession – and even those are not strict divisions among our people." She paused, setting aside a still heavily laden plate. "But we Synths were birthed in laboratories, with technology integrated into our brains and genetic differences that grant us lifespans many times that of normal humans. These are the things they fear."

"And now they hunt us," added Jessica. "Once there were many Synths; now only a few dozen remain, and we have scattered ourselves throughout the Hundred Worlds in an attempt to survive."

My sister-friends had given me much to consider, and I silently rose from my cushion and moved toward the door, barely taking note of Satish's nod of deference as I passed. Before I left, I turned toward the two Synths, studying them with every facet of my vision.

"I give you my word," I said, "no harm will come to you or your companions while you are guests of this warren."

Would that my words had been true.

✳✳✳

Elliot Gar was the first of the Synths to die.

I remember the warm summer afternoon through the eyes of Hilal, one of the large, brown-and-green speckled warren-brothers of the cultivator caste. Elliot and I were in the amaranth fields with dozens of the cultivator warren-brothers, tending to the crops as we did every day when a blocky-shaped, unfamiliar shuttle flew in from the west and abruptly landed in the field, crushing precious crops beneath its weight.

"Run," Elliot said to me, his voice urgent. "Tell your warren-brothers to run. Now." His smell had changed from one of salty sweat and hard labor to the sharp bitterness of adrenaline, and the hand that rested on my speckled carapace trembled ever-so-slightly.

He recognized the markings on this shuttle, that much was obvious, but I did not waste time asking questions. My warren-brothers and I feared nothing on our world, but Elliot was our brother-friend and we trusted him – and he said we were in danger.

I quickly chittered out the warning, rising to my full height to extend the folded layers of my upper thorax to reveal the bright red and yellow markings displayed only in times of threat. As Elliot shouted beside me, I repeated my warning again and again as loud as I could over the sound of the shuttle's growling engines, waving my forearms to catch the attention of those of my warren-brothers who stood there staring, mesmerized as I had been by the strange vehicle.

At last the warren-brothers heard us and began to flee – myself and Elliot following them as the shuttle's ramp descended. As I ran, I looked back several times, snatching glimpses: a large party of humans running down the ramp... lifting large-barreled weapons to their shoulders... firing, a series of deep, throaty 'pops' of sound that reverberated across the field. I felt the vibration in my antennae, heard the thud of projectiles impacting in the ground around me, the crack of carapaces as warren-brothers were struck and fell mid-stride.

Then Elliot was struck, one of the projectiles hitting him in the back and exploding through his chest in a splatter of hot, wet blood. My steps faltered as he fell against me and slid to the ground.

Before I had a chance to react, hot metal pierced my carapace, driving me into the ground. I gasped for air... struggled to stand... and then my memories that came from Hilal faded into pain and darkness.

✳✳✳

I am tens of hundreds of black-shelled warriors, pouring from the warren to rescue our dying cultivators and defend the crops that sustain our warren.

We are solid and strong, and march toward the invaders with pincers extended, surrounding them like a deadly, living wall. For a moment, we stand there, staring at each other, our antennae waving, the late afternoon sun reflecting off our glossy black carapaces in hints of blue and green and gold.

"Give us the Synths!" one of the humans shouts, speaking in the common language they call Standard, "and we will leave you in peace!"

But we have found the murdered shell of Eliot Gar, the Synth who had become our warren-brother, lying amid the fallen cultivators, and we do not believe the invaders.

"We will not give up our own!" we reply, the whisper from our collective throats like the rush of wind across the trampled amaranth field. We snap our mandibles and click our pincers in a show of force.

They fire into our numbers with their projectile weapons, thinking to kill us as easily as they killed our cultivator warren-brothers, but our shells are stronger, and we stand there, unharmed.

The humans put away their weapons, and first we think they are afraid – as they should be, for we are hundreds and they mere dozens.

Then several of them step forward carrying strange objects we do not understand, and begin hurling huge, blazing orbs into our midst, which splatter off our shells in a spray of oil and set fire to the broken amaranth beneath us.

Again, and again they rain fire down on us, and while our carapaces are impervious to the flames, our underbellies are not so heavily protected and the longer we stand in the burning field, the more we begin to feel the effect of the heat. But we do not give ground.

We cannot. For if we falter, the invaders will have access to our warren, to our Synth warren-brother and sisters, and to our Queens, and that we cannot – we will not – allow.

So, we advance, moving forward, legs soaked in the flaming, oily substance, thoraxes smoldering, bubbling in the heat, the sickly-sweet smell of scorched chitin soon tainting the smoke-filled air.

Many of us fall long before we reach the humans, but we do not stop. They retreat, wisely staying just out of reach of our pincers, then advance again, dealing out more of the fiery oil, roasting legions of us in our shells. The battle continues thus, a slow push-and-pull of shadowy figures moving forward and back through the smoky haze, inching ever closer to the mouth of the warren.

✳✳✳

I am a score of golds, the intellectual caste of our warren, who think beyond instinct to guide the lesser caste-members and provide counsel to the Queens. One of our number fell with the cultivators, another was lost with the great army of blacks, and the memories that have come to us from the few who survived those encounters has left us silent and fearful.

The sun has slid through the sky slowly on this day, but it now hangs heavy on the horizon, casting long shadows through the smoke-filled sky into the single remaining entrance to the warren. We have collapsed the other entrances, and now wait in the shadows, clinging to the ceiling, caked mud covering our golden shells to obscure us from sight until we jump down onto our enemies.

We are too few to survive if the bounty hunters succeed in penetrating deep into the warren. Our strength is in hardened carapaces and overwhelming numbers, pincers that can snap a limb in two and sharpened forelegs with which to decapitate an enemy. We are the masters of close combat; but we have no weapons for fighting at a distance, as the humans do.

And so, we lie in wait, like patient predators, for them to come to us.

We have been told that the bounty hunters want us to hand over the Synths, which is something we will not do. Our warren-brother, Elliot Gar, has been lost to us already, his lifeless body carried away by the invaders; with no memory molecules to pass his knowledge to the members of the warren, his loss fills us with a profound sadness. Kara Jem and Loren Kol are missing, and we can only hope that they and the greens that were with them have found shelter far from this warren, for we cannot protect them.

Our warren-sisters, Jessica Lim and Brianna Rei, we sent to the Queens, deep in the warren, where the bounty hunters cannot reach them. Or such is our hope. We think and we plan, and we strategize, but we have also seen the odds, and know that our success is by no means certain.

And then we hear the crunch of heavy boots on the rocky path, see the flicker of the artificial lamps the bounty hunters carry. The Synths had carried similar lamps when they first came to the warren, before they learned that the glare was uncomfortable for our multi-faceted eyes and abandoned them in favor of the softer glow of phosphorescent plants to light their way. But we expected no such courtesy from the bounty hunters and are not surprised by this.

The smoky scent of our fallen warren-brothers filters to us now, ahead of the bounty hunters, and we are enraged, fighting against all instincts that cry out for us to jump out early and alert them to our presence. We wait, long, agonizing moments, for our prey.

They come closer.

They enter the warren.

They are cautious, which is wise, shining their lamps down the passage and along the walls, moving forward slowly, not thinking to look above them, not seeing their light reflected in our eyes as we watch them advance.

They fill the corridor, from entry to the first bend, one bounty hunter for each pair of us, more pressing in from the mouth of the warren.

As one, we drop from the ceiling, slicing off heads and piercing through their soft, shell-less bodies faster than they can react, then turn to take on their companions, counting on the advantage of close-combat and sharp pincers.

But they have other weapons we do not expect them to use here – small projectiles pepper our bodies, piercing our shells, gouts of flame wash over us, melting our chitin.

We fight as long as we can, reducing their numbers by more than half, but it is a losing battle, and soon they have finished us, crushing the last light from our eyes as their boots stomp over us and they move deeper into the warren.

* * *

I am a thousand thousand greens. We are each no larger than the head of one of the human attackers, and by our caste more suited to running errands and delivering messages than fighting battles, yet we will die before we allow them to harm our Queens.

We swarm, filling the tunnels of the warren and covering the invaders, slicing with sharp forelegs, cutting with pincers, biting with small but powerful mandibles. We drop on them from above, climb the tunnel walls and leap on them as they pass us, pour upward under their feet as they step across downward-branching passages. They peel us from their bodies and throw us into clusters of our kin, stomp on us, cracking our carapaces, smash us into the earth under their heavy boots, and still we come.

We will defend our warren.

Other humans come with different weapons, small rock-like objects that explode moments after being thrown into our midst, shattering our shells and blowing our bodies apart, killing many of us in an instant.

"Just give us the Synths!" the humans cry. They say other things, too, but not in any language we understand.

But the Synths are our warren-brothers, our sister-friends. Our Queens have named them members of our warren, and it is not our way to give our own over to bounty-hunters.

We continue to swarm, brushing antennae as we climb over the shattered shells of our fallen. We know the pain of their deaths before we experience the pain of our own.

✳✳✳

I am a Queen of the Callibrini – and I am five Queens and all Queens, from the youngest of our Council to the eldest. I am Val'en and Le'tar and Mi'rel and D'lor.

And I am Y'reui.

We stand together on the Council dais, receiving the memories of the greens who have come to us, and experience the flight of the cultivators, the pain of the warriors, the cunning of the golds, and the bravery of the greens who are now all that stand between us and the bounty hunters.

We know, too, why they are here – that they want the two warren-sisters who stand before us, Jessica Lim and Brianna Rei, and that they are destroying our warren to reach them.

"Had they come to us in peace," said Val'en, staring down at Jessica and Brianna, "I might have given you to them, even though you are our sister-friends, for matters that extend beyond the bounds of the warren are of little consequence to me."

She paused, rustling her antennae and tapping a razor-clawed foot on the ground.

"Instead, they chose to kill all in their path, never thinking of what they might have had simply for the asking. And that I will not tolerate."

"We cannot drive them out," said D'lor clicking her pincers nervously as she spoke. I was the youngest of the Queens, but D'lor was a mere decade older. "The fire they carry with them is too powerful."

"Then we put it out," I said. The others turned to me. "We know where they are in the warrens, and can collapse the tunnels on them from above, with no risk of being burned by their flames."

Val'en nodded. "It is a good plan."

"Until others come," said D'lor anxiously. "How much of the warren will we collapse?"

"All of it, if it comes to that," said Val'en. "We will stop them. And then we will build a new warren."

"How can we help?" asked Brianna.

We all looked at her in surprise. No one ever interrupted the Queens when we were in Council.

"The bounty hunters are here because of us," said Brianna. "How can we help you drive them away?"

"Brianna Rei, you will go with Y'reui," Val'en said. "Take the smaller tunnels that we cannot and leave the warren from the east." She held up her foreleg to prevent further interruption. "Jessica Lim, you will go with D'lor, and leave the warren from the north."

She turned her attention the two young Queens she had named.

"You are young, and if you escape, will outlive us all. One of these golds will accompany each of you, together with a dozen greens and browns. If you find any warriors or cultivators, take them with you as well. Establish new warrens, far from this place."

Then Val'en came to us and laid the great fronds of her antennae over our own, strands winding around each other, binding us to her.

Unlike the warren-brothers, who share all their memories whenever their slim, segmented antennae connect, we Queens can choose what memories we wish to share.

Val'en chose to share everything.

My legs buckled under the onslaught as hundreds of seasons of memories flooded into my mind – both her own, and the memories passed on to her from previous Queens – together with the wisdom and experience they carried with them.

Then another brush of antennae, as Le'tar and Mi'rel linked their fronds to ours, adding their memories to those Val'en shared.

The memories pressed into me, blurring my vision, and I cried out, a single, keening wail. The note rose, twining with Val'en's and D'lor's own cries, harmonizing with Le'tar's and Mi'rel's as the five of us saw through each other's eyes, knew everything the others knew, felt all the others felt.

Where our experiences would take us, what choices we would make from that moment forward would mold us, change us, again separate us into unique individuals. But in that single moment, we five were one mind, one Queen, holding the knowledge and memories of our entire warren from its very beginning.

And then Val'en released us.

"Go," she said, moving away, her steps faulty. "Go now."

A low rumble shook the cavern, dust raining down on us from the ceiling.

"There is no more time, my sisters" said Val'en. "Go!"

D'lor, Jessica, and a group of warren-brothers headed toward the northern exit. I reached out to Val'en, briefly clasped her forearm, then turned away, unable to look long into the gently whirring eyes of Le'tar and Mi'rel, the sister-Queens I was leaving behind, as we gently brushed antennae in farewell.

"Come with me," I said, nodding to Brianna, Satish, and a cluster of greens and browns that stood nearby.

Not waiting to see if they followed me, I left the dais, taking the tunnel that would lead to the eastern exit, while Le'tar and Mi'rel collapsed the passage behind us.

***

We fled through the darkness.

With no light to guide her footsteps, I carried Brianna on my own back, the warren-brothers with us being too small to carry a human. She clung to me, gripping my carapace with her knees, her arms wrapped around my upper thorax, just below my forelimbs.

"Y'reui, we can't just leave," she whispered.

"What would you have us do?" I asked.

"Save the other Queens," she replied. "You said you knew where the invaders were – we should follow your plan and collapse the tunnels on them now, before they reach the Great Cavern."

I paused, then made my decision, turning down a side path that led away from the east exit and toward the invaders.

"But Val'en commanded—" began Satish.

"I am Val'en," I said, cutting him off. "I am all Queens of this warren. And this is my command."

***

Racing now against time, we sped toward the place where we last knew the invaders to have reached, staying in the upper tunnels. From time to time, we felt the ground shake from their explosive devices, and I would pause, spreading the fronds of my antennae across the walls of the tunnels to sense the direction of the tremors, and adjusting our course to guide us through the labyrinth toward them.

At last I felt the rhythmic tromping of their heavy boots. "There are seven," I said. "Ahead of us, one level below, moving forward. Many greens still delay their progress."

Again I reached out, trusting the sensitivity of my antennae, aware not only the vibration of the bounty hunters heading our way and tremors deeper in the caverns that I couldn't identify, but feeling for the tiny fissures in the tunnel floor and walls, the places where we should dig to collapse the tunnel completely on the invaders.

"Here," I called out, pointing to several locations both above and below. The browns and greens with us immediately set themselves to the task at the points along the tunnel floor, pincers put to work scooping great gouges in the dirt, while Satish began to demolish the ceiling.

"Where do I dig?" asked Brianna, sliding off my back. "I can't see."

I pressed her soft hands against a point on the tunnel wall that would require little strength. "Here," I said, moving to assist Satish in his labors on the ceiling.

If we timed our efforts right, the collapsing ceiling would fall into the weakened floor and carry it down, crushing the invaders as they passed through the level below. Some of the greens that harried them would perish, but most would be able to dig themselves out unharmed.

I kept one antenna pressed against the tunnel wall and felt the ground beneath our feet weakening as the invaders approached. I was reaching out to pull Brianna out of the way when one of their explosive devices went off directly below us.

At the same moment, the plan Val'en, Le'tar, and Mi'rel had put in motion also reached its peak, and I suddenly understood the deeper tremors I had felt beneath us. The Queens had destroyed the pillars supporting the Great Cavern and everything above it.

The tunnel floor collapsed, and we fell.

* * *

I awake to weak sunlight, and a small swarm of greens digging the rubble away from my body. Each breath feels like a pincer slicing through me, and I cannot feel two of my legs.

I am afraid to move and do little more than blink in recognition of the greens, but they take note of the motion. One of them approaches and cautiously dips a broken antenna toward my dusty blue fronds, the memories he shares filling me with grief.

Satish is dead, his shattered carapace lying half excavated from the debris a short way from me. I can see him without moving my head.

Val'en and my sister-Queens, Le'tar and Mi'rel, who remained with her have not been found, nor will they ever be, entombed under tons of earth and rock when the Great Cavern collapsed.

D'lor had been found, as well, and Jessica Lim, their broken bodies peppered with the fragments thrown by the bounty hunter's explosive devices. Of her warren-brothers who accompanied them, only the single gold survived, though his injuries were severe.

The bounty hunters, themselves, are no more; the bodies of six of their seven have been found. The seventh was seen, limping through the field, carrying another human to their ship, and I fear it was Brianna Rei that he took away with him, as we have found no trace of her. I grieve for her loss – but the ship no longer sits in the burned and blackened amaranth field, and for that at least, we are grateful.

The greens continue to excavate the debris covering me as other survivors gather, more greens and browns tunneling their way to the surface, a handful of speckled cultivators who had survived the massacre in the fields, and a single, charred, black-shelled warrior. One by one, they come to me and touch their segmented antennae to the feathery blue fronds of my own.

I am Y'reui. I am their Queen.

* * *

In the weeks that followed, we gathered our dead, collecting their antennae into a single mound and plowing their burned and broken bodies deep into the ground, in the hopes that one day this place of so much death and destruction might again be filled with life.

But before grinding the mountain of antennae to dust and scattering it on the wind, as is the way of the Callibrini, I gently brushed each broken antenna with my own, experiencing both the lives and the deaths of all the warren–brothers we had lost and making their memories mine.

And then we left this place and its memories and went east.

###

About Leigh Saunders

LEIGH SAUNDERS GREW UP AS A "military brat." And while she's long-since settled in her Rocky Mountain home (with her husband and a pair of feuding cats that vie for her attention), her life-long wanderlust regularly inspires her to write about the people and places that spark her imagination. When not writing speculative fiction for a living (her day job is writing computer software manuals), Leigh enjoys writing "social science fiction" – stories that focus on people (or "things" that are also people) in distant places, and how futuristic events or advances in technology impact their lives.

A 1993 Writers of the Future finalist, her recent short fiction can be found in multiple Fiction River anthologies.

Connect with Leigh here:
www.castrumpress.com/authors/leigh-saunders

AMBASSADOR T
By Quincy J Allen

- Part 1: Investigation -

JANUARY 17, 2098 – ROSS 128-B

"I wonder what happened to them," Commander Ramirez said, his voice filled with awe. A dark-haired native of North Carolina and geologist by training, he barely filled his environment suit with a tall, thin frame built for teaching at University. He'd always believed his acceptance into the space program had been a miracle, even more so when they assigned him to be the lead landing party commander.

He stared up at a monolithic sculpture made of something his scans identified as titanium bonded to a polymer unknown to human science, and he still couldn't believe his eyes. The structure—he assumed it was as sculpture—rose nearly a hundred meters into the air, was riddled with holes, and gave off a chorus of lyrical moaning whistles as the alien breeze passed through it. Contrasted against a deeply azure sky, it reminded him of the Washington Monument in his hometown of D.C. back on Earth, but this one was octagonal, silver, and had a much wider base in proportion to the apex, making it look more like an elaborate pyramid than a phallus. He glanced over his shoulder at their resident doctor, Lieutenant Cohen.

"Disease, maybe?" she suggested from where she stood atop a parked vehicle across the street. It had a rounded top, spherical wheels set into the undercarriage, and seats built for an occupant half the size of a human. They hadn't found any remains whatsoever, and some of the vehicles looked like they'd stopped in the middle of the street. Cohen believed the people of that world would have been bipedal and, based upon the controls of the vehicle, possessed of more than two arms. She was the landing party's medical doctor, and one of three assigned to the mission. "A global plague?" Like the rest of the thirty-person crew of Patrocles, she'd opted for a buzz-cut, which made her look like she had a black skull cap inside the polyglass helmet of her environment suit. She was short, trim, and looked completely natural in her suit, a feat Ramirez had always been jealous of.

"I don't know...." Ramirez said slowly, shaking his head. "Maybe?" He felt a slight headache coming on. He tried to scratch the back of his neck and remembered—for the fourth time—that he was in an environment suit. There wasn't enough oxygen and too much helium in the atmosphere for them to move around without them. "Dammit," he grumbled under his breath. He'd told the techs back at Luna 5 that something on the neck ring poked him. Apparently, they hadn't believed him. "And you're sure the scans haven't picked up any fauna other than the insects and the beasties?" he asked, looking at Lieutenant Sparks.

The scans from orbit around Ross 128-b, as well as those taken both on their approach and groundside, indicated that there was no sentient life left on the planet to appreciate the remarkable sight or sound of what had clearly been a focal point for the people who once inhabited the massive city spread out for kilometers in every direction. Hundreds of such cities dotted the planet's four continents, many of them arrayed along the extensive coastlines, and they all seemed to have been constructed out of the same material as the monolith—titanium and polymers. Every city was devoid of any sign of their creators, overgrown by vegetation—to the point of obfuscation in some cases—by a wide array of thick flora. The only fauna they had found on the planet was a short list of hearty and predatorial insect life, plus an entire ecosystem of pale-green, tardigrade-like organisms the team had affectionately labeled "beasties." The creatures ranged in size from microscopic to about thirty kilos, appearing to subsist on every kind of vegetation in sight, and they paid the landing party little or no heed at all.

They were everywhere.

"You saw the data yourself, Commander," Lieutenant Sparks, the resident botanist, said. His short, tight, red curls were a flash of color inside his helmet. He pushed a beastie aside with his boot as the thirty-centimeter organism inched toward him from beneath a nearby vehicle. "Whatever sentient race used to be here, assuming there was one, seems to have been replaced by these guys at some point in the distant past."

"Assuming there was one?" Lieutenant Akashi asked, her voice full of sarcasm. "Who do you think built the cities? The trees? Or maybe it was the beasties." Akashi held advanced degrees in both biochemistry and chemical engineering. She was also the smart-ass of the group, delighting in wisecracks almost as much as she did chemistry. Raised in Tokyo, she had a peculiar sense of humor that always seemed to elude Ramirez's sensibilities, but she was one of the smartest people he'd ever met.

"I'm just saying that we don't know," Sparks retorted. "If I didn't know any better, I'd conclude that the inhabitants were wiped out by the beasties, but that doesn't jibe either. Any race capable of putting up satellites like the ones we saw

THE DAYS ANTHOLOGY, BOOK 2

should be capable of dealing with these things.... Cohen's right ..." he added "it had to be a plague of some kind that wiped out the higher life forms, and the beasties filled the vacuum afterward."

"Again... maybe?" Ramirez said, looking to where one of the gray, puffy, insect-like creatures undulated slowly, warming itself beneath the red sun. It was a half-meter long and looked all the world like a giant tardigrade, excepting for the color and the fact that it had five segments rather than the four exhibited by the microbial versions back on Earth. Theorists had long speculated that the bizarre and exceedingly hearty life form had possibly entered Earth's ecosystems via a meteorite or other celestial body after impacting the planet's surface. It was well known they could survive just about anywhere. Like those on earth, the beasties' rounded faces folded inward like the flaps of a male orangutan, and their cylindrical mouths held small, bony white stylets for chewing up any vegetation they could reach. Their bodies were boneless, and they looked more like swollen caterpillars than anything else.

"They're kinda cute, in a horrifying sort of way," Cohen added. "Will we be taking some home with us?"

"Looking for a new pet?" Akashi asked with a chuckle. "You could call it Spot and teach it to fetch," she added.

Cohen turned and rolled her eyes at Akashi through her faceplate.

"I suspect we will," Ramirez said, hoping to cut off more banter. The two were always at it in one way or another. "It's part of why we came, after all.... I just never expected to find such the flora and fauna on humanity's first visit to an Earth-like planet, let alone the lost civilization we have here."

"We all figured it would be water, rocks, and maybe some basic vegetation," Akashi said.

"The questions alone will keep scientists talking for decades, never mind whatever we decide to take back with us," Cohen replied, stepping away from the beastie that had apparently taken a liking to her boot.

"Captain?" Ramirez said, "Do you copy?"

"Affirmative, Ramirez," Captain Abimbola replied, her voice washed with only a thin layer of static. "Go ahead." She was an astrophysicist of the highest caliber and one of the best astronauts to come out of the Global Union's Earth Space and Research Agency in the past thirty years. She was the golden child of ESRA, instrumental in planning the eleven-light-year-journey to Ross 128, and had been the natural selection to command the mission when it came time to make the decision. She'd even had the full confidence and support of the GU's Council.

"We're about two klicks from the lander," Ramirez reported. "This city is abandoned, just like the scans showed." Ramirez lifted his eyes skyward, looking to where the Patrocles was in stationary orbit above them.

"We've been monitoring," Abimbola replied. Her tone was calm and cool, as if the discovery of both life and a lost civilization on a new world was the sort of thing she'd done her entire life. "What's your recommendation?"

"Send down the other team down and have them set up in that wide delta along the coast south of here. They can start gathering data and specimens in a more natural setting while we do the same here in an urban one. They get the flora and fauna. We'll gather as much anthropological and archeological data and objects as we can fit in the lander." He shifted his gaze to Soon, the mission anthropologist. "Is that alright with you?"

"Yes, sir!" Soon said, his face beaming through the faceplate. He hadn't said a word since they'd landed, simply taking images and making notes on his tablet as they walked through the city. The running joke was, Soon preferred dead people to live ones.

"We'll relocate the lander and set up our environment shelters at the base of this big sculpture," Ramirez continued. "We can use it as our base of operations. I suspect we can gather an inordinate amount of data in the two weeks that we have down here. I also recommend that Patrocles alter orbit and begin slow passes to do as much geophysical scanning as possible. It will put us out of contact intermittently, but I think we're relatively save down here."

"Copy that," Abimbola said. "Stand by."

"Roger that," Ramirez replied, trying to rub his neck again. His headache was sharpening a bit, but not any worse that a sinus headache.

"I can't help but wonder if we're standing on the first colonized world of Terra," Sparks said.

"Possibly," Akashi added. "It would take years to swap out the helium in the atmo with nitrogen, but that's just an exercise in engineering when it comes right down to it."

"And the indigenous flora and fauna?" Cohen asked.

"Earth is crowded," Ramirez said cautiously. "And you know as well as I that the colonies on Luna and Mars are far from being long term and self-sustaining. This place is a green world with water on it.... Fortunately," he added with a sigh of relief, "such decisions are light-years above my pay grade. I'm just a dumb dirt-digger."

"Ramirez," Captain Abimbola broke in, "your recommendation is approved. "Murphy's team is prepping their lander now and should make landfall in a few hours. Get set up as quickly as possible and report in every two hours." There was another pause. "One more thing.... I want Richards to do a full sweep of the area out to a few hundred meters before anyone goes wandering off. Let's make sure there aren't any obvious surprises."

"Yes, Captain," Ramirez said. "We should have the shelters set up before the sun goes down, if we hump it."

"Understood," Abimbola replied. "Patrocles out."

Ramirez looked to where Lieutenant Richards stood, gently poking at a cat-sized beastie with the tip of his rifle. Everyone had side-arms as a precaution, but Richards, a marine pilot and biologist, was the only one of them with an autorifle and combat training. "Take two with you when you do the sweep" Ramirez said.

Richards nodded and gave a sloppy salute. "You got it, sir," he said, slinging the rifle.

Ramirez turned to the rest of his team. "Well, you heard the lady. Let's get moving."

***

– Part 2: Realization –

JANUARY 19, 2098 – ROSS 128-B

"You're the third person to complain about a headache in two days, Commander," Cohen said, shining a small light Ramirez's eyes. "How bad is it?"

They were inside the medical module that opened into one side of the main habitation module where a secondary air lock and the mess hall was housed. Each module, made primarily of a tough, carbon fiber material, could be sealed and self-contained in an emergency. Rigidity was sustained by narrow channels of high-pressure atmosphere that lined the interior in a crisscross pattern that could be inflated and deflated as necessary. A variety of equipment and cabinetry lined the module, all of it done in a very sterile white that made up the entire seven-module habitat.

"Barely noticeable but there," he replied, leaning forward on the collapsible examination table. "On and off again since shortly after we entered the city. Who else?"

"Soon and Akashi ... and they said the same thing." Cohen placed a small monitor to the side of Ramirez's throat, just over the jugular, and watched the readouts for a few seconds.

"Do you think it's environmental?" Ramirez asked.

"All seals remain unbroken on both the suits and the modules. And all decon protocols have been followed to the letter, so I'd have to say probably not, unless we missed something really, really small. But I've been checking the air every thirty minutes, and I take blood samples whenever they return to the modules."

"You should ask the others if they've noticed anything and just haven't mentioned it. You know what a hard-asses Sparks and Richards are."

"I'll check with Sparks as soon as he returned from his sweep. He and Soon were investigating what they thought might be an arboretum of some kind about a kilometer to the southeast. And I'll check on Richards once we're done here."

Ramirez nodded. "Could it be from radiation, maybe?" he offered.

"Negative." Cohen shook her head. "That bloody, great monstrosity in the sky might be ugly to our eyes, but what we receive groundside from it is actually a little less intense than what we get from Sol back home. And the suits still apply."

"Well, maybe its just stress. We are on an alien planet, after all."

"These readouts would seem to agree with your assessment, Commander," Cohen said, motioning for him to get off the table.

The headache at the base of Ramirez' skull suddenly intensified with a sharp spike and then faded. He winced at the pain and then sighed as it dissipated like the bursting of a bubble.

"Are you alright?" Cohen asked, clearly concerned.

Ramirez stood up straight and took a few breaths.

"Yeah," he said finally. "I am. It's gone ... like it lit up for just a moment and then disappeared completely, as if it had never been there."

We wish words... the voice, although that term didn't really apply, filtered into Ramirez's thoughts, almost as if he'd thought them himself, but he knew he hadn't.

"Did you hear that?" Cohen asked, looking around the module.

Ramirez nodded, and he looked spooked. "Yeah. 'We wish words,' right?"

Cohen nodded.

"Hey," Richards said, poking his head around the module entrance, a sandwich held in one hand. "Did you two just hear something in your head?" He had a truly perplexed look upon his face.

"Commander, I think you better get out here," Akashi's voice came over the speakers spread throughout the habitat.

Ramirez moved quickly over to the comm panel on the wall and hit the actuate button.

"Is everything okay?" he asked.

There was a long pause.

"I'm not sure .... I think so?" It was Soon's voice this time. He sounded a little worried but not frightened. "You better bring Richards, sir."

"I think we're good out here," Akashi added. She'd been just outside the habitat, taking air samples. "But I wouldn't dawdle."

"Copy that," Ramirez said. "We're coming out ASAP." He released the comm actuator.

"Richards, gear up and grab the rifle" Ramirez said, brushing past him. "You're coming too, Cohen," he ordered over his shoulder. He marched across the mess and into the suit bay where everyone's environmental suits hung along the walls.

All three of them suited up as if the habitat was losing atmosphere, checked each other's seals, and then stepped into the primary airlock in record time. None of them said a word, but there were plenty of worried glances exchanged as the seal closed behind them.

"It followed us from the arboretum, sir," Soon said as Ramirez, Cohen, and Richards exited the outer hatch. "And it's just been sitting there since we got here, as if it was waiting for something."

"Or someone," Akashi added a bit ominously. She was seated in the rover, her hands on the controls, staring at something on the ground just beyond the hood. Soon and Sparks stood off to the side a half-dozen meters, looking down at the same spot.

When Ramirez stepped around rover, he saw what they were looking at. He gasped in surprise, stopping dead in his tracks.

It was the mother of all beasties, over two meters long, two-thirds of a meter thick, and with a head the size of basketball. As Ramirez came into view, it raised its strange-looking head and lifted its first segment off the ground, pointing its mouth straight at Ramirez.

Richards immediately raised the rifle reflexively, aiming down the barrel at the beastie's face.

"Easy, Richards," Ramirez said, placing his hand on the barrel and lowering it gently. He turned to and locked eyes with Richards. "Stand over there," he motioned to a spot a few meters off. "Where you won't have a problem with line of fire."

Richards nodded, a stern expression on his face.

"Don't do anything unless I say so or if it attacks anyone. Understood?"

Again, Richards nodded.

You hear. We think.

The words hit Ramirez' brain as clear as a bell, and he saw that everyone jumped at them.

Ramirez realized that everyone could hear the 'voice,' and there was little doubt that the big beastie was the source.

Take time to learn thoughts. Will take more. No more head pain.

"It's talking to us," Cohen said.

"Apparently," Ramirez said. "It seems our mission of exploration has just become a first contact mission." The implications staggered Ramirez's imagination.

"Holy shit," Akashi whispered, but everyone heard her through the comms.

"You can understand me?" Ramirez said, taking several steps toward the beastie. He stopped only a few meters away and went down to one knee, getting on an eye to … well … snout level.

You hear. We think, it repeated.

Ramirez didn't know what to say next. They'd gone over some scenarios about meeting space-faring races and how to handle any sort of contact, but this was different. Was this a primitive species with a rudimentary language, something on par with human intelligence? Or was it something greater?

We think like you, it said.

It had heard his thoughts.

114

"Everyone," Ramirez said slowly. "Do us all a favor and try not to think of anything aggressive toward the beastie or which might compromise to the mission."

"It can read our thoughts, can't it?" Cohen said.

Ramirez nodded slowly. The mission just became a whole lot more complicated.

"Cohen," Ramirez said. "Would you go back inside and let Patrocles know what's going on here. Don't alarm them, but they need to know. Tell them I have a Level 4 Omega situation on my hands, but that I don't expect trouble. Abimbola will know what it means. And think quietly," he added.

"Yes, Captain," Cohen replied as he moved back toward the airlock.

Ramirez stared at the beastie for a moment, and it looked like it was staring right at him, although it didn't have any eyes. "We come from another world," Ramirez said. "And we come in peace." He couldn't believe those words just passed his lips. Was this really happening?

Other world. Yes. Peace. Yes. Home here.

"This is your home?" Ramirez asked, feeling a bit confused by the conceptual way it injected thoughts into his mind.

Yes. Home.

"Are you the only one who can speak to us?" Ramirez asked.

Yes-no.

That didn't make any sense to Ramirez.

I think. Yes. No pain. Others speak. Some. Yes pain. I speak you now. No pain. You we learn.

Ramirez nodded his head. It made sense. It was the one speaking, and there were others of its kind who could send their thoughts to the landing party. It might explain why some of them had experienced the headaches. He assumed their telepathic communication required the beasties to send in a manner humans could perceive. Or humans needed to adapt somehow to receive the messages. Or both. And only the big one was able to communicate as clearly as it obviously could without causing the humans any discomfort.

I and we same think, it said.

Ramirez cocked his head to the side, not understanding. Did 'we' mean the beastie and the humans, or all of the beasties combined?

"I think it's a sort of collective, sir," Richards said. "When we speak to it, we may be speaking to all of them ... and vice versa."

Ramirez nodded his head.

Why here? it asked.

"We're explorers," Ramirez said. "We came to see what this world was like."

You want live here? It asked.

The question hung in Ramirez's thoughts. It's ability to communicate with him was already improving. It was adapting quickly to alien minds.

"I don't think that's possible anymore," Ramirez said, carefully. He had to assume they'd been listening to the landing party the entire time, and there had been conversation about colonization. The truth was, with the world inhabited by a sentient species, there was no way the GU would ever even consider sending a colony. An embassy, maybe, but never a colony.

"Not anymore," he said. "We might have, but now that we know you are sentient, such a thing could never happen."

Agreed. Never happen, it said. The words were firm but not angry or even meant as an ultimatum. Somehow, he knew that.

Ross 128-b was now off-limits to any future human colony.

"We would like to learn more about you. About your world," Ramirez said.

You welcome to learn. We learn too, it replied We learn together, it added.

"We don't have much time here," Ramirez said. "We will be returning home in about twelve days."

Twelve days good, it said. Learn what you can. I will stay here and we learn together.

"I would like that," Ramirez said. "Will it be okay for some of us to move about the city while the rest of us stay here and learn from you?"

Yes. It is okay.

"Thank you," Ramirez said. "I look forward to learning more about you and your people." He was astonished. The whole thing seemed utterly surreal, and he could only hope he didn't botch what was now the most pivotal mission of exploration humankind had ever undertaken.

***

– Part 3: Invitation –

JANUARY 25, 2098 – ROSS 128-B

For six days, Ramirez, Cohen, and Richards sat around a small folding table they'd set up just in front of the rover. The rest of the team was exploring the city. They were gathering botanical samples, doing their best to capture at least some of the elusive insect life that inhabited the world, and collecting a broad range of archeological artifacts for later study. The other landing party also continued gathering data and specimens. They'd found a diverse ecosystem of flora but little fauna, excepting the preponderance of the beasties and nothing like T.

They'd given their new friend the name T and decided to call the other members of its race "Tardis." They'd asked if they could refer to it that way, and it said that it liked the idea, although its species didn't have distinct names like humans. It differentiated between others of its kind by a sort of mental signature. It had all been Akashi's idea, actually, but the names stuck.

T had acquiesced to Cohen taking a skin sample on the second day, and they'd discovered that the DNA of the Tardis made them distant cousin of the tardigrades on Earth. That revelation alone had made the trip worth it. It proved a number of theories and disproved others. It also alleviated some of their concerns about dealing with an alien species that wasn't so alien after all.

All the while, Abimbola and the rest of the Patrocles crew listened in, posed questions through Ramirez, and recorded all of it for posterity. This was the greatest moment in human exploration, and it was taking place over, basically, a picnic table.

They learned about the Tardis' life cycle—virtually identical to tardigrades—as well as their social interactions, such as they were. And T learned a good deal about human civilization. It seemed curious about humans, but not overly concerned about their existence.

"There's something I've been meaning to ask you," Ramirez said carefully. He kept his thoughts as neutral as possible for fear that it might be a touchy subject. And the answer might impact how the landing party treated the Tardis that, thus far, had been as docile as caterpillars and as friendly as puppies.

The builders, it said. It had taken some getting used to, but Ramirez was finally accustomed to it knowing what he was thinking.

"Yes," he replied. "The civilization that built these cities—we believe they were at about the same level of technology as humans, maybe a little farther ahead, and we're reasonably certain they had at least begun exploring the stars. Out scans found several launch installations that are very similar to our own. What happened to them?"

Our memory is long, it said from where it perched on the hood of the rover, basking in the sun. But there is nothing in it that includes those who lived here before. It lowered its head to the hood and chewed upon a clump of leaves Richard's had collected for it and left in a pile. The two had become fast, if not odd, friends. He had gone out every morning and collected large leaves from a nearby tree that T had said was its favorite.

"Do you have any sense of time?" Ramirez asked. Their scans of the buildings, vehicles, and tools of the civilization indicated they'd been built and abandoned a little over twenty-five hundred years earlier, when mankind was deep into the age of bronze, iron, and conquest of neighboring lands.

Neither time nor generation holds any meaning to us, it said. As individuals, we come and go over countless rotations of our world, what you call days, but we do not keep track of such things. We eat, we breed, we listen to the sky, and we sing to one another. It is enough, it said simply.

Ramirez nodded his head. T's people were not unlike many of the indigenous peoples of his own world before technology instilled within them a desire to advance even further. Every discovery had let to another. And another. Humans, as a species, seemed to possess a drive that T's people did not. There was even a part of him that envied their way of life. He'd often read about several of the South American tribes who still lived in that manner, isolated and protected by the GU so that their way of life remained uninterrupted.

Were T's people so different?

"I can certainly appreciate that," Ramirez said.

"Me too," Richards agreed. "Hell, I've spent a few summers in the back country of Alaska, just surviving and enjoying that connection to the natural world. There's nothing like it."

"It's too bad we can't take one of you with us back to Earth and show you more of our way of life," Cohen said. "I'm sure it would be very interesting to you, although, perhaps it would be more appalling than anything else."

The three humans chuckled at that.

Why not? T said.

The question hit all three of them like a shot.

Would it even be possible?

There was no way they could build a suit for T, although they could fabricate a large enough cargo pod to carry it, and they had equipment to modify a cryo-chamber.

"Cohen," Richards said, "do they even respirate?"

"The ones back home don't," Cohen replied, looking thoughtful. "I'd have to do some thorough scans of T, and we could set up another module and see if it could exist in our atmosphere. I'd also want to take a good deal of samples of its body and excretions to see if there were bacteria, viruses, or anything else that might be harmful to humans. From the work I've done thus far, I'm inclined to say that they are harmless to us. But I'd also want both of the other doctors as well all of the biologists and biochemists involved."

"Agreed," Ramirez said. "We'd have to be absolutely certain." Ramirez looked at T. "Are you sure about this?"

You once mentioned an Earth ambassador here on this world. Would you consider an ambassador of my people coming to your world?

T had a point.

They wouldn't be able to leave an ambassador behind—not yet at least. Future missions, however, could come equipped to set up a permanent research station with an ambassadorial presence. It could be the first step toward an interstellar alliance.

"You have to understand, T," Ramirez said slowly, "for this to happen, we'd have to find a way to get you back to Earth. The journey takes three years. That's over a thousand rotations of your world. And we go back in a sort of frozen sleep. You're related to our tardigrades, so I don't think there'd be a problem, but in all honestly, it might kill you, and that's a terrible risk. Three years to get home, and I don't even know when another mission might come back to Ross 128. It could be a decade or more before you would be able to return home, if at all"

I live a long time, and knowing what I know of your people know, I would think your curiosity would bring more of your missions back to our world sooner rather than later. And if I never returned, I could accept that. I have my songs, and you said yourself that there are some of my kind on your world. Perhaps I could learn to sing with them.

Ramirez thought about it ... about the discovery and what this would mean to the people of Earth. It was the next big step for human exploration, and if T was willing and Abimbola approved it, then humanity would be changed even further ... and forever.

He glanced upwards. "Patrocles, have you been listening in?"

"Affirmative, Commander," Abimbola's voice broke in on the comms. "We've been discussing the matter."

"T says he's willing to accept the risks. Are we even authorized to bring back an alien? Ambassador or not?"

"I presented this very scenario to the ESRA administrator five years ago, and protocols were created that make it possible." There was a pause. "For the time being, have Cohen begin preparations. We're sending down the third lander with a medical module that can be used to do the work at your location. Doctor Cohen?" Abimbola asked.

"Yes, Captain?"

"I want you to pull up a data file entitled 'Dinner Guest.' Use decryption key Tango Bravo Delta Five Seven Niner. I'm sending that information to your tablet now. You've got lead on the research effort, and I'll have both of the other doctors to you within a few hours."

"Understood, Captain," Cohen replied.

"I'm authorizing a full mission revision," Abimbola said. "All crew are hereby reassigned to support the effort to bring Ambassador T with us back to Earth." She paused for a moment. "Ramirez?"

"Yes, Captain?"

"Please inform the ambassador that upon our return, there will be a two-to-six-month decon process on Luna with a team of our specialists. They will ensure that it is safe for both him and the people of Earth to walk around freely among our people. He is hereby granted full Ambassadorial status and is to be treated as such. For our purposes, I want you and Richards to just keep doing what you're doing."

Ramirez was almost disappointed, but not quite. He enjoyed talking with T, and where initially it had been almost scientific discovery, he was now finding they were sharing philosophies. Not much just yet, but it was growing. He had a unique opportunity before him. A sentient race with awareness of the stars and space travel, but which had no interest in it. Did they have laws? Crime? Politics? Were such things even possible with a hive mind? And if it was truly a hive mind, how would the whole react when the one had been removed from it. And vice versa.

He had a strange feeling that he and T would be friends for a very long time, and he found himself wanting the captain, ESRA, and even the GU to permanently assign him as T's liaison upon returning home.

I would like that too, T said.

***

– Part 4: Revelation –

JUNE 18, 2101 – SOL 3 (EARTH)

Are you sure you're ready for this? Ramirez asked as the shuttle made its final approach to the spaceport. They'd come a long way together, and their friendship had grown into a comradery unlike anything he'd ever known. He'd even learned how to converse with T by thought alone. He'd discovered, purely by accident, that by only thinking his words, they were able to make their conversations private. Ramirez called it their private mode, and he'd discovered quickly that they could exchange information more quickly that way. T could still broadcast and have conversations with multiple people simultaneously, but there were times when Ramirez preferred the private mode. In it, he actually received sensory impressions, emotions, and even visual images from within T's vast memory. It was always a heady experience, and he was coming to understand the peace and tranquility of a hive mentality.

I am ready to meet your people, T said. I am experiencing a strange sensation, though. I believe you would call it nervousness. It is new.

I can feel it, Ramirez replied, I wouldn't worry. They're all here to see you. He looked out the window at the Mediterranean as the coastline of Athens raced by beneath them. Athens had become the center of planetary and interplanetary travel. There were other spaceports, of course, but Athens was the jewel in the crown of the GU, which is why the celebration was being held there. Get ready for a jolt, he added.

I am ready, T said, but the feelings coming through were far from calm.

The shuttle touched down with a single, gentle bump, and then the breaking pushed them forward slightly. T swayed with the deceleration, but he didn't tumble.

An interesting sensation, he said, and there was a sense of delight in his thoughts.

I'll see if there's a way to get you onto a roller coaster, my friend, Ramirez said. He visualized one, remembering his sensations as a youth at an amusement park near where he'd grown up in North Carolina.

!! T's surprise at the imagery and emotions was palpable. You do this on purpose? he asked.

I used to. People still do it... for fun. Ramirez would make it a point to ask their GU contact if it would be possible to get T onto one during his visit. He thought it likely.

He wanted T to experience as much of what it was like to be human as was possible. He'd spent almost every waking moment with the Ambassador for nearly seven, waking months. He'd accompanied it up to the Patrocles back on Ross 128-b and helped get it situated in a modified cryochamber the crew had prepared for it. They had a week of wake-time heading out of the system, three years of cryo-sleep, and then a week of wake time as they entered Sol's system.

When they finally contacted ESRA command in Berlin and reported what was going on, the news spread like wildfire across the entire system. Humans had not only made first contact with an alien race; the first alien ambassador was going to visit Earth ... eventually.

Ramirez was no longer a commander, although he was still a member of the ESRA. At his request and Captain Abimbola's recommendation, he'd been permanently reassigned as T's liaison. From that moment on, Ramirez went everywhere with Ambassador T.

Ramirez travelled with it to the isolated Luna Research Complex over-looking the Sea of Tranquility. He worked with a wide assortment of scientists there and assisted in the laborious process of making sure that Earth was safe for T and T was safe for Earth. Atmosphere turned out to be a non issue. Like its microscopic cousins, it could withstand extreme temperatures, pressures, and even the vacuum of space without any ill effects. And its tissues, taken at the request of T, were impervious to every pathogen humanity had stored at the LRC. It was also devoid of such pathogens.

They took the full six months to everyone's safety, and a massive amount of data was accumulated about T's genetic structure and biological makeup. They'd also discovered that it could consume just about any organic matter as a source of nutrition. It didn't seem to matter what it was, so long as it had been alive at one time. It endured every test and exercise the scientists wanted to perform, and over the course of those six months, T had become quite a celebrity. Nearly the whole of the human race wanted to meet T and learn more about his people on Ross 128-b, eleven light-years away.

There were protests here and there about alien invasions, the dangers of exposure, and even several demonstrations from the more extreme religions claiming that it was all a hoax, because some still believed humans were the only life in the universe. For the most part, however, Terrans—Ramirez had forced himself to think in those terms—were excited to meet or at least see the ambassador from another world.

And here they were, finally reaching Earth.

The two of them had travelled on the shuttle alone, and when they walked down the jetway and entered the terminal, there was a crowd of GU dignitaries as well as a large assemblage of media teams who were quick to grab as much video footage as they could. They were kept back a discreet distance, but there was no mistaking the excitement they had at seeing their first alien.

As the two of them approached the crowd, Ramirez walking and T undulating forward with is caterpillar-like gait, a petit man of Indian descent stepped up to them.

"Ambassador T!" he said in a faint Indian accent. "It is a sincere pleasure to finally meet you." He made a formal bow and then smiled. "I am Chancellor Prassad of the Global Union, and on behalf of the GU and all Terrans everywhere, it is my honor and privilege to welcome you to our world."

Thank you, Chancellor Prassad, Ambassador T replied. I am very happy to meet you.

A collective gasp rolled through the group, including the Chancellor, as everyone in the vicinity received their first telepathic message. Chancellor Prassad's eyes went wide, and then he grinned like a child.

"Remarkable," he said.

Ramirez smiled. This was going to be one more for the history books.

"I believe you have a vehicle ready to take us to the amphitheater?" Ramirez asked.

"Indeed!" Prassad said, motioning toward a red carpet leading up to an electric airport cart. It had been modified with a single seat for Ramirez on one side and a long platform for Ambassador T on the other. They even had a small ramp for the ambassador so that he could simply crawl up into place. "This will take you to a vehicle outside, and it will take you to the amphitheater. I will give an introduction speech and then you can take all the time you want to introduce yourself to the people gathered there as well as much of the rest of humanity. We are broadcasting your speech across the entire system. Once you give your speech, I am hoping you will have time to meet with me and the rest of the GU council for a casual gathering we've prepared in your honor."

I believe I will enjoy that, T said, nodding his head.

Ramirez smiled again. During their time together, T had picked up quite a number of human mannerisms, including nodding and shaking his head whenever he communicated, although he sometimes got it wrong.

Ramirez and T moved up to the cart together. Ramirez took his seat quickly, but as T undulated up the platform, he paused at the top and looked out over the group of humans who had welcomed them.

I would like to thank you all for such an agreeable welcome. You have made me feel immediately at home, and my gratitude is without bounds. He lowered his head once, mimicking a human bow, and the crowd erupted into cheers and applause. He took his place, and as the cart pulled away, Ramirez turned to his friend. That went well.

Agreed, T replied. They are a friendly people. Noisy, but friendly. He added.

Ramirez's laughter flowed through the airport as they rolled past one gawking face after another.

✳✳✳

They stood together in a side passage behind the amphitheater stage, waiting for Chancellor Prassad to finish his speech to the thirty-thousand people seated beneath blue skies and a warm, yellow sun.

Will you be able to speak to them all? he asked.

I believe so, T replied. On my world, the range of our communication went beyond the confines of the city. In fact, I can hear the minds of more human minds than I thought possible. It's actually a little disconcerting.

Ramirez felt a sharp pain at the base of his skull, but he realized the pain wasn't his. He turned to his friend, a concerned look upon his face.

Are you alright? he asked suddenly worried for his friend.

Ambassador T's body twitched slightly, almost like a shiver across his entire body.

I believe I am fine. We experienced a similar sensation back on my world when your landing team first arrived. I suspect it is just an adjustment to being exposed to so many human minds in one place. T's thoughts were steady, but there was an underlying strain that Ramirez could clearly sense.

If you are in distress, Ramirez said, we can postpone this. You don't need to give a speech. I have no doubt they will understand.

No, T said emphatically. This is important to your people, and I can endure a bit of discomfort for the good of interplanetary relations.

Ramirez felt T's determination and a strong sense of good will.

If you're sure, he said.

I am, T replied.

A thunder of cheering and applause reverberated throughout the entire amphitheater, echoing against the walls around them.

As I said, T gave a mental version of a chuckle. Noisy.

Ramirez laughed again as T's body vibrated once again and another sharp pain hit Ramirez's mind.

Pay it no heed, T said. I will endeavor to make sure they do not feel the sensation.

A young woman with long, dark hair and a flowing gown appeared at the top of the steps a short distance away, smiling at them both.

"They're ready for you, Ambassador," she said. "If you will both follow me, I'll take you onto the stage."

Let us proceed, T said, and he shuffled after her.

Ramirez followed, suddenly very worried for his friend, but T's insistence left him with no recourse other than to see it through.

As the curtain was pulled aside, they both walked onto a wide stage. Bright sunlight shined down from a virtually cloudless sky. Chancellor Prassad stood before a podium, facing them both. He immediately began clapping as Ambassador came into view, and when the crowd spotted him, they, too applauded.

T shuffled across the stage, and as he did, the entire audience rose out of their seats. Many started cheering and whistling as he neared the center of the stage, and as they did, Ramirez felt another pain lance through his mind. He glanced at T, but there was no telltale shudder across his body. He hoped that he would be the only one to feel it. He opened his mind, doing his best to lend T all the mental fortitude he possessed.

If you need to channel it, please use me. I will support you in any way I can, Ramirez said.

Thank you, my friend. There was a strain to his thoughts. I may just do that.... So many minds...

I'm here for you, Ramirez added, opening himself even further.

They made their way to the center of the stage, and T stopped in the middle, right beside Chancellor Prassad. As they came to a halt, the crowd stopped applauding and seated themselves. Ramirez looked out to a sea of faces. A stiff wind blew through the amphitheater causing a dozen flags lining the back of the amphitheater to flutter at attention. The wind blew straight toward the starport beyond, only a mile away. As he watched several planetary and orbital aircraft rose into the air, taking people not only across the globe but to Luna and even Mars on their regular runs.

Ambassador T nodded once to Prassad.

Thank you, again, Chancellor Prassad, T said.

A collective gasp ran through the entire audience, and Ramirez could tell that even the people in the back row reacted to their first telepathic communication.

Pain hit Ramirez hard, pressing from the base of his skull and lancing over the top. He tried not to wince at the intensity of it. He opened himself further, willing his mind to become the conduit for T's pain.

I would first like to thank every human here for such a wonderful greeting, Ambassador T said. I could never have imagined that so many entities on a distant world could be as welcoming to one of my kind.

Pain hit Ramirez again, and this time he saw T's body shudder.

From the first moment we encountered my friend Ramirez and the crew of the Patrocles, we sensed nothing but goodwill. Indeed, their kindness and willingness to learn from us as we learned about them was one of the reasons I was willing to make such a great journey across the stars to meet you.

Pain.

Ramirez thought his head was coming apart, and as he glanced at T, he saw a slow vibration running along his skin. As he looked out at the audience, he saw a number of people in the front rows wincing.

I ... T paused, as if he were collecting his thoughts, but Ramirez knew his friend was having difficulty. I would like to extend our warmest ... pain ... greetings to each and every ... PAIN ... one of you.

PAIN.

Ramirez dropped to his knees in agony, and Chancellor Prassad staggered forward, grasping at the podium to support himself. Several in the front row cried out, grasping their heads.

I ... T started, and then he flopped forward, his legs crumpling beneath him. I ... seem to be ....

Another wave of intense pain washed through Ramirez's brain.

Ramirez? T cried on the private mode. I think ... dying....

Many in the front row screamed as Ambassador T's body shuddered violently. His skin color rapidly shifted from the pale green to a deepening hue that in seconds turned black.

Ramirez crawled over to his friend.

T! he cried.

Dying.... T said. Dying.

T's head disintegrated in a cloud of black dust, and as it did, the pain immediately subsided in Ramirez's skull. He gasped as it a wave of relief washed through him, and then he watched in horror as Ambassador T's entire body disintegrated into a large cloud of black dust that was quickly carried by the breeze into the audience and onto the wind.

Many in the audience screamed, and a number of them rose from their seats, ready to bolt at the sight of what had happened.

All Ramirez could do was kneel in front of what had been his friend and weep.

"Everyone!" Prassad's voice, carried over tumult of the frightened audience by the PA system, boomed throughout the entire amphitheater. "Everyone, please!" He tapped the microphone several times. "Stay calm!"

The audience turned frightened eyes toward the Chancellor.

"What we have seen here today is a terrible tragedy, but we must not panic."

The clamor in the audience subsided slowly.

"I do not know what has happened to here, and I grieve for the loss of such a brave individual as Ambassador T. He travelled so far, and he brought with him the hope and enthusiasm of two peoples. We must all honor his sacrifice and take it into our hearts."

Ramirez felt hands lifting him from the stage.

"As Chancellor of the GU, I promise you we will do everything in our power to discover what has happened. I must ask you all to make your way to the exits and go home. The Council will provide you any and all information available as we investigate what has happened here today. I would also ask that you keep Mr. Ramirez here in your thoughts and prayers. He has suffered a greater loss than any of us, for I know that the Ambassador was a dear friend of his. His loss is ten-fold greater than any of our own, and we must do what we can to support him as he navigates the days and months ahead."

The crowd rose slowly, and all of them applauded as Ramirez was gently led off the stage.

He never did recover.

***

It took nine months for the spores, borne of Ambassador T's disintegrating body, to gestate into the microbial versions of itself that would wipe out the human race. Within days of the gestation, a host's body began suffered first from organ and brain failure, and it didn't take long for human doctors to realize what was eating them all from the inside out.

But by then it was too late.

The spores, carried upon the breeze that day, had infected the entire audience. It had infected the travelers at the space port. It had infected every person they came into contact with, wherever they went.

Within twenty-four months, the inhabitants of two worlds, one moon, a half-dozen space stations, and the mining colonies in the Asteroid Belt between Mars and Jupiter, were devoid of human life, and their bodies were the first things consumed by the rapidly growing descendants of Ambassador T.

The last human alive died alone, afraid, and screaming in a cargo bay in the Asteroid belt around Mars. She became the last human meal in the Sol system for what had long-been the most dominant life form in the Milky Way.

***

– Part 5: Investigation –

3,000 EARTH ORBITS LATER – SOL 3

"I wonder what happened to them?" Sub-Adjunct Koytail said, his voice filled with awe. He was thick-bodied, like most of his species, with pale blue mottled skin and a crest of red spines running over his flat head, each tip glowing faintly within his environmental suit. The oxygen and nitrogen-rich atmosphere was close to that of his home world, but they his team had to concern itself with possible contamination and infection.

The exo-team commander and botanist by training, stared up at a monolithic structure made white stone. Its surface was darkened by patches of green moss and streaks of gray that had accumulated over a long period of time. The structure, a tall, narrow, four-sided pillar with a pointed top, rose above an ancient city full of what had once been white buildings decorated with thick columns. Contrasted against a pale blue sky, it reminded her of a history marker back home.

"Disease, maybe?" Tertiary-Adjunct Vess suggested from where he stood atop a parked vehicle across the street. It had a flat top and seats built for an occupant twice the size of a sugan. He'd suggested that the indigenous species of the alien world would have been bipedal and, based upon the controls of the vehicle, possessed with only two arms. "A global plague?"

"I don't know...." Koytail replied. "Maybe?" She felt a slight cranial pang coming on. "And you're sure the scans haven't picked up any fauna other than the insects and these green life forms?"

She glanced over to a set of stone steps where one of them chewed on a patch of moss in the shade. It was small, maybe half the length of her arm, with a folded in face, a cylindrical snout full of bony white dentia, and reminded her of a microbial life form found in some of the more extreme places of her homeworld.

"Hello, my little green friend," she said. "Can you tell me what happened here?"

She winced again as a mild pain shot up into her cranium.

###

About Quincy J. Allen

NATIONALLY BESTSELLING AUTHOR QUINCY J. Allen is a cross-genre author with numerous short story publications in multiple anthologies, collections, and magazines. His first short story collection *Out Through the Attic*, came out in 2014 from 7DS Books. He made his first short story pro-sale in 2014 with *Jimmy Krinklepot and the White Rebels of Hayberry*, included in WordFire's *A Fantastic Holiday Season: The Gift of Stories*, and his most recent short story sale, *Sons of the Father*, appears in Larry Correia's *Monster Hunter: Files* from Baen, published in October, 2017.

Chemical Burn, his first novel and the first volume of the sci-fi detective noir series *Endgame*, was a finalist in RMFW's Colorado Gold Contest in 2011. His latest installment of the *Blood War Chronicles*, *Blood Curse*, is book 2 in an epic fantasy series starting in the Old West and featuring a clockwork gunslinger.

He is the publisher and editor of *Penny Dread Tales*, a short story collection in its fifth volume that has become a labor of love. He also runs RuneWright, LLC, a small marketing and book design business out of his home in Charlotte, North Carolina, and hopes to one day be a full-time writer in Baen's stable of fantastic authors.

Connect with Quincy here:
www.castrumpress.com/authors/quincy-j-allen

ALIEN DAYS

DISCOVERY
by PP Corcoran

The churning brilliant blue cloud which surrounded the first stable wormhole known to exist held the crew of the Discovery fixated with its ever moving, intermingling clouds. More than one person had remarked at how similar it was to one of Earth's own turbulent hurricanes, the clouds madly racing this way and that but always, at its very heart, the completely still eye.

This hurricane, however, was caused by no earthly phenomenon. The Singularity was the result of an ultra-secret government project with the express purpose to back engineer alien technology recovered from a ship which crash landed in the Arizona desert in 1947.

It had taken the best brains the United States military could get together in one room the better part of a century to reproduce a working prototype. Though a prototype of what none could say for certain because nobody had the faintest idea what would happen when the device was switched on. The scientists best bet was that the device was a type of inertia cancelling engine. However, for all they knew it could very well have been a rather complex garbage disposal.

With a caution which many at the time had though unduly over reactive the prototype was, in the darkest secrecy, loaded aboard a resupply ship headed for the fledgling Martian colonies and, when the ship had reached what was deemed a safe distance, this distance being several million miles, the crew donned space suits, opened the wide cargo bay doors and removed the device from its storage container. Attaching a small chemical motor to the device it was allowed to float free of the ship of its own accord before the engine ignited slowing the devices forward velocity and allowing the supply ship to accelerated away. On a command from Mission Control the power supply to the device was activated and everyone waited with bated breath to see if anything would happen or if the past hundred years had been a colossal waste of time. They were not disappointed. What happened next was best explained as breathtaking. With a flash as brilliant as a star going supernova the alien device functioned and in the blink of an eye a stable wormhole appeared in the solar system.

With the secret out of the bag the government had been forced to reveal the whole truth. For the better part of a century they had not only known that aliens existed, but they had been running a secret program to reverse engineer and replicate the alien technology. The conspiracy theorists jumped with joy and pointed fingers at those who had dismissed them for so long while governments around the world expressed outrage that they had been deceived for so long. Scientists and engineers demanded the release of all the previously classified material.

Under such massive pressure the government caved and then came the second great revelation. The device that had generated the singularly was only the beginning, the government had already taken the next step and constructed its own hybrid spacecraft based on the pieces recovered from the crash in 1947 and the most advanced human technology. And it was ready to fly.

This second revelation only served to fuel the demand, for international oversight and reluctantly the government handed over control to a multi-national space agency who would operate under the auspice of the United Nations however, the only people currently trained to fly the Discovery were a US military crew, this would not do cried the UN, but this crew had been years in the training responded the US. Years of detailed research had gone into tearing the Ralak technology apart figuring out how it ticked. Doctors had poured over the remains of the four dead Ralak's who had crewed the original crashed ship. Linguists had taken decades to build up working knowledge of the alien's language both written and spoken through long tortuous hours of frustrating conversations with the damaged ships Artificial Intelligence. Conversations that had left more questions than answers. According to the AI the ship had been a one of a kind probe. Designed specifically to travel through the wormhole in search of a new home for the Ralak whose home planet faced some sort of impending cataclysm. What form that cataclysm took was not clear, that part of the data banks had been wiped clean, presumably as a result of the crash. The only way to find out was to travel through the wormhole and that was precisely what Colonel Diane Kielty and her crew had spent the past five years, day in day out, training to do.

Compromise was now the word of the day. Bolt an extra couple of seats into the already cramped cabin and there you had it. Room for a couple of observers.

Kielty surreptitiously ran her damp palms along the leather arms of her command chair. The Singularity cast its bluish tinged light all across the cabin, the light played on the already blue jump suits of her crew making them apparently fade into the background of the cabin, fleeting glimpses of pale skin the only thing alluding to their presence.

However, the two brilliant white jumpsuits of the international observers, Colonel of Cosmonauts Joseph Molanokov representing the Russian Federation and Dr Mi Lee So, China's leading astrophysicist and, in Kielty's opinion, far more approachable than the gruff Molanokov. The observer's jumpsuits had taken on a vibrant electric look to them which only served to highlight their... Kielty's search for a suitable word eluded her so she settled on the first descriptor that popped into her head... wrongness she thought with a wry smile.

That wrongness was reinforced by the years of layer upon layer of security that had surrounded the crashed Ralak probe and the Backstop Program. The significance of the ship and the possible advantages its advanced technology could provide in the middle of the heightening tensions of the Cold War was not lost on the more shadowy parts of the United States government and military. The decision was made to keep the ships very existence a secret. Squirreled away on the uninhabited mid Pacific island, more an atoll than an island really, of Gilo. Surrounded by thousands of square miles of empty ocean Gilo dated back to the early fifties when US Air Force engineers descended on the small island. Originally conceived as an alternate landing strip for US bombers they constructed an extra-long, all weather runway and array of hardened buildings. For three decades for all appearances there was a minimal Air Force presence at the base, just enough to maintain the infrastructure before, finally, the base was closed and gifted to a privately financed marine research charity. In truth, Gilo had effectively been hollowed out and a warren of underground facilities held research labs, living quarters, a nuclear power plant and everything you could possibly need to operate a state-of-the-art facility. The research charity was nothing more than a front for the ongoing Backstop Program.

So, while every inquisitive eye in the world had been focused on the famous Area 51 in Nevada the true work was being carried out tens of thousands of miles away in the middle of the Pacific. Well it had been thought Kielty. Gilo was now a throng of scientists, engineers, military men and the inevitable nosy, preening politicians from every corner of the globe. All with something to say about how it was disgraceful that Backstop had been kept such a closely guarded secret and, of course, how if they had been in charge, they would be so much further along in their understanding of all the Ralaks' secrets.

A small harrumph escaped Kielty's lips at that. Was she not sitting in the center seat of the most advanced spacecraft that humanity had yet to build? Sure there was still some systems that they had yet to completely understand but the best minds had assured Kielty and her crew that those systems were so integral to the functioning of what the scientists had dubbed the R Drive, probably because nobody could be bothered saying Ralak all the time, that during trials the drive had simply failed to function without them so they had left them in place.

Discovery herself was built completely around the R Drive hence its shape, the bow of the ship was triangular in shape, raking back sharply until it met the spherical engine bay. Unlike conventional manmade space craft there were no protuberances at the tail of the craft which would indicate an engine exhaust. The R Drive worked by generating a bubble of null space around Discovery which could be controlled to 'pull' her along in any direction. The drive worked just as effectively in atmosphere as it did in vacuum. The added bonus was the negating effect the drive had on acceleration. Whether in atmosphere or vacuum the null space 'bubble' formed around Discovery by the drive cancelled out any feeling of acceleration within the 'bubble' so the normal g forces which a crew would experience at high acceleration did not apply, this also allowed Discovery to make radical maneuvers which would rip normal atmospheric or space craft apart, ninety degree, or more, changes of direction were the norm for the Discovery. A fact that many an observer to a UFO sighting would attest to.

"We are green across the board, Colonel. Ready to proceed." Intoned Commander Henry DeSotte in his, to someone who had not grown accustomed to it, nasally voice.

Kielty felt a shudder of trepidation run down her spine. The moment of truth was upon them. The crashed ships AI had only given them a very vague insight into what lay on the other side of the singularity. A fact that had struck many as oddly perplexing. Kielty included. It had felt that the AI was deliberately... Hiding information from them. The consensus was that the AI had been programmed to reveal the minimal amount of information about its origin so as not to aid any foreign species that may gain control of the ship. A prudent precaution when you considered that that was exactly what had happened.

"Okay, Henry, take us in, keep us at a steady hundred KPS." Kielty was surprised at how steady her voice sounded as with no perceptible feeling of movement the Discovery surged ahead, racing for the still, dark eye of the singularity at one hundred kilometers per second. With every passing second the singularity grew larger in the cockpit windows. The veil of silence that had descended on the cabin was only broken by the steady clicking coming from old fashioned naval timepiece which the first, now long retired and probably dead, admiral who had overseen the Backstop program had gifted to them in the hope that one day the timepiece would travel to somewhere he could only dream of. Well today his dying wish would be fulfilled.

"Event horizon approaching. Twenty seconds." Said DeSotte.

The third member of the original crew, Lieutenant Commander Chan Lou, spoke without lifting her head or averting her eyes from the instrument panel in front of her. "Radiation levels are stable, Colonel. Hull integrity is good. It looks like the R Drive is doing its thing."

"Acknowledged, Commander."

The Discovery sped ever closer to the beckoning maw of the artificial monster and Kielty unconsciously gripped the armrests of her seat as the oncoming blackness filled the cockpit windows.

"Event horizon in five... four... three... two... one..." DeSotte's voice seemed to fade into the distance as a strange tingling feeling spread throughout Kielty's body. Her vision narrowed to a pinpoint, the instrument panel lights before her dimming, melding into one single multi-color blur. The tingling crawled up her body and her brain registered that although not uncomfortable it was leaving her limbs numb as it passed through them, heading steadily up her body until finally it reached her neck. Unable to control her muscles any longer Kielty's chin fell forward onto her chest. The last thing she saw before lapsing into unconsciousness was a single point of light hovering at the center of the wormhole.

Is this what death is like?

***

From somewhere in the cobwebs that filled her brain a steady, demanding tone was calling out. Calling to Kielty like a beacon it took her considerable effort to gather herself and force her eyelids which felt as heavy as lead open. The blackness of the singularity's heart was gone replaced by bright, eye hurting light forcing her to squint against the harsh light. Kielty raised a hand and by sheer muscle memory tapped the smooth reactive glass surface of her control panel. At her command the cockpit windows polarized enough to make the light streaming through them more bearable. Only after her hand had returned to her side did Kielty realize that an unaccustomed weight tugged on her body. With a shake of her head to clear away the lingering fog she realized that the Discovery must be near a gravitational source. And a massive one if it was affecting her bodies movements. A gravitational source of this magnitude could easily drag Discovery into it with fatal consequences.

"Ugh..." Kielty's attempt to talk died in her parched throat. A side effect of their transit through the singularity Kielty wondered. Swallowing heavily, she licked at her dry lips before attempting to speak again.

"DeSotte. You still with us?" She managed to croak.

"Yeah. I'm still here." Peering through the cockpit windows the commander tried in vain to locate any readily identifiable stars. "Though pretty sure I don't actually know where 'here' is."

"We've got a bit of a more pressing problem than that. I think we are in the pull of a gravity source. Something pretty big. Let's get the engines back online ASAP."

A gloved hand tapped Kielty on the shoulder and in heavily accented English she heard. "You mean something like that."

Kielty followed the direction that Molanokov was pointing and her breath caught in her chest. The entire right-hand side of the cockpit window was filled with the curve of a planet. So close that Kielty thought that she could reach out and touch its brilliant white clouds with her bare hands and that was too damn close for her liking. A glance at the radar display spurred her into action.

"Where's my engines, Henry?"

DeSotte was resting the engine start up procedure manual on his lap while tapping away at the controls with his free hand. "I'm working on it."

"Well work faster." Kielty said with another glance at the radar display and the numbers indicating Discovery's height in rapidly decreasing numbers.

"Here let me help." Said Lee So retrieving the manual from DeSotte and coolly beginning to rhyme off the startup sequence in a calm and orderly fashion while DeSotte's fingers flashed over his board.

The R Drive engine status lights swiftly went from red to green. "Move us to a high orbit, Henry." Kielty ordered as the last light went green. DeSotte tapped a control, fingers flexing around the joystick. Kielty felt the reassuring pressure of being pushed back into her padded seat as Discovery made for high orbit.

✳✳✳

"Shit!" Diane Kielty said softly, half to herself though in the silence which had descended upon the cockpit of Discovery it was almost certainly what the rest of the crew were thinking too.

They had been in orbiting the planet for hours and, after the days otherwise traumatic events, the sight of a dead planet felt like a massive let down.

The astrogation computer had eventually been able to identify their location. HR 6847, a solar system with a G2 primary just like our own sun. However, the planet Kielty was gazing upon lay roughly seventy-four light-years from her own planet of birth. Without turning her head, she addressed See Lo.

"Well, Doctor?"

"I'm afraid my observations leave me in no doubt Commander. This world has suffered an Extinction Level Event and," Lo spared her compatriots a forlorn look, "sometime in the planets recent past."

"How recent?" Grunted Molanokov.

See Lo shrugged her thin shoulders. "My guess would be perhaps the last fifty years or so."

"The Ralak AI did allude to some kind of impending threat." Clarified DeSotte. "It looks to me like whatever that threat was they didn't find a way to avert it."

Kielty continued to stare at the dead world which hung so serenely in the sky before her. Hard to believe that below their white majesty the Discovery's radar had detected the ravaged remains of mighty cities now lying decimated by an unknown fate. A surge of resentfulness welled up inside her and she clenched her jaw in frustration. They had spent so many years and uncounted fortunes to get here... and for what. Nothing. The thrill of First Contact was gone replaced by the specter of loss for the Ralak species.

"Let's go home."

✳✳✳

"The humans had made transit." The Untarl at the detection grid said respectfully.

V'alk bent a single antenna in polite acknowledgment. The Untarl were only recent additions to the Union and, though V'alk was not amongst them, some of his own species, the Opki, resented the speed at which they had amalgamated the technology that entering into the Union had given them access too.

135

V'alk's lower mandibles clicked softly together as he considered the High Council's reaction when they learned that the Humans had managed to not only construct a working singularity drive but successfully incorporated it into a vessel of their own design and fly it to the world chosen by the council as the First Test. It had taken his own species twice as long to understand the secrets of the singularity drive and achieve the first steps on the road to joining the Union.

"Please signal the AI that it may disclose the information to begin the Second Test." A Pokalaa at communications input the required codes. On distant Earth the AI of the fictional Ralak species sat deep underground on the Pacific island of Gilo came to life and began chirping. Human scientists rushed to interpret the information which, much to their combined astonishment, proved to be a tweak to the R Drives navigational software which would allow the R Drive to access a second destination.

If the speed at which the humans had completed this first task was a gauge of their inherent aptitude then V'alk was certain that it would not be long before he was able to stand before a living representative of their race rather than the long distance observing that Union protocol insisted he hold himself to.

First Contact was only a baby step away.

###

About PP Corcoran

AUTHOR OF THE AMAZON BESTSELLING Saiph Series, PP Corcoran writes fast-paced military science fiction because he gets to mix his two loves; shoot em ups and science. A twenty-two-year-veteran of the British Army, Paul began his writing career in 2014. After serving all round the world, this native of Scotland now lives in Northern Ireland and writes epic space opera for a living; in 2018 he reached the heady rank of #10 in Amazon's Sci-Fi Authors.

Paul loves to hear from readers. You'll find his hangout on Facebook.

Connect with Paul here:
www.castrumpress.com/authors/pp-corcoran

A BOLT FROM THE BLUE
By S. K. Gregory

– 1 –

"Behold, Planet Earth!" Tyler announced, sweeping his arm dramatically at the landscape that lay before them.

Iris giggled at her boyfriend. "Or Vista Falls as it's actually known. I think we'd have to hike a lot higher to see all of planet Earth," she said.

Tyler pouted at her. "You're no fun. I'm trying to make this impromptu day of exercise more fun." He hopped off the rock he stood on. He wore baggy shorts and a sweat soaked t-shirt, despite the fact we had only been walking for ten minutes.

"That's a big word for you," she teased.

"What, exercise? You were the one that insisted we get healthy, so you're the one I'm going to blame when I drop dead in this heat."

"Stop complaining. It'll be cooler the higher we go. Come on."

The hills overlooking their hometown were beautiful this time of year. Iris loved nature, but Tyler preferred Netflix and Chill. She finally convinced him that a hike could be fun, and she wasn't turning back now.

A blue sky stretched above them, and Iris had packed them a picnic lunch in her backpack. She felt good, being out in nature, getting away for the day. Years ago, her father used to take her and her brother on hikes all the time. Until she turned ten and he died of an aneurism. Her mother fell to pieces and for over a year, she felt lost. Slowly, she started to recover, but even now, she wasn't the same. Iris missed him terribly. Being out here, made her feel close to her dad again. Like he was watching over her.

She pulled her phone from the back pocket of her denim shorts and shot a quick selfie. She hit upload to Instagram, then she noticed that there was no signal up here. She didn't think about that.

"No internet. Now we're really doomed," Tyler joked.

She scowled at him. "I'm not a slave to social media like you are. I can go a few hours without posting something."

"Is that a fact?" he said, crossing his arms. "I doubt that. I give you twenty minutes before you're racing back down the hill in search of some bars."

Iris made a show of switching her phone off and stowing it in her backpack. "Wanna bet?"

"Yes, actually. I bet you want to turn around in the next half hour to go home."

"Fine, what's the stakes?" she said, playing along.

"If you win, I will be your slave for a whole day."

Iris laughed. "A week. And if you win?"

He smirked at her. "Well, I think you can guess what I want."

Iris shook her head at his dirty mind. It's always about sex with him. She wouldn't give him the satisfaction of winning.

"Guess I'm getting a slave," she said. She pulled her baseball cap lower and started walking. Tyler lagged behind her as they made their way to the top. If anyone would give up, Tyler would.

Sweat poured off Iris. She did regret this, but she wasn't going to admit that to Tyler. If I can walk for another thirty minutes, I'll have my very own slave.

The thought spurred her on.

"Oh my God, Iris, stop!" Tyler groaned after a while.

She glanced back at him to find he had a desperate look on his face.

"I need water," he pleaded. The idiot hadn't even thought to bring his own.

Laughing, she passed him her canteen and he gulped the water back. "Don't drink all the water," she snapped.

"Let's stop and rest a while," he said. He poured some water into his hand and rubbed his face.

Iris glanced at her watch, thirty-two minutes. "Okay, Slave. But just for a bit."

They found a spot near a ledge to sit. Iris spread out the blanket she'd brought with her and Tyler flopped down onto it, his hands behind his head. "Ah! Much better."

"I don't think so. You can lay the food out," Iris said.

Tyler pouted at her. "You know there's other things we can do, besides eating."

He waggled his eyebrows and she giggled. "Dream on. I'm not an exhibitionist."

"There's no one up here."

"No chance. Now get the food." She tossed her backpack at him.

Sighing, he started unpacking the food, while she lay back and closed her eyes. The sun made her feel sleepy and she started to doze off.

"Are you going to eat any of this, or not?"

Tyler's voice startled her awake. Groggy, she sat up to find that he had eaten most of the food himself. "Thanks a lot," she grumbled.

She grabbed a bag of chips out of his hands and checked inside the bag. Almost empty. She grabbed the leftovers and shoved them into her mouth, crunching loudly. "You're a pig," she said around a mouthful of food. The sandwiches were gone too, and he drank the cans of soda. How long was I out?

"Walking makes me hungry," he said.

She rolled her eyes and turned her attention to the view. Such a beautiful day, but now the blue sky was marred by one lone gray cloud that floated in their direction. She stared at the cloud curiously. It looked weird.

"Look at that," she said.

Tyler tilted his head back. "Is that a cloud?"

"I don't know. I've never seen one like that. And it's the only one up there."

Tyler climbed to his feet, sending a cascade of crumbs onto the ground. He swiped at his shirt with his hand and moved to the edge of the cliff for a better look. The cloud began to pick up speed, moving until it stopped directly over Tyler's head.

"Dude, this is so weird. Come see," he said.

"Come away from it, Tyler. Please," Iris said. A knot formed in her stomach. It looked artificial. Could it be a disguised drone?

Getting to her feet, she noticed orange sparks running through the cloud. There was a sudden flash and a bolt of lightning exploded from the cloud, striking Tyler below.

"NO!" Iris screamed. She ran forward to help him.

Tyler fell to the ground and rolled onto his side, where he lay still.

"Oh my God, Tyler! Please don't be dead. Oh my God. Someone help!"

She knew she was screaming into the empty air, but she didn't care. She dropped to his side, reaching out a shaking hand to search for a pulse. Shockingly, she found one, although the pulse was erratic and way too fast.

"Tyler?"

She looked up, but the cloud had disappeared. That's not normal. Turning, she scrabbled for her backpack, searching for her phone. It took an eternity to switch back on and it was only when the screen lit up, that she remembered there was no signal.

"Shit. Tyler it's going to be okay. I'll go get help."

As she got to her feet, Tyler let out a groan. "Tyler? Can you hear me?"

His eyes snapped open.

"Tyler?"

He pushed himself up and stood, looking confused.

"Oh my God, Tyler. A lightning bolt struck you. Are you okay? Say something?"

He blinked once, his head turning to look around him. Is he brain damaged or something?

"Tyler? Say something," Iris said, placing a hand on his arm.

He glanced down at her hand, then back up at her. The next thing she knew, she was on the ground after he shoved her.

"Hey!" she cried, more from shock than pain.

He ignored her and started walking down the hill. What the hell is wrong with him? The lightning must have fried his brain.

With no other choice, she hurried after him. He walked stiffly, arms swinging at his sides. Something's seriously off about him. More than his behavior, it was something else. She couldn't put it into words.

"Tyler, please talk to me. We have to get you to a hospital."

He stopped walking. "Confirm location. Vista Falls. Planet Earth."

Iris let out a relieved laugh. He was messing around. "Damn it, Tyler. You scared the shit out of me."

"Awaiting further scouts."

"What?"

Iris followed his gaze. Hovering over Vista Falls were four more weird clouds like the one that almost killed Tyler. She watched as they moved in different directions, positioning themselves at the four corners of the town.

Clouds don't do that. They can't move like that.

"Begin."

Four flashes of light, four lightning bolts erupted from the clouds, striking something in the town below.

"Tyler? What is going on?" Iris whispered.

He ignored her and continued his journey down the hill. Iris stared out at Vista Falls. Those clouds weren't natural and if the lightning struck other people...

She ran after Tyler.

***

– 2–

"Tyler, if this is some joke or sick game, you need to tell me right now!" Iris snapped.

Angry, she grabbed the back of his t-shirt and pulled hard. He stopped walking, straining forward. Her fingers slipped and he continued walking. Like a robot.

Why was he heading back to town? Was he going to meet up with others? Thoughts were racing through Iris' brain as she tried to keep up with him.

It was then she realized what was wrong, what was bugging her. The way Tyler walked, the way he held himself, it was like looking at a completely different person.

"Who are you?" The words came out of her mouth before she knew it.

He half turned his head in her direction but didn't answer her. So, he could hear her, he was just ignoring her.

"Where's Tyler?" she demanded.

She didn't expect a reply, but she got one. "Dead."

Iris stopped, her breath catching in her throat. "What? You're lying."

But was he? Who could survive a lightning bolt to the head? Don't be stupid, he's walking, moving. It must have scrambled his brain.

"H, I'll play along. If you're not Tyler, then who are you?"

"Four one five eight designation – Communication's Scout."

"What the hell does that even mean?"

He appeared to be done talking. He carried on walking, not stopping to rest. Iris lagged behind him.

"Where are you going?" she asked, exasperated.

"Leave, Human. Or face the consequences."

Human? He's human too, unless...

She couldn't let him reach town. Whether he had a scrambled mind or something else, she felt this overwhelming certainty that if he reached town, something very bad would happen.

I can't stop him, he's too strong. I need a plan B.

She stumbled as her foot hit a rock. A thought popped into her head.

She lifted the rock and hurried after Tyler. I'll knock him out and then I'll get help.

It seemed like a good plan, but as she raised the rock, she hesitated. Could she do it, hit him? What if she killed him?

You can't think that way. Do it.

"I'm sorry," she whispered.

Bringing the rock down hard on his head, Tyler immediately stumbled and fell. He grabbed his head and let out an unearthly cry. Iris backed off fast.

"Tyler?" she said.

His head still in his hands, he groaned softly. His head rose slowly, eyes filled with fury. "You shouldn't have done that."

Iris dropped the rock and ran.

***

– 3 –

Iris skidded to a halt at the edge of a steep drop. She turned back to find Tyler closing in on her.

"Stop!" she cried, holding up her hands. To her surprise, he did. He still seemed to be having trouble with his head, he kept shaking it as if trying to clear something.

"You have damaged this vessel," he growled.

"Vessel? That's my boyfriend you are talking about," she snapped.

He glared at me. "He is a vessel. A broken one. But I will complete my mission."

"What mission?"

"To establish a home base, subdue the population and await the arrival."

"The arrival of what?"

A horrible grin spread across his face. He pointed a finger at the sky above them. I knew it. He's not Tyler. He's... What? An alien?

She tried to push the thought away but couldn't. What else could he be? If aliens existed, she always expected huge ships like in that movie Independence Day. But taking people over? With lightning? She felt the overwhelming urge to laugh suddenly. This is crazy, totally crazy.

"What are you going to do to me?" she asked, knowing he could easily push her off this cliff.

"You will be annihilated, like the rest of your species."

He grabbed her by the arms, pushing her back to the edge of the cliff.

"NO!" she screamed, as he started to tip her backwards. She grabbed hold of his arms tightly, trying to save herself. He gave her a shake, trying to get her to let go.

Desperate, she dug her nails into his arms. When he pulled her closer, in an effort to shake her loose, she used the opportunity to bite him on the nose.

He yelled in pain and threw her aside. She almost went over the edge but managed to scrabble onto solid ground. She got up to run, but he grabbed her by the hair.

"Get off," she screeched.

Rather than pull away, she spun and lashed out with her foot, catching him in the groin. He grunted, releasing her hair. He took a few stumbling steps backwards.

"I'm sorry, Tyler," she sobbed. Right before she shoved him, hard. He toppled backward off the cliff, landing on the rocks thirty feet below.

Shaking, Iris moved to the edge and peered down. She saw the angle of his neck. He's dead.

Iris sank to her knees, her body trembling. She started crying and couldn't stop.

I killed him. I killed Tyler.

How could this be happening? A short while ago, they were happy, they were...

She got to her feet. She couldn't stay here, she needed to move, to get back to town. In the back of her mind, she knew that she needed to warn people about what happened, but all she could see was Tyler's face.

In a daze, she started walking. She had no water with her, and her things were still back at their picnic spot. It didn't matter though, she would keep walking.

Keep moving, don't think, just move.

By the time she reached the edge of town, she was ready to collapse from fear and exhaustion.

She paused at the top of Main Street. "The Sheriff. I need to speak to the Sheriff, explain what happened," she mumbled to herself.

She needed to make him understand what Tyler had become. I hope he believes me.

Unless he's one of them.

The thought stopped her in her tracks. Four lightning bolts, four more aliens or whatever they are. The Sheriff could be one of them. It would make sense wouldn't it? To take control of the man in charge.

Then why pick Tyler?

He worked at the arcade; he didn't have any power. So, could it be about proximity? They chose the first humans they came into contact with. That didn't rule out the Sheriff though. If the Sheriff had become one of them too, he would probably shoot her on the spot.

I need to figure out who has changed and stop them.

But what did that mean? Would she be forced to kill more people? Her stomach roiled at the thought and she vomited on the ground. With her stomach empty, she wiped her mouth with the back of her hand. Whatever came next, she couldn't do this alone. She needed help.

As she approached the Sheriff's station, something caught her eye. Mr. O'Neill, the man who owned the bakery, was walking on the other side of the street. He was an old man and for as long as she'd known him, he walked hunched over with a cane for support. Now, he strode down the street in that same stiff way that Tyler did back on the hill.

He's one of them.

Maybe it would be easier to spot them than she thought. She jogged across the room, careful to avoid him seeing her. If she could figure out where he was going, she could tell the Sheriff. He ducked into an alley, beside the pawn shop with all the TVs in the window.

Iris peeked into the alley. Mr. O'Neill wasn't alone, Jared Tate stood before him. Iris knew him from school, he worked in the garage now.

The two men weren't speaking, they stared at each other in silence. What the hell were they doing?

Jared's head turned in her direction and she quickly ducked back out of sight. She waited to see if they are coming, but they hadn't moved.

She leaned against the pawn shop window. Okay, I know who two of them are. It shouldn't be too hard to find the others. I need to go to the police.

She felt slightly more hopeful. I can stop them. Who else is going to do it? As she turned to head back to the station, she glanced at the window. A news report played on the TVs.

The banner headline, 'Strange Lightning Strikes' caught her attention. It must be about Vista Falls?

A map appeared on screen and the news reader highlighted the areas where lightning struck. Iris stopped breathing. It wasn't only Vista Falls. Lightning bolts struck all over the country, in every state. They were everywhere.

How many are there? How can we stop all of them?

A hand clamped down on her shoulder. She had time to see Jared's face, a fleeting glimpse, before being struck across the face. As she crumpled to the ground, her last thought was: They're here.

###

About S. K. Gregory

S. K. GREGORY IS THE AUTHOR OF SEVERAL urban fantasy, paranormal romance and young adult novels. She runs a blog that supports indie authors by offering book reviews and promotions.

She is an editor and proofreader with JEA Press.

With a background in journalism and film making, she recently worked on an arts-based radio show called Lisburn Reads, with a focus on local writers.

Connect with S. K. here:
www.castrumpress.com/authors/sk-gregory

FIRST FRIENDSHIP
by A.N. Myers

Robert always found meeting the Shoma unsettling, and yet he struggled to pinpoint exactly why. What was it? Shoma induced a vague panic in him, that was certain, and whenever he was face to face with one, his hands would sweat as if he had been rolling butter in his palms, and he would experience a most uncomfortable burning in his chest. Perhaps it was that were so tall, three meters from huge feet to luxuriously coiffured head when fully grown. Was it their hands, those seven fingered creeping explosions of bone and joint whose jerking movements he studied with no little disgust as they flicked through the papers on the desk? Robert didn't like their bulbous green eyes either, with the sideways blinking lids that reminded him of slamming windows; nor the greasy alabaster skin; and the chirping, child-like voices, which combined wheedling sympathy with crushing threat, were utterly loathsome to him.

The most likely cause of his anxiety, Robert concluded, was that the Shoma were such slave driving alien bastards, and that any encounter with one was inevitably followed by weeks of miserable, pointless, hard graft for Robert Pell.

"High-rise window cleaning?" said Robert, trying to stop his voice from quavering too much. "Friend Shoma, I'm merely the caretaker of the Block, the caretaker, that's all. I look after the boilers, the elevators, and organize the maintenance crews. I don't know anything about high-rise window cleaning." Robert wiped his moist hands on his rough workman's trousers, adjusting his tight community collar, in order to allow the chunk of concrete in his throat to descend through his esophagus.

"But, Hoo-man Robert, it says here, you are the estate manager. So, this task would fall into your zone of expertise."

"You are mistaken, Friend Shoma." It always struck him that the courtesy term Friend by which humans were expected to address Shoma, and which was never reciprocated, was entirely inappropriate. "The estate manager is Keith Spungeon."

"Hoo-man Spungeon is dead."

"Dead...but...I just saw him yesterday. He was fine...how?"

"Oh, it is very sad," cooed the Shoma. "He was in here. This very office. And he died. In the very chair that you yourself are sitting in."

Robert shifted in his seat staring past the Shoma, to the cityscape beyond the window. They were very high up, nineteen floors. There, close by, was the North End of the city, with its gleaming, imperious office blocks, where humans labored and Shoma, on the whole, managed them; to the South, hunkering in the shadows, the human residential districts, dilapidated and grimy. A tug of a breeze swayed the open window and for a moment the impeccable black locks of the Shoma lifted from its dome-like skull. With barely a blink, the Shoma eased its alien curls back into place.

"Why-why did Keith die?" asked Robert.

"A heart attack, that is what hoo-men doctors say. Just one heart, that is problem for your species. You should have three hearts, like Shoma!" It laughed. "So, now his task falls to you. You have not been informed of your promotion, we see, but of course we Shoma are so busy. So, you learn this now."

"You want this done for the centenary of First Friendship? I'm not sure how, in three weeks..."

"Ah yes, First Friendship! The joining of our two races, the beginning of our glorious alliance! An occasion well worth celebrating, and the more so here in London, the site of the first arrival! All Shoma and Hoo-men leaders will be here, and the Shoma Marshal himself! Essential that all business blocks will be shining, shining, and this one will be the brightest!"

The burning sensation in Robert's chest had ignited into tongues of flame which leapt up his throat. "But Friend Shoma, this building is...enormous...it must have five thousand glass panels. It will be time consuming- and very expensive."

"Hoo-man defeatism! Hoo-man laziness!" squealed the Shoma, its voice rising to an indignant whistle. "You complain of injustice, how we Shoma take your opportunities. But surely, is it not that you don't work hard enough, that you would prefer to laze about in your hoo-man pits, while we Shoma generate the wealth? You are a fool to spurn Shoma offer!"

"I am grateful, Friend Shoma, of course I am, but- will you guarantee me that the funds will be available from the building budget? Because last time –"

The Shoma waved its giant white knuckle airily. "There are no guarantees of anything, Hoo-man, but we are sure if you speak to the correct authorities, the funding may be arranged. In the meantime, we assume that you agree to this challenge?"

Robert nodded.

"Good. You will report your progress to us here in seven days. Do not let the Shoma down."

Robert left the office and for a moment or two leaned against the wall. He felt sick and dizzy. He pressed the button for the elevator but nothing happened. He would have to order a maintenance team to repair that. Last time it took two months.

Robert made his way to the stairwell and began descending the eighteen flights of stairs, his mind crowded with miserable possibilities.

✳✳✳

Instead of going straight home to Brixton, Robert made the decision to visit a human bar he knew, on the edge of the business district, in order to clear his head, settle his nerves with a couple of drinks, and maybe come up with a solution to his problem. He phoned home from a booth in a squalid alley near the tube station. His seventeen-year-old daughter, Dora, answered.

"Dad, mum's been really bad today. She hasn't got up, hasn't eaten. Just keeps crying and saying she wants to die. I didn't know what to do and I couldn't get hold of you at the block. I couldn't help out at the food bank today."

"Dora, I'll only be an hour- it's- I had a meeting with a Shoma." He paused, feeling the constriction in his throat again. "It didn't go well."

He heard Dora's breathing down the line. "A Shoma? Okay, Dad, but please come home as soon as you can. I'm supposed to be going out tonight."

"Yes, Dora. Thank you. Just an hour. I need some time to think. Look after your mother till I get home."

"Dad..."

"Yes?"

"Don't get drunk. Not again."

It had started to rain. Robert pulled up the collar of his thin coat and made his way along the edges of light-smeared lanes, keeping clear of the main roads, splashing through glistening puddles. He kept his head down, trying to keep the world out, to drive all his thoughts inward. But it was impossible. From high above, he could hear the rippling, arrogant laughter that could only be a group of young Shoma, celebrating some deal clinched, some welcome acquisition to further brighten their lives. Pausing in a doorway Robert watched the sparse crowds drift by; he noticed that the humans seem to cling, like him, to the edges of the pavements, while the few Shoma that loped past occupied the center of the road, their smart business suits and perfect hair undampened by the rain.

Robert soon arrived at his destination; a tired, beaten-up sort of joint with peeling paint and a broken awning from which a stream of rainwater sloshed into the gutter. He knew there would be no Shoma in here- there never were, and its low door hinted that Shoma weren't welcome anyway. Most pubs and restaurants these days, if they wanted to remain in business, had raised their door height to the mandatory three meters, often at considerable expense.

Robert took his usual seat by the bar and ordered a whiskey and soda. He kept his eyes fixed on the grain of the wooden table top, trying to achieve that balance in his head between thought and anger, to drive away the fear that was still sticking to him after his meeting with the Shoma, to warm away the moisture in his clothes that was more sweat than rainwater.

What should he do?

He racked his brains for minutes and minutes. Robert knew he'd end up paying for a big chunk of the job up front, like he had done in the past; the Shoma would refuse to stump up for it. This time it might ruin him. Could he do the clean himself? He wouldn't know where to start. And if he did nothing at all, refused to attempt a task outside of his expertise, he would lose his job, his family would be evicted, and poor Becky with her health problems...ever since they'd stopped giving her the pills, the pain had become unbearable for her.

Robert stared at the beer stained swirls of the wooden grain, going around and round, closing into tighter and tighter spirals, ending where they began.

"LIE!"

Someone was shouting from a dark alcove at the rear of the bar. Robert glanced up from the tabletop. A shaggy bearded old man, hunched over his pint, was pointing drunkenly at the TV screen. Robert had noticed this guy here a couple of times before but had never spoken to him. Now he found himself marveling at his reckless anger.

"Another bloody lie!"

"Shut your trap, Gary," remonstrated the woman behind the bar. "Do you want me to get shut down again?"

Robert glanced at the TV screen. The Shoma news anchors were introducing another story about the celebrations. A blue banner rolled across the screen; 100 YEARS SINCE FIRST FRIENDSHIP.

"That's another lie!"

"One more time, I swear, and you're gone!"

On the screen now was a grainy still photograph Robert had seen many times before; the old, long dead President of the USA shaking hands with a towering male Shoma in red robes, at least three feet taller.

"Bullshit! That photo is bullshit!" Screamed Gary.

"Right, that's it..."

"Yeah, I'm going..."

But he didn't. Thirty seconds later Robert was being interrupted from his reverie by this old chap Gary sliding along the bench next to him and extending his hand.

"She's only kidding. Me and her, we've got an understanding. I'm Gary."

Despite Robert's interest in this guy, he wasn't really in the mood to get drawn into any unwelcome conversations. "Robert," he replied, a little stiffly, shaking the proffered hand.

"You look like you could do with some company. Seen you here before. Let me guess the cause of your obvious misery. Shoma?"

Robert nodded grimly.

"Yeah well. They're liars." Gary pointed at the TV. "And that's a lie, too. The centenary. Big, fat, stinking lie."

"How?"

"Because it's only been seventy-eight years."

"And you know that because?"

Gary grinned, showing his yellow crooked teeth. "Because I was there. Buy me a beer and I'll tell you all about it."

***

"Course, when they arrived, nobody was expecting it. The Shoma just.... rolled up. I was only eight years old, a little kid. I remember my mother crying, holding me to her chest as it was announced on the TV, her warm breath as she murmured the Lord's prayer in my ear, over and over again... but my Dad- he took me and my sister to London, in his old BMW, to Tower Bridge, to watch them arrive. There was music- somebody playing a trumpet- pretty girls dancing, all in blue- and lots of old men with placards- End of the World, that kind of stuff. The police couldn't stop the crowds. Then we watched it come through the clouds over London Bridge. I guess my Dad was irresponsible bringing me along, but that was the kind of guy he was.

"Overall, I reckon- even then, as a kid, I picked up on it- amid all the fear, and the racket, we felt- well, more excitement, and hope, than anything else. That whole day- it kind of- smelt of it! We watched the grey clouds break apart, and this colossal silver dome slowly push downwards, and it felt like the moon was coming down to say hello! The river was roaring, it seemed like the water was rushing upwards, the clouds were moving and billowing and swelling, and there was wind and noise all around- but- my Dad held my hand, and he shouted, Don't worry, Gary! They're here to save us! From ourselves. See? They're just like angels! And as that huge, huge, silver ball slid through the clouds toward Big Ben, like the fist of God, I remember thinking, even though I was so little- of course, he's right. He's my Dad, and he's always right. Just like angels.

"I don't remember much else- but my Dad would tell me years later about all the joy they brought with them after arrival, and why they were here. Their spaceships, see- they were broken, needed fixing. The Shoma wouldn't stay long, and in the meantime, they would give us...things in return- like machines, and cures."

"Which we never got." Interjected Robert.

"That's right," said Gary. "And they told us they were going to leave- but they didn't. They stayed. Their spaceships, rotting in junkyards in Essex, we've all seen them. The Shoma never intended to leave, ever. And what about us? Humans? What's happened to us? We've dwindled. It's like something they've brought with them- is sucking the life out of us! And when was the last time you saw a baby, for Christ's sake? There's less people around now than there used to be."

Robert nodded. "I guess I knew all this already. But you don't think about it, do you? It's just normal, just what is. And nobody ever talks about it anymore. I remember, a few years ago- but now- it's like we've forgotten."

"So much for hope," said Gary.

On the TV screen was that picture again, the one with the Shoma shaking the hand of the President, but this time as a studio backdrop behind two Shoma newscasters. "Look at this," said Gary, reaching into his jacket pocket and drawing out a rectangular piece of card. "My Dad took it."

It was an old, crumpled photograph, yellowed and stained. He held it up, aligned with the TV screen, and Robert and the bartender woman stared at it. An old white man was shaking hands with a Shoma, like the famous photo on the TV. But this was different.

"The Shoma," said Robert. "It's tiny. Is this a baby one, or-?"

"No. That's what they were like. All of them."

This Shoma was a wizened little thing, with shriveled, sallow cheeks and redly weeping eyes, whose head reached no higher than the man's waist, and whose hands were tiny, like pale moths.

"I remember," said the woman, "that they were smaller. Not as small as that, but no bigger than a normal person."

"They've grown," said Gary. "Something here's made them grow. Maybe the same thing that's made us not care, made us forget. And that image- "he nodded at the TV- "fake."

"But- surely," said Robert, "people should know about this. Shouldn't we be doing- something?"

The old man fixed Robert with a steady gaze from the shadows.

"What have you done, Robert?"

Robert looked downwards in shame. "Nothing," he said.

Gary bought Robert another drink while Robert told him all about what had happened that day, and then he wasn't terrified anymore, instead finding himself animated, excited, and strangely hopeful. At the end of the evening, Gary laid his liver spotted old hand on Robert's arm and said, 'I may have a proposition for you, Robert. You'd like to do something, yes?'

"Yes," said Robert, charged with an unexpected sense of rebellion.

"Find out how much it will cost you to hire a firm to do this cleaning work," said Gary, his eyes glittering. "Then meet me back here tomorrow. I'll see what I can do to help you. To help all of us."

***

When Robert arrived home, it was well past midnight, and he was mildly drunk. He stared at Dora's bedroom door, resolutely shut, remembering with a pang of guilt that he'd promised to come home early so that she could go out with her ex-college friends. She would have had to stay home and look after Becky, as she often did. She would be angry with him for days.

Robert paused swaying outside his open bedroom door and watched Becky sleeping in the gloom for a few moments. She was so narrow- so small- beneath the thin sheets, barely a shape at all, almost a ruck in the bed linen. Robert moved to the single bed and reached out his hand to touch her, to check she was there. The angular shoulder twitched away irritably.

Going into the bathroom Robert stared at himself in the mirror for a couple of minutes. His face, he considered, was an unremarkable one. Round face, small nose, scrunched up grey eyes, thinning hair. He was far from handsome. But there was something else. His face was more than unremarkable and unhandsome, it was unambitious. The nose an unattractive gnarled blob. The chin, weak, almost absent. His was not the face of a man who made things happen, who changed things- it was the shapeless face of a nobody, a man whose ambitions never exceeded the bare maintenance of life, a man who would let others push him around.

"What have you done, Robert?" he said to himself.

The next day was Robert's weekly day off, unusually he got up early, despite his hangover, and spent the morning researching high rise cleaning techniques online and poring through Yellow Pages and business directories for cleaning companies who would be able to do the job by next month. Only one company could fit him in- they'd had a cancellation- but they were reluctant to deal with a Shoma Corporation without fifty percent up front. Robert swallowed so loudly he was sure the woman at the end of the line must have heard him. He told them he'd call back.

After a strong cup of coffee Robert put through a call to the Shoma Estate Bursar's Office. He spent the next fifteen minutes arguing with a bored sounding female Shoma who refused to honor any invoices he might send them for the cleaning, especially for a whacking great ten thousand pounds. She suggested he take out a personal bridging loan, and at some point, in the far future her office might repay him. Robert knew what that meant. The loan repayments he took out for an electrical job his Shoma had insisted be completed had ruined Roberts finances for two years, and some smaller payments he'd made and later reclaimed had never been refunded at all.

"All I can suggest, Hoo-man. Be grateful for the advice."

Robert sat in the half-darkness for twenty minutes, drinking more coffee, absorbing this injustice, listening to the sound of Becky shuffling around in their bedroom, dreading her getting up, having to face her incessant misery, her endless complaints.

A short time later Robert heard the scratchy sounds of a key turn in the lock. Dora. He listened to her busying herself in the hall. She didn't know he was there. He could see her in the gap of the door, sorting out her bag. He loved to watch her sometimes, his wonderful, pretty daughter. The slow, certain way she moved, the serious expression she wore when she thought no one was watching her. He admired her so much, her determination to improve herself, to help the less fortunate at the food bank, and the other charities she volunteered for. Robert remembered the terrible day just three months ago when she came home in torrents of tears to tell him her public college had been closed. It was to be reopened as a Shoma Technical School. Two and a half years of hard work on that Anthropology course- gone. He loved her and he had so much hope for her although he knew deep down, she had very few opportunities at all for the future. Dora was so stern and determined, always talking about restarting her course, despite knowing only too well that private human colleges were the only option for her, and her father could never afford the fees on a caretaker's salary. Even though he admired her courage and positivity, sometimes when he looked at her, he saw her mother staring back causing him to shiver with despair.

Robert called out to her, but she was gone up the stairs, and his words stalled in the dead air.

***

Robert didn't quite know how he ended up at the bar that night. Couldn't remember leaving home, the long walk, the pouring rain that soaked through his thin coat and into his trousers as he spoke to Gary and that female bartender- all he knew was that somehow he was there, as though a mysterious destiny had propelled him toward that moment, and erased everything in between.

The woman was middle aged, stout, and spoke with a warm Australian accent, nodding politely as he spilled his guts about the terrible day and his poor daughter. "I mean- Ingrid? How am I meant to come up with ten thousand quid? Ten thousand quid, to keep my job and my wife alive." He buried his head in his hands. "It's just so fucking unfair."

Gary smiled. "Rob, you said you wanted to do something. Make a difference. Is that still the case?"

"Yes," said Robert, "More than ever. I've got nothing to lose now, anyway."

"Okay," said Gary, his voice suddenly quietening. "When you told me your story the other day I immediately thought of Ingrid. She's got experience in these sorts of projects. She used to clean high rises in Melbourne. Isn't that right?"

Ingrid nodded. "I know everything there is to know about this sort of stuff, sweetie. They used to call me Swinging Ing."

"And I've done some work on high buildings too," said Gary. "Scaffolding, that sort of affair." Gary's moved close to Robert; his cratered face was like the surface of some ancient, unfriendly world. "Rob, you organize the equipment, and me and Ingrid and some other guys will do the whole job for you. And this is the thing. I'll pay. I'll pay for the lot."

Robert's head was swimming. This afternoon an alien bureaucrat had threatened to ruin him. Now an unknown old man was promising to rescue him. It was all too much. "Why? Why would you even do that?"

"Gary said there was no crane on the roof. Is that right?" Asked Ingrid.

Robert nodded.

"I suppose the firm you spoke to was going to use either bosun's chairs or mobile elevated work platforms?"

Robert nodded. "The second one."

Ingrid wrote something in a notebook. "We just need the equipment, Rob. The platform. We'll provide the labor and everything else."

"I'll pay for everything," reiterated Gary. "I'll even send money to your wife and kid, to pay for the medication and a private college course. Whatever you need. I can afford it."

"But why- "

"Imagine this," said Gary huskily, grasping Robert's forearm. "It's the big day. The day of the celebration. All the bigwig Shoma will be in London- including the Marshall and the Chancellor- congratulating themselves on their victory by stealth, and all the human collaborators with 'em. Drinking their pricey wine, nibbling their canapés, snorting their cocaine, whatever; and they go out to watch the fireworks, and then- they look up at the smartest, brightest building on the Thames, overlooking the entire city- and there's a message for 'em. Written on the block in giant green fluorescent letters. A, massive, lovely, obscene message, the biggest fuck you in History!"

"What, like graffiti?"

"More than just graffiti!" Ingrid laughed. "A protest. A message that says- we're not going to be shit on anymore!"

"What- what would it say?"

"Something really insulting. The ruder the better!"

"What," said Robert, "something like- Fuck the Shoma, piss off back home, that sort of thing?"

"Yes," laughed Gary. "Just like that, Robert. In ten-meter letters. You can even compose it if you like!"

"But you'll be caught. You'll be seen."

"We'll do it at night," said Gary, "after the clean is finished. The night before. Under the guise of a final polish before the big celebration. No one will bat an eyelid."

"We'll use specialist paint," explained Ingrid. "With a chemical ingredient that glows when illuminated by lights behind it. During the day, it'll be a shimmering veil, barely perceptible. But when they switch the lights on for the celebration- ta da!"

"It sounds great. But...when it's over, I'll be caught, arrested for conspiracy," sighed Robert. "I can't risk it, not with my family."

"I'll put my hands up to everything," said Gary. "You knew nothing about what we were doing. You were completely innocent." He glanced at Ingrid, then back to Robert again. "I'll be honest with you, Rob. I'm ill. I've got cancer. My lungs. I've not got long, six months at best. I want to go out with a bang, understand?"

"Well, I'm sorry," Robert said softly, somewhat discomfited better understanding Gary's motivation.

"The prospect of imminent death confers a certain freedom on the victim," chuckled Gary. "And Rob- even if you did get arrested- so what? Your family will be looked after- I'll take care of that- and for you- there will be the sense that you've done something, stood up for to them, been true to yourself. That's worth five years in prison, surely?"

Robert contemplated Gary's proposition. He thought about his Shoma boss, the impossible, unreasonable demands. He thought about Becky, suffering without her pills. But most of all he thought about poor Dora, her dreams smashed when they closed her college. Robert knew now that the Shoma were invaders, not Friends, and it was his duty as a human to stand up against them, even if only in a small way. And what were the alternatives? Financial ruin, and further disgrace?

Robert gave a curt nod. "Okay. I'll do it. I'll set it up."

Gary and Ingrid exchanged smiles. "Good man."

"But there's just one condition."

"Name it," said Gary.

"For that last night- the night when you finish it- I want to be there with you. I want to paint the words. That's my condition."

"Accepted," said Gary, and shook Robert's hand.

✳✳✳

That night, Robert slept soundly for the first time in months. And his sleep abounded with dreams, marvelous dreams of shimmering skyscrapers, around whose snow-topped peaks thousands of doves circled; and then of black craggy mountains, engraved with huge, stern letters of fire, forging words that he could not read or remember, but which dripped rivers of molten lava onto the heads of shrieking packs of demons below. Of course, it didn't matter if he didn't remember it; the message would write itself on the day, and although it might be obscene and childish it would become transformed in the minds of those who read it. Its meaning would escape the words themselves, to become a source of hope and liberation.

Awake now, he lay on his narrow single bed, ignoring the sleepless sounds of misery from Becky not far from him. The idea of the message grew and grew in his head. He could imagine the reaction of the human crowds as it appeared before them- first horror, then amusement, then delight- and then incipient rebellion. The Shoma wouldn't like it- they'd be outraged, and immediate efforts would be made to shut down the message, to eliminate the offenders. But by then it would be too late. The message would have been seen and absorbed. The humans would now know that they didn't stand alone, there were others like them who felt the same way, and things would change. There would be demonstrations, riots, as people saw for the first time the injustices visited upon them. It would be the beginning of a new movement- and he, Robert Pell, would be responsible for it.

At seven o' clock in the morning there was a ring on his doorbell. He opened the door to find a shoe box on his front step containing twenty-five thousand pounds in large denominations, a hand-written note atop the notes read- More to come. Rob bagged up the money and set off for work, his heart soaring with excitement. Two hours later he'd made all the arrangements for delivery of the cleaning platform, a massive hydraulic rig that unfolded from the back of a truck. He rushed over to the company in Clerkenwell and paid them in cash. Then, thrilled with his decisiveness, spent his lunchtime planning for Dora to be enrolled at one of the most expensive colleges in London, where she could restart her Anthropology course, and then bought twenty courses of pills online for Becky, using his newly stoked up debit card. By the time he went home he felt he'd done more in a day than he had in a lifetime.

The day of the celebration grew nearer. Gary and Ingrid along with another couple of workers turned up on Friday morning in a van, dressed in matching blue outfits and equipped with all sorts of mysterious cleaning apparatus. Robert spent his lunchtime watching them from the sidewalk, as they crept up and down the sheer glass face, scrubbing and soaping industriously. Presently he was joined by his Shoma, who nodded with satisfaction.

"Any difficult task can be completed with the correct application of willpower, yes, Hoo-man Robert?"

"Yes, Friend Shoma."

Robert smiled. If only you knew, you arrogant alien fuck.

When he got home that evening, Robert brought with him a plan of the North Face of the block and all its 1,500 panes. He reviewed the twelve words that Gary had approved, and which formed a simple, obscene message. The next three hours were spent plotting out his wonderful design, and the best and most efficient route for the moving platform to follow during the ten hours available for the operation. When he finished, Robert sank back into his chair with a sigh of satisfaction.

Over the next few days, Robert took every opportunity to gaze upon the platform and its tiny occupants as it rose high above the city, the sun twinkling on its metal surfaces. He longed to be with them, to be above everything, to be part of the execution of their clandestine plan. Once- a Wednesday- he rushed up to the seventeenth floor and watched the five of them through the glass for fifteen minutes. Robert waved at them, but they ignored him, and he felt sad as the platform climbed up to the next floor, leaving him behind.

And sooner- sooner than he could have imagined- the cleaning was over, and the great task lay before him, that very evening. Robert was so choked with anticipation he could hardly think or speak, and it was with extreme difficulty that he managed to get through his working day without throwing up with excitement.

"Are you ready?" asked Gary, through the window of the van. Robert, dressed in the blue overalls he had been loaned the night before, had been standing in the basement car park of the block for two hours, so immersed in his fantasy that he hardly noticed them pull up. "Rob?"

"Yes. I'm sorry. Miles away. We're doing it now?"

"Of course. Are you sure you're okay?"

"Yes," Robert replied, climbing into the back of the van.

"The platform's all set up?" asked Ingrid. "You've got the keys? The window plans?"

"Yes, of course." Looking around him, half-dazed, at the shadowy towers of paint cans that surrounded them. "That's a lot of paint."

"We've got a lot of work to do," said Gary. "Rob, this is an all-nighter. You sure you're up for this?"

"Yes. Yes. It's just that- I can hardly believe it. At last, I'm contributing. To the struggle." He rubbed his eyes; he was thinking he might cry. "I just wanted to say..."

"Mmm?"

"Thank you. Thank you for everything, the money, listening to me- and the opportunity. This opportunity."

All was quiet in the back of the van; they jolted over a speed bump; an embarrassed cough from Gary. "Don't worry about that. You just concentrate on what you've got to do."

It seemed like a ridiculous remark. He'd pictured the moment a million times, it felt like. And soon, he would be up there, living it- high above the Shoma, high above the city, with his new friends, in their tiny swinging cradle- painting out a bright message of hope that would transform his life, and the lives of every human on Earth.

***

It was late morning. Robert was at his desk as usual, his momentous task complete. He had not gone home, having crept into the office at five thirty; he'd left his suit, shirt and tie folded in one of the reception rooms, and had even managed an hour of sleep curled up on the sofa before everyone else started turning up. Now he sat at his desk, unable to concentrate on this day's humdrum tasks, basking in the pleasant glow of exhausted achievement, his shoulders aching with the physical exertion. His imagination ranged ahead in time to when the lights would be switched on, and his fateful message would be broadcast to a grateful population. As he dozed, the images of the previous night fluttered through his sleepy brain; the moonlight glittering on the silver platform rail; the gentle nocturnal hum of the hydraulics; the murmured instructions from Gary; the rocking of the cradle, its soft jerks as they moved ever higher; the flashing of the torchlight on the blue plans; the sloshing of the silvery paint on the black glass. As they descended, the sun had peeped over the City's skyscrapers, and the security guards who'd watched them all the way down didn't have a clue. No one would know until the grand switching on tonight!

Robert had stood in the basement car park and watched the white van trundle away into the dawn light. Gary and the others had not even said goodbye to him. But of course, everyone was so tired, happy but tired!

***

The day passed all too slowly for Robert. He hardly noticed anything that was happening around him, unaware of the anxious buzz that pervaded his office that afternoon. He picked up on some vague talk about an 'announcement'- but what did he care? It was probably to do with the celebrations tonight, celebrations that would be crowned with his wonderful protest! But as the afternoon drew on, he did admit to himself that people did seem to be louder and more emotional than usual, and by the time he resolved to finish his work and ask someone about it, the office was empty. He looked at his watch. Half past five. Usually the office would be pretty much full at this time. Only two hours before the grand switching on. He felt a surge of pride as he examined the translucent smear, like the trail of an enormous snail, weaving across his ninth-floor window. His own work, that. Strange, though, where were they all? Nobody here had been talking about going to the celebrations. Getting a little worried now that somehow his scheme would be foiled, Robert tried to ring Dora at home. No reply. However, she'd left an answer phone message.

Dora sounded breathless, stressed. "Dad? We've been trying to get you all afternoon. Have you heard the news? Ring us Dad, please! Mum's in pieces!"

Robert left the deserted building. It was probably nothing. It wasn't unusual for Dora to get a little over-emotional. He'd ring her again from his bar, maybe have a little something to eat, even though he felt far too excited to swallow anything. But as he marched along those familiar alleys, he became aware that something was different; people were running- no one walking- and the voices that rose from the murky twilight were screams, and sobs, and incoherent wails of despair. And another sound, a terrific roaring, distant, yet loud and persistent; Shoma voices, lots of them, a chanting that rose above the rooftops. There was a phone booth in front of him, and, hands shaking, he pushed a coin into the slot and dialed Dora.

"You're back. What's-" Robert began only for Dora to cut him off.

"Dad, where have you been? They're evicting us! Haven't you heard?"

"What? But we paid the rent, they can't- "Robert half stammered in disbelief.

"Not our family! Everybody! The Shoma are evicting us-humans- from the whole planet! They're saying they were here first! We're the aliens now! Dad! Dad!"

Robert left the phone swinging and rushed into the bar. It was empty- a few turned over tables, the signs of a recent commotion. On the television, a Shoma newscaster cheerfully delivered the headlines.

"To summarize the Marshall's announcement- on this anniversary of First Friendship, the Government is pleased to announce that the repairs to all one thousand thirty-nine hoo-men starships have been completed, their hyperdrives restored. Hoo-menity is now ready to begin its long return journey to its home world. In one year's time, this repatriation will begin, and our happy association will come to a sad end, both races enriched by their brief but fruitful encounter...."

The old First Friendship picture was on the screen again- but this time, the dead President was a shrunken dwarf, and the Shoma which beamed benignly down on him was a golden God - an Angel.

Robert remembered Dora's words. We're the aliens now. And then his message, the beautiful tidings that were due to appear in the next few moments, popped into his head again, resplendent in their awful, irresistible power.

Oh my God!

Rushing back to the phone booth Robert crammed in coins, dialed the number that Gary had advised him to ring in case of dire emergencies.

The line was dead.

And then he was out into the street again, dodging blindly through the rain, struggling through the screaming crowds. He had to get back to his block- before- before-

Oh Christ.

It was before him now, and across its glittering surface, dominating the skyline, dominating everything, in savage ten-meter letters of glowing green, was his message-

SCREW YOU ALIEN SCUM. FUCK OFF HOME AND LEAVE US IN PEACE.

In front of the tower hundreds and hundreds of Shoma danced and celebrated beneath his message; and there were more aliens on the building itself, on the balconies, above and below the cruel words, and all of them were chanting, and now he knew what it was he'd heard in the street earlier- FUCK OFF HOME. FUCK OFF HOME. FUCK OFF- On the fringes of the concourse, terrified humans fled into the shadows.

Robert ran the other way, toward the crowd, into the mass of shouting Shoma, pushing them aside. He had been tricked- somehow. "I've got to- I'm the caretaker- got to switch the lights off – " He screamed to be heard over the Shoma.

A huge male alien grabbed his shoulder and hauled him backwards, off his feet, tossed him to the wet pavement. Robert sat up, dazed. They were all around him now.

"What are you doing here, Hoo-man?" One alien demanded.

"You shouldn't be here. Shoma only." Cried another.

"Hoo-man scum."

"Can't you read, Hoo-man? Can't you read the words?"

Robert looked up as the vicious kicks and blows fell upon him, he could read the words, his huge green letters- but they were changing, just as his dream had foreseen, dissolving with every Shoma punch into a cataract of glowing alien sludge that swamped and drowned him.

***

Hours later, Robert found himself back in the Shoma's office on the nineteenth floor. He was sitting down, and his broken arm had been roughly shoved into a cast, his cuts and wounds had been briskly patched up by a reluctant Shoma doctor. Now his Shoma was talking to him. There was something about its voice, something he'd never heard before. A quality akin to, but not entirely like, pity.

"It is very sad, Hoo-man. Very regrettable, that this foul racist message appears on what should be a day of happiness, final reconciliation. Some young roughneck Shoma must be responsible, one of those who attacked you. And this terrible slander appears to have inspired wider acts of violence against hoo-men. I would like to apologize, on behalf of my people. It is not how guests should be treated."

"Guests?" Asked Robert in confusion, looking up, too bludgeoned and exhausted to argue.

"We would like you and your family to stay here until the end. We need you to manage the block. You can leave in one of the final ships."

"Those ships," Robert muttered, "they're saying they're not flightworthy. They won't even make it into space before breaking up."

"Hoo-man defeatism! Hoo-man laziness!" hooted the Shoma, but with a little less malice than before, Robert thought. "You should exercise some of the determination that you demonstrated in cleaning the block," it added artfully.

"And your planet- where you're sending us- it's destroyed, burned up. It's why you came here in the first place."

"You are mistaken. This is our planet," insisted the Shoma.

Robert stood up. "I should go. Do you need me to clean off the letters?"

"No. There is no need. They can remain." The Shoma stood falling into step beside Robert as he walked toward the lift, dragging his aching limbs, his broken arm numb and useless. He passed a window that gaped invitingly open. Below he could see columns of humans being led by huge armed Shoma guards to the internment camps.

He could jump. Here and now. End it all. Death below right now, or death above, in one year's time.

Robert sensed the Shoma watching him.

"Thank you again, Hoo-man," it said in a low voice, "For all your service to the Shoma people."

Robert stood by the open window for a few moments before turning away, toward the elevator. Dora and Becky would need him, and he intended to be with them at the end– whenever that might be.

###

About Andrew Myers

ANDREW MYERS WAS BORN IN London and educated in Reading and Oxford. Since completing a MA in Prose Fiction at Middlesex University, he has won and been shortlisted for several literary prizes, including Momaya, Dark Tales, and Hammond House International Literary Prize, and his short fiction has been seen in such publications as 101Fiction.com, Speculative66, and the British Fantasy Society bulletin. His gothic science fiction play Nineteen Hertz was recently performed by a radio theatre company in San Francisco.

The Ides, his gripping YA science fiction novel, published under his pen name of A.N. Myers, is currently available on Amazon and through his website www.anmyers.com. He is currently writing its sequel, Open Locks Whoever Knocks, the second of the Fugue series. He is a member of Clockhouse London Writers.

Andrew Myers works full-time as a secondary school English teacher in East London and lives with his partner and two teenage sons.

Connect with Andrew here:
www.castrumpress.com/authors/andrew-myers

ALIEN DAYS

PHOBOSTEUS
By Dennis Mombauer

- ACT I -

The curtain rose, and the first act began.

Falb stood in one of the claustrophobic hallways of the cruiser, surrounded by other soldiers. The projection screens in the walls had come alive and commanded everyone's attention. Falb took a deep breath and clenched his teeth. Until a moment ago, the screens had only shown star-speckled emptiness and the yellow glow of the colony world: now, there was something else.

Sensor domes protruded from it like bone spurs and superstructures covered the immense hull like fins as it plowed through space toward them. Radiant stripes of light illuminated an endless mass of dark metal, its prow the closed jaws of a horrific sea creature. This was an Apparition ship, a Phobosteus, named after a species of armor fish that only went extinct because there had been no more prey left.

The enormous vessel had charted a direct collision course with the cruiser however, something was wrong with it. Falb allowed himself the briefest of smiles. The protective plating and parts of the engine had burst open like flower buds, and cold brightness leaked out into the vacuum. The damages were greater than the furrows of small rocks and interstellar plankton the Phobosteus must have dived through. They were combat wounds.

Falb had seen all he needed to see and began moving toward the staging area. "Put on your costumes," he shouted. "Curtain's calling."

Falb and his brother trekked through the trees of a dark forest. They treaded on the soft soil without noise and followed the well-traveled path. Danger inhabited these woods, but the brothers felt no fear, for they had crossed them many times before.

Soldiers streamed through the hallways toward the cruiser's staging area, their steps accompanied by warning sirens and announcements. Falb strode into the high-ceilinged staging area and toward the boarding shells, where men and women changed into combat gear. Falb already wore the thermal underlay and plating of his own effigy suit, and hundreds of tiny needles painlessly sunk into his flesh, preparing to pump drugs and stimulants as needed.

The room jerked as gravity tightened and pressed the soldiers against the floor. Their cruiser maneuvered against the Phobosteus, and Falb needed to assemble his unit.

The forest grew darker, and wind rustled above the treetops, imbuing their leaves with a choir of whispers. Old waystones rose by the road, overgrown with moss and lichen, but the brothers knew them by heart.

"There you are," Deuteros called. She was Falb's second-in-command, a career soldier and veteran who shouldered her rifle and stuffed extra magazines into her pockets.

"Here I am." Falb marched right by her. "Get Tritos, Tetartos, and Pemptos. I'll find the new guy and meet you at the shell."

The artificial gravity shifted as the cruiser turned to the side, and the projection screens along the bulkheads showed the Phobosteus simultaneously changing its course. Falb glimpsed the planet below with a dark shape hanging in lower orbit, a converted corporate freighter almost as big as the cruiser. The colony world's evacuation was progressing, but it would be hours before they had ferried up half the population.

"Boarding position in T minus five minutes," the announcement system proclaimed. "All units, prepare for launch."

Ceiling lights rotated in deep orange, and Falb discovered his missing man on the wrong side of the staging area, staggering between soldiers that advanced in orderly lines. He called to him: "Hektos!"

Heads turned, and a few looks lingered: Falb's complete lack of hair made people nervous. He had permanently removed it from his body, although single hairs still sprouted in one place or another, which Falb had to pluck out with a pair of pincers. Nothing was medically wrong with the hairs, but Falb couldn't stand them, didn't want them as a part of himself, and he removed them as soon as they appeared.

"Hektos!" Falb strode toward him, and this time, his newest recruit turned around, the faint blue of his eyes so spotless they gave him an even more boyish appearance. Falb reached Hektos with a few steps, grabbed him by the shoulder and dragged the young soldier along.

The announcement system continued to count down: "Boarding position in T minus three minutes."

All the organs in Falb's body attempted escape in different directions, the familiar sickness that always accompanied combat maneuvering. It was just the heavy oil swashing through the tanks of the cruiser's Flüstermeer engine, but he never got used to it.

"All right, come on, come on." Falb herded his soldiers down a ramp and toward the open hatch of their boarding shell. "Everyone to their positions."

Deuteros climbed in first, followed by Pemptos, Tritos, Tetartos, and finally young Hektos. Falb checked the shell's gauges while everyone strapped into their padded holding clamps. Once the cruiser reached boarding position, it would fire the shells at the Phobosteus, still connected to the cruiser by their tethers.

Everything read out operational, all shell functions normal: however, the situation was anything but. Falb recognized an opportunity when it presented itself, and this might be the biggest one he would ever get.

He stepped into the shell and closed the airlock behind him before he addressed his soldiers: "You have all seen it. The Apparitions have sent a damaged ship into battle. First time that's ever happened, and we'll take advantage of it."

In the beginning, no one had believed the stories, dismissed them as the yarn of space sailors desperate for attention: then, the incidents piled up. A cruiser of the Amaranthine Fleet reported an immense ship that had projected the faces of dead men on its screens; a corporate freighter with inaccurate Flüstermeer calculations spotted a ghost ship drifting far outside its target system; a smaller cruiser vanished without a trace. The oneiromancers received images of towering waves and broken seashells; and then, without any declaration, the attack waves began.

Falb held the wide-eyed gaze of his soldiers and finished his address: "We'll go in and do what no one else could do before: We'll find and capture an Apparition."

✳✳✳

Underneath the ceiling of leaves and branches, the path reached the most remote region of the forest. Falb looked at his brother Timeon, but Timeon didn't look back, and they both continued onward.

"Hold tight." At Falb's command, his soldiers fastened their grip on the handholds and braced for the shell's impact on the Phobosteus' outer hull. They waited like young actors before their first performance, and Falb remembered his own early battles: how the anxiety had throbbed hot through his nervous system, how he had dreamt of fighting creatures like the companion in a Larvosis play.

He had known that those theatrical dreams didn't equal reality and the odds of returning from a combat mission against the Apparitions were slim—but as far as Falb was concerned, probabilities only mattered to people without vision.

A shock traveled through the shell as it touched down, landing like an angry hornet on the skin of the immense Phobosteus. The central ring corridor of the Apparition ship should stretch below them, and as the magnetic claws pulled them closer, the shell's welding lasers heated up.

Falb closed his eyes, inspected his emotions, and arranged them before his inner eye, a shimmering armory of tools and weapons. There was his thirst for knowledge, long and barbed, his urge to get answers: What the Apparitions were? Why they had descended upon humanity? What they looked like? Next to this, a double-edged blade: Falb's anger at the Amaranthine Fleet and its petrified hierarchies, at the oracles who only ever saw the same; and finally, the spearhead of Falb's ambition, his desire to rise above such restraints.

Deeper than these emotions, Falb's relationships secured him like the shell's tether secured it to the cruiser: His brother Timeon, who had stayed behind to command the cruiser, and his sister Larea, whose whereabouts Falb didn't know but whose face he remembered vividly even after all those years—siblings not by birth, but by choice.

He listened into his body, to the steady rhythm of his heart, the muscle contractions when he clenched his fists and relaxed them, the creeping of the metal shell at his back.

Pemptos' voice yanked Falb out of his meditation: "Let's stage the play."

He opened his eyes and took stock of his unit: Deuteros, the veteran; Tritos and Tetartos, the owl and the otter; the tall Pemptos; and finally, Hektos, the boy with the blue eyes. Tritos tried to straighten his shaggy hair, Tetartos mumbled something inaudible, Pemptos caressed the grenade launcher on her rifle. Hektos stared at Falb's bald head, and Deuteros looked down at her effigy suit, into whose surface words had been burned with acid.

Deuteros noticed Falb's attention: "The survivors," she said. "Everyone who returned from a mission with me. They're my mantra."

Falb nodded. To do this job, to fight against the Apparitions, the soldiers of the Amaranthine Fleet needed control over themselves. They needed to rely on their bodies and minds to withstand the nightmares, and they needed something to hold onto, some object or idea. Deuteros had the names etched into her armor, Pemptos her weapon, Falb the pincers he used to remove hairs from his body.

Falb activated his effigy with a thought and summoned the floating holographic representation of his body, visible only to himself. He made the organs glow, visualized his blood flow, and the major areas of activity in his brain, all the 'fuel stats,' as the soldiers called it, before the image dissipated into the air again.

"Boarding Shell 7, touchdown." The prompter filled the background of Falb's consciousness and created a rough picture of the Phobosteus and the substantially smaller Fleet cruiser, the space between them crisscrossed by tethers. "Shell 3 and 4, welding process completed. Shell 9, touchdown in T minus ten seconds. Nine. Eight."

Every moment now, their own announcement would sound, and the anticipation in the men and women under Falb's command was palpable. An icy lump grew in every one of them, getting bigger and colder by the minute. For some, it inhabited the stomach, made their legs weak and spoiled their appetite days before the mission; for others, it occupied the lungs or the heart.

Hektos shouted "Curtain up!" in an uncertain voice, far too loudly, and the others joined in: "Curtain up!"

The last sparks glittered as the welding lasers finished their work, the pressure adjusting with a hiss that pierced into Falb's eyeballs.

***

– ACT II –

"Go!" The airlock opened, and Falb pushed himself into the next act, followed by the rest of his unit. He leaped through the freshly opened hole, the edges still glowing, landed hard and panned his rifle. The ring corridor looked the same in both directions, broad and as clinically sterile as an operating theatre, punctuated in regular intervals by open airlocks. There were no isolated light sources, only long tubes that flooded everything with the same, contrastless brightness.

Above the forest, the moon came up, and its pale light trickled down between the treetops while the wind chased away the clouds. The moonlight illuminated a trail of footprints in the soft forest floor, and Falb followed it. It was said that a network of hidden paths traversed these woods, only visible in special nights: and that one of those paths would lead to the tree of visions.

"Faster!" Falb shouted at his soldiers. The heavy effigy suits made them look like archaic divers sinking down into the Apparition's realm. They hit the ground, went through a trained sequence of movements, and trudged to their positions.

Falb glanced at curved crossbeams, perpendicular hallways, and round columns that harbored the ventilation fans. In the distance, he could see a second unit jumping in through another welded hole, just before the airlocks came down. It was the usual pattern: once foreign matter boarded the ship, the Apparitions segmented the ring corridor and separated all boarding teams from each other—and with this, the countdown started.

Nobody knew the reason for it—maybe tactical considerations or a psychological predisposition—but when the Apparitions attacked, they always followed a fixed hierarchy of targets: Intruders on their own ship, ships in orbit, and, at the very last, the world they had come for. Even if several Apparition ships opposed a single defense cruiser, they only initiated their surface attack if the cruiser had been destroyed, captured, or forced out of the system.

The trail meandered between trees and bushes into a wilderness that neither Falb nor his siblings had ever explored. The silvery reflection of puddles guided him on his way like a series of beacons, without providing any meaningful illumination.

The soldiers formed a semi-circle around Falb and aimed their weapons at the perpendicular hallways that led further into the ship.

"Incoming!" Deuteros cried, pointing her weapon as several hatches opened along the inner wall. With a low-pitched whirring, fist-sized drones dashed out, their glowing sensor antennae rotating in the air as they skimmed over them in formation.

Under Falb's feet, the wet forest floor turned to mud as he followed the trail from puddle to puddle. Trickles ran down the tree trunks and combined with other trickles from swampy wells. Water sloshed between the trees like an inland tide, swelled and flowed into a reed-covered lake.

Six muzzles lighted up, the noise of ejected cartridges and reloading mechanisms filled the Phobosteus. Falb couldn't tell if the drones were autonomous or if the Apparitions controlled them, but they were transmitting data: and that meant that the Phobosteus was aware of Falb's every move.

Falb's soldiers fired again. Two drones exploded, the rest swiveled sideways to fan out, speeding up above their heads.

Falb steadied his hand as he aimed at one of the drones, followed its flight path and pulled the trigger. The insect-like machine tilted in the blink of an eye and narrowly evaded the burst of fire, falling back into its horizontal position increasing speed with an audible hum.

The rat-a-tat of rifles cleaved the air, but no more of the tiny machines went down.

Shapes moved in the algae-green water of the lake, nearly transparent fish with eyes that glimmered like streaks of gold. Could the fish see him? Were they responsible for his feeling of being watched? And most importantly: would they reveal to him the tree of visions?

"Fields of fire! Cover your quadrants!" Falb exchanged hasty glances with his soldiers and indicated angles with his hand. A brief silence washed through the room, allowing Falb to take a few quiet breaths. Beating the Apparitions was about being smart, to outmaneuver them at their own game.

The units' weapons barked, and three drones turned into smoke and wreckage when they found no escape.

"I got one!" Pemptos cheered as she hit another target and continued to fire at the next. Tritos and Tetartos synchronized their volleys while Deuteros lowered her rifle and waited.

The remaining drones sped toward their hatches in the wall and slipped in. Tetartos rejoiced: "They are retreating!"

But Falb knew that they would have done that no matter what, that this was only the first stage. It was a small victory, and it was their high point: everything that followed would be worse.

***

"Stay sharp. Hold your positions." Falb pivoted the barrel of his gun to keep his section of the ring corridor in sight.

"Puppets!" Blue-eyed Hektos aimed into one of the perpendicular hallways, where half a dozen figures in scarred battle armor advanced stiffly.

"Take cover!" Falb shouted ducking behind a nearby ventilation column as the enemy opened fire. He knew exactly how the next minutes would go, he had played through them in simulation and live action a thousand times, and still his heart pounded. He peeked through an incredible window of opportunity, and these dead men in metal blocked his view. He had no time to fight them, but there was no way around, no shortcut to the Apparitions.

The puppets in their armored suits moved with the cumbersome momentum of a cargo train. They made a series of heavy steps toward him, bracing their boots against the floor and firing their weapons as if their arms were being lifted up on strings. There was no organic flow to them, just a sequence of separate motions without hesitation and consciousness. Their rifles howled with supersonic acceleration as they hurled out volleys of projectiles. Servomotors hissed as the puppets moved their feet and their metal soles touched down.

Falb let his reflexes and muscle memory take over: acquiring targets, firing short bursts, diving back behind cover. The puppets came like waves breaking against a sea wall, and their projectiles hit everything around Falb.

Falb's nerves twitched without provocation, his fingers clawing together, and his breast trembled. The nightmares flooded in with the puppets, the subliminal presence of the Apparitions. A shiver ran through Falb, as if he had touched the golden ornaments of an oneiromancer, and his arms and legs began to cramp.

He could see in his soldiers' faces that they felt it as well, that their bodies rebelled against the Apparitions. Hektos scratched at his armor, trying to wrench parts of it free, while Tritos tore out his shaggy hair and Pemptos ground her teeth.

The fish in the lake grew restless, whipping their scaly fins, darting back and forth with faint splashes. They filled the lake with movement, but their golden eyes never left the human following his trail along the shore. Falb saw a shadow of the tree of visions floating below the surface, but he sensed that the tree itself wasn't here.

Falb concentrated on his breathing, using the deliberate tensing and relaxing of his muscles to slowly bring his body back under control. The Apparition's nightmares always came in waves, each one stronger than the last, but they were nothing more than illusions. Falb wouldn't be stopped by such trifles, not when he finally had a chance to get answers, to reach the center of this damaged ship.

Nobody understood the Apparitions. They emerged like the darkness in a Larvosis play, a faceless and formless threat, and as far as scientists, military, and the oneiromancers could tell, there was nothing the Apparitions gained from invading human space. They didn't take any resources, they didn't occupy territory, they showed no interest in slaves, wealth, or technology. They abducted some people and turned them into puppets, but one colony world alone would've been more than sufficient for that.

"Target Alpha." Falb directed his unit against the Apparition's revenants. One puppet came to a standstill, its armor porous from bullet holes, before it tumbled down in a cascade of crashing metal. The remaining puppets didn't turn their heads, and Falb's soldiers cowered under a series of supersonic booms as they returned fire.

"Forward!" Falb ran toward the puppets till he reached the next ventilation column, dropped on one knee and took a shot. The Apparitions had the servo-assisted armor and the sophisticated weapons, but they commanded only the remains of men, broken toys that lacked speed and reflexes.

Deuteros and Pemptos advanced behind Falb, and another puppet fell. The remaining puppets tried to turn, then Falb was right next to them. The salvo missed his arm by a hair's breadth as he pulled his own trigger.

Armor plates and necrotic flesh tumbled under a barrage of close-distance hits collapsing like a stage prop. The rifles died down, and the sharp stench of smoldering tissue wafted from the hallway into the ring corridor.

Falb stopped to wait till the rest of his unit had passed the fallen puppets.

"Should we establish defensive positions, Commander?" Asked Tritos.

"No. Follow me. We go farther."

"This isn't procedure." Tritos kicked one of the destroyed puppets, checking for any reaction. "Our orders are only to hold the line, to buy time for the evacuation."

"Since the very first encounter, every Phobosteus has been flawless and fully functioning. This one is damaged. It has weak spots." The artificial gravity wasn't uniform, it had tiny currents and whirls that tugged at Falb's armor. It was hard to stand steady, harder still to ignore the opportunity that this implicated. "I told you we're going to capture an Apparition, and we will."

✳✳✳

– ACT III –

The third act contained the first major transition in every Larvosis play. There was conflict, often between the characters of the companion and the creature, but never without ambiguity. Larvosis theatre had left the realism of earlier forms far behind, venturing toward a refined symbolism, in which everything and every character represented something other than themselves.

The fish in the lake stopped moving and drifted in the water as the path curved into the forest again.

The unit marched through the perpendicular hallway into an immense room. This was it. Falb's skin prickled in the freezing atmosphere. Tilted panels and heavy strutting lined the walls while huge metal blocks towered up from the floor. Surgical lightheads glided on ceiling rails between them, creating corridors of high-lux illumination and leaving keel waves of diluted shadows.

Parts of the floor lost themselves in gray shadows where lamp tubes had been destroyed by explosives. There were no other signs combat, no dried blood or ejected shells, but it was clear that this room had seen fighting in a previous battle.

Falb's voice was but a whisper in the vastness of the room, the only sound except for the ventilation and the steps of his soldiers: "The thing's been gutted already."

Other entrances gaped on the far sides of the room, and Falb ordered his unit to fan out between the enormous blocks. They moved with him, they trusted him, and he would never throw away their lives without purpose.

"Shh." Tritos seemed to listen to something that only he could hear, turning his round head. "Is that you? I waited for you, I took care of her, like you wanted. No ... it can't be, no, no."

His eyes squinted as he stared at the empty air, obviously manipulating his effigy. "Commander, I ... the nightmares show me my brother, and I ..."

Falb's muscles tightened, and their involuntary activation began to heat up and stew him inside his armor. The pores and glands in his body took on a life of their own, and Falb drowned in his armor even as he tried to control them.

Sweat poured over his skin, soaking the thermal underlay. Tears and snot ran over his face, his eyes burned, and the saliva in his mouth accumulated so fast he had to constantly swallow.

The golden eyes of the fish flared their light piercing Falb's head like the rays of a sun. He staggered under the tree canopy hands pressed to his temples. In the murky lake, the fish eyes dimmed again as they sank between the reeds.

The effigy appeared before Falb's watery eyes, and he tried to close the floodgates. Hundreds of microscopic needles released chemicals into his organism, while the suit tried to sponge up his body fluids pumping them into small tanks. He tried to concentrate on a single point while the armor did its work, imagining his pincers pulling every last hair from him.

He reduced his body's outcry to mere data streams, to visual input and sound waves, nothing more than warning lights and sirens without emotional attachment. He controlled the onslaught of his senses like he controlled his mind and flesh, mastering them like he had mastered his hair growth.

As the storm calmed in him, Falb saw Deuteros moving her hands over the etched-in names on her armor, and young Hektos trying to bend back his fingers from his face, where they had left bloody scratches. As his soldiers fought against the nightmares, metallic clangor rose up from the ship's depths, like a dozen kitchen knives hacking down rhythmically.

Pain surged from Falb's right arm up into him. His muscles were pulled out and furled, and Falb pinched the right biceps of the floating effigy to prompt the mechanisms in his real arm to block neural transmission, preventing any input from reaching his brain.

"Falb." A voice hissed in his ear, its anger audible through static interference and the high tide of the nightmare effects: Timeon, Falb's brother back on the cruiser.

"What are you doing, Falb?" A light head passed by over Falb blinding him for a second. "You are too far away from your shell. If you go any farther, we will lose you."

"The Phobosteus is damaged. There's a way inside."

"This isn't in our orders, and you know it."

"We can't keep following orders. Not while the Apparitions overrun system after system."

Massive spider-machines stalked into the hall, their heavy armament swiveling toward Falb's unit. They advanced between the towering massifs of metal, and where they put down their legs, air filters began to roar in the walls.

Falb called for his soldiers to take cover and used his effigy to force his own legs to move with artificial nerve impulses. Timeon kept talking to him the entire time, but Falb only paid attention once he reached the nearest column and its rotation vibrated through his bones. A bright light glided past on the ceiling, then the shadows flooded together again. His brothers voice returned to his ears.

"... where every part has to work, or the whole engine jams. The Amaranthine Fleet is under a lot of pressure, and we cannot relieve it, lest the Apparitions burst through and drown us all. You cannot win the war on your own, Falb, but you may be able to lose it."

The armed spiders opened fire, releasing streams of super-heated projectiles in wide arcs across the hall.

"Keep your heads down!" The wave of nightmares ebbed down, and Falb released the effigy to regain natural control over his nerves and muscles. "Timeon, I can't discuss this now. The oracles are broken. Our orders didn't foresee a damaged ship. You need to trust me."

The moon's pallid reflection vanished as the forest closed around Falb.

Falb shot a blind volley toward the spiders and pulled back as a staccato of impacts thundered against the column.

"If we believe the Apparitions made a mistake, we believe what the Apparitions have fed us." The detached voice of a gold-emblazoned oneiromancers trickled in Falb's ear, one of the advisors of the Fleet. "We know one thing about them: They do not change their pattern without intent. Our orders are unambiguous, and so are the omens. We hold the line until evacuation is complete, and then we disengage. Everything else is certain doom."

It was time to act, not talk. If Falb didn't do something, his unit would be pinned down and die here, with more puppets trudging in from across the ship.

He took his gun and sprinted forward while Deuteros and Pemptos laid down covering fire. The guns of the robotic spiders blazed, their hail of bullets hammering down behind Falb, pulverizing the floor where his feet had been.

As Falb dodged the salvoes, the rest of his unit joined the shooting, and the roaring of small explosions meant that Pemptos was launching grenades from her rifle. The impacts caught up to Falb, and he leaped forward toward another block, rolling over the ground in full armor. The collision knocked the breath out of him, but when he got back up, the spiders fell silent.

"Timeon. Are you still there? You're telling me about probabilities, rules, fears. I know you are better than this. I hope you remember why we joined the Fleet: to do the important things. You're my brother, Timeon: wait for me. I will return from the abyss."

✳✳✳

"Let's go." Falb called to the others as he changed his magazine and stepped over the scrap metal carcass of a spider robot. It reeked of rotten meat and decay, of mold and fungi proliferating within its hardened shell.

Tree trunks and undergrowth stretched in all directions, monochromatic in the pale moonlight. Falb had lost his brother, and now he couldn't find him anymore. He called his name, but the leaves swallowed his voice and didn't return an echo.

"Should we really go further?" Tritos reminded Falb more of an owl than ever, his eyes widened, and his hair glued together by sweat.

Falb stared at him and shuddered at this disgusting mess of hair. He turned to the rest of his soldiers stepping out of cover. Dark spots disfigured Pemptos' arm, and red fluid leaked over her hand.

"You're wounded."

"A few pieces of shrapnel, Commander."

Falb gathered his unit and checked their status, but everyone else seemed fine. He had never lost a soldier under his command, and he wouldn't start today. Pemptos was strong, nonetheless Falb could see her face losing color, paling like the eyes of young Hektos.

"Go back to the shell and seal it behind you. Wait for us. If the cruiser leaves and we're not there, don't stay behind. You understand?"

Pemptos nodded absent-mindedly, probably releasing painkillers through her effigy.

"Go." Falb watched Pemptos shoulder her heavy rifle and hurry away. "No other injuries? Good. Follow me: time is not on our side."

He started to march, and his soldiers trailed him through an entrance and into one of the petrified arteries of the Phobosteus.

The undergrowth closed around Falb and whispered with tongues of grass, feeling for his legs.

Falb started to speak, but stopped as a shock traveled through the corridor, shifting the floor under his feet. He wrestled for his balance as the metal shuddered under a series of tremors.

"What's happening? Is the Phobosteus being hit?" Asked Tritos.

Falb shook his head: "The cruiser's weaponry can't penetrate the shielding. This is the Apparitions' doing."

Another quake, followed by mechanical noises in the walls: things twisting themselves, rotating in steady rhythms, snapping into place with a click.

Behind Falb's soldiers, heavy gates closed like rows of teeth while new entrances opened elsewhere, as if the Apparition ship was a theatre stage changing scenery between acts.

Falb would never find the way back, he could only go forward to find the tree of visions. The treetops trembled as birds landed on them, crows with inky plumage and snow globe eyes.

Rectangular blocks rose up from the floor, and Falb and his soldiers had to tread carefully toward the exit. When they were almost in reach of it, the corridor tilted like the board of a seesaw, suddenly connecting two different levels of the ship's interior maze. They stumbled as the ground inclined beneath them.

"Marin," croaked the birds, "Marin. Marin. Men like you are the victims of darkness." They plucked out their jet-black feathers and whet their beaks on the tree's bark. "Marin."

"We should go back, Commander." Hektos pleaded. "Please."

"Can't." Falb clambered down the corridor-turned-ramp. His skin was sticky with dried body fluids, and every movement rubbed against his armor. "Only one way left. Toward the final act."

In a Larvosis play, the creature was the one that came at the companion in a series of random attacks while the darkness followed an intricate plan, a byzantine conspiracy to corrupt and erode the seer's will.

This nightmare architecture was like both, evoking a sense of spontaneous improvisation while at the same time having been prepared long in advance.

Falb and his unit continued through the lower corridor: and all at once, as if they had crossed an invisible border, the lights went out.

***

- ACT IV -

The Phobosteus was a stage, and Falb was stepping into the next act.

Without the moon, the forest underwent a metamorphosis. Branches, vines, and roots coalesced to form a mass of clawing tentacles, a nest of snakes and writhing worms. The wind roared between the tree trunks and carried bright bells, a melody from the tree of visions.

"Lighting!"

Rifle-mounted spotlights flared, transforming the hallway into a maelstrom of restlessly swaying shadows. The geometric blackness shifted like the inside of a kaleidoscope.

"Commander? What's the next act?" Hektos' pale eyes had lost all color now resembling bleached-out pearls.

"Catabasis." Deuteros stood next to Hektos and squinted over the rifle barrel while strafing her spotlight methodically along the corridor. "The descent into the underworld, the journey along the river. The seer's fight against the darkness."

Noises resounded in the distance, whirring and scraping.

Falb knew the world was spinning for his soldiers, and he had to become their fixpoint. "The Apparitions turned off the lights. So what? Are we children? We have our own lights."

"Marin." The birds in the treetops turned their heads with eyes like luminous marbles, their call as spiteful as if they were saying: "We warned you." Their little bodies formed feathered silhouettes in a pandemonium of gray, and Falb could barely distinguish them from the shreds of sky.

They moved on with careful steps, Falb at the front, followed by Deuteros, Hektos, and the rest. Before them, a chamber opened, so vast that the brightness of the spotlights perished part-way. Rows of drawers lined the stainless walls, their screens flickering with numbers and data readouts, while high voltage cables as thick as Falb's leg twisted over the floor.

"Stop." Falb grouped everyone in a tight circle, guns and lights pointing outwards, heads and bodies as close together as possible. "Listen to my voice. Think of why you're here. Think back to the plays you've watched, the roles you wanted to perform."

Every Larvosis play had four main characters: the seer and the companion, the creature and the darkness. The companion had to overcome the creature, the seer the darkness. The basic constellation was simple, but the audience didn't know the distribution of roles. The story-path turned into an intellectual challenge because underneath each of the many skins—played by a real actor or a robotic substitute—could be the companion, the creature, the darkness, or the seer.

There were countless people who wanted to be the companion and fight the creature, to be the trailblazer who made the seer's metaphysical struggle possible. The conflict with the darkness on the other hand, the unknown, utterly alien, inhuman, amoral other ... this conflict only spoke to a select few, to extraordinary individuals like the ones that had led humanity into the outer dark.

"For long stretches of my life, I was satisfied with serving. A son to my parents, a soldier to the Fleet. But there have been times I wanted to achieve more. To take on the role of the seer." Falb let his words sink in. He could only hope that Timeon wouldn't disengage the cruiser and flee the system, that he would give Falb the time he needed.

This was uncharted territory, because nobody had ever penetrated this far into a Phobosteus. Anything could wait for them here.

"Every one of these times, I succeeded. The seer needs the companion, and I need you. No turning back now, only success or failure. Aren't you curious what an Apparition looks like? What it is?"

The drawers moaned, as if corpses turned inside their tombs. The numbers on the monitors changed, and some readout lines spiked. "Come on."

It seemed to take hours to cross the chamber, but according to Falb's suit, it was little more than a minute. The spotlights peeled an exit from the gloom, a corridor that branched out into three directions.

In the brightness of their lamps, every step felt detached, as if they were controlling themselves through their effigies, watching their bodies from outside. Tritos and Tetartos secured the left branch, Deuteros and Hektos the right one, while Falb walked straight, like divers exploring the wreckage of a long-lost submarine.

Tetartos gave his "All clear," and Falb turned to the other side: "Deuteros? Do you–"

A door slammed down and cut Falb short. The corridor to the left turned into a wall, cutting of Falb, Deuteros, and Hektos from Tritos and Tetartos. Falb swiveled around to see another wall where the chamber had been, imprisoning them in a cul-de-sac.

"Tritos? Tetartos?" The radio inside the suit returned only white noise, like waves breaking over rocks. "Tritos! Tetartos!"

"It's the darkness." Hektos muttered to himself, and coldness radiated through Falb's body. In the Larvosis theatre, the perversion of expectations was a major theme, and it was always caused by the darkness.

"Remember the end." The darkness deceived and manipulated throughout all the acts, but ultimately, the seer and the companion emerged triumphant. Larvosis theatre was more than mass entertainment, more than a complex riddle: It was a common myth, a story about ambition and success, about the seer's vision and the companion's endurance. It had made humanity reach for the stars, build the first Flüstermeer ships and colonize worlds so distant they hadn't even been dreams before.

Deuteros and Hektos rushed toward Falb, only to witness the next metamorphosis of their surroundings. The walls glittered and bathed the corridor in radiological light as they turned into x-ray mirrors. Falb barely recognized his own skeleton: his bones so friable, the rifle enormous in his bare knuckles, his eye sockets hollow and gaunt.

The birds had vanished from the branches, and the memory of their voices was fading.

"We shouldn't be here." Hektos' eyes flickered amidst red scratches. "This place is inhuman ... it isn't meant for us."

"But it is." Deuteros stroked gloved fingers over one of the mirrors. "It is made precisely for us. Do you think the Apparitions built all this for their puppets? It's a trap."

Predators scurried through the foliage on all sides, only vaguely perceptible from their rustling. Falb turned around, searching for his brother, for the trail, for the moon in the sky. The clearing with the tree of visions had to be close, the forest's treasured secret: but would he be able to find it?

"We don't turn back." Falb strengthened his voice and purged it of any trembling or hesitation. If he didn't hold on, his unit would fall apart, and the enemy would pick them off. Tritos and Tetartos waited for them somewhere behind these walls, and so did the Apparitions. "The mirrors are here to lead us astray."

Hektos cried: "What if you are wrong? What if we are dead already?" Falb let the voice bounce off his skull. All doubts in this place were part of the nightmares, not real, and Falb had to stick to the beliefs he remembered from the cruiser.

✳✳✳

The heavy steps of puppets approached through the corridors like the incoming tide in the hours after midnight.

Falb, Deuteros, and Hektos moved their spotlights around, the first two steady, the third shaking, and advanced into a dome with multiple levels of walkways.

The floor was two stories below them, the ceiling two or three above, only faintly touched by their lamplight. There were no elevators, stairs, or ladders, only an exit on the other side: and so, they moved along the stainless-steel ledge.

The vast darkness of the dome seemed to echo back at Falb, to make him feel increasingly lost. Was the dome spinning, slowly revolving against their movement, or was it just a matter of perception?

"We are never getting out of here." Deuteros stopped a few steps behind Falb and Hektos. "The Apparitions will capture us and turn us into puppets. In the next battle, we will fight for them."

"We can find an Apparition and bring it back to the cruiser. Timeon will wait for us."

"Even if he waits, there is no way back." Falb had never seen Deuteros so shaken. "Do you know who they use? The ones that are best-preserved. The ones with a still functioning brain they can rewire for their purposes. At the very least, we should make ourselves useless to them."

Falb had heard this piece of fiction before, a lie that soldiers told themselves before boarding a Phobosteus: but the statistics didn't support it. The Apparitions picked at random or according to their own inscrutable designs, and their machines could repair any damage humans were capable of inflicting.

"We'll do this when there's no other way. The time hasn't come yet." Falb put a gloved hand on Deuteros' shoulder and flinched as the next wave of nightmares rolled over him.

He had no proprioception anymore, no sense of the position of his limbs and their movements on the narrow ledge. He almost stepped over the edge but managed to activate his effigy at the last moment and hurled his body against the wall with a neural shock.

He felt warmth on his left arm and turned to see his armor melting. The metal liquefied and ran down his wrist and elbow, at first in drops, then sizzling streams. What was left of the underlay and plating formed trickles and rivulets, revolving vortexes that bubbled and steamed without Falb feeling pain.

Thousands of pin-prick lights glowed on Falb's exposed skin, rose like thin filaments of smoke. Hairs grew where they weren't supposed to, all over his arm, as if he was regressing into an animal.

Falb tried to blank out his senses and concentrate only on the effigy floating before him. He squinted and imagined his pincers hovering over him, removing one hair after another, but they were too slow, too inefficient.

The hair growth was as much an illusion as the melting armor, but he still convulsed in disgust. The hairs turned into a fur, obscuring his skin with a dark, asymmetrical mass, a chaos of curved lines that stuck out in all directions.

Timeon. Falb visualized the face of his brother before his eyes, his perfect teeth, the strong jaws, his gold-rimmed glasses. He floated over the abomination that Falb's arm had turned into, lighted by the molten effigy suit.

Larea. He remembered her mouth, which could contort in such a unique way when she was angry, her sharp intellect, her disdain for money.

As long as his brother and sister were with Falb, the Apparitions couldn't keep him back, not with their puppets and not with their nightmares.

"Deuteros. Take–"

Something whizzed past Falb, and the wall splintered outward in a hail of fragments. A swing of the spotlight revealed a dozen puppets on the ground floor, aiming up and shooting in short bursts. There was no cover here, no scenery to hide behind. Only one way to go.

"To the other side! Move!" Falb fired one volley at the Apparition's mindless soldiers, but his bullets only hit ground. All around him, impacts turned the wall into clouds of shrapnel, and still the nightmare effects hadn't worn off.

Behind Hektos, Deuteros was hit by a series of projectiles that came too fast to evade. Holes burst open between her breasts and down to her navel, effortlessly piercing the effigy armor. Soundlessly she plummeted from the ledge and was swallowed by gloom when her lamp broke on impact.

"Jump!" Falb ran and dove through the entrance at the end of the ledge. "Hektos, come on! Don't stop now!"

Hektos stared at him, his blue eyes gleaming: "I want to go home."

"Not yet. We came here for a reason, remember?"

"No ..." Hektos took a few steps back, then stopped. "I can't do this."

Falb tried to grab him, but a door came down and cut him off, instantly clearing away all sounds and motion.

***

– ACT V –

Every Larvosis play had one more act than the actors played out, the spectral act. In five normal acts, the play escalated toward a climax, but only the sixth act, the one that took place exclusively in the audience's imagination, unraveled all threads and unveiled the true perspective.

There was a trail again, a set of alternating imprints in the earth underneath grass and dead leaves. Falb searched for his brother and any other human, even for the birds. The forest lurked around him with bared teeth and scraping claws, but he was close, and he could still reach the place he wished for.

Falb stood in the corridor and tried to reach Hektos on the radio. The door gleamed in stainless steel and wouldn't budge, no matter how hard he hammered against it.

"Hektos!" Falb shouted, and the name echoed along the walls: "Hektos!"

Deuteros was dead. Hektos was lost, Tritos lost, Tetartos lost as well. Falb had no sense of direction anymore and all his instruments had ceased working. He could be anywhere, merely a few rooms from the center or close to the outer hull again.

A part of the wall flipped and revealed another x-ray monitor in which Falb's skeletal likeness floated as if over a bottomless well.

The bushes parted, and Falb saw yellow eyes, not like the molten gold of the fish, but dirtier, more feral. Inside them, like a fly caught in amber, trembled his own reflection.

More x-ray mirrors appeared as wall panel after wall panel turned in a sea of blackness where miniature versions of Falb flickered like candlewicks. He closed his eyes for a short moment, let oxygen sink into his lungs and carbon dioxide eject again.

He opened his eyes once more, raised the muzzle of his weapon, aimed at one of the mirrors and pulled the trigger. The glass exploded noiselessly in a shower of glitter. In the strange silence, Falb pivoted, destroying one mirror after another until the floor was carpeted with shards.

The wind howled, and the forest reared up against Falb.

In space, there were people who couldn't stand the void, who were overwhelmed by it and recoiled from it even on projection screens—but Falb preferred the emptiness over the maze of reflections.

The corridor led Falb into another hall, but his legs trembled under him. He pressed his back against the wall and let his body slide down to the floor.

When he turned his lamp off, the inky blackness around Falb was absolute; when he turned it on, he sat on a mountaintop, surrounded by a crawling precipice, by steep slopes and valleys of shadow. The spotlight illuminated his arms and a section of the floor, but little else, no walls or ceiling. It was hard to believe that he was inside a spaceship, and harder still to imagine why it had been built with this changing labyrinth as its interior.

Something shimmered in the light, a single hair between Falb's thumb and index finger that had somehow found its way through the glove. With his other hand, Falb took his pincers, grabbed the hair at its root and yanked it out. The pain was so faint he only felt a familiar tingling.

He moved his arms, stretched his skin and found another hair. The gap of the suit's elbow joint. The pincers removed it and made Falb more comfortable, even here and now. If he gave up, his unit would have perished without purpose. If he gave up, the Apparitions would keep coming, and no one would know why. For Hektos and Deuteros, for Tritos and Tetartos, for Timeon and Larea, he had to have faith.

Falb took one deep breath, slowly got up and continued.

***

The room yawned enormously, a disturbing parody of a Larvosis stage: tiers of audience seats descended with stairs in between, a platform rose in the center of the floor, and two bridges connected it to the walls.

The wind fell silent, as if it had never existed. The trail ended where the trees had stopped growing and the forest opened into a great empty space with a carpet of grass and something alien in its center.

Two figures stood on the stage, and Falb recognized them both: his brother Timeon and the oneiromancer.

"Timeon!" Falb took several stairs with each step between the tiered audience seating but slowed down when Timeon didn't react.

"Falb ..." Timeon didn't look away from the panorama of painted trees that formed the backdrop of the stage, whispering the name to himself and not as an answer.

The oneiromancer studied Timeon: "There is only one boarding team left on the Phobosteus. We have to retreat."

"We stay."

"This is not a decision you can make."

"Am I not the commander of this cruiser? Am I not in charge?"

The oneiromancer said nothing, his face betraying no emotion.

"Maybe it holds risk, but every person aboard is aware of the dangers of their job. Falb isn't alone inside the Phobosteus. If we save him, we may gain valuable information, even a specimen. It could be the breakthrough we are all waiting for."

It was a dialog that could happen, that had to be happening right now: but whoever stood there on the stage, it wasn't Timeon, only an actor or a robot inside a skin. In a Larvosis play, you never knew who played what role until the end, who was the seer and who the companion, who the creature and who the darkness. This uncertainty interrupted the strictly formalized sequence of acts, but it had no place in reality. In reality, you always knew who you were.

"It isn't even that, is it? Not one life against hundreds ... not Falb as the counterweight to the crew of this cruiser. It is his death, or his death and the death of everyone else. We can't save him anymore."

The oneiromancer nodded, and Falb continued his movement down the stairs, his weapon raised. He reached ground level when he sensed movement behind him, turned, and froze.

"We do not lie to you." The Apparition stilted between the audience seats toward Falb, its body indiscernible under alien armor. "What you see is real, has really happened."

A faceless and eyeless head mask stared at Falb, and coldness steamed from its exhaust slits. Long, segmented spider fingers dissected the air, sharp as razors, then the creature continued to speak:

"All life is suffering." Its voice was evocative of clinking ice cubes, temperature less, but impregnated with a sophisticated horror, as if floating in spilled blood. "All suffering is learning. How much have you suffered? How much have you learned?"

Falb stood before the tree of visions and saw its fruits. Darkened glass bloomed from the branches, globes that held only one image: a reflection of Falb oscillating on their curved surface.

Falb tried to order his thoughts, to arrange his emotions into a shimmering armory again. His weapons had vanished, thawed away without a trace. The trees of the forest backdrop loomed on all the walls though they had only decorated the stage before.

"A nightmare is a dream from which you cannot wake. You suffer and suffer, but there is no way out." Thin vapor from the exhaust slits drifted over the Apparition, shrouding it with ice crystals that briefly flourished. "Do you believe that?"

Scalpel fingers scraped against each other in the air as the creature approached, folding its hands like a bag of surgical instruments. "Do you believe there is no way out of the nightmare?"

Falb glanced over his shoulder to see two motionless puppets with shrunken, half skeletonized faces.

He looked back at the Apparition, which continued its speech: "Do you believe the forest is without end, and that the darkness stretches further than you could ever run?" The Apparition came to a standstill before Falb and turned its polished head, so that Falb could see his own reflection gliding across it.

He aimed his rifle: "Come with me. If I must, I'll shoot you." The gun in his hands felt useless, but he pointed it at the abomination.

The tree bent its branches, and the mirror-fruits chimed like bells, clear and hollow. Falb's image in them radiated, his spine and ribcage visible through paper-thin skin, his heart beating a million times a minute.

"Again, and again you make the same decisions. Again, and again you lose yourself without learning, without having changed anything. You cannot fight us. You do not see the world as it truly is."

The Apparition's torso opened like a blossoming flower of blades, with cold petals that seemed to cut air molecules themselves. "Do you know what you are doing here?"

"I'm taking you prisoner." Falb couldn't recognize his own voice anymore.

"Tell me, Falb: What do you believe in?"

"I believe in my brother Timeon."

"You are lying. If you believed in your brother, you would have come here with his consent. What do you believe in?"

"I believe in myself." Falb tried to pull the Apparition's suggestions out at their root, to keep himself clean and orderly, a smooth plane without impurities.

"If you believed in yourself, you wouldn't need such control. Why restrain and subdue yourself? We are telling you this: True intelligence doesn't believe in anything."

"Is this a riddle? What do you want?"

The forest vanished into stylized lines and dried paint, receded into two dimensions onto the stage walls. The eyes of the fish and the birds became one with the tree's fruits, the grass withered away like the hair on Falb's body. Everything fell silent.

"You have come here of your own free will. We did not force you, but still you keep coming. You want to know if you are the seer or the darkness. You can sense the stain deep inside you, a thing that needs to perfect itself, and you seek an answer. If you are patient, we will give you this answer: We will show you what you are in the dark."

###

About Dennis Mombauer

DENNIS MOMBAUER CURRENTLY LIVES in Colombo as a freelance researcher and writer of speculative fiction, textual experiments, and poetry. His research is focused on ecosystem-based urban adaptation and sustainable urban development as well as other topics related to climate change. He is co-publisher of a German magazine for experimental fiction, *Die Novelle – Magazine for Experimentalism*, and has published fiction and non-fiction in various magazines and anthologies. His first English language novel, *The Fertile Clay*, will be published by Nightscape Press in late 2019.

Connect with Dennis here:
www.castrumpress.com/authors/dennis-mombauer

ALIEN DAYS

THE LAW OF THE JUNGLE
By Mickey Ferron

Now this is the Law of the Jungle -- as old and as true as the sky; And the Wolf that shall keep it may prosper, but the Wolf that shall break it must die. As the creeper that girdles the tree-trunk the Law runneth forward and back -- For the strength of the Pack is the Wolf, and the strength of the Wolf is the Pack.

RUDYARD KIPLING

As the sun set on the vast Alaskan forest, a piercing sharp fracture sound, shattered the prevailing silence. As the sound echoed around the emptiness, a singular dot of nothingness appeared, so small as to be indistinguishable from the surrounding darkness. The dot measured one micron in diameter. To cover the point of a hypodermic needle would take one thousand microns. It is difficult to explain in scientific terms the technology needed to create this dot when that knowledge is so far beyond us. For this one-micron diameter dot had penetrated our planet's space/time fabric, the way a mosquito finds a way between the stratified layers of the epidermis making up our skin. Like a mosquito, micro-mechanoreceptors probed, searching for areas of least resistance, pushing and prodding through layers of invisible strata. Until, eventually, they found an infinitesimal point, where the Earth's space-time fabric was thinnest and simply punctured a hole through it.

At the instance of origin, the hole appeared one meter above the forest floor holding its position while gradually expanding. In under a minute, the hole increased in size a thousand-fold to a millimeter, continuing to expand exponentially. At two minutes, the hole had had grown a million-fold to a meter. Upon reaching a perfect circular diameter of two meters it halted its expansion. Raw energy hummed around the peripheral edges of the aperture. Electrical discharges of bright yellow light arced from edge to edge in kaleidoscopic patterns.

A Creature emerged through the aperture. Traveling from its own planet to enter ours. Passing between thresholds, crossing into our universe. Existing for a nanosecond in two different realities across space and time. The opening to another world closed behind it. Simply ceasing to be, leaving the Creature behind, to deliver a response to Earth's Invitation.

November 16, 1974, the Arecibo Radio Telescope in Puerto Rico. Scientists broadcast a three-minute-long interstellar radio message; the aim of the message was for it to be received and deciphered by extra-terrestrial intelligence. In simple ones and zeros, these 1,679 binary digits informed alien life precisely where in the universe to find humanity and what we look like. The message contained details of the chemical elements of humanity's genetic building blocks, along with Earth's environmental and population demographics.

The message was carried by the radio waves travelling at the speed of light aimed into the center of the Milky Way Galaxy. With space being so unimaginably vast, the scientists did not expect the message to reach the center of the galaxy for twenty-five thousand years. Given that a reply by the same means would take another twenty-five thousand years it was safe to say the scientists at the Search for Extra-terrestrial Intelligence (SETI) Institute did not expect to receive a response anytime soon. They were wrong. Very wrong.

The naivety of these so-called space experts in sending such a message is astounding. Credulous in both its intention to randomly provide an unknown alien lifeform with important information on our existence. More importantly, they expected these intelligent, extra-terrestrial beings to be benevolent toward us. To welcome us warmly, with open arms. Not once stopping to think that our own history teaches important lessons in what happens when different civilizations meet. Ask the Carthaginians or the Babylonians; ask the Egyptians or the Assyrians. Ask the last South American tribes, sheltering in their shrinking rainforests, or the indigenous people of North America who once roamed the plains alone for twelve thousand years before the arrival of the white man changed their way of life forever. Our History tells us repeatedly and emphatically, when an established civilization meets a more advanced civilization, the lesser civilization ceases to exist.

Travelling at three hundred thousand kilometers per second, the Arecibo radio message reached the edge of our solar system in May 1975, passed Alpha Centauri in March 1978 and Ross 128-b in October of 1985. June 1988 saw the message race past Wolf 1061-d in June 1988 and Gliese 832-c in 1990, the broadcast travelled through the Eridian Stars in 1994, and beyond 61 Virginis-b in July 2002. Still undetected and unheard.

The unrequited Arecibo broadcast endured its journey for another seventeen years. In 2019, within the Aquarius Constellation the message reached a planetary system orbiting an orange dwarf star humanity designated Trappist-1. Similar to our own solar system, gravity arranged the Trappist planets in different orbital positions from their star. One planet, Trappist-1e, meets the Goldilocks principle criteria and by coincidence, is approximately the same size as our own planet. Like Earth, Trappist-1e has a compact atmosphere with a comparable mass, along with a parallel density, temperatures and gravity. The planet surface is covered in areas of liquid, very similar to water on Earth. Trappist-1e looks like Earth: it could be Earth, except being thirty-nine light-years away, rotating around a different, dying star. Here, at last, the Arecibo message was intercepted and deciphered, by a world 369 trillion kilometers away from Earth. However, as the broadcast continued its mission, ever deeper into space, the inhabitants of Trappist-1e, did not send a reciprocal radio message to Earth. Instead, they sent the Creature who now stood alone, in the dark Alaskan wilderness.

Two meters tall and mainly cylindrical in shape. With overlapping membranes at its base, the Creature used a form of undulatory locomotion, similar to Earth's snake species, to move silently across the forest floor. The Creature did not possess the equivalent of a mouth, having no need to breathe, nor ingest liquids or solids for fuel. The Creature's civilization long ago adapted to harness the power of its dwarf sun, converting solar energy through an advanced process of photosynthesis. They did not converse in an audible language, having evolved telepathy, allowing instant communication between groups and individuals. Its body was a robust design, evolved and adapted to the gravitational forces existing on its home world. Apart from a circular array of sensors, at the top of its body, hefty, thick overlapping scales protected its exterior. While the Creature did not have legs, it did possess what a human would have interpreted as arms, although tentacles would be a closer comparison. Around its tubular shaped body, seven tentacles were positioned equidistantly, nine centimeters thick and over three meters in length. Each tentacle ended with a broad flat pad, similar to the shape of a human hand; and across the inner surface of each pad, thousands of tiny sensitive filaments, which filtered the surrounding environment, doing the job of a human's senses.

The seven tentacles wrapped around the Creatures torso, in a downward ivy-like formation and slowly unfurled, with synchronized elegance the Creature began carrying out the tasks it had been sent to Earth to accomplish. Cataloguing all types of life inside a fifty-meter radius of the emergence point. The Creature detected small fauna inside the flora, insects and various small mammals, but no organism matching the biped mammal, calling itself human.

The Arecibo message stated the average height of a human to be 1.753 meters, with a genetic make-up of principally Hydrogen, Carbon, Nitrogen, Oxygen and Phosphorus. The message confirmed the genetic structure of all Earth life, structured via a double helix ladder, the same as life on the Creature's home planet. The demographic information contained within the Arecibo message had been used to select the location for the Creature's arrival on Earth. The absence of heat signatures meant an absence of technology, which in turn meant an absence of human activity. It appeared that there was no human activity within one hundred kilometers.

The Creature continued its scan of the surrounding vegetation, assessing the different types of trees, bushes, plants and grasses. Fundamentally, silicone based, the Creature shared more similarities to plants on Earth than the carbon-based fauna, which made up seventy-five percent of Earth's life. The ambient temperature confirming this area of the planet habitable.. Delicate sensor filaments across the Creature's pads measured the chemical components of Earth's atmosphere. Nitrogen at seventy-eight percent proved uncomfortable but bearable. The twenty-one percent Oxygen level would be a greater problem. While not needing to breathe in any environmental gases to exist, the corrosive proprieties of such a high level of oxygen would become difficult to endure. Scheduled to remain in place for 2.42 Earth hours, the Creature calculated that its exterior should be able to withstand Earth's atmosphere for the required amount of time to complete its mission.

The Creature concluded its atmospheric evaluation: Argon at 0.93 percent, Carbon Dioxide at 0.04 percent with trace elements of helium, hydrogen, methane, neon and krypton. Though not ideal, Earth's atmosphere would not hinder The Plan.

If the Creature found Earth suitable then upon its return home then preparations would begin to mount an offensive to eliminate Earth's human population. A minimum populace would be retained, to perform various terraforming activities, reducing excessive nitrogen and oxygen gases from the atmosphere. Subjugation of the human race would be swift. Completed in three Earth days.

The Plan called for portals to pierce the space/time fabric between Home and Earth in thousands of remote areas, around the entirety of the planet. Through these portals vast armies would invade and wipe out all resistance simultaneously. Humanity would have no hiding place; eradication and near extinction would occur concurrently across the planet.

The Creature felt no animosity toward the human inhabitants of Earth. Emotions such as animosity, along with every other emotion, long ceased to exist amongst the inhabitants of Home. The decision to remove humankind from this planet, being purely requisite and logistical. Earth possessed a similar planetary environment to Home and the inhabitants of that world, needed to expand to survive as a civilization.

They had sent their own probes into the darkness of deep space, searching in vain for habitable planets. Four of its moons ago, the Arecibo message had reached Home, providing a possible solution to their obstacle of expansion and survival. A new world. A new planet. A new beginning. Earth.

The Creature was passing fifty-two percent of mission time duration busily mapping the positions of the constellations in the sky above when its senses identified multiple lifeforms approaching from the polar north. Through a series of pulse snapshots the Creature monitored the lifeforms progress, sensors concluded the trajectory of their advancement. The lifeforms were on a direct path to its current position, reaching its location in 0.19 Earth hours. Unperturbed; the Creature carried on with the scheduled evaluation of Earth's position and surrounding solar system.

At the top of the Creature's body the skin separated revealing a dome shaped quivering muscle. This muscle was embedded with millions of pixel-like receptors providing 360-degree vision. The Creature's version of vision operated by interpreting objects, using various light wave frequencies, each adapting to individual environments. As the lifeforms drew closer, the Creature finessed sensors to an infrared wavelength, enhancing the poor light conditions with the ability to detect heat signatures. A check of its internal chronometer showed 1.18 Earth hours until the portal opened again. Estimated contact with the approaching lifeforms in 0.16 Earth hours. In the silent darkness of the Alaskan timberland it resumed gathering data on the surrounding environment.

✳✳✳

M12 sat cocking its head to one side as it used a hind leg to scratch at the GPS collar around his neck. Details of his progress and locations was transmitted hourly to a monitoring satellite. Downloaded remotely, the information was used to map his range and his whereabouts, at different periods throughout the Alaskan seasons.

M12 had been shot with a Telazol dart from a helicopter last year and collared as part of the Wildlife and Fisheries program to monitor the Alaskan wolf population. It had been many years since such an initiative had been undertaken due to the remoteness and inaccessibility of the area. However, during the previous decade, the success of the Yellowstone program to reintroduce Canadian Timberwolves back into the national parks, ignited America's and indeed, the world's imagination. Yellowstone wolves became canine celebrities through award winning documentaries, so, people wanted to know more about wolves. No other wolf remained more unknown and more mysterious than the Northwest McKenzie Wolf.

M12 had become a minor celebrity himself amongst the Wildlife and Fisheries program due to him being only the twelfth McKenzie Wolf, collared in the McCarthy region of the Wrangell St. Elias National Park. If M12's signal maintained the same position for two days or stopped transmitting altogether, the Wildlife and Fisheries Department, would use the last transmission to scour the Alaskan woodlands for him to find the cause. M12 belonged to the McCarthy pack, which lived in a valley, straddling high mountains, between the American and Canadian borders. Sharing a protected wilderness, stretching over thirty million square miles covering an area bigger than Scotland making it North America's biggest and most isolated National Park.

Evolution had hardwired synchronized sleeping roles into wolves with alternate pack members sleeping at different stages throughout the night, ensuring the safety of the pack from a surprise assault. The McCarthy Alpha male and female did not sleep in stages, one of the many privileges of being leaders. Instead, they slumbered, back to back, contently in the middle of the den, bellies full of the two caribou they had brought down that day. M12 sat guardian like on the pack's periphery. Eyes focused, ears swiveled one way and then another, sweeping the Alaskan night for sounds, his nose filtered the evening breeze for anything not his pack, not his valley, not his forest.

M12 froze as still as a statue as he detected something not forest to the southeast of the den. The first indication was an audible sharp crack, similar to the sound glacial ice makes when an inner flaw fails, resulting in a loud, and ripping facture sound. Measured in time, the millisecond long splinter soundwave, condensed into a short high frequency, well above the audible reach of humans. But not M12's two million years of evolution hunter's hearing.

Stretching his neck high, M12 let out an intense howl rousing the entire McCarthy pack from sleep. In seconds, all were barking and growling at some unidentified and unseen presence that dared enter their forest. Something unknown invading their homeland. The territory controlled by the pack provided them with a plentiful food supply throughout the seasons making it a prime real estate. Other wolf packs constantly probed and raided and each and every incursion was met with the full ferocity of the entire pack. This valley, their territory and their existence depended upon maintaining their dominance. With the two Alphas in front, the McCarthy pack set off to investigate the source of the intrusion.

Travelling at a steady trot of five miles an hour, switching back and forth across well-worn deer trails in the direction, of what their canine perception understood as a disturbance of their forest. It did not take long before the breeze brought them a strange, never encountered before scent. The unfamiliar spoor provided a clear direction of the disturbance and the pack increased their pace to reach it.

M12 brought up the rear, accompanied by two sisters, who would soon be leaving the McCarthy pack with him. When the light time returned, M12 and his sisters would move to the edge of the valley and form their own pack. Both strong dogs, one a dappled mixture of grey and white, the other, a uniform shimmering silver from head to tail. M12 himself was a mirror image of his brother, the Alpha male. Three-years-old, thick fur the color of the darkest night, weighing over a hundred thirty pounds. The only difference between M12 and his brother was a small patch of white on M12's forehead, earning him the nickname of 'Black Beauty' among the Wildlife and

Fisheries rangers. The remainder of the McCarthy pack were a motley mixture and patchwork of thick fur, in hues of every variation and shade, of grey, silver, black and white. Numbering forty-two, they seamlessly coordinated together as one company, one pack. Each individual being born with an instinctive, inherent cognizance, understanding survival depended upon functioning together, as one.

Rudyard Kipling's poem 'law of the jungle' encapsulates it probably the best. 'The strength of the pack is the wolf, and the strength of the wolf is the pack'

The pack reached a clearing, and without pause, began spreading themselves around the periphery, forming a loose circle around some unknown Thing. As one, they began closing the circle, preventing any escape, taking their lead from the two Alphas. Each standing tall, stiff legged, their ears erect and pointed forward. Lips drawn back with incisors exposed, their fur standing erect on their backs and their tails horizontal to the ground.

***

If the Creature perceived a threat from the surrounding lifeforms besieging it, its stationary stance gave no outwardly indication. Its 360-degree infrared vision calmly assessed the surrounding forty-two unknown indigenous lifeforms. The Creature factored in each individual's size and mass, based on their body heat signatures. The lifeforms encompassing circle maintained a firm distance of ten meters. Sensing no immediate danger, the Creature kept gathering information, while waiting for the portal to reopen in 1.02 Earth Hours

***

The wolves understanding of their environment and its inhabitants was simplistic. They lived in the forest, where all animals belonged and all had their place. The packs territory encompassed the valley and surrounding forest. Beyond that existed other packs, with their own territories. There were animals within their territory, and some of those animals could be dangerous to the pack. The wolves did not have a name for the Grizzly Bears who roamed through the forest at will however, they associated a bear with wolf known facts. Being big and powerful, stronger than many wolves. Having ferocious teeth and claws and a specific scent. A scent which triggered a survival warning mechanism inside each wolf's brain. When the pack encountered a bear, their strategy evolved to avoid the large brown animal with vicious teeth and claws. If necessary, they could attack and kill it, but they would lose many brothers and sisters.

The Thing standing in front of them now however, stretched so far beyond their understanding of their environment it forced them into a rare behavioral reflex. Fight or flight.

Throughout the wolves' evolutionary journey, neophobia has been a tried and tested survival approach. When encountering new things, neophobia, generates an extreme, irrational fear or dislike of anything new or unfamiliar. The normal neophobic behavior would be to detach themselves from this unknown Thing. Observe it from afar to gauge the threat level it posed to the pack. The intruder might be as deadly as the bear or might be benign and harmless. However, on some lower, primeval level, the wolves' sensed this Thing standing in their forest to be an abomination to nature; not belonging to their forest environment. On a deep subliminal level, they sensed this Thing a threat to their way of life and their very survival. Fear set off a hormonal chain reaction, electrical synapses bridging neurons and chemical receptors, inactive for many millennia in wolf history.

Closer to the Thing, the wolves fully registered the smell, a strong stench, similar to rotten vegetation. The foreign aroma triggered neurotransmitters, generating huge quantities of Oxytocin and Vasopressin chemicals. Pituitary Glands, deep in the base of the wolves' brains, adrenocorticotropic and corticosteroid hormones flooded across cranial receptors and coursed through their bodies. In short, the presence of the Thing set off an electrical storm inside each wolf brain, sending a surge of aggressive steroids across mind and body. The neophobic strategy of the wolves' normal behavior was overridden. Evolution chose fight over flight. A fight to the death.

The male and female Alphas approached gradually, from opposite sides of the encompassing circle. Halting periodically to ascertain if there was any reaction from the Thing. Bodies low to the ground. Back legs compacted, each loaded with compressed energy, ready to release, ready to pounce. Edging forward, paw by paw.

***

The Creature remained motionless, providing no acknowledgement of the encircling presence, noting the two lifeforms at a range of four meters, with another forty, ten meters beyond.

***

As one, the pack growled at the strange Thing in front of them, having no shape resembling any animal living in their forest. Betraying no behavior signaling either aggression or submissiveness to the wolves. The Thing stood silently in the gloom, absent of visible defenses or obvious areas of weakness. However, the Thing's scent sharply penetrated their olfactory receptors, registering a mixture of rage, fear and death. Without warning. At incredible speed. The Alphas launched themselves into the air. Intent on tearing apart the invader.

***

The Creature responded in a blur. Rotating its core ninety-degrees, barbed tentacles flashed out. Needle-sharp spurs, as long and as thick as a man's finger, punched through rib cages. Each spur injecting lethal doses of curare poison, more potent and toxic than any poison dart made by South American tribesmen. In a blur of motion the Creature rotated ninety degrees, two additional barbed tentacles penetrated the wolves' ears entering their skulls, releasing poison into the Alpha's brains. Death was instantaneous.

***

The pack was stunned by violent deaths of the Alphas who now lay still on the forest floor. Instinct pushed them back. Like a ripple from a pebble dropped into a pond, the wolves backtracked a few meters, to safety. Except for M12. The Beta wolf raised his head to the stars and let loose a deafening howl in lament of his brother. One by one the pack joined his chorus of despair the haunting sound reverberating up and down the valley. The pack had a new Alpha.

With the packs anger and remorse still echoing in his ears M12 began slowly trotting in a wide circle around the Thing. His keen eyesight searching out a weak spot. Any difference Any indication of a head or a flank that could provide a target for attack. He found none. Upon returning to his original position, the pack looked to M12 for direction. Baring his incisors he began to inch forward. Following his lead all forty wolves began closing in on the Thing. After a few steps, M12 stopped and reevaluated the situation; the pack mirroring him. Advancing the length of a wolf M12 paused once more. The Thing remained motionless in the center of the circling wolves. M12 and the pack cautiously advanced again, reducing the space between them and the Thing by another wolf length.

***

The Creature evaluated the decreasing gap between it and the surrounding forty lifeforms, measuring each individual distance with precision. Gauging that distance against the reach of its own tentacles still hanging loosely by its sides. The lifeforms remained beyond its effective reach. 0.92 Earth hours until the portal reopened.

***

M12 and the pack had now closed to within what he now judged to be a gap of four wolves from the Thing. To his left stood his grey and white sister. On his right, the silver sister, the lifeless bodies of the two dead Alphas lay in front of them. This close to the Thing, the reek of rotting vegetation, intensified the release of aggressive steroids, inducing a feral rage M12 could barely contain. Tail straight out, horizontal to the ground behind him. Fur along his back erect, incisors bared, he steeled himself for the onslaught. But before he could launch himself at the Thing, the grey and white sister leapt into the air, only to be struck down dead by a tentacle spur tearing through her throat. This close to the Thing, the wolves' aggressive rage overrode any lingering survival impulses; only the law of the jungle endured. 'The strength of the pack is the wolf, and the strength of the wolf is the pack'. While the grey and white sister, lay bleeding out, on the ground, the pack leapt to the attack.

***

The Creature met the onslaught with deadly precision, more than matching the ferocity of the lifeforms. With incredibly efficiency, the barbed spurs struck, dispensing lethal poison, killing wolf after wolf. All the while the wolf's teeth and claws ripped and slashed at the Creature.

***

As a tentacle spur killed the pack mate in front of M12, he seized the opportunity to clamp his teeth tightly around the tentacle. The McKenzie Wolf's jaws are the most powerful of all wolves, forty-two teeth, with massive molars capable of crushing moose femur bones. Exerting 1,500 pounds of bite pressure, M12 tore the barbed pad of the Thing's tentacle before retreating to a safe distance of four wolves.

***

If the Creature felt pain, it did not exhibit any indication which might alert the lifeforms to the damage sustained from the concentrated assault. Twelve additional dead lifeforms had joined the original Alphas scattered across the forest floor but the Creature had lost a tentacle pad to them. The lifeforms razor sharp teeth had repeatedly torn deep into its thick scale-like skin. The open cuts now exposed to the caustic oxygen of Earth's atmosphere which ate into the raw lacerations and the soft flesh below. Running diagnostics on the overall extent of injuries, the Creature channeled a treacly sap to congeal and protect the wounds. Thirty lifeforms remained as the Creature analyzed amending its current defensive strategy to one of offense. Concluding for the moment that defense remained the most appropriate. 0.79 Earth hours until the portal opened.

***

The condensed vapor from the surrounding wolves' heavy breathing in the cool Alaskan air shrouded the Thing in a cloud of mist. M12's heartbeat slowed as he focused completely on the Thing, trying to gauge any sign or indication their foe might be hurt. His hunter's experience told him that it could be a good tactical decision to withdraw from a dangerous prey. If the quarry were sufficiently wounded, the injuries inflicted, would take their toll, weakening the prey and lessening the danger to the pack. However, the Thing in front of M12 showed no signs of impairment, with the exception of the missing paw, M12 tore off. He might have waited longer. Continued to assess the condition of the Thing, but he could sense the anger flooding through the pack. They wanted this Thing dead, and they wanted it dead quickly. As new Alpha, his role became recognizing the needs of the pack and acting upon them.

'The strength of the pack is the wolf, and the strength of the wolf is the pack'.

With an ear-piercing howl he flung himself and the pack once more into the fray.

***

As the lifeforms retreated, the Creature counted twenty-two dead on the ground while the remaining twenty encircled it, at a distance of four meters, averaging seventeen degrees apart. The last assault was as ferocious in its intensity as it had been its savagery. The Creature was unable to rationalize the aggressiveness of the repeated suicidal strikes. Any sane lifeform should have withdrawn after sustaining such horrific losses. The Creature ran diagnostics on its own fresh injuries and channeled additional sap to aid protection from the corrosive atmosphere. Once more, it reviewed the options available to it. Defense or offense. Both were dismissed considering the extent of the injuries it had sustained from the lifeforms. Only one option was now available. Survival. 0.54 Earth hours until the portal opened.

***

M12's eyes regarded the ground before him. Another ten of his brothers and sisters lay dead amongst the blood-spattered leaves and brush that made up the clearing. A decision needed to be made. Twenty wolves strong, the pack remained a formidable force. Strong enough to fend off any incursions by neighboring packs. M12 could acknowledge their losses against a remarkable adversary and retreat. Should M12 decide to withdraw, the pack would follow him back to the valley, and life for the McCarthy wolves would endure. However, if he persisted, even killing the Thing in the next offensive wave, based on its defenses so far, there would undoubtedly be additional losses. The consequences of further depleting the packs numbers would mean the McCarthy wolves would lose their valley. They would become a rouge pack, having to travel with stealth through other wolf territories, always wary and fearful of contact from aggressive enemy packs. Warily new Alpha made another circuit of the clearing, methodically gauging the damage inflicted upon the Thing standing motionless at its center.

During the last assault, they had bit off another two deadly paws, leaving four, just as lethal. Completing his circuit of the Thing, he now understood with a certainty, this strange Thing did not belong inside the forest, or the world of the wolf. Listening to his wolf brain, he slipped into a space beside the silver colored sister. M12's honed senses told him that victory was within his grasp. 'The strength of the pack is the wolf, and the strength of the wolf is the pack'. M12 lunged forward a baying howl, filling the forest. The McCarthy pack charged again.

***

The Creature counted thirty-nine dead. The three, still standing, lifeforms spaced themselves evenly around it, a bare four meters away. The last attack had developed into a desperate and fraught struggle. The lifeforms were weakened and slowed by their previous assaults, but for each one the Creature struck down, another two managed to breach its defenses. Biting and clawing. Incisors gnawing, digging deep through the protective scales. Tearing mouthfuls of sensitive inner layers from its body. Ripping and renting fresh wounds open, exposing them to the unforgiving oxygen. As the assault endured, the Creature's multiple scenario analysis concluded that it had the upper hand and the death of the attacking lifeforms was only a matter of time. Without warning, the lifeforms broke from the fray, retreating to safety.

If the Creature possessed emotions, they might have registered disappointment with victory so close. Dispassionately it noted its worsening health status, confirmed by the severity of multiple bites and lesions, resulting in a life-threatening situation. The damage had reached such an extent that it prevented the application of protective sap to the new lacerations, letting oxygen etch, even deeper into open wounds. The relentless forays had torn off six tentacle pads, severely limiting its defenses. Unremitting visceral assaults ripped and shredded numerous areas of the 360-degree visual array, leaving numerous zones completely blind. The Creature rotated ten degrees to compensate as best it could. 0.38 Earth hours until the portal opened.

***

M12 strained to regulate his breathing back to normal. The last wave formed a different pattern than previous tactics. Darting forward. Inflicting damage before retreating rapidly to avoid retaliation. Push forward again, bite, and retreat. However, the packs rising sense of desperation, escalated and changed the organized foray to a rabid chaotic melee. A kill or be killed; fight to the death. Amid the blood and carnage, something within M12's intrinsic leadership quality, something within the madness of the protracted conflict, screamed at him! Withdraw and evaluate the condition of the remainder of the pack. Only at his direction, did the remaining wolves relent.

By one shoulder, an old grey stood Elderly, but strong and experienced. On his other, stood the silver sister, who time after time, proved herself worthy of the female Alpha position. Realization of the lethal impact, the Thing had dispensed to his pack, stirred an additional aggressive boost as M12 dug deep inside himself. Maximizing his anger and hostility. He would need all available rage for the imminent, final assault. For when finished, only the wolves or the Thing would remain in the forest, nothing else. Focused, he began to trot around the perimeter, wary of the deadly reach of the Thing's paws. Searching for weakness, target areas, anywhere the Thing might be vulnerable. The silver sister fell in behind him, followed by the old grey. Together they circled the Thing, looking for flaws or faults in the Thing's defenses.

***

The Creature watched the three lifeforms circling. After a few circuits, the black lifeform accelerated, pulling away from the other two. The silver lifeform allowed a gap to open between itself and the black lifeform before it too increased its pace. Once a third gap had been established the grey lifeform matched the other two lifeforms pace. All three now raced around the clearing. Visually following the lifeforms proved problematic for the Creature due to the visual sensory damage it had suffered during the numerous assaults. Monitoring each of their individual paths became impossible. Away from the Creature's last remaining tentacle pad, the lifeforms reduced the boundary from four meters to three meters, then back to four meters. The Creature recognized the systematic testing for visual gaps, an urgent problem needing correction if it was to survive long enough to get back home.

Starting at a subdued ultra-frequency, the Creature began pulsing multiband soundwaves, ricocheting of the encompassing trees, registering stationary solid objects. This basic form of echolocation had limited effectiveness, but provided the Creature with a form of binary information, filling the voids in the damaged visual

THE DAYS ANTHOLOGY, BOOK 2

sensory system. Between the gaps, the lifeforms were there or they were not. If there, the sonar pinged into their soft body, registering its presence. When not there, the sonar pinged on solid trees. Satisfied it had secured a potential failing in defenses, the Creature continued to monitor the progress of the three lifeforms. In an effort to improve the quality of echolocation transmission, it incrementally increased the ultrasonic frequency range. At the sixty-seven-megahertz level, the quality of echolocation, marginally improved, so the Creature increased the range of ultrasonic frequency, toward seventy-megahertz. 0.25 Earth hours until the portal opened.

***

As the wolves circled, probing for vulnerability, M12 sensed the Thing might be waiting on something. Something about this specific spot must be important. Throughout the protracted fight, the Thing remained fixed exactly where the pack had first encountered it. Even when the wolves had been their most ferocious, the Thing did not move into the safety of the forest, which would have made contact more difficult for the wolves, because of the trees. Using the protection of the forest, the wolves could only have reached through narrow openings, limiting their effectiveness. This puzzled M12; what is so special about this exact spot? What made this strange Thing refuse the protection of the forest?

As they persistently probed the safety limits, they discovered areas absent of a response, if a wolf drifted in a little closer. Areas, where the Thing did not even raise a limb in preparation to repel an attack. This was new. In the continuing long drawn battle with this strange Thing, where nothing changed, new was good. Could the Thing be weaker in these areas?

Even without the poison paws, the Thing's limbs and reflexes proved enormously effective, thrashing wolves unconscious to the ground, with preciseness throughout the fight. M12 prepared to launch himself into an identified weak area, when the Thing started screaming. At first, the scream stayed level, loud as the cry of a wounded coyote. After a moment however, the screams increased in pitch and volume. M12 felt the screams batter at his ears. Quickly the screaming sounds went from mildly annoying, to irritating to unbearable pain. For the first time since the fight began, the screams forced the wolves to retreat beyond the four-wolf distance they had maintained.. However, increased distance, only provided M12 and his surviving pack mates meagre respite from the pain inflicted by the intensifying screams of the Thing.

***

The Creature went through the ultrasonic frequencies, observing that once beyond the sixty-seven-megahertz range, the lifeforms ceased their circling. Using the last of its limited energy, the Creature increased the frequency. In response, the lifeforms not only ceased their predatory intentions but withdrew, increasing the distance between them.

***

Beyond the Thing, originated a loud fracturing sound. The same noise which initially alerted M12 causing him to wake the pack from their sleep and had led them here to this bloody battle site. M12 focused through the excruciating pain, seeing nothing behind the Thing except darkness. He sensed that whatever was the source of the sound, it and the Thing were connected. M12 forced his brain to work through the pain which threatened to push him into unconsciousness. Could this sound be the reason why the Thing chose to in the openness and not seek the protection of the trees? The rules of the fight had shifted. Something happened; something changed to the Thing's advantage. M12's perception on the change of events grew, as the Thing, with subtle slowness, began to move toward the growing black dot of darkness.

***

The portal began to open. The Creature calculated 0.13 Earth hours until the opening was large enough to allow it to pass through. In six Earth minutes, it could return home, leaving Earth and these aggressive lifeforms behind.

***

Incensed the Thing which had killed so many of his brothers and sisters might somehow live; the Alpha howled a rallying cry into the Alaskan night sky. M12 would die before he let the Thing escape. Frustration provided the spark which ignited and drove intense anger. M12 ignored the increasingly painful screams of the Thing. The pain now fueling his rage and fury. M12 howled again, signaling engagement. Deep in his wolf brain, he knew the Thing must not live. Howling one last time, calling on the law of the jungle to aid him one last time.

"The strength of the pack is the wolf, and the strength of the wolf is the pack."

***

As the Creature moved toward the portal, two separate events registered on the remains of the sensory array. Firstly, the absence of all three lifeforms from its remaining visual sensors. Second, all three lifeforms hurtled directly toward echolocation pulse points. The Creature ignored them as it concentrated on reaching the portal and home.

***

Pain converting to wrath, M12 directed every residual ounce of energy to his rage and tore into the Thing. Dodging tentacles, which previously would have slammed him to the ground, M12 tore into what he perceived to be a head. His teeth ripping into already open wounds. The Things screaming stopped, the excruciating pain disappearing like the sun burning the early morning mist from the valley floor. Reinvigorated, M12 felt the full force of his bloodlust course through his veins as he continued savaging the Thing, tearing ever deeper into the wounds his teeth and claws had already inflicted. He would not stop mauling this Thing, not until it lay lifeless on the forest floor.

THE DAYS ANTHOLOGY, BOOK 2

Sensing victory, M12 ripped ever deeper into the Thing, as tentacles pounded him relentlessly, blow after blow.

***

Exhausted from the prolonged fight and with its reflex responses diminished to almost non-existence. The Creature struggled on with depleted energy and its last remaining tentacle spur. In a final, desperate attempt to secure victory it prepared a three echolocation pulse targeted at its attackers in a synchronized strike. Too late. All three lifeforms reached it at once, inflicting critical damage to the pulse projectors.

The combined weight of the three lifeforms was simply too much and the Creature shuddered to a halt within reach of the ever-enlarging portal.

Using the last vestiges of its strength the Creature swung its tentacle to bring it crashing down on the grey lifeform cracking its skull open with a sickening crunch. The silver lifeform managed to avoid the full force of the swinging tentacle however, the glancing blow it received dropped it to the forest floor unconsciousness. If the Creatures external auditory sensors had still been functional it would have registered the black lifeforms howl of despair as it saw its brother and sister struck down. Able to fully concentrate on a single target the Creature wasted no time in pummeling its last remaining attacker unconscious.

As the black lifeform lay on the ground, the Creature rammed the spur home piercing the body through and through. At last, the battle with these aggressive lifeforms was over. The Creature dragged itself wearily toward the portal and survival. It attempted to retract the tentacle from the impaled life form only to encounter resistance removing the spur. A second attempt also resulted in failure as fatigue and whatever resistive pressure, on the spur, continued to prevented retrieval of its last armed tentacle. With increasing difficulty the Creature dragged itself forwards, the black lifeform, still impaled on its tentacle spur, trailing heavily along the ground.

Passing the unconscious silver lifeform the Creature wrapped two tentacles around its still body. Logic dictated that Home would need to assess the threat to any pending invasion posed by these lifeforms which had proven so difficult to overcome. The assessment on the biped beings, detailed on the signal received, omitted information on belligerent, indigenous lifeforms, as dangerous as these. Home would need to reevaluate their understanding of Planet Earth.

If the biped lifeforms, who sent the radio message, were the dominant specifies on this planet; where in the hierarchy of Earth, did these lifeforms, which so nearly killed the Creature, exist? Where there more dangerous lifeforms, than those just encountered and fought? The Creature pondered this question, swaying and struggling to stay erect, as painfully slow it advanced toward the portal. 0.05 Earth hours, or three Earth minutes, until the portal reached full magnitude.

***

M12 regained consciousness. The Thing's paw penetrated the GPS tracking collar, puncturing through the leather exterior and wedged into a metal strip, sandwiched between the leather. The stainless-steel metal strip was designed to protect M12 from the multitude of snares which trappers placed in the remote wilderness. Now, the foresight of the Wildlife and Fisheries Rangers, had saved the young Alphas life from a more extraterrestrial threat as the Thing's spur had become wedged on the strip failing to penetrate M12's neck instead the blow had only knocked him senseless for a few moments.

As the Thing trailed him across the forest floor, M12 could see the silver colored sister, dragged along beside him. Coming fully awake, he realized the Thing must be still alive. The fight with this Thing unfinished. M12's stupor receded; replaced with the now familiar aggressive anger. Beyond the Thing, he could make out a shimmering blackness. M12 did not understand what the blackness might be, only that it felt wrong; not forest. With a concentrated effort, he rolled his body into the Thing, providing some relaxation from the pull of the spur. With the tension of the spur relieved, he managed to regain his feet. Summoning the last vestiges of his strength he launched himself into the attack. Teeth clamped down on the restraining limb with the last of his strength, taking three bites, to sever the last paw. Once, twice. Three times finally severing the Things paw. Free, he bolted to the limbs wrapped around the sister attacking them in an all-out frenzy. One by one, M12 bit through them, while the Things limbs flailed weakly and ineffectively upon the thick fur of his back.

The Thing appeared close to death. M12 sensed a final weakness, lacking the strength to bring the Thing to the ground. Instead, he collapsed upon the body of the silver sister and could do nothing more, watching as it slowly advanced upon the wide circle of flickering blackness.

✳✳✳

The Creature left the two lifeforms sprawled exhausted on the ground concentrating whatever meagre energy remained into reaching its. The portal.

Once Home, the Creature would recount the discovery of the belligerent lifeforms encountered on its reconnaissance mission. It would recommend a detached aerial assault on the planet's population, from portals opened in space above the planet. The radio message had portrayed a population of friendly, nonaggressive lifeforms, eager to reach out to other life. The Creature now understood the content of the message to be false; in reality, many lifeforms on the planet Earth were aggressive. A land invasion may encounter similar resistance to its own reconnaissance mission and end in failure.

The Creature was within a centimeter of the portal and completion of its mission. Its two remaining visual sensors showed the two prone lifeforms behind it and the shimmering periphery of the portal ahead of it. Without warning the view of ahead radically changed as the portal disappeared to be replaced with the twinkling stars of the Alaskan night sky.

The Creature had a brief second to attempt to understand what was happening before it ceased thinking forever.

***

The grizzly bear's last meal had been four days ago. It tried to manage hunger through sleep and had succeeded in part until an alien screaming sound had ripped it from its slumber. The empty ache in its belly reminding it of its hunger so it set off to investigate the sound. Perhaps, the four legs had brought down something big. Something big that now screamed in pain. Something to sate his own hunger for he was bigger than the four legs and was willing to fight them for food.

He quickly reached the clearing and the sight before him brought him to an abrupt halt. The crumpled bodies of Four Legs lay everywhere. Confronted by so many dead Four Legs, a deeply ingrained survival instinct nearly made the bear bolt for safety. However, the fear vanished, when the bear focused on the Thing, moving toward a strange twinkling black shape, hanging in the forest air.

The same primeval instinct which had triggered the intense aggressiveness of the wolves, elicited the same belligerence and ferociousness from the bear. The bear charged. Loping over the scattered bodies of dead Four Legs. Reaching the Thing in seconds. With a weight of over 1,500 pounds, the bear hit the Thing with the impact of a wrecking ball. As the Thing tumbled to the forest floor, the bear brought down a massive forepaw with all its might, six-inch razor-sharp claws severing, what the bear assumed to be the Things head. The bear turned its attention to focus on the shimmering black hole. A sound akin to that made by the thousands of tiny winged insects which worked so hard to produce the sweet soft food the bear craved so much assailed his ears beckoning him forward with its rich promise. Rearing up on its hind legs, the bears head towered a full eight feet above the ground, the bear roared defiantly into the all-consuming blackness of the portal. With a backward glance at the two Four Legs lying side by side on the forest floor he stormed into the blackness, slashing left and right with colossal claws leaving Earth forever.

***

M12 watched the big brown animal with teeth and claws, knock the Thing to the forest floor, kill it with one blow from its massive paw. He had registered the fear mingled with hate and anger in the bear's eyes as its victory roar assailed his ears, before the bear rushed into the blackness. After a few seconds, the strange spitting sound ceased, the circle of blackness disappearing. Silence filled the void and the forest became just the forest again.

Tenderly getting to his feet, M12 examined the silver sister, lying still on the forest floor, seeing her chest moving and knowing she was still alive. He began licking around her muzzle, in an attempt to bring her back from unconsciousness. Her eyes flickered open, looking into his own. There gaze met, eyes communicating a meaning beyond their ability to pass vocally. M12 gently nudged his sister as she struggled to her feet.

His sister seen too M12's attention turned to himself. Something sharp was scratching at his neck every time he moved his head. Sitting back on his haunches he kicked at the irritation with his back paw however, it refused to budge. Back on her feet his sister noticed his struggle. Padding over to him she let out a low growl as her eyes lit on the cause. Jutting out of her brother's collar was a piece of the Things paw. Clamping her teeth around it she shook her head violently from side to side her head filled with the memory of the monster that they had so recently fought.

In an attempt to aid his sister, M12 braced his hind legs and pulled backwards for all he was worth. With a sudden jolt the entire collar came away complete with the Things paw still imbedded in the metal strip falling to the leafy ground.

M12 limped to the dead Thing, lying a length of three wolves away. Sniffing around the severed head, he confirmed the Thing to be at last dead. Lifting his rear left leg; M12 urinated long and hard, marking his territory. Other wolves would find this Thing and know the new Alpha male of the McCarthy Pack claimed its death. M12 looked across to where his new Alpha female stood. Together they would begin a new pack. Slowly, he picked his way through his fallen brothers and sister until he halted by his brother's inert form. Bowing his head he gently licked his dead face before raising his head to the cold Alaskan night sky and releasing a despairing howl. His sister picked up on his howl which echoed along the valley walls. In the distance a wolf from another pack joined in. Then another, and another until it seemed the entire forest was filled with the sound of wolves honoring a fallen leader. "The strength of the pack is the wolf, and the strength of the wolf is the pack."

***

2038

Fifty-nine years after its transmission the Interstellar radio message from the Arecibo radio telescope in Puerto Rico, reached the Dorado Constellation. Around the dwarf star Gliese 163, three planets orbited sedately within the stars habitable zone. One of these planets, named by Earth's astronomers as Gliese 163c, held sentient life. Life advanced enough to have evolved a civilization capable of intercepting and translating humanity's primitive transmission. The inhabitants of this world discussing the information contained in the message at length for contact and communication between different worlds, especially such a primitive one as this Earth appeared to be, was not an enterprise embarked upon without thoughtful consideration of the possible wider impacts. After six solar years, they decided upon their response. This Earth planet and its human inhabitants were not ready to make first contact yet. The message was filed away with a note to open it again in five millennia.

###

About Mickey Ferron

WHEN NOT WRITING SCIENCE FICTION, Mickey Ferron pays his bills working as an Aeronautical Engineer. For over thirty years, he has been travelling the globe, working with all the major Aerospace companies. His only career regret is not being part of the current Space X program to Mars, but he would consider it, should Elon Musk ever contact him with a job offer.

His lifelong love of Sci-Fi began as a child, reading pulp comics such as 'Out of this World', 'Uncanny Tales' and 'Astounding Stories'. He still maintains a respectable comic collection (if that's not an oxymoron) of these old treasures. From comics he graduated to the Sci-Fi classics; H.G. Wells' masterpieces, The Time Machine and The War of the Worlds. For his tenth birthday, his father gave him a battered copy of Arthur Conan Doyles' 1912 The Lost World, he has it still. It shares bookshelf space with other prized possessions; sandwiched between Jack Finney's 1954 Invasion of the Body Snatchers and John Campbell's 1938 Who Goes There, (brought to the silver screen as The Thing) These three books alone inspired a passion of shapeshifting aliens, space adventure, time travel and dinosaurs, into adulthood.

When not troubleshooting around the world, he likes nothing better than clashing plausible, conceivable science with believable fictional stories. He fervently believes in the existence of alien life in other worlds, time travel, alternative realities and different dimensions, we just haven't discovered them yet.

Mickey is a 'self-taught' Jedi Knight, sworn only to use his powers for good. He resides Ireland, as he awaits the call from the Rebel Alliance. He shares his life with his wonderful wife, two fantastic children and a dog that someone needs to have a serious conversation with, informing him, that he isn't human.

Drop Mickey a line on anything Sci-Fi.

Connect with Mickey here:
www.castrumpress.com/authors/mickey-ferron

ALIEN DAYS

AND THE LIGHT FADED
By Lisa Fox

Rosa Santos focused on the road ahead as she ran. Her feet ached, pounding heavy on the cracked pavement, her strides as labored as her breathing in the icy air. She ignored the clouds of dust billowing through the woods around her and the trees swaying in violent protest against the advancing swarm.

***

Rosa had looked forward to ringing in the new year quietly - Netflix, popcorn, and a warm blanket. She clicked on the television; it painted her living room in a soft glow. The light cast shadows in the empty corner; dust collected in the space where her Christmas tree usually stood. It flitted over a mantle devoid of decoration – not a card, a holiday stocking, nor a candy cane hung from the fireplace. She hadn't seen the point of displaying her Nativity scene, either. Baby Jesus still lay sleeping in a cardboard box stacked at the top of her closet.

This year, Santa Claus was not a symbol of giving; he was a reminder of all that had been taken from her.

Rosa hadn't felt like celebrating – she wanted it to be over.

***

An Earth-shaking BOOM had jolted Rosa awake. It sent the popcorn bowl skittering off the coffee table and a photo frame crashing from the wall to the floor, the faces in the photograph distorted by the broken glass. A siren screeched outside, piercing through the flash of heat and gooseflesh that washed over her body. Rosa leapt from the couch and ran toward the window.

Graffiti covering the walls of the bodega across from her apartment glowed a sickly green. An odd radiance painted the sky, it was as if midnight were dueling with dawn. She turned away as the floor rumbled beneath her and cracked. Through a massive fissure, the face of her downstairs neighbor stared up at her.

Rosa grabbed her coat and raced outside, greeted by a street full of stunned neighbors staring at the sky. The invaders descended like giant hailstones; the hulking multi-legged creatures crashed down with such fury; Rosa felt as if the Earth had been knocked from its orbit.

The year twenty twenty-three arrived not with bursts of confetti or popping champagne corks, but with a firestorm from space. The aliens invaded just as the Times Square Ball began to drop. The world counted down its final moments, and a thousand fireworks exploded simultaneously in a grand finale gone horribly wrong.

And there was nothing to do but run. Or die.

✱✱✱

Three days had passed since New Year's Eve.

Rosa needed rest and shelter, and her options were limited. Few structures remained intact after the onslaught. When the aliens swarmed, they devoured everything in their path, like cockroaches on stray crumbs.

She pushed forward, her focus on breathing and moving one foot in front of the other. Through eyes blurred by tears and lack of sleep, she thought she saw a crumbling mansion in her sightline. It must be a mirage, she thought, or maybe I'm desperate. Le Château was the place to see and be seen; a threshold she had never expected to cross, unless it was through the service entrance.

Or unless it was the end of the world, Rosa thought.

Though a section of the outer wall had collapsed, and a massive hole was blown through the roof, the building still stood. Like the few survivors she'd encountered once the sirens had stopped, it too was crooked and broken.

Rosa's legs quivered as she approached the fractured marble steps. She leapt over a body splayed between the blown-out double doors. His tuxedo was soaked in blood, his face twisted in the scowl of a man surprised by his own death. Taking two steps at a time, she raced into the building.

Shards of glass from a broken chandelier shimmered across a cracked floor strewn with tattered paintings, chunks of brick, and abandoned personal effects– high-end handbags, shattered cell phones, the keys to luxury cars mashed like tin cans in the parking lot. A tremor sent Rosa tumbling into the rubble. She landed with her cheek pressed against the face of a dead woman, fresh blood oozing from beneath perfectly coiffed hair.

Trembling, Rosa pushed the body away and stood, her foot landing on a small metal object. She looked down at the cracked face of a Rolex, its hands frozen, the links of its metal band broken and jagged. She kicked it away.

So valued by the living, so useless to the dead, she thought.

She turned and ran down the hallway, glancing into the open doorways for signs of life. The grand rooms stood like mausoleums, some with their ceilings blown away, others pulverized into twisted masses of steel and wire and plaster. Well-dressed bodies lay everywhere, gathered in their finest to usher in the end of the world. Like civilized people. She pushed through a metal door and found herself in a kitchen.

Dust coated the black and white floor, though the stainless-steel appliances still shone under the grayish glow of a skylight. A sliced tomato wilted on the countertop; a butcher knife lay next to it, still wet with juice. Curious, Rosa thought as she shoved the warm fruit into her mouth. She couldn't remember the last time she'd eaten.

As she chewed, Rosa heard movement in a cabinet beneath one of the kitchen's many industrial-sized sinks. She took the knife and crept toward the noise. More shuffling. Her heart thrummed in her throat as she raised the knife.

The cabinet door creaked open and banged shut just as quickly. From within, a muffled sound arose, something like a groan. With a thump, the door burst open and a woman's leg shot out, her stockings ripped, the heel of her shoe broken off. "Oof!" a voice cried. The leg retracted and the door closed.

Rosa released her breath, though she still held tight to the knife.

"Hello?" Rosa called.

After a pause, a woman's voice rasped from within the cabinet. "Are you... human?"

Rosa relaxed her grip. "The last time I checked."

The woman's feet jutted out, scrambling to find the floor, and two hands covered with liver spots and glittering jewels grasped the framing of the cabinet as the woman attempted to pull herself out. She fell back into the cabinet again with a grunt.

"My legs are all pins and needles," the woman said.

Rosa reached out a hand to help. The woman trembled as she rose, her designer dress in tatters.

"Mrs. Parker?" Rosa said.

"Rosa?" Frown lines broke through the woman's Botox-smooth skin. "How did you get in here?" She brushed off her dress, scattering a few errant sequins to the floor.

"Free trial membership." Rosa scowled and folded her arms. "Guess they'll let anyone in these days."

"I'm sorry," Mrs. Parker said. She wrung her hands, avoiding Rosa's glare. "I didn't mean it like that." Rivulets of smudged mascara streamed down her cheeks. "William is dead – they're all dead. I'm the only one left."

Rosa nodded. Mrs. Parker was the only living person Rosa had seen since the prior evening, when she and a group of strangers spent the night hiding under a highway overpass. They fled at the first rumblings of the swarm, and Rosa was on her own again.

She placed a hand on the elder woman's shoulder. Mrs. Parker shuddered, then relaxed with an audible sigh.

"I thought I might be the only one left, too," Rosa said. "But we're not alone now."

Pots and pans rattled on the walls. Rosa felt the building vibrate through her clenched teeth. She wondered how much time they had.

"The aliens are on the move again. We need to hide until they pass," Rosa said.

"Won't there be anyone to rescue us?"

Rosa shook her head. "I don't think so." In limited exchanges, other survivors had told her the National Guard was destroyed; the enemy cut through their steel wall of armor like it was paper. She gestured toward the cabinet where the elder woman had hidden. "But we'll need to find someplace bigger than that."

Mrs. Parker nodded. The women looked around the kitchen. Next to an oversized refrigerator, Rosa found a wooden door leading to a small pantry.

"Here," she said. "This should do."

"I wish I had seen this earlier." Mrs. Parker grimaced. "My knees are killing me."

Still holding the knife, Rosa opened the door. The air was damp and musty, and there was enough room for the two women to sit cross-legged, facing each other. As her eyes adjusted to the dim light, she noticed rows of shelves lined the walls; kitchen aprons and clean dish rags crisply folded amid black and white oven mitts. And stacked in the corner, almost like contraband, were a half dozen cans of fruit cocktail.

"Eureka!" Rosa grabbed two cans.

"Canned fruit at Le Château." Mrs. Parker wrinkled her nose. "I never would have imagined."

Rosa shook her head, glaring. "Not good enough for you and your friends?"

Holding the can securely, Rosa used the pointed edge of the knife to puncture the lid. Inch by inch she turned the can, cutting into the metal with each rotation until the lid came free. She bent it back slowly to avoid cutting herself, and snapped it off with a swift motion.

Mrs. Parker stared at her. "I've never seen anyone do that."

"I'm sure there's a lot you haven't seen." Rosa smirked, and raised the can to her lips, gulping the sweet liquid. She thrust her fingers into the juice and retrieved a slippery peach.

"Here." Rosa worked on a second can and handed it to Mrs. Parker, then laid the knife down. The fluid sloshed as the building shook; the metal blade rattled against the tile.

"Thank you." Hesitantly, Mrs. Parker picked a cherry out of the can, holding it between her thumb and forefinger. She took a bite, a look of disgust crossing her face. Rosa hunched over her meal and ate in silence.

"It's been so long since we've seen each other." Mrs. Parker cleared her throat. "How have you been? Since..."

Rosa looked up. She tucked a strand of hair behind her ear and stared at Mrs. Parker for a moment before she replied. "Since giant aliens invaded the world? I've been great."

"I wasn't referring to the aliens."

Rosa bit her lip and placed the fruit can on the floor. She reached into her pocket and removed a toy building block. Laying it in her palm, she ran her thumb over the chipped pink letter 'D' painted into the carved wood.

"I've carried this with me, every day, for the past 267 days," Rosa said softly. "It was her favorite. 'D is for Dottie,' she'd say."

Mrs. Parker nodded, solemn.

Rosa leaned back against the shelves and hugged her arms across her chest as if to warm herself with a memory – Dottie, her only child, who'd shined with the life and light and love only a four-year-old could.

"She had my mother's eyes."

Mrs. Parker smiled. "She had your spirit."

Her daughter's zest, her light, was ended by a tumor that appeared as suddenly in her small body as the aliens did in the sky. Yet another predator, she thought. Satiated by pain. No purpose but destruction.

Mrs. Parker sniffled and played with the hem of her dress. "I'm sorry I didn't bring you back on after Dottie passed. You kept my house in order like no one else could." She paused, covering Rosa's hand with her own. "You were almost like family."

"That's rich." Rosa huffed. She snatched her hand back. "Let me guess. Being around me was too difficult for you."

"I didn't understand what you were going through," Mrs. Parker said. "The loss of your daughter was so tragic. But before...all this... I had never watched anyone die. I didn't know death."

"No one knows death until they've felt the absence it leaves behind." Rosa placed the wooden block back into her pocket. "It's like a hole in the sky."

Mrs. Parker reached up for a clean dish towel and dabbed at her nose. She continued, her breath catching. "It happened yesterday. He'd made up his mind to go outside. I begged him not to, but men like my husband are used to taking charge. Then, one of those... things... grabbed him. It tossed him away like he was nothing."

Rosa recalled the dead man lying on the stairs in the bloodied tux. Mr. Parker. She hadn't recognized his face. Death had robbed him of the confidence, the arrogance, she'd remembered him wearing so well.

"I understand, now, Rosa. And I'm sorry." Mrs. Parker grabbed Rosa's hand and squeezed hard. "All those hospital bills..."

Rosa sighed, a melancholy smile playing on her lips. "Maybe it was best Dottie left us when she did," she murmured. "Her light faded in its own time." Like a sunset, she thought. Gradual and serene, sad and beautiful.

The ground shook hard. Mrs. Parker covered her head as linens bounced off the pantry shelves on top of the two women, covering them like a shroud.

A screech – metal on metal – pierced the silence.

Mrs. Parker gasped.

"Closer," Rosa said.

"What do we do?" Mrs. Parker whispered.

"We wait."

"For what? Those things to get us, too?" Mrs. Parker began to cry. "We can't stay in here forever."

"Forever is relative. Let's worry about now." Rosa leaned forward and embraced the older woman, one hand stroking her back to soothe her. Her sobs quieted.

Just like Dottie's had, at the end.

Rosa had clutched her daughter's hand as Dottie's small body wilted into the pristine white sheets of her hospital bed, and hummed a lullaby to calm the rapid, gasping breaths which ushered in their final moments together in a cold room far from home. A mother willing the hands of the ticking clock to slow, to stop, and to hasten – terrified of the inevitable but wishing it to come to end the pain. Rosa closed her eyes, pushing aside the memory and replaced it with a specter of happier times – Dottie's soft brown curls bouncing as she sang and played in her footed pajamas that last Christmas morning, her tiny hands building a tower with her precious blocks. Dottie beamed as the letters proclaimed her name.

Mrs. Parker straightened, her deep shuddering breath bringing Rosa from her thoughts. "I never thought I would die this way, hiding in some god-awful kitchen pantry."

"Eating canned fruit. With the help." Rosa chuckled. "Heck of a way to go."

"I always thought my death would be more...dignified." Mrs. Parker smoothed her gown. "I suppose at least I'm dressed for the occasion."

"Me too." Rosa tugged at her stained sweatpants. "See? No holes."

"You do know you're violating the club's dress code." She nudged Rosa. "Three strikes and you're out."

"But, Mrs. Parker, I didn't realize I was in."

"You are now. Please, call me Evelyn."

Brow furrowed, Rosa slowly nodded. "I'd be happy to. Evelyn." The name lay foreign on Rosa's tongue and, at the same time, comfortable.

"New Year's used to make me sad." Evelyn leaned her head back and smiled. "Every time the ball dropped, it was like a rock pushed itself through an hourglass. One year closer to old age. Seems silly now, sitting here as we are."

Evelyn closed her eyes and sighed.

In that moment, Rosa saw beyond the elder woman's glittering jewels. She noticed the fine lines cracking at the corners of Evelyn's mouth and eyes as if time had indeed caught up with her. She observed how the woman's shoulders, once perfectly postured, rounded as she sat slumped on the cold floor. Rosa envisioned an alternate reality in which Evelyn and William Parker glided across a glowing marble dance floor, their gazes fixed upon each other, hypnotized by the ghostly croon of a saxophone.

She pictured an alternative life in which her own Christmas night had been spent gathering scattered toys under the glow of Christmas lights instead of grasping at memories in an empty room. And she thought about how shared sorrows connect us in ways shared joys never do.

She picked up the half-full cans of fruit cocktail from the floor, handing one to Evelyn as she raised the other in a toast.

"To the end."

Evelyn nodded. "To the end."

The metal cans connected with a soft ting. The women sipped the juice in silence.

"Promise me something," Evelyn said. "If these creatures should..."

BOOM.

The ceiling broke apart. Chunks of plaster rained down, the dust covering to their hair and eyes. The women clung to each other, a last hold on their humanity.

"They're here," Rosa whispered. She felt Evelyn's breath hot on her cheek, her body trembling.

"Do you think they'll –"

BOOM.

The tile cracked beneath them; fractures spread across the floor in a wave. Evelyn yelped. Rosa took a deep breath, desperate to calm the pounding in her chest.

BOOM.

Bright light leaked through a fissure in the wall, glinting off the knife on the floor. Rosa grabbed it, her knuckles tight around the handle. Her knuckles turned white as the blood drained from her face.

"This is it."

Evelyn reached out and grasped Rosa's taut fist. She spoke rapidly. "It needs to be on my terms. Not theirs."

Their eyes locked.

"Whether we succumb to the flames or leap into the abyss, the outcome will be the same." Evelyn squared her shoulders. "I need to die with dignity."

Rosa nodded, grim. She knew Evelyn was right.

"Will you do this for me?"

Rosa's breath caught like it did the moment after Dottie lay still. When time stopped, and the world was quiet. When the screams that threatened were quelled by the lingering peace of her daughter's final breath.

Soft wisps of silver hair entwined between Rosa's fingers as she placed her hand at the back of Evelyn's neck. Her pulse thumped against Rosa's wrist – steady, calm. Resolute. Rosa leaned in, feeling the woman's warm, even breathing, soft as a breeze.

"Thank you." Evelyn closed her eyes.

With a swift stroke, Rosa slit Evelyn Parker's throat.

Rosa kissed the woman's forehead and laid her down gently as blood and life drained from her body; death had taken her quickly. Peacefully.

BOOM.

Chunks of wood and splinters exploded as the pantry door blew open. The massive alien hovered, filling the doorway. Its claws clicked against the remaining tile. Rosa beheld her own face reflected endlessly in the multi-faceted surface of the creature's enormous eye. Green steam emanated from its gaping mouth. Its fangs glowed. Acrid breath enveloped her.

Rosa smiled at the creature.

She plunged the blade into her chest.

She felt the touch of a tiny hand.

A wooden block pressed into her palm.

And the light faded.

###

About Lisa Fox

LISA FOX IS A PHARMACEUTICAL MARKET researcher by day and fiction writer by night. She enjoys crafting short stories and short screenplays across genres, but her passion is for Sci-Fi/Drama hybrids. She thrives on the thrill of creating something out of nothing, in transforming life's 'what ifs' to prose that people can relate to – even if it involves robots, aliens, or clones. Nothing makes her happier than having readers say that her work made them feel something or look at the world in a different way.

Lisa won the 2018 NYC Midnight Short Screenplay competition and placed third out of over 3,000 writers in the 2018 NYC Midnight Flash Fiction contest. Her work is featured in various online publications, including Theme of Absence, Credo Espoir, Unlikely Stories Mark V, Ellipsis Zine, and Foliate Oak Literary Magazine, among others. She also has a short story in the Devil's Party Press anthology, Suspicious Activity. A resident of northern New Jersey in the USA, Lisa relishes the chaos of everyday suburban life. She and her husband Dan are kept busy by the comings and goings of their two sons and by the demands of their couch-dwelling golden retriever. Lisa hopes to begin working on a novel in the foreseeable future – she just needs to get those first few words on the page.

Connect with Lisa here:
www.castrumpress.com/authors/lisa-fox

ALIEN DAYS

RECIDIVISM
By Charles E. Gannon

D an stared out across the rolling green fields, over two vaporous snippets of cloud and up to the faint ghostly disk that hovered high in the vault of the deep blue sky. He held his breath and then sighed it out very slowly. A daytime moon always made Dan think of traveling in space. At night, the white disk was solid, not spectral, its bold materiality inviting an exacting consideration of the starkly detailed craters. Dan craved a telescope at those times, felt an amateur astronomer's call draw him from the moon to the stars. He imagined swiveling the telescope and adjusting the lenses until those distant suns no longer twinkled but shone fully and frankly at him.

But a moon in the daytime sky was an object of haunting fancy; it seemed to beckon rather than reveal. And so, he always daydreamed of travel up, up into the seamless skies that began as cerulean, deepened to sapphire, fell through to blackness--adorned only by the stars that there, as in the telescope, would have shone rather than winked at him. But that was all a dream--at least for one such as himself. Had he been allowed to study for the doctorate--well, his life might have gone differently. Indeed, everything might have gone differently.

Dan lowered his eyes back down to the rolling green fields, wondered if he now detected a faint limning of grey-brown at the horizon, and wondered if a doctorate, his doctorate, really would have made a difference in his life--or in anyone else's. It might at least have made a difference in how he was addressed: since failing to be accepted for doctoral study, he had also failed to hear anyone address him formally, using his proper name. He was just Dan—-his full name as forgotten as his early promise and potential, his life and services now always at the beck and call of the powerful and the successful. So, because time was shorter today than it ever had been before (although time was always short for a data entry clerk with no reasonable hope for advancement), he forced himself to look one last time at the document which had been the catalyst for his afternoon reverie: his rejected dissertation proposal of thirty-seven years ago.

The application form had begun to yellow with age, but there was no degradation in the clarity of its catastrophic content. He smiled——mostly inwardly——at that adjective: 'catastrophic' indeed. Dan had written about catastrophe-—and reaped as he had sown. He read the lines again, wondering how he could have ever been so naïve as to believe that his proposal and his project might have been perceived merely as prudent scientific query, rather than as an apocalyptic challenge to the social and cultural norms that had been the bedrock of civilized behavior and thought for more than three centuries. He skipped over the sheets listing the names-—his, his mentor's, the department head's-—and the long (and somewhat archaic) addressing of the sub department-—Political Science and Synergistic Applied Technologies-— and reached the first page of his fateful proposal:

A PRECAUTIONARY COMPARATIVE ANALYSIS OF STRATEGIES
FOR PLANETARY BIO/GENO-CIDAL STERILIZATION:

PROJECT OVERVIEW:

This project proposes to identify threat vectors that invading xenosapients might use in a campaign of pre-colonizing bio- or geno-cide. Although no evidence of xenosapience has been recorded, contemporary social factors make such a study both pertinent and prudent.

Since the Great Renunciation of 308 years ago, the related environmental decision to decrease our presence in, and use of, space has achieved its stated goals of reducing our debris-intensive encroachment upon the pristine exoatmospheric environment. An inevitable consequence of this laudably eco-conscious initiative is a proportionally decreased capability for advanced detection or intercept of potential intruders. With any potential warning interval thus shortened, it behooves us to consider—in advance—what forms of attack are likely to be mounted by aggressors, particularly those who might employ 'preemptive sterilization' prior to taking possession of new worlds. By identifying and modeling these 'threat vectors', we may be able to pre-craft defenses that achieve the dual purposes of frustrating such attacks while also minimizing the loss of life on both sides.

This latter criterion, implicit in the universal pacifist mandate of the Great Renunciation, is one of the key motivations of, and explanations for, the highly speculative nature of this project. Experience has shown that unanticipated conflicts pose serious challenges to violence mitigation techniques, usually because there is insufficient time to adapt them to the specific challenges of the crisis at hand. Given the scope of destruction presumed by this project, advance planning becomes not only advisable, but ethically imperative. To do any less is to undermine both our odds of survival and our ability to minimize the damage we might inflict upon any potential aggressors.

Dan blinked, shocked, not having read the earnest (and awkward) doctoral-candidate prose in almost a decade. Had he ever really believed that the senior Academics who decided his fate could see past the horrors of blood and war that his investigation invoked, that they would be able to glimpse the scientific and moral practicalities that lurked behind it? Did he himself really see that anymore——or was it just something he believed he had seen, like a hallucination of youth that age magically promotes to the status of a genuine "memory?"

He skipped much of the careful, carping diction with which he had made his obeisant bows to innumerable cultural shibboleths, and reached that section where he had committed the cardinal sin: to think like the monsters he had invented, to adopt the mentality and objectives of the threat force in order to predict and understand them. His careful contextualization's-—that this was the necessary prelude to designing effective and merciful responses-—had been completely ignored or had gone unnoticed. He had been surprised at that, back then: now, he was surprised he could have ever been so gullible to hope, much less expect, otherwise. He read his thumbnail sketches of Apocalypse, couched in the layman's prose that had been optimally congenial to the non-scientists on the review board . . .

SELECTED ATTACK METHODOLOGIES:
(in ascending order of likelihood)

MATERIALIZATION OF MATTER WITHIN PLANETARY OR STELLAR SPHERES:
Agency: A fundament of quantum physics is that various subatomic particles do not transit actual space during changes in energy states, but disappear from their first location, and reappear in their new, probabilistically predicted second location. A weapon which could accelerate a large, dense shower of these high-energy subatomic particles (e.g. mesons) out of normal space-time so that they would then reliably re-express within the target body of either a planet or star would have utterly devastating results. Planetary core disruption could

lead to catastrophic seismic events and sudden tectonic deformation; stellar core disruption could result in massive flare(s), a sharply increased radiation hazard, possibly complete stellar destabilization.

ADVANTAGE:
- Defender interdiction of the weapon effect is highly improbable, since the attacker's offensive energy does not transit the intervening expanse of space-normal.

DISADVANTAGE:
- Scalability of effects unreliable, due to uncommon complexity of variables; therefore, this is a preferred attack method only if the aggressor is willing to accept complete annihilation of planetary (or system) resources.

PRE-ACCELERATED KINETIC BOMBARDMENT.
Agency: Massive solids accelerated to high, even near-relativistic velocities, may be launched to impact the target planet. Attacks by relatively low-mass/high velocity objects have a number of distinct advantages, making this the probable preferred variant. High speed objects will be virtually impossible to intercept or even detect (if they are traveling at near-relativistic speeds). Also, higher impact velocity is likely to reduce atmospheric ablation (and premature fragmentation) of the accelerated object, and also reduce susceptibility to atmospheric deflection.

Aggressors conducting such an attack would probably commence their acceleration of the object in the trans stellar planetoid belt that extends as far as one light-year beyond the heliopause. This great remove makes their preparatory activities almost completely undetectable; it is also unreachable by any of our current technologies. Careful charting of a clear acceleration track through this planetoid field, and then the system itself, is a prerequisite for mounting such attacks: therefore, detection of the aggressor's preparatory survey activities might be the only means of acquiring advance warning.

ADVANTAGES:
- Very high ratio of destruction: cost, due to simplicity of acceleration, repeatability, and use of cheap, indigenous resources;

- Some scalability of effects, if a sequence of smaller objects is used, with post-strike determinations of whether additional attacks are required.

DISADVANTAGES:

- Imprecise control over planetary impact points, due to difficulty of long-range precision and limited options for terminal vector correction;
- Considerable lag time between commencement of offensive operations (charting, observation, and acceleration) and actual completion of attack (impact).

DEADFALL KINETIC BOMBARDMENT.

Agency: Massive solids released on planetary reentry trajectories without significant prior acceleration. Although impact sites could be infrastructure targets (cities, defense facilities, power generation centers, transport and communication nexi), a maximally destructive target list would call for a mix of tidal flat, deep-water, and polar ice-shelf strikes in order to facilitate widespread coastal inundation, rain, flooding, and consequent infrastructure and crop failures. Another, but more destructive approach would involve deep penetrations of the planetary mantle, with consequent ejections of dust into the high atmosphere, triggering a nuclear winter.

ADVANTAGES:

- Some scalability of effects (destabilization of biosphere may range from null to severe, but is controllable by varying the number of attacks and their impact points);
- Minimal delay between commencement of operations and practical access to indigenous resources.

DISADVANTAGES:

- Uncontested access to orbital bombardment points must be secured, possibly requiring conventional (and expensive) military operations;
- Low probability of complete extermination predicts a post-strike insurgency by survivors.

TAILORED BIO-/GENOCIDAL MICROORGANISM

Agency: Options range from long-duration agents (e.g.; a sleeper virus which renders all offspring sterile) to fast-acting, broad-spectrum ecocidals (e.g.; an aggressive and non-selective reducing bacterium).

The latter would logically be geneered to be hardy, rapidly self-replicating with a high mutational rate (so as to defeat pharmacokinetic countermeasures), swift to spread to and affect new organisms. Optimal employment would be covert seeding, rather than overt bombardment, which could be interdicted at two points: pre-impact intercept and post-impact zone containment or sterilization. Lastly, the organism could be designed to completely die-off after exhausting all available nutrients, leaving a thoroughly sterilized world.

ADVANTAGES:
· High selectivity and scalability: geneered organisms can be narrow or wide spectrum in their effects upon indigenous biota;
· Most resources, and select elements of the biosphere, remain intact.

DISADVANTAGES:
· Considerable advance preparation required (collection of indigenous biotas, gene-equivalency identification, fabrication of aggressor organism, lab testing, operational observation).

Other, less likely methodologies include...

And so, his proposal had unfolded, pursuing dreadful and diverse nightmares of apocalypse down every per mutative path. He had imagined weapons as theoretical as a quantum-based device that would function as a 'gravity bomb' --devastating either to a planet's tectonic plates or to the immediate substrata of a star's photosphere. He had even advanced the admittedly bizarre concept of a 'time bomb.'

The sheaf of papers sagged in his hand; if only he could change the flow of time, how different things might have been. Or would they? Knowing what he now knew, would he have done anything different? And would--—could—-the Academic Review Board have heard him any differently than they had? The Great Renunciation had remade the world, ended the strife between nations, eliminated famine, created an unparalleled equity of wealth and opportunity. Instead of embarking on a quest to find new biospheres, all attention had focused on preserving the blue and green globe that everyone called 'home.' In a world where violence had at last become not merely wicked but vulgar, in which weapons were forgotten implements of a barbaric age, his inquiry had had no place. It was the clangor of a sword upon a shield in an age where cultural harmony depended upon the all-pervasive music of the pipes. And he had been foolish—-or perhaps just 'young' -—enough to think that science (or rather, scientists) were living embodiments of the objectivity they preached and taught and swore to uphold. He never did understand how the Renunciation of violence as a behavior necessitated its repudiation as a subject of investigation, any more than he ever understood the complex rhetorical figurations which-—so his mentors claimed- —provided objective proofs of the pointlessness of violence in all its forms, in all situations. He had wanted to behold that Transcendent Truth, that touchstone of the Great Renunciation, but his intellect remained innocently intransigent. All his mentors could offer were expressions of sympathy (but no empathy, since they were not so cognitively benighted), and the consoling assurances of a future as a government functionary in a world where no one starved, no one knew pain, and no one who had failed so miserably as he had would ever reproduce. It was all for The Best, they had assured him; it was his part to play in the continuing achievement that was the Great Renunciation.

That standard of golden wisdom remained absolute and untarnished until, thirty-six years later, the first starships appeared at the edges of the heliopause. Evidently, interstellar space was not wholly devoid of other intelligences, after all. And evidently, not all these races were as committed to a policy of peaceful non-expansion. The creatures debarked, more strange than horrible to Dan's tolerant eyes. They professed good will, which they attributed in large part to their worship of an all-loving deity. But they also expected cooperation, and ultimately, willing cooption into their expanding interstellar sphere of influence. The many nations of the globe met to consider this offer (which daily seemed more akin to an ultimatum) but, in the end, that international council felt ethically compelled to decline membership. The loose articles of confederation put forth by the newcomers contained explicit contingencies for war-making, suppression of insurgency, and the imposition of martial law. It was of little or no consequence that the aliens (who now seemed more like intruders or even usurpers) were informed of this decision in the politest and apologetic of terms; they perceived it as a rebuff. With few words (none friendly, and few enough civil) they returned to their craft. So departed the intruders.

Who, one year later, returned as subtle, indeed undeclared, invaders. As Dan had predicted in his long-gone youth, they had found the option of a tailored biocidal microorganism the most appealing. During their first visit, they had had ample opportunities to collect a wide range of samples: evidently, even as they had spoken of brotherhood, peace, and mutuality, they had also been preparing for a one-sided war of extermination. But, upon the occasion of their second visit, their former invocations of a supreme deity of peace (in whose image they predictably asserted themselves to have been made) mysteriously transmogrified into something far more ominous. It was now a creed of duty to a higher purpose, of a manifest destiny, of a (regrettably) militant responsibility to bring their notions of peace and tranquility to the rest of the universe—-even if they had to kill every other sophont in that universe to achieve it.

Dan held the paper up to eyes that refused to focus as quickly or as surely as they had just a moment ago; he resisted a subtle but sudden rise of utterly pervasive pain—

--Or was that the forbidden emotion of anger, maybe even . . . homicidal rage? And why did it feel so right, so just, so like an awakening rather than a descent into troglodytism? And after all, it wasn't he who had behaved like a troglodyte.

For as Dan had predicted, even as the invaders stepped down from their returned ships, offering stonily blank faces and almost diffidently issued ultimatums, they had surreptitiously seeded a timed-release version of the blight that, days after their departure, erupted into what became universally known as the Rot--which had, in the time that Dan had watched, moved half of the distance from its first position as a brown line at the edge of the green fields. As if to witness a final, fearsome act in a tragedy, the second moon was now peeking timidly over the horizon: too horrified to look full upon the scene, but also too compelled to look away.

The Rot---misnamed, for it was more akin to accelerated bacterial reduction—- was already here, in his room, although Dan could not yet see it. But the door's plastic frame had started to warp; a bad sign. Plastic took longer than wood or animal tissue, but ultimately, its origins in organic molecules condemned it to the same fate as all flesh. Not long, now.

Dan felt his anterior heart flutter, followed by the predictable consequent weakness in the complex muscle junctures necessitated by his equally complex radially hexapedal physiology. He sagged, but pursued his final question with a final, fleet-footed yet fleeting thought: who were the troglodytes?

His race, which had foresworn weapons, war, and violence in all its direct and indirect manifestations? Or this pestilential species of duplicitous bipeds who had been patchy-furred apes only a few hundred thousand years ago, and whose ventures into space were not yet four centuries old?

But he who had been spawned as Dan'ytk Kr!k could no longer distinguish the searing pain of the Rot from the burning irony of its conquest. As the edges of the paper began discorporating in his wavering grasp, and his sight began to fail, he saw one last time his failing grade, and the note that had been scrawled beneath it in the tongue-painted quatrefoil sigils of the argot of the Academicians' Caste:

Sadly, the motivation and reasoning behind this project is not merely dysfunctional, but wholly recidivistic. The devolution it implies in its author regrettably compels us to conclude that you are not suitable for further advancement, nor for inclusion in the breeding pool.

With regrets,

Hzuult'yk Ktraa, Academician
Caste-Patriarch, Primus-ultra-Pares

Dan felt the papers fall from his palsied hands.   Thirty-seven years ago, the Academicians decreed that 'Dan' had failed as completely and ignominiously as was possible for his race.

And now, so had they.

###

About Charles E. Gannon

DOCTOR CHARLES E. GANNON IS A Distinguished Professor of English (St. Bonaventure University) and was a Fulbright Senior Specialist in American Literature & Culture from 2004-2009.

Doctor Gannon's series include hard-SF interstellar epic (the Caine Riordan series, set in his Terran Republic universe, nominated for three Nebulas, two Dragons, and winner of the Compton Crook Award) and epic slipstream fantasy (the forthcoming Broken World series). He also collaborates with Eric Flint in that author's New York Times Best Selling series *Ring of Fire series* as well as with Steve White in the NYT Bestselling *Starfire series*. He has also worked in universes/shared worlds such as *War World, Man-Kzin Wars, the Honorverse*, etc. and in various anthologies and Analog SF Magazine.

Along with about fifty other SF writers (such as Larry Niven, Ben Bova, John Hemry/Jack Armstrong, and Greg Bear), he is a member of SIGMA, the "SF think-tank" which advises intelligence and defense agencies (cf. www.sigmaforum.org). In his role as a subject matter expert on advanced military/defense/intel concepts, he has been featured on the Discovery Channel, NPR, Fox, and a wide variety of other national media outlets.

His earlier work includes various products and flash fiction for the gaming industry. He worked as both author and editor for Games Design Workship on their award-winning games *Traveller, 2300 AD, Dark Conspiracy* and *Twilight: 2000*.

Doctor Gannon has many credits in non-fiction; his most noteworthy is his book *Rumors of War and Infernal Machines: Technomilitary Agenda Setting in American and British Speculative Fiction*. Now in second edition, it won the 2006 American Library Association Award for Outstanding Book, and was the topic of discussion when he was interviewed by NPR (Morning Edition).

Doctor Gannon has been a Fulbright Fellow at Liverpool University, Palacky University (Czech Republic), and the University of Dundee. He also received Fulbright and Embassy Travel grants to these countries, as well as The Netherlands, Slovakia, England, and Italy. Holding degrees from Brown (BA), Syracuse (MS), and Fordham (MA, PhD), he has published extensively on the interaction of fiction, technology (particularly military and space), and political influence.

Prior to his academic career, Doctor Gannon worked as a scriptwriter and producer in New York City, where his clients included the United Nations, the World Health Organization, and The President's Council on Physical Fitness.

Connect with Charles here:
www.castrumpress.com/authors/charles-e-gannon

A MISSION OF MERCY
by Mark lynch

Human nature is complex. Even if we do have inclinations toward violence, we also have inclination to empathy, to cooperation, to self-control..

— STEVEN PINKER

Sweet mercy is nobility's true badge.

— WILLIAM SHAKESPEARE

S econd Lieutenant Christopher Taylor opened his eyes slowly, attempting to identify his surroundings. His entire body ached, and he was cold...freezing in fact. A bright artificial light shone above his head, nearly blinding him. He needed to blink several times to adjust his eyes to the glare. The first thing which became apparent was his total nakedness, with not even a rag or blanket to cover his dignity. No wonder he was freezing. He tried to move but discovered he could not. That was when Taylor started to panic.

When he attempted to lift his head, Taylor felt a tightening around his throat. He soon realized that a tight leather strap was secured across his neck. Likewise, his wrists and ankles were similarly secured. Taylor fought and struggled but to no avail. The straps were tight and escape impossible. His mind raced as he tried to come to terms with his predicament.

Stay calm, he told himself, there must be some kind of logical explanation. He took in his surroundings; his eyes scanning from left to right and back again. Taylor discovered he was secured to a metal slab set in the middle of what looked like a surgery or an operating theatre. He glanced to his right-hand side and was horrified to see a tray of sharp utensils laid out; surgical knifes, scalpels and a variety of horrific looking instruments which he couldn't identify. Taylor experienced a cold chill of terror running through his body as he continued his vain struggle against the restraints.

He realized where he was now. Taylor wasn't sick or injured. He didn't require surgery, nor was he under an anesthetic. They'd finally come for him. The officer knew all too well what would follow, he'd seen it before - the hideous and barbaric 'experiments' carried out against his fellow American and British POWs, a number of captured Russians and so many wretched Chinese peasants. He knew the pain and horror they would put him through. He opened his mouth to scream but couldn't make a sound.

What had the bastards done to him? Taylor lay helpless on the metal slab, secured by his restraints but otherwise totally naked and exposed. He was nothing to them – nothing but a living, breathing and conscious body, prepared for vivisection.

The surgeon entered the theatre a few minutes later. He was a small and slight man dressed from head-to-toe in medical garb and wearing latex gloves. A surgical mask covered his face, only exposing his dark, oriental eyes – eyes that were cold, pitiless and entirely devoid of humanity. The surgeon calmly advanced over to the operating table, looking over Taylor's exposed body as if it were a slab of meat. Taylor tried to engage his captor - to plead with him - but the words wouldn't come. He remained speechless and entirely helpless.

The cruel medic paused when he reached the side table and took his time to look over the collection of vile instruments. After careful consideration the man choose a long and sharp scalpel. He held his gloved hand up to the light to examine his foul tool in more detail. The terror pulsated through him; his breathing became labored and his body drenched in cold sweat. The surgeon leaned over the table, carefully lowering his scalpel to a point just below Taylor's ribcage. The Lieutenant felt the cold steel against his skin, the knife cutting through his exposed flesh. He watched his own blood flow from the incision. At last Taylor found his voice, and this time his horrified scream filled the room.

He awoke in an instant, his head shooting up from his sweat drenched pillow. It took several moments for Taylor to compose himself and to realize where and when he was; his bed, his quarters located within the Roswell Army Airfield. He switched on the tableside lamp before checking the clock on the far wall of his bedroom. The time was 4:32 a.m., and the date July 7...no, July 8, 1947. The war was long over, and it had been almost two years since Taylor's liberation from the hellish Pingfang prison camp. He was safe, but still the nightmares were frequent and so vivid.

The man was alone in his bed. Anna had left him a year ago and he'd agreed to the divorce a couple of months back. She'd no longer been able to tolerate his vivid nightmares and violent mood swings. Taylor couldn't blame her. They'd been high school sweethearts, marrying two days after Pearl Harbor and just before he'd taken up his commission. They'd both realized he might not survive the war, and Taylor often wished he hadn't.

It could all have been very different had it not been for that one fateful and tragic mission. On April Fool's Day 1945 Taylor's B-29 super-fortress set out from Saipan with the rest of the 17th squadron. Their bombing target was an enemy military base in Eastern China, except Taylor's plane never made it back. They'd experienced engine troubles on the return flight – a sick irony that the B-29 was almost impervious to A-A gunfire, yet a mechanical failure had brought them down. Their plane crash-landed deep in enemy territory and Taylor was the only survivor. Some would say he was lucky but, given what happened after...

A Japanese patrol had found him soon after the crash, taking him prisoner. Taylor had been frightened at the time. He knew how the IJA treated their prisoners, having heard all about the Bataan Death March and numerous other atrocities. Nevertheless, nothing could've prepared him for what was to come.

They took him to a facility deep in Manchuria, far from the front line and from prying eyes. It didn't take Taylor long to realize this place wasn't a normal POW camp. The inmates were under the 'care' of an obscure section of the Kwantung Army named the Epidemic Prevention and Water Purification Department but known by most as Unit 731.

Conditions within the facility were predictably terrible; The cells medieval and unfit for human habitation, the food sparse and inedible and the guards all sadistic thugs. Taylor and his fellow POWs attempted to adjust to the brutal conditions, but it soon became clear that something even more sinister was occurring behind closed doors. It wasn't until his captors forced him to work as an orderly that Taylor experienced the full horrors of the evil facility.

He'd discovered that Unit 731 were responsible for developing new biological and chemical weapons for the Japanese military and also for conducting human experimentation, specifically to test the limits of a human being's physical endurance. The vivisections were just one of the vile experiments conducted by the surgical division. Prisoners, mostly Chinese, were strapped to operating tables and cut open while still alive and fully conscious. They'd made Taylor watch while they did it. He'd heard their blood curdling screams and smelt the foul stench of creeping death.

He witnessed so many horrors during those dark days – people mutilated and tortured, women raped and deliberately infected with syphilis and gonorrhea, and POWs tied to stakes and brutally murdered with grenades and flamethrowers, to name but a few. To this day he didn't know how he'd survived those horrific months. They'd beaten him, starved him and tortured him, but he wasn't strapped to a table and cut open like the others had been.

Taylor survived up until August 1945. The end of the war was close, not that the prisoners knew it at the time. The guards took Taylor and the remaining POWs out into the countryside one afternoon. He was certain that they meant to kill them all, to eliminate all witnesses to their atrocities. It had only been by blind luck that they'd survived, having been found and freed by an advancing unit of the Red Army, just moments before his captor's intended to shoot them.

The Japanese lost the war but the monsters of Unit 731 evaded justice. That bastard MacArthur had made a secret deal to keep these war criminals from ever facing trial, and now the animals worked for Uncle Sam, passing on the 'knowledge' they'd gained from their sick and sadistic experiments. Taylor and the other survivors had been ordered to keep their mouths shut, and the whole ugly incident was covered up.

After the war he'd returned to active service and got posted to an out-of-the-way USAAF airbase in Roswell, New Mexico...left to live alone with his nightmares.

Taylor tried in vain to return to sleep but he realized his efforts were futile. Eventually he gave up on his attempts at slumber and got out of bed, intending to go to the kitchen sink to get a glass of water. He was halfway down the corridor when he heard the sound of his phone ringing. The loud bell gave him a fright. Who the hell would be contacting him at this ungodly hour? It must be some kind of emergency on the base. He apprehensively picked up the receiver and listened to the voice on the other end; "Taylor? Taylor, it's O'Neill."

Captain O'Neill, his commanding officer. The man was a decent CO, understanding enough and not the type to phone you up in the middle of the night without a good reason.

"Sorry to call you so early, Lieutenant. I hope I didn't wake you?" said O'Neill.

"No, sir," Taylor answered, "I was up anyhow. What's happening?"

There followed a lengthy pause before O'Neill answered. Taylor swore he heard O'Neill sigh down the phone before he spoke. "There's been an incident...A report of an aircraft crashing about thirty miles north of the base. A rancher called it in earlier this evening. Apparently, he saw a disc-like object falling from the sky and an explosion on the horizon. He phoned in the report to Chaves County Sheriff's Department and they contacted us, thinking it must have been one of our planes that went down. Trouble is, we didn't have anything in the air at that time. Anyway, the commander wants it checked out right away."

"Jesus Christ!" Taylor swore.

"I know! I know!" O'Neill said apologetically. "Chances are the report is bullshit. Either that or its some experimental plane or balloon which Special Weapons haven't told us about. However, there's a chance it might be something the Soviets have cooked up – a spy plane or a rocket, or something like that."

"Oh, come on!" Taylor exclaimed, "The God damn Russians! Here in New Mexico?"

"Why not?" O'Neill asked, "The Reds captured a lot of German scientists at the end of the war. Who knows how far they've come? Look, I know it's a pain in the ass Taylor, but I need a good man out there to check things out. I'm assigning you a security detail and a couple of jeeps. The Sheriff's Deputy will meet you outside the perimeter gate and escort you to the site. Okay then?"

"Sure." Taylor replied, in the full knowledge that he had no choice but to obey his orders.

He replaced the receiver and returned to his bedroom, where he proceeded to get dressed, and all the time wondering what kind of wild goose chase he'd been drawn into.

✳✳✳

Forty-five minutes later, Taylor was on the road, heading north through the arid desert landscape of rural New Mexico. As always, the atmosphere was dry and hot, but with an hour until dawn, the land remained cloaked in darkness. Taylor and his team travelled in two open-top jeeps which followed behind the Deputy's patrol car. O'Neill had taken no chances when organizing the security detail. He'd assigned Taylor a seven-man squad under a young corporal called Fischer. All of the USAAF troops were armed with either M1 Garand rifles or M3 'grease' guns and dressed in full combat gear.

It was almost as if the brass were expecting trouble...Did these lunatics really believe the Russians had landed in New Mexico? It seemed implausible to say the least. The great 'Red Scare' was all over the papers and radio these days. Taylor didn't hold any resentment toward the Soviets himself – After all, they'd saved his life back in Manchuria. But, after Hiroshima and Nagasaki, the whole world was living in an age of intense paranoia and fear. Taylor would have to make sure Fischer and his men didn't get trigger happy on this morning's mission.

They had to drive off-road for a couple of miles before they reached the crash site. The Deputy's patrol car slowed to a crawl as apparently the policeman didn't want to get too close. Taylor told his driver to overtake the police vehicle and keep driving.

Taylor set eyes upon the wreckage and was immediately mesmerized. The aircraft, if indeed that's what it was, appeared circular in shape, looking like a saucer in fact. It wasn't overly large in size, perhaps measuring thirty-odd foot in length. The craft had clearly crashed into the ground at great speed judging by the size of the crater it occupied but, as far as Taylor could tell, the body was still largely intact. It had no wings or propellers and he'd no idea how it flew.

Taylor stood and observed the site for several moments before the most obvious thing struck him – the machine was glowing! It remained dark out, yet the downed flying saucer was illuminated by a light green glow which could only have been produced artificially. Taylor had never seen anything like it before.

The two jeeps came to a halt about fifty yards in front of the downed aircraft. The men hopped out of the vehicles with their weapons at the ready. Taylor could tell the boys were uneasy, scared even – "Man, it's weird." "What the hell is it?" "I don't like this, guys!"

"Pipe down, men!" Taylor proclaimed in an authoritative voice, "We're professionals and we have a job to do, so keep it together!"

The command seemed to have the desired effect but in truth the very same thoughts and questions were going through his own head right now.

"You guys, set up a defensive perimeter here." He ordered, while facing his detachment of enlisted men. "Corporal Fischer, come with me."

Taylor and Fischer cautiously advanced in the direction of the downed aircraft. The Lieutenant was alert, not knowing what to expect. Taylor became fixated on the illuminated metallic exterior of the vessel. He almost tripped over a piece of debris lying in his path, leaning down to take a closer look at this scrap of loose metal. He waved his bare hand over the debris, expecting it to be burning hot – but instead the material was ice cold. Taylor threw caution to the wind and reached out to touch the piece. As soon as his fingertips made contact the material lit up and Taylor felt a surge of energy pulsating through him. It was like nothing he'd ever experienced in his life.

"Jeez, Lieutenant!" exclaimed Fischer, "Are you sure that's a good idea?"

Taylor ignored the man. He proceeded to lift the piece of debris up with his one hand. The part was about four or five-foot-long and yet as light as a feather. The material was so thin it looked as if it would snap in his hands and yet was strong and seemingly robust. He didn't know of any metal with these properties. Taylor had no idea where this vessel came from, but he was sure it wasn't a Russian spy plane. He'd seen first-hand the Red Army's troops when they invaded Manchuria and knew they didn't have technology as sophisticated as this – not even close. But, if the aircraft wasn't American or Soviet, then who the hell did it belong to?

"It looks like something from another world." Fischer muttered, "Hell, maybe they're God damn Martians!"

The soldier laughed nervously at his own quip. At first, Taylor thought the suggestion was ludicrous, but then he got to thinking. He recalled Orson Welles' famous War of the Worlds radio play which they'd first broadcast back when he was a kid. Taylor remembered the mass panic the play caused, as thousands of people thought the Earth really had been invaded by little green men. Taylor never had much time for those trashy science fiction pulp novels and comics, with their far-fetched stories of little green men and flying saucers, but now the evidence was here, right in front of his eyes...What other explanation could there be?

Taylor pondered this question as he moved closer to the downed craft. Corporal Fischer carefully followed in his trail, clutching a tight hold on his submachinegun. Taylor approached the side of the vessel, observing and admiring the perfectly formed spherical shape, tarnished only by the damage inflicted when it hit the ground. The metallic glow intensified the closer he got. Taylor felt the power flowing through him, as if his body and mind were both feeding upon the potent energy emanating from its metallic exterior. Was such a thing possible? Why not? After all, the advanced beings who had constructed this extraordinary machine must be capable of producing any number of wonders.

Taylor continued to circle the saucer, closely examining the curved exterior. He was searching for something, but for what he couldn't say. It happened suddenly – a surprise, but yet not entirely unexpected. There was a soft buzzing sound, closely followed by movement, as a panel on the exterior of the saucer began to slowly open, revealing the inside of the alien craft.

Taylor and Fischer both stood back and watched in awe as the hatch opened fully, as if by magic.

"Sweet Jesus..." Fischer swore.

Taylor shared the man's sentiments. He felt nervous but yet did not fear for his own safety. He didn't feel under threat at all. The way Taylor saw it, he'd come this far, and so he might as well go just a little further. It was as if the flying saucer and its inhabitants were calling out to him – inviting him to enter. The officer began to walk toward the open doorway, taking in every iota of his surroundings. He was irritated by the sudden interruption from Corporal Fischer.

"Hey, Lieutenant!" said Fischer in a meek and nervous voice, "I'm not sure that's such a good idea. We don't know what's in there...they could be dangerous!"

"Fine." Taylor snapped impatiently, "You can stay outside. I'm going in."

He began to turn away before the soldier interrupted him once again. "But, Boss, Captain O'Neill gave me specific orders. He said we're to stay alert, proceed with caution and take prisoners if there's any survivors. Use lethal force only as a last resort, those are the captain's orders.

"Are they indeed?" Taylor replied thoughtfully. He found it interesting that O'Neill hadn't communicated this order to him – what the hell was the man's agenda?

"Well, Corporal," he answered, "O'Neill's not here. I am in command and I'm going inside this vessel. Under the circumstances, I think its best you stay out here. Is that clear, Fischer?"

"Yes, sir." Fischer responded uncertainly.

Taylor detected a hint of relief in the Corporal's voice. With this unwelcome distraction behind him, he ducked his head and entered the craft's interior.

The heat was the first thing he noticed, that and the thick smoke. He could also hear a slight ringing noise, something like a fire alarm. With some difficulty he advanced through the dark and smoke-filled interior, climbing over assorted debris and wrecked machinery. He made his way toward a dim light at the front of the vessel, which he assumed marked the location of the cockpit. Taylor cast his eyes upon a control panel filled with monitors, switches and dials; almost all of which were dead and inactive, producing only the occasional spark of electricity from their broken circuitry. The only light emanated from the one cracked monitor which appeared to be working, although all the screen displayed was a black and white static.

The cockpit set-up was familiar to Taylor, given the hundreds of hours he'd clocked up flying B-29s during the war. That said, the equipment, instruments and controls of this vessel looked many times more sophisticated than the USAAF's best bomber. But what really drew his attention were the three seats contained within the semi-circular cockpit. The trio of chairs all faced forward in the direction of the control panel. Taylor stood directly behind the seats so was unable to see their occupants. What struck him was how small the chairs were, as if they'd been designed for children. Come to think of it, the whole interior was compact, and his head almost touched the ceiling.

The Lieutenant felt anxious but also extremely curious – He needed to see what these creatures looked like. Taylor crept around the three chairs and cast his eyes upon the occupants. He could not believe what he saw. The aliens (and he was now certain they were beings from another world) appeared surprisingly human-like. As one would expect, they only had one head, two arms and two legs. They were small and frail in appearance. Taylor estimated their height at four foot at most. Their bodies looked slim and lean, and their skin was a light grey color. He noted how the aliens' heads looked out of proportion, appearing too big for their diminutive bodies.

Three aliens in total, all still strapped into their flight chairs. He could only guess at their respective jobs on-board the ship. Presumably one operated as the pilot, the second might be a navigator and the third a weapons specialist, assuming the vessel was a military one. Two were undoubtedly dead since their eyelids remained firmly shut and their bodies completely motionless...But the third was clinging to life. Taylor saw its chest moving in and out, an indication of labored breathing.

The creature sluggishly turned its head and looked upon him. Taylor was astonished by its eyes – gigantic, oval-shaped and jet black. This being was obviously in pain; Taylor could sense it. In spite of the extraordinary circumstances the American veteran found himself reminded of another place and another time. He vividly recalled lying bruised and concussed inside the wreckage of his B-29, before the Kempeitai, the IJA military police, took him as their prisoner...And now, two years on, he was the captor.

Now Taylor understood what was happening. The USAAF, the government – they wanted this alien alive. Surely, they would do to him what the Japanese had done to Taylor and so many others during the war – cage him up like an animal, torture him, run sick experiments on him...probably dissect him. Taylor wouldn't accept this. He couldn't inflict this suffering upon another living being, even if that being was not of this world. He locked eyes with the alien creature and experienced an intense wave of empathy. Taylor had no way of communicating with this lifeform but somehow, he knew what it wanted – to be free...free from pain, free from fear.

He reached down to his leather holster, carefully removing his Colt .45 pistol and making the gun ready to fire. They'd probably court martial him for this, maybe throw him in prison, but Taylor no longer cared. He raised the gun and held it against the creature's forehead. It or he didn't flinch...this was what it wanted. Taylor wondered whether these beings believed in an afterlife. Hope you make it there, buddy.

He pulled the trigger. BOOM! The sound of the gunshot reverberated around the vessel's interior and dark, hot blood splattered across his uniform. The ugly task was completed, but Taylor did not know how he should feel. Suddenly he could no longer bear to be inside this damned spaceship. He felt claustrophobic, as if the walls were closing in on him.

Taylor darted back to the open door of the craft, nearly tripping over debris as he went. Soon he found himself back out in the open air and experienced a great relief. Corporal Fischer stood there, shouting something about gunfire and prisoners. Taylor ignored him. Dawn had come. The exhausted Lieutenant looked to the far horizon and saw the bright yellow sun rising; its light and warmth spreading across the land. Taylor savored the immense beauty of the scene and, for the first time in years, he felt at peace.

###

About Mark Lynch

MARK LYNCH WAS BORN IN 1983 and hails from the beautiful coastal town of Holywood in County Down, where he lives with his wife Jackie and cat, Jet.

Mark studied History & Politics at Queen's University Belfast and maintains a keen interest in these subjects. His fascination with the 'What ifs?' of history and his love of the genre classics (such as Philip K Dick's The Man in the High Castle and Robert Harris's Fatherland) inspired him to develop his own alternative history timelines and transform them into works of fiction.

Mark currently works as an information analyst in the health service and writes in his spare time. His long-held ambition was to become a science fiction author and he achieved this goal in 2014 with the publication of his first novel, The Rogue Colony. This publication was closely followed by the first book in his Red Ulster Trilogy, imagining a 1960s Ireland controlled by the Cold War superpowers.

His 2016 novel, Reich of Renegades, ranked in the top #30 Alternative History books in Amazon US.

Connect with Mark here:
www.castrumpress.com/authors/mark-lynch

ANOTHER DAY, ANOTHER DOLLAR
By Juleigh Howard-Hobson

Now that we've got ourselves a Federal Alien Replicant Disaster on our hands, we have what the government refers to as emergency measures all over the place. Which aren't as fancy as they make them sound on the news sites, with their talk about all the registered Centre for Disease Control humane holding units implemented for the collection of infectious non-earth-based animated materials related to replicated posthumous human remains showing anthropomorphic mutations. We call them trap trenches. Like I said, the reality doesn't match much.

Trap trenches are long holes we dig anywhere there's been infection introduced into an area. I was given a rule book which says to dig them six-feet deep, but we dig them nine-feet deep. By we, I mean any of us employed by the Fed to catch these suckers.

The official procedure is to bait the traps with material containing the aroma of formaldehyde-infused corpses. We aren't given actual pickled people, no. This is some soy-based stuff that comes in a can, like cat food. We're supposed to open the can up, leave it like an aromatic lure in a snare—which these are, sort of—and come back in a few days and see what we managed to catch.

Of course, the cans don't work. These ET-things can tell embalmed body scents from whatever smelly gluten-free garbage the authorities give us. I made an arrangement with my local funeral parlor. I only need a little dab at a time, so I can last a few weeks on one embalmed foot, and no one is any wiser because nobody looks in the shoes of the departed, especially when they are laid out in their coffins. I buy feet cheap, because the owner/operator over at Holmes Funeral and Mortuary wants to get rid of the problem just as bad as the powers that be do. Plays hell on his business.

Citizens, such as me, are hired to stand at the edge of traps, where we fire guns at the funny looking aliens. At their necks. With rubber bullets. Shooting doesn't kill them, nothing does except pulling their eyes out and stabbing them in the optic

236

nerves. But shooting them in the throat shuts them down. And it's fun. About the most fun thing about all of this, really.

Like target practice.

The thing is, before this outbreak, this space borne infection, whatever they call this invasion, there wasn't much about the rest of the world I liked anyway. I always hated other people, and they didn't like me much back either. All the time, getting in the way, telling me what to do, how to do it, nagging, nagging, nagging me to get a real life. Like somehow being a loner was a one-way ticket to Loserville. They don't understand me. I like the way it is now. People leave me alone. I'm paid to do what I like to do. Be alone. And I get to shoot Furries. Sorry, extra-terrestrials. But hey, they look like freaks in furry suits. For a few days at any rate, before they start falling apart because they replicate themselves on corpses injected with formaldehyde. No one knows why they start to replicate embalmed human bodies then add on other anatomical stuff from different creatures, they could end up with pig snouts in the middle of their faces, or antlers on the top of their skulls. Some do the whole anamorphic thing—and come off looking like cartoon dogs and squirrels. Isn't my problem. My problem is they can do a lot of damage in the few days they have to run around on our planet before the embalming chemicals break down and they literally fall apart.

The immediate damage they do is negligible. Unless you are the family of the corpse. People don't like when you copy their deceased uncle and add on bear paws and some sort of lion tail. No, the problem is the Furries tend to bite people.

People who are chomped on—even a small nip-- swell up, like they got stung by something massive and venomous. After a while they begin to turn purple—makes zero difference what color skin they had to begin with, every one of them goes violet and lavender streaked with yellow in a couple of hours. Then comes the complaining about how much they burn inside. Some rave and rant, others fall silent. In the end, they simply drop dead. The internet sites say it's like they were drowning in embalming fluid from the inside out. No agency has confirmed or denied this.

People who die alone, before anyone realizes they were chewed on, are duplicated faster and they have weirder add-ons than the formaldehyde-soaked bodies in the funeral parlors. No one knows why this is. Let me repeat, no one knows why or how; seems like we only know what happens.

Not that the government is doing much research to find out why. They hire people like me, and pass legislation against putting preservative chemicals in dead people anymore.

Embalming happens, though. On the side. For the families.

I don't blame the embalmers, most aliens these days are made through mastication. And more are made every day.

I counted four of the Furry weirdos in my trap this morning. And, dang if one of them didn't appear to be the spitting image of my nephew's Little League coach, Mr. Karrol. If Mr. Karrol was a huge brown dog who walked on his hind legs and had two sets of horns on his head. This one wasn't pleasant to look at, seeing as how the original Mr. Karrol died about three days ago, and the corpse lifestyle had been rough. The left ear, right under the first of the horns, was half torn off, flapping away. And the fingers, excuse me, toes because dogs don't have fingers—well, I couldn't see them. Its front paws sort of stopped at two raw meat looking black dog pads. I imagine the Furry wore them off somehow. Probably trying to burrow back into the funeral home to infect somebody else's embalmed coach. Not this season, Karrol-copy. Not on my watch.

I loaded my grandmother's Enfield rifle with the rubber bullets the current administration issued for us to use. Grandma had gotten the rifle from my great grandfather who went to fight in France back in Double U Double U Two. I never got to go to Europe, and now I never would—too many Furries in Europe these days. Serves them right for laughing at us and saying the space-bugs couldn't cross the oceans when we said it would. The Europeans simply left us here, to deal with the first outbreaks of infection by ourselves. Their official view being we only had ourselves to blame. Just desserts. For Area 51 and our general arrogance about the Moon Walk.

Of course, the Europeans forgot about the cruise ships already headed out their way. Cruise ships loaded with senior citizens, and every one of those ships has a nice working morgue, tucked away below decks. Old people get sick quickly and die on cruises all the time. Only took the one bad port of call on the Texas gulf where some enterprising interlopers looking like over-fed pet chihuahuas got on board after a few elderly women ate dodgy shrimp, one of which wanted to be laid out in her coffin up on deck (the old lady, not the shrimp).

Well, Europe was over run fast. The remainder of the world quickly followed. It's completely infected, chewed up and reanimated in that half-ass way the off-worlders work. The gerbil-faced sharp-fanged hoof-waving duplicates are biting everyone, before falling apart in droves as their copycat bodies break down, covering the streets from Paris to Algiers, Edinburgh to St. Petersburg. And I mean this quite factually: they are laying on the streets. Their eyes wide open. And no one has any idea what they are going to do next, besides rot into mush and bones. Which is what they are doing right now. Add to that the chaos of each of them having the capabilities of the organisms they resemble as well (and some resemble quite a few all at the same time) ...and there's a whole bunch of problems to deal with.

We are not going to let that happen here though. I don't care how many traps we need to dig. No planetary invasion is going to be able to take hold and stay here. That's where my job comes in. I clear them out of Washington State and send them on—to wherever unwanted visitors from outer space who look like cartoon animals go. First stop CDC lockers. Second stop Hell.

Or, is hell only for human beings? Somehow, I doubt it.

I took stock of what I had in the hole this morning. Three males. One female. I mean, to me they seemed like male and female whatever they were. Who knows what genders they really were? We say gender is fluid now, could be they were saying those things all along.

Either way, I aimed for the neck of the female-looking one; a faithful representation of somebody, doubled right down to the bright yellow sports suit outfit the original corpse had on. You know... the kind some women buy in shopping malls to wear to the supermarket but not to the gym. I couldn't figure out why anybody would want to bury the real departed person in that hideous outfit until I remembered that the odds were, she never got to the embalming table. The original lady was more than likely bitten by whatever was walking around looking like her now. She sported a beak where her nose should be and fluffy canary feathers were coming up out of her neckline, and where her feet should be, I saw what looked a little like yellowish snake tails. One coming out of each pant leg. They reminded me of a pair of ripe bananas---black spots and all. The Furry stared at me; maybe the original lady was a decent person, but there was nothing in those bird-brained copy eyes but raw anger now. I squeezed the trigger. Bingo, right between the dirty chin and the dirty collar. Feathers flew. Bird-woman dropped like a yellow sack of sand.

One more space nasty hit the dust. For a little while at least.

The other three Furries started shuffling around in that weird jerky way they do. I think it's because they can't get their unnatural legs to move as fast as they want, so they push their chests out as if puffing up will send them where they are going any quicker.

I don't know why they do. They just do. They seem only interested in three things: being able to run around our planet, looking like people who somehow merged with local wildlife, and gnawing on warm bodies. The one thing they sure as heck don't want is to be shot at. Even though shooting them can't kill them, they don't want any part of it. And that's why my traps are nine-feet deep. Furries check in but they don't check out.

I lined up my next shot. The Mr. Karrol-look-alike was digging away at the walls of my trap. Trying to tunnel out, I reckoned. Without any dog claws on the end of those paws, things weren't going too well though. I decided to let it keep itself busy while I took aim at the one that wasn't moving around as much as the other two.

This Furry replicated a hipster and a fish: lumberjack beard, flannel shirt, skinny assed jeans, motorcycle boots and greenish speckled scales on its face. Webbed fingers, no eyelids, the whole aquatic get-up. Gills too. It was ugly. Granted, the whole rotting briny flesh thing didn't help... but... man-o-man, what with the groper profile and the beard...hipster fashion gone bad.

Bang!

Good riddance sushi man.

Only Mr. Karrol and a wrinkled old-man wannabe remained. The old man Furry looked like a living version of them Easter time battery operated toys. You remember, the kind that came with the cheap thin 'pink fur' cloth and a drum to bang. That's what the old guy looked like. Long ears on his head, a little peachy colored fuzz covering his exposed body parts. Twitchy nose. I guess he had a cotton tail, but he was dressed. Nobody would want to play with him though, not with those blood shot rolling non-mammalian eyes, creepy rodent-paw hands and all the lurching around. Given the general dilapidated appearance, the space-invader dug the original body up and out of its own grave, before it took the form and added essence of bunny; it wore a Marines uniform, with dirt and splinters all over its filthy self.

Mr. Karrol was still pawing away, making weird noises. Not words, not dog barks: noises. I figure the rotting tongue stopped working properly but it didn't notice because aliens don't speak human. Or, could be I was actually being told something about why they picked my planet to infect. Are we the only world with formaldehyde and fun fauna?

Whatever, I let the hollering continue while I dealt with the old looking dirty splintery nose-twitcher in the Marines uniform. This guy was getting wiggly and agitated before I had hit the hipster but seemed fresh out of steam now. No doubt needed a fresh nibble as a pick me up, which was never going to happen again. I could feel it dead eye balling me.

I aimed for the scraggly part under the quivery chin wobble, but the Furry tripped before the bullet hit. Instead I took off the top of Mr. Karrol's right dog-haunch shoulder. He stopped making noises and looked right up at me. I almost felt bad. Like it knew that was a first taste of what was coming.

Those noises started up again, and the antler shaking... My relatives might really have liked their late baseball coach however, this one was only an echoed piece of meat, falling apart and liable to gore me hard. I never liked the original guy in the first place. He was a dick. If you catch my drift. Three strikes you're out.

Mr. Karrol's look-alike got a rubber bullet smack in the Adam's Apple. The body thrashed around like a chicken with its head cut off - even though the head was still on for a while. I waited, thinking about how much each of these star-bugs was worth in cold hard non-electronic cash. Ca-ching.

Took two whole minutes before the dang thing was laying quiet. Still. Not an antler shaking, not a paw twitching. Silent. Like the corpse it partially cloned. Down, boy!

Usually, the last of them will begin acting up—stumbling in circles, doing whatever aggressive feral semi-beast things do. Chewing, cawing, roaring, yapping, barking, snapping.... This old-looking Furry was different, standing upright, in the dirty uniform, its little velvety nose wrinkling, while I aimed. I knew there wasn't any real thinking or feeling going on. Merely a doomed space-germ in a rotting meat bag, looking forlorn and smelling to high heavens. Nothing else. I couldn't think about the fact this astro-copycat seemed to understand it was a doomed space-germ. No. This Martian marine was nothing. Some vicious animated infection on bunny legs...legs that never really belonged to it.

The infection on bunny legs saluted me.

My heart stopped. My brain went into worry mode. Was what I was looking at an alien? Was he a real Furry? Could a real Furry have Alzheimer's?

I hate when stuff like that happens. Damn. Was he someone's grandpa having a final fling in the seedy world of plush anonymity? Were they looking for him? Could I see a zipper anywhere on his downy parts? Why would he wear a fuzzy animal costume and a uniform? Talk about fetishes. Oh man. Damn it. I was counting on the money for whacking four of them today.

He was an alien.

I needed the money. He had to be an alien.

I shot him in the throat. Whatever.

Semper Fi, Peter Rabbit. I let him twitch a little, watching to make sure the others were all still stone cold out. Nothing like the gut wrench of having a paw grab your leg as you go to pull its eyes out. We lost people that way, early on. Good men and women I needed to watch and whack myself, after, once they swelled up. I earned a tidy bunch of cash, but I wish those events never happened.

I put on my gear, which consisted of a pair of latex gloves and a disposable face mask—some people go all out with body suits and leg protection, but I can't work like that. I'm a hand's on, face in, kind of gal.

I went down into the dirt with my stuff: government issued plastic bags, machete, marker, gallon sized zip lock baggies, twine, a long thin knife ...and my special antique cooking spoon that I use instead of the regulation scooper I was assigned. My spoon is better. I sharpened the bowl along one side. Reshaped the long handle so the cutting edge fit snugly into sockets. It used to belong to my mom.

Everyone has their own method of killing these freeloading alien fiends. Me, I open each eye lid, (if they have eyelids, some of the fish faces don't), slip my spoon in behind the ball, and tug. Out pops the eye, in goes the long knife, and there goes the optic nerve. Since I got the hang of it, I can remove and sever in two moves. It's fast, and less disgusting than other things I've done. Trust me. They aren't finished until that nerve is cut.

Today, because I still felt uneasy about old Hippity-Hopper, he got his peepers popped and his optic nerves severed first. Out, in, stab, he was done. No more worries. Now for the rest of them.

I put the detached eyes in zip lock bags and use the twine to tie them around the neck bases. Good and tight. Regulations require hunters to take off the heads and bag them, too. Which is a pain in the ass, particularly when they come with horns or long bills or forehead shark fins. But we must. Too many politicians watched too many zombie movies back in the day. It's annoying though, these critters aren't undead. They're made from copies of the dead with assorted livestock images thrown in. It's nothing but a waste of time decapitating them. The whole mojo is in the optic nerve. Sever the nerve and it's all over. You're left with a flesh bag with horns or fur. And no eyes. I'd stomp the round squishy suckers into juice if it was up to me. Just because. But that's the government, we're not allowed to do the whole job our way.

I whacked each of the copied craniums off, and stuck the baggies of eyeballs around the spinal stumps. Like I said, pointless work. Mr. Karrol was a nightmare with his double antlers. The long-eared Marine didn't make things too easy either. Still, I did my job. I always do.

As far as I'm concerned, all the fun is over as soon as the scooper comes out. After that, it's work: tagging, bagging, dragging. But work pays the bills.

The decapitated trunks with their tie-ons are lined up for disposal trucks to pick up. The noggins are placed in special double-thick see-through plastic bags. Labeled clearly with time and place of removal. These are delivered to the CDC office up by the county sheriff's. Everyone is afraid they'll regenerate if a molecule of visual nerve is left inside so, the Furries heads, no matter what they look like, stay with the trappers.

I get the willies, driving with them sitting in a row on my passenger seat. One of these days one of them will open its lids and those eyes will be back in, unpopped again. Staring back at me. I drive as fast as I can to the sheriff's office. Where somebody else takes them out and logs them in ...and pays me.

Keep coming, you animal looking withered-corpse copycat fucks from outer-space. I'll get you. I'll get you all.

Because I hate people, and I hate you, but I like money.

###

About Juleigh Howard-Hobson

A POST-MODERN DROP OUT, Juleigh Howard-Hobson lives on a farm, nestled besides a dark forest, with her family and a black dog named Grimm. There are secrets whispered in the woods. Magic falls from the clouds. The dog may or may not be mortal.

She is a Million Writers Award "Notable Story" writer, a Predators and Editor's top ten finisher, she holds an Anzac Award and an Alfred Award, and has been nominated for 'The Best of the Net', The Pushcart Prize and, most recently, a Rhysling.

Her speculations can be found in in Devolution Z, Bewildering Stories, The Liar's League, Danse Macabre, Leading Edge Science Fiction and Fantasy Magazine, Every Day Stories, Glory of Man: The Rise and Fall of the Reality Soldier (Cockroach Conservatory), History is Dead (Permuted Press), Loving The Undead (From The Asylum), Lost Innocence Anthology (Niteblade), Return of the Raven (Horror Bound) and many other places, both in print and in pixel.

Her fifth book --a numinous formal poetry collection-- is Our Otherworld (Red Salon Press).

For the record, she was born in England, raised in New York City as well as just outside of Sydney, Australia. She currently lives in the Pacific Northwest of the USA. It rains. A lot.

When not writing, she tends to her private gardens—one of which grows dark shadowy plants and the other archaic ones (an alexander potage anyone?) -- while she does not dig trap trenches, there is a lot of composting. Beware.

Connect with Juleigh here:
www.castrumpress.com/authors/juleigh-howard-hobson

ALTERED
By Alexander Harrington

Y ou blink away the remains of dreamless sleep and sit up. The room around you slowly comes into focus, dull and milky around the edges of your vision. For a moment you have no sense of where you are, but familiarity quickly asserts itself: you're in the living room of your home; a small, two-bedroom house in an unremarkable suburb-built years before you were born.

Stretching, you look out the bay window at the evening sky, gradually turning a soft orange, troubled by accents of bruised purple. The street outside is still. It's peak summer, and your town has been strangled for weeks by a record-breaking heatwave with temperatures unheard of in decades.

Across the street your neighbors' two children run back and forth through a sprinkler, their hysterical bouts of laughter punctuating the languid stillness of the quiet neighborhood. Your house is within walking distance of a train depot which serves as a way station for the surrounding counties' negligible industry; beneath the echoing laughter of the children, comes the sound of distant clanking freight cars starting forward on a rusting track.

An unfamiliar black car with tinted windows meanders past your house, then speeds up as it passes the stop sign, tires squealing obnoxiously. One of the older children shouts something obscene in response.

At first mistaking it for a train, you hear thunder rumbling, it's tones low and stealthy, as if it's preparing to sneak up on the world.

It is remarkably hot inside your house, considering your expensive air conditioning is already at its highest habitable setting. With the back of your hand, you wipe sweat away from your brow and neck; there are dark patches of perspiration on the couch where you have just been sleeping.

Rising on unsteady legs, and with a slight limp, you wander listlessly to the kitchen. Opening the fridge door you grab a bottle of cheap domestic beer, the only thing guaranteed to give some relief from the heat that clings uncomfortably to your body. Downing half of the bottle you set it on the counter, knowing the flack you'll get from your partner if you leave empties lying around.

Next to the sink sits a small Pioneer stereo system with an iPod dock. The radio is on, tuned to an AM news station.

"Meteorologists have reported atmospheric disturbances on both East and West Coasts," a voice that last knew the splendor of youth sometime around the 1960s intones. "Listeners all over the country have been calling in and sharing details of sightings as far inland as Canmore and Lethbridge..."

You switch the stereo input to its iPod setting and select a playlist of Van Morrison's greatest, keeping the volume low.

The door to the patio and backyard is just to the left of the kitchen window — a window that cracked during one of last winter's more severe ice storms. You run your fingertips over the fracture from where it branches out from the corner of the frame; it's something you've put off fixing for months now, in spite of the relative simplicity of the task, and you can feel an irrepressible frown tug at the corners of your mouth, frustrated that yet another item has cropped up on your ever growing to-do list, derailing what little free time you get to yourself these days.

Knowing that procrastinating any further on the matter will only spark a blow-out with your partner — of the sort occurring all too frequently lately — you resign yourself to visit the hardware store and put the matter to rest. Your partner is laying down in the upstairs bedroom before they have to work, so you'll have a couple of hours to slip out unnoticed and get a start on it.

Maybe, if you're lucky, you can score brownie points with this little project and alleviate some of the tension that's been kicking around between the two of you over the last couple of weeks. Besides, it feels like they're always complaining about your lack of initiative, your lack of drive, so why not prove them wrong for once?

Energized, you reach for your keys on the counter, but hesitate, deciding to indulge in a quick cigarette before you leave. You're motivated but still groggy, in no mood to rush; not in this heat.

Locating the cigarettes next to the pig-shaped cookie jar your partner made you buy for them at a yard sale; a ghastly eyesore you often think of smashing to bits with something blunt whenever you see it. Ignoring the pig's risible stare, you grab your smokes and step outside.

Outside now you sense a malaise hanging over everything — a sudden and definitive silence punctuated only by the buzzing of cicadas. The children across the street have gone quiet, likely having been ushered inside by their parents to stave off heat exhaustion.

Craning your neck you look up to the darkening sky, a drop of rain alights gently on your forehead. The air feels damp; a stark relief from the oven the inside of your house has become. Another drop lands on the weathered deck boards beneath your feet. Then another. You light your cigarette, holding the first drag in your throat slowly letting it out as lightning illuminates the backyard like an incredibly bright camera flash. You tense up for a second, waiting for an ear-splitting crack that never arrives. There is only silence.

Suddenly the storm clouds overhead are illuminated by a collection of bright, green-hued lights. You can't discern a source for these lights, but their flashing seems oddly coordinated, like fireworks sequenced to music — you almost expect to hear a symphony by Wagner bombastically fill the air around you.

The lights flicker in and out of the clouds, dancing and bouncing off each other like drunken fireflies. Your mind searches feebly for an explanation for this strange display: aircraft, extreme light pollution, aurora borealis. Nothing in your experience quite matches what you're seeing, though a popular acronym almost slips past your lips...

The sound of rattling tin causes you to jump. The noise is close by. From over the short fence that separates your properties, you see your neighbor — a genial old fellow with a doting wife and a runty dog that may or may not be deaf. He's putting the garbage out, which rest assured is no easy task for a man of his advancing age.

The sight of him fills you with an abiding sense of endearment: he's a charming man with a handful of amusing anecdotes in his repertoire, though you're convinced by now that you've heard each one at least three times. Not that you'd ever tell him that — you enjoy the man's presence in your life too much to run the risk of offending him.

Waving toward the man, you expect him to seize the opportunity to offer you a beer on his rickety and decaying back deck. However, he only smiles and nods his greeting, turning back to the house and disappearing behind the glint of his screen door. Standing there for a moment, you feel slightly put out; certainly not offended but nursing a childish feeling of rejection you know is uncharacteristic.

Finishing the last of your cigarette, you're about to step back inside when the rain begins in earnest.

The black cloud above the house seems to undulate like an artificial lung; the air ripens with ozone. Then the rain begins to fall, heavy, with a sound like marbles clattering down a set of wooden stairs. Only a few drops land on you before you close the door with a heavy thump.

The torrent hammers relentlessly on the world outside, droplets spattering through the screen of the open window as you stand, safe and dry, in the darkening kitchen. You watch the rain fall, transfixed, struggling to remember the important task you set for yourself just minutes ago.

A sudden rush of nausea washes over you, dizziness makes the room reel violently. The ozone smell from the rain intensifies, filling your nostrils with an unpleasant, sickly sweet scent. Bile rises in your throat and you swallow hard to suppress it. You quickly close the distance between yourself and the window, slamming it shut.

You feel a pulsing headache forming; a writhing sensation beneath your eyelids, like tiny insects scurrying en masse. Pressing your palm to your forehead in a vain attempt to suppress it, wincing at the inexplicable aches now tugging violently at your muscles, your joints, your bones, even your skin.

Deciding to postpone your plans you take a hot shower instead, hoping it will help restore your balance. At least it will cleanse you of the unpleasant feeling of grime and sweat coating your body.

You head down the hallway to the bathroom, passing the open doorway to the master bedroom where your partner's still sleeping form lies on the bed. Entering the bathroom you flip on the light switch to the left of the door. Peeling off your sweat-dampened clothes, you step into the tub, and turn the water on. The warm, comforting patter of the water against your body is an almost instant antidote to the pervasive feeling of clamminess that's been haunting you since you woke up.

After a minute or so of just standing under the water, the lightheadedness you experienced in the kitchen returns. The headache without warning violently builds momentum, your temples throb, a buzzing sound like a hive of angry bees fills your ears. Your vision begins to blur and distort as building steam from the shower cloaks the room in white. Your thoughts begin to race with worst-case scenarios: heart attack, stroke, aneurysm.

You need to get to your phone and call 911, but in your confusion and pain, you can't remember where you left it. A trembling hand reaches out in a feeble attempt to draw back the shower curtain, but the cheap plastic slips from your grip as you begin to go numb, the beehive of noise in your ears building to an excruciating cacophony. You anticipate a flood of pain as the shower floor rushes toward you, but it doesn't come...

There is only darkness.

✳✳✳

You come to. You are lying on the couch in the living room, fully dressed. The television is on, the screen bright blue with no input. Confusion and terror settle over you like a black pall, and it takes a long time for your eyes to adjust to what they are seeing, like a newborn registering its world for the first time.

Standing up you call out your partner's name. All you hear in return is the steady tick of the clock above the television. Everything around you swims in and out of focus. You manage to focus enough to make your way down the hallway to the bedroom, where you stand at the door, a trembling hand hovering over the knob. After a moment's hesitation, you enter.

The curtains covering the open window billow above the sleeping form of your partner. Stepping closer, you see the reassuring rise and fall of their chest with each steady breath. They stir slightly and turn away from you, conscious, perhaps, of your presence in the room.

Heart racing in your chest, you command it to slow sensing that normalcy is still holding reign, even if your head is swimming with troubling possibilities regarding what has just happened to you.

You try to clear your mind of clutter in order to get a better handle on the situation. Something off has happened, something you can't explain or simply let slide. But what can you do about it? Waking your partner is out of the question, they work nights and would not appreciate being disturbed from their pre-shift slumber; going to the hospital is a possibility, but you're not exactly sure what good it would accomplish. What would you tell a doctor? That you had a vivid and extended dream you confused with waking life? That in said dream you experienced a distressing series of physical phenomenon, the catalyst being some unexplained lights in the sky?

Closing the door to the bedroom you head back down the hall. Plopping down on the couch you spend a few minutes trying to concentrate. Shaking your head in resignation, you make your way to the front door, deciding that fresh air is what you need most.

Opening the heavy oak door you step outside. Night has fallen and with it a shroud of fog thicker than any you have ever seen. Overhead, restless clouds move swiftly across a jet-black sky.

Your attention focuses on a car, stopped in the middle of the road directly across from your house. The driver and passenger side doors are open, and the interior light is on. Slowly, with unease knotting your insides, you make your way down your front porch and across the path that splits the front lawn. As you hit the sidewalk, you hear the incessant ping, ping, ping of an open-door sensor.

With deliberate, slow steps, you approach the car. Looking inside the interior appears to be a jumbled mess of random objects: garbage, clothes, dog toys, a toolbox with its contents spilled all over the back seat. A deep-fried smell, pungent with age, rises somewhere from within the car's depths. Hesitantly, you slide into the car on the driver's side.

The digital face on the car's expensive looking satellite radio reads 1:17 PM — roughly the same time that the episode in the shower happened. If that episode even happened at all.

Something must be wrong with the stereo. The minute kept alternating between 1:17 and 1:18, as if time was struggling to inch forward in its usual implacable march.

You turn up the volume on the radio. The stations are all awash with static, save for one: a twenty-four-hour satellite news station.

"—something in the rain" a clipped and barely audible voice pronounces. "Government authorities have determined—"

Static overtakes the signal. You adjust the tuner, and the voice returns, clearer, but only for a moment.

"Health officials have issued a warning that all citizens of the greater—"

The rest is swallowed by white noise.

Fumbling with the keys you kill the engine before your eyes settle on the windshield. Rivulets of a dark liquid run down the glass, but you can't tell if it's on the inside or the outside, so you wipe the pane. Examining your hand you find the palm to be stained red, a rich coppery smell rising from it. In a horrified instant you realize what the liquid is. Breathing heavily, your heart banging in your chest your eyes search the mist-enshrouded street struggling to make out familiar shapes and forms.

You see three dark figures standing in a circle on the sidewalk four or five doors from your home.

"Hello?!" you call out, voice echoing in the stillness. There is no response, no movement, and after a moment the shapes simply dissolve into the dark and roiling mist.

Sound, like an exploding tire, rings out. Turning in the sound's direction you make out an indistinct figure emerging from your neighbor's house. The figure moves with an unnatural, limping stride that reads of panic or agitation. You quickly give chase, calling out your neighbor's name. The figure unlatches the gate to the backyard and disappears into the darkness, gate hinges squeaking in its wake.

Reaching the gate, you open it and step through. A floodlight clicks on, illuminating the yard. The sudden brightness confuses you, and you trip over a plastic lawn chair, almost doing a faceplant onto the wet grass.

Your neighbor is standing in the center of his lawn, back turned to you. There is a long object in his left hand that glimmers dimly in the emerging moonlight. You approach him slowly; his attention seems to be fixed on the sky above, as though he were searching for stars in all that cloudy dark.

You're only a few yards away from him when he raises the long object in both hands and places it under his chin. A startled cry tries to escape your throat, but is choked off as you recognize what the object is.

The entirety of your neighbor's head explodes in a red mist as a deafening report bounces off the surrounding houses.

A hoarse scream escapes you, the exclamation deafened by a painful ringing in your ears. In a gruesome display of post-mortem vitality, your neighbor's headless corpse stands perfectly upright for a moment before crumpling soundlessly onto the grass, hands still gripping the stock of the smoking shotgun.

Bile rises insistently in your throat. You clasp a hand over your mouth, but it's no use — an intense coppery smell hits you and you double over, the reeking contents of your stomach spilling out in a steady stream covering your shoes. Falling to your knees, choking and retching, an unrestrained torrent of warm tears spills from your eyes. You stay doubled over, sobbing, gasping, trying and failing to regain composure.

The absurdly redundant idea that you need to call an ambulance comes to you right then, and you can't help but emit a hysterical little giggle. Your whole-body trembles violently as you. wipe the acidic taste of vomit from your lips. Still in a daze, you walk back in the direction you came, opening the gate to the backyard as the floodlight clicks off behind you. Rather than returning home you move steadily toward the side door of your neighbor's house. Finding it unlocked, you enter, navigating around a pile of shoes left on the mat. It's been a long time since you have been inside of your (now former) neighbor's house, so everything is unfamiliar. Before you a long hallway runs, a light shining dimly to the right where it ends. The master bedroom.

Cautiously you make your way down the hall and enter the bedroom. The first thing your eyes register is a single slipper discarded on the floor; pink with a tuft of white fur on top. You search for its match until your eyes light on a smeared red spot on the carpet. With growing dread your eyes follow a trail of red splotches until they reach a figure sitting slumped against the wall, its entire upper body covered with a curtain torn hastily from one of the windows. It's your neighbor's wife, legs splayed in an unnatural fashion beneath her; dark blood soaking through the curtain covering her face. There is a riot of red all over the bright yellow wall behind her.

You register a dull shock at the sight of the body, mind unable, or unwilling, to grapple with what it's seeing.

Taking a tentative step forward you know you shouldn't touch her, but some horrible force within compels you to move closer, extending a trembling hand toward the bloody curtain. You pinch the soft fabric lightly between forefinger and thumb, pulling the curtain away with a flutter.

What remains of her face is a tattered red concave filled with shattered bone - one of her eyes, still intact, dangles loosely from a thin thread of connective tissue. He must have shot her at close range. You pray, idly, that she felt little or no pain as her brain fired its last neurons.

Leaving the room, you make your way back down the hallway in a half stupor. Stopping where a landline telephone hangs from the wall you lift the receiver from its cradle, press it to your ear, and dial 911.

The line is busy.

You hang up and try again with the same result, then you walk down the remainder of the hallway and back out the door. You head down your neighbor's driveway and crossover onto your own property. You feel weak, drained, on the verge of collapse.

Reaching your front porch steps you register a figure out of the corner of your eye: a tall, thin man approaching from the sidewalk, features blurred, made indistinct by the tears still welling in your eyes. He begins to move toward you, his hand outstretched imploringly.

"Help," you manage to croak, not sure if the man hears you. "Please, I need help. There's been a-a-"

The figure steps into full view, hideously bathed in the sickly hue of your porch light. The face that stares in your direction is a mockery of the human form, its waxen skin painfully tight against bulging and distorted bones; lifeless black eyes, insect-like in their size and prominence, gazing from too large sockets; a gaping, lipless mouth revealing a manic arrangement of sharp yellow teeth; thick drool clinging to the pocked skin over its chin.

You back away swiftly, heel catching on the runner of the first step and sending you sprawling backward onto the porch stairs. A jolt of pain courses through your back, even as you struggle to crawl away from the approaching figure.

The thing — surely the only word for what it is — moves steadily toward you, extending arms that terminate with long nails that have no business being attached to a human hand. A dry wheeze escapes from its throat as the vocal cords pathetically attempt to form words that must be "Please help me," but come out more as "Preese hurp muh."

Frantically you scramble toward the door and heave yourself by the handle onto your feet. Sweaty hands fumble with the knob, the hair on your neck rising as you feel the thing closing the distance between you. For a terrifying moment you're sure the door is locked. At last it opens, and you hurl yourself headlong inside. Slamming the door shut, you press all your weight against it, still feeling the thing's presence on the other side.

After a moment you hear footsteps descend the stairs, pausing a second before moving away from the house.

Your heart rate begins to slow to a tolerable jog, and you close your eyes against the all too bright lights inside your house. Van Morrison belts out "Wild Night" from the stereo in the kitchen.

All the lights are on. You only remember the light in the foyer being on when you left. Your partner must be awake. A long shadow falls over the hallway wall, bobbing up and down before moving out of sight. You move through the living room toward it and catch a quick glimpse of your partner as they turn toward the bedroom.

You think you hear them sobbing, though the sound is muffled, indistinct.

You call their name. No reply.

Entering the bedroom, you notice the curtains fluttering. The air is damp, acrid with the scent of freshly fallen rain.

Your partner sits on the left-hand side of the bed, opposite the dresser, their back turned to you. You call their name several more times.

Still no reply.

Reaching out you place a firm grip on their shoulder. Finally, they turn toward you.

Something inside of you snaps, but you don't scream. Unappeasable horror pushes all rationality down inside of you, like gravity, to that comfortable, buried place where madness resides.

Your partner stares back at you with pleading insectile eyes, one hand gingerly caressing their new face and its obscene features, trying to make some sort of sense of them. A single tear runs down a strangely protruding cheekbone. They open their mouth to say something, to beg, perhaps, for some sort of explanation — all that comes out is a dry croaking sound that couldn't possibly be words. You turn and walk toward the bedroom door, almost seem to float toward it.

You've gone completely numb now, the terror and confusion receding, in their place a sort of pleasant understanding. An acceptance.

Passing the open bathroom, you catch the reflection of a stranger in the mirror above the sink. It's funny, really. The stranger shares many features similar to your own, including the very clothes on your body, but there's a taut translucency to the skin, a bulging quality to the eyes - they seem to grow larger as you stare into their jet-black surface.

You smile at this stranger, and the stranger smiles back at you with yellowing teeth that don't quite seem to fit properly.

Your partner appears behind you, placing a hand on your shoulder. It almost feels reassuring.

Outside, barely audible beneath a growing din of emergency sirens, you hear thunder rumbling...

###

About Alexander Harrington

ALEXANDER HARRINGTON, BORN APRIL 12 1989 in London, Ontario, will never forget the fateful night his young self was sat down in front of a grainy television set to watch a late-night airing of Howard Hawks' The Thing from Another World, an experience that still resonates powerfully in his imagination. Raised on a steady diet of comic books and age inappropriate film and television, the Examination Day segment of the 80s Twilight Zone still triggers him, he is a journalism major who has contributed freelance movie reviews and entertainment articles to several publications.

Alexander has also created works in the world of independent theater, writing, directing and acting in a number of limited engagement stage plays, including the surreal and macabre thrillers Last Echo and Painkiller, both of which deal with twin obsessions in his writing: identity and the nature of reality.

He is currently working on a play anthologizing several short stories by the great H.P. Lovecraft, and is also developing a podcast with a focus on pop culture and the murky and problematic politics currently plaguing it. He is a rabid genre fan, particularly of weird and pulp fiction and spends a potentially unhealthy amount of time in bargain basement book dealers, amassing a collection of obscure, B-grade VHS tapes and musty paperbacks.

Alexander divides his time between a busy work schedule in the industrial sales industry, writing, travelling, drawing, volunteering, and stalking the floors of horror and science-fiction conventions. He lives with his wife and two children in the greater Toronto area. Altered is his first published short story.

Connect with Alexander here:
www.castrumpress.com/authors/alexander-harrington

WITHIN THE STORM
By Beth Frost

The sun is rising high in the cloudless blue sky, turning the white buildings into pillars of molten gold. The automaton in the corner deals with the remnants of my meal as I take this moment to stand and look out over the city.

Below me, the streets are thronged. Bright colors abound, and I know if I open the window, the sounds of the festival will rise up to me, borne on wings of laughter. There is always a carnival on Rest Day.

I don't think this will be the day that I leave my suite and descend to the party. I'm getting too old to dance in the street anymore, even if I would love to celebrate. Today, the carnival will come to me.

I watch the people below, letting the time pass in reverie, until I hear the stampede of footsteps outside of my door. They don't stand on ceremony, and my door is flung open. Little Alyson is first in, dressed in vivid orange, waving a handful of streamers around, trailing glitter behind her in a cloud. Markus is beside her, smart in dark blue, and with his face painted with a crystal and green mask. Polly and Paul, my beautiful twins are in sunshine yellow and sky blue, their hair braided with bells that sweetly chime with every movement. Baby Ruth is in the arms of Anne, a giggling scarlet vision as she tries to catch the ribbons in Anne's hair. And lastly, my oldest grandchild, Nocturne.

He wears silken blacks, translucent greys and sparkling white, and is desperately trying to pretend he doesn't want to be here, for the benefit of the two friends I can spy lurking, unsure of their welcome. But I know him, and he comes to me for a hug as eagerly as any of his siblings do.

They sit around my feet for a while, telling me of all the things that they have done and seen in the days since I've seen them. Nocturne and his friends sit together, heads bent as they whisper and gossip amongst themselves. But the conversation fades, the pauses longer, the silence deeper, until they all watch me with wide eyes.

They want the story.

And so, I begin.

***

It was common knowledge that trouble comes in threes. When my Dad tripped and fell over a particularly ornery sheep, that was the first sign. If it had only been a strain or a sprain, then Dad would have just shrugged and carried on walking the hills. But he broke bones, and even for my Dad, that was a bit much. And so, he was housebound with my very patient mother hovering around him, trying to keep him distracted.

It couldn't have come at a worse time. We were in Life Season now, and everywhere on our farm, new life was coming into being. Our herds and flocks had survived the Cold Season well, and Dad was hopeful for a good number of babies. Ours was only a small farm, and every life, especially a new life, was precious.

Thankfully, for me anyway, most of the lambs had already been born, and there were only a few stubborn holdouts in the hills, which became my job to watch. So, on the morn of the Rest Day, I trekked into the hills with my bag on my back, and our dog Saf frolicking at my heels. Our bothy was an hour away, and the neighbor who was there was expecting me.

The weathercast I heard before I left the house was the second sign of trouble. There was the promise of rain, and a bit of wind. Dad had listened, sucked his teeth, and then shook his head.

"Ain't be listening to that," he told me. "Twill be a storm, and a bad one. City folk don't understand our weather. You take care of yourself out there, lass. Wouldn't ask this if 'tweren't important."

I trusted my Dad's weather instinct more than I trusted the soft voice over the air and made sure to take my waterproofs and a few other things to make my life easier.

Our neighbor was not one for conversation, so as soon as I arrived, he departed without even a goodbye. I didn't take it personally, left my bag in the bothy, and set off to check the sheep. None were in labor, or looked anywhere close to being in labor, so I returned to the bothy to wait.

Every hour I did another tour of the flock, every hour I checked the weather again. Every hour I could see the clouds boiling over the mountains. Dad had been right.

As the wind started to gust, and the clouds started to move down the slope one of the ewes decided this was the perfect time to go into full labor. She was Dads prized ewe, had lambed a dozen times with perfect results. I knew he'd want me to watch her closely to make sure nothing went wrong. And so, I, in my infinite young wisdom, brought her inside while the rest of the herd clustered on the leeward side of the building.

Saf, our dog was rather confused about this, but tolerated the wooly interloper in front of her stove, settling beside the heat, one eye on the door, and one on the ewe. Barely had I closed the door when the full fury of the storm hit.

The building was sturdy and solid, and the wind howled outside the door but inside we felt no chill. Rain thundered on the windows, but we were dry and warm. The ewe was laboring away herself and required no intervention. I was slumped in the old chair, half asleep in the heat, when Saf raised her head.

She made a noise, not quite a growl, not quite a whine, and her tail twitched.

"What is it?" I asked.

Thump.

Thump.

Thump.

The third trouble.

Three knocks on the door, hardly heard over the thundering storm. If it hadn't been for the attention of Saf, I might not have heard anything.

No one should be out in a storm like this. All our neighbors were at least as weather wise as my Dad, and none of their lands were anywhere near us. Saf didn't think there was a threat, the ewe was busy with her own business, and no one should be out tonight.

I stood up from the chair, crossed to the door and unbolted it, bracing myself as I opened it. The wind screamed as it gained entrance, racing inside and sending loose objects flying. Rain poured down, splashing over the threshold and leaving puddles behind. However, I wasn't paying attention to the vagrancies of the storm. Outside was a figure, tall, lean and wrapped in a dark cloak for protection against the raging downpour. I couldn't make out his face.

"Shelter," he rasped in a low growl/hiss, and I saw from the corner of my eye Saf cocking an ear in attention, but she still wasn't growling.

Old stories told on dark nights sprang to mind, and I simply stepped to one side, opening access to the room without speaking a word. The man needed no words and he stepped inside, ducking to avoid the lintel.

Saf sniffed at his cloak as it passed her nose, before laying her head on her paws again. Reassured, I forced the door shut against the wind slamming the bolt home.

I was used to tall men. My Dad was tall, old William in the village was taller still, but this stranger towered above them all. Beneath the thin cloak, his figure was slender, and he moved with a strange gait as he crossed to stand in front of the stove.

"You picked a bad time, Stranger," I told him as I took up my seat again. "What brings you out here?"

The stranger shook his head and did not answer. Some people were like that, I knew. Maybe he was as wary of me as I had been of him.

"Tis a wicked night for walking, but it should blow over by morning." I tried to make conversation again, and again, silence met me.

This time I chose to honor the strangers need for silence and kept my mouth shut, begging my mother's forgiveness for not offering hospitality. Maybe when the man warmed up a little, he would be better tempered.

We sat in silence for some time, until the wind caught the door a heavy blow, rattling the iron hinges so as to make you think they were about to shatter. The noise in the silence was so abrupt it startled the stranger. He whirled around, and his garment began to slither free. With concealed hands he tried to stop the movement, but failed, and the fabric fell away from his form.

It froze, revealed to my disbelieving eyes for the first time.

Under the cloak it had passed for human, but without the concealment...it looked like a huge insect, standing upright and staring back at me with huge multifaceted eyes.

It had three fingers on each hand, and the cloak hung useless and forgotten from one hand, black against the shiny green of its hard skin. A pair of gossamer wings fluttered frantically from behind it, and it stood as if to run on its three jointed legs.

I was shocked, yes, but not horrified. With the scream of the wind outside, it made my world hold an unreal quality, emphasized by the figure in front of me.

The sheep lying beside the stove chose then to groan, a tearing sound that set fire to all the instincts my Dad had trained into me. I darted up from my seat and to her side, ignoring the creature. It skittered out of the way, claws clicking on the floor as it dodged away.

Luckily for me the ewe was just being a drama queen, and was still laboring away quite happily, requiring no intervention from me. Just as well, as my mind was still grappling with the reality of the being which was currently trying to blend in with the stonework. As it was green, it wasn't doing such a good job.

Now my initial shock had passed, I could easily take in the creature. It was like nothing that I had ever seen before, whether in person, or in books. Nothing like it had been mentioned in the stories passed down through families, or the stories passed around in the tavern. It pressed tight against the stonework as if trying to hide and was hunching over as if to conceal its true size from me. And, looking intently, I could see it trembling. That would never do.

I moved away from the fire, toward the wooden cupboard on the wall feeling its eyes watching me cautiously. The door creaked as it opened, causing the creature to flinch once more. Inside the cupboard, I blessed my mother again, before pulling out a well-worn patchwork blanket. I draped it over my arm and turned back to face the creature.

"You must be freezing," I told it calmly, in the same way I talked to the sheep, walking toward it, unfolding and holding the blanket out in front of me. With slow footsteps, I approached the creature as non-threateningly as I could. It didn't move as I got to within arm's length, and to my surprise allowed me to wrap the blanket around it. I had to stand on tiptoes to reach its shoulders even with it hunched over. It held the edges of the blanket in its three fingered hands, and I could see it relaxing into the warmth.

"Come back to the heat," I suggested gesturing it forward, moving back to my seat to give it space. When it moved, it moved with slightly less hesitation, crossing to the stove and crouching down to get the most heat. It was hard to read, but I thought maybe it was relieved.

I leaned back into the seat and took a deep breath. I was trying to work out what to ask it. 'What are you?' seemed to be far too rude to ask a guest, but it was only thing I really wanted to know.

"I thank you," the creature saved me from thinking too hard as it pressed a hand to its chest and spoke in that same growl, almost hiss it had spoken in before. "Regret disturbance. Weather unexpected."

"No disturbance," I told it. "I was here, and it certainly isn't a night for being out."

It made a peculiar clicking noise as it took in my words, before turning away from the fire somewhat in order to face me. "Curious," it said. "No fear. Good, but why?"

"Why should I be frightened?" I asked it and could hear the confusion in my tone. It clicked again, and I realized it was laughing at me.

It gestured to itself, and then pointed at me. "Strange," it hissed. "Fear expected. Unknown. Different. We are not like you."

I could see what the creature was saying, but I couldn't help but shrug. "Not that different."

It clicked with laughter again, and looked around, seeming to be far more relaxed as it took in the bothy. I didn't think I had said anything special. Saf decided now that the creature was more settled, it was worthy of investigation. She rose and padded across the floor to sniff curiously at it.

The creature tilted its head to watch, before carefully reaching out a hand. Saf, ever keen for attention, insinuated her head under those three fingers, closing her eyes in pleasure as the creature tentatively scratched her ears.

If anything, I felt that proved my point.

From in front of the fire, the ewe let out another bleat, and this time, there was something I could see happening. A pair of hocks were protruding, and the ewe was pushing busily. The creature noticed the shift in my attention and looked over.

I wasn't skilled at reading it, but in this, curiosity was visible. As I moved to kneel beside the ewe, bringing an old blanket with me, the creature came to stand behind me.

The ewe required no help in labor, and I caught the lamb as it was born, setting it down on the old blanket. There was another one following close behind, and I laid it down beside the other. The ewe was already up and turning to tend her new babies, and I caught the afterbirth as it was delivered before it could land on the floor.

The creature leaned over my shoulder, making a strange noise, like the crickets in the fields. It reached out over my shoulder to touch the mass with a three fingered hand, and then withdrew again.

"Curious," it noted quietly.

I smiled at it, and moved to the door, bracing myself before opening it.

It was still raining outside, although it was a softer rainfall, silvery in the moonlight. The wind had died down to a gentle breeze as the storm moved on. The world smelled clean as without us realizing it, the tempest had passed.

I buried the afterbirth in the wet soil beside the bothy and checked on the rest of the sheep. None of them were in labor themselves, and so I returned to the bothy to wait out the rest of the night.

The creature was now kneeling in all its strange glory beside the ewe, petting the newborn lambs with a gentle hand.

When it turned to look at me, its multifaceted eyes were sparkling with an emotion I couldn't read. Rising to its full height, its beautiful gossamer wings spread open to their full extent, glittering in the candlelight.

It hugged me.

It was all sharp angles and smooth plates and smelt of dusty soil and static. It shivered as I raised my own arms to hug it back, churring nonstop, almost like a cat's purr. We stood together in the middle of the room, and just...held each other.

***

My grandchildren are mesmerized by the story. Little Ruth has fallen asleep, and now lies in my arms. Nocturne and his friends have abandoned their pose of indifference and chatter.

Although I didn't know it then, I was the first to meet them, these aliens from another world. My friend had been with the diplomatic corps his ship having been blown off course in the storm. He returned to his fleet after the disturbance had passed, and they had made their grand entrance to the city under their peace banners.

My friend had done his duty then, bridging the gap between our species, working out the details of the peace treaty that still holds to this day. And then, he had come in search of me.

When the ship had hovered over our small yard, my father had stared slack-jawed for but a moment, before he had been calling orders to my mother, myself and my siblings. Even here, in the wilds, we had heard of the K'has'vor and this strange new peace that was descending. But my father was always cautious.

In my heart of hearts, I knew it was my friend coming back to me, and had stepped forward to greet him, even as my father yelled at me to step back. Saf had emerged from the house, her tail held high as it wagged in delight.

As I fall silent now, my tale told, there comes a fresh knock at my door, and I can see my grandchildren looking curiously at each other. This is something new. As if an old lady can't have friends!

"Enter," I call, and rise to my feet, shifting Ruth to rest in the crook of my arm.

His carapace is blackened with age now, and one of his eyes no longer sparkles, but my friend of the K'has'vor is very much the same as when I met him so long ago. Bright colorful handprints decorate his abdomen, and his wings are sheathed in glimmering jewel tones, ready for the Carnival.

We hug each other, in our familiar routine. He cannot come as often as he would like, or as often as I would like to see him. But I know that within eight Rest Days, he will be here.

We're getting older now, as time passes, and one of these days our friendship will come to its physical end, and we will dance at Carnival for the last time. Nonetheless, when I go to meet my Maker, and he travels the Desert of Stars, we will always remember each other, and that night within the storm.

###

About Beth Frost

BORN IN ENGLAND, RAISED IN Scotland and now living in Northern Ireland with her husband and a space-mad child, Beth Frost always knew that she wanted to be a teacher. Which is why she now works as a secretary by day, and author by night.

Raised on a diet of fantasy books by the likes of Anne McCaffrey and David Eddings, Beth started out by writing fanfiction, and then moved onto creating her own worlds and characters. She hasn't stopped since.

She has dabbled her toes into the waters of self-publishing, having shifted genres into paranormal romance for a number of years, but now is heading back to her first love of fantasy & science fiction.

Besides doing accounts and writing, Beth enjoys crochet, taking long walks in the nearby forest, and firmly telling her plotbunnies to stop multiplying.

Connect with Beth here:
www.castrumpress.com/authors/beth-frost

SONGS SWEETER STILL
By David M. Hoenig

F im dropped the rock she carried into the hopper, then lifted her face to eat some of the tasty snowflakes falling from the sky. She moved on to allow the next person to drop their rock in, and listened to the peculiar sound as it banged down to follow hers. She ate more of the snow which came down, rich and wholesome and nutritious, and considered her feelings.

Rocks didn't make such a sound anywhere other than when they went into the strange boxes of the hot ones. She'd been hearing the noise all her life, but today, she realized, the sound was wrong in some way. This odd feeling persisted and grew stronger, to the point where she could not simply dismiss it as she usually did. Instead of returning to get her next rock, she ate a few last flakes and moved toward one of the hot ones.

'Gray' walked amongst her people as she did most days, asking questions of them, all the while tapping at something she held in her hands.

When Fim reached the hot one, she tapped it on the arm to get its attention. "Why do we give you our rocks?"

Gray turned quickly, as though surprised, and Fim saw the odd face of the creature, similar to, but so different from her own. "Oh! Hi there, Fim." The voice came from a patch on its neck which seemed to gleam in the same way as the hopper did, though the hot one's mouth seemed to be moving so as to fashion the words. "What did you ask?"

"I said: 'Why do we give you our rocks,' Gray?"

The hot one looked down and tapped the thing in its hand before responding. "That... is a very interesting question. I'll trade you: an answer to your question for an answer to one of mine. Agreed?"

Fim considered before she nodded agreement.

"Well, because we need the 'rocks.' It's one of the main reasons we're here at all." Gray waited a few moments, but Fim remained quiet so the hot one went on. "My question is this: Why did you call the rocks 'ours'?"

"Isn't it obvious, Gray?"

The hot one's lips drew thin. "No. Please tell me why you think they are."

Fim moved her arm in an all-encompassing gesture. "The rocks are part of this world, yes?"

"Of course."

"We are part of this world?"

"Also true, but..."

"But you and your boxes are not, Gray. Nothing like them exists in all the rest of the world. They are unnatural."

The hot one remained silent for a few moments, and when it spoke in a monotone. "Your point?"

"You are not of this world; the rocks are not yours. They're ours because we are." Fim turned and walked away.

She did not hear the hot one murmur behind her. "Fascinating."

***

Doctor Maya Agramonte hurried from the airlock storage compartment where she had left her suit and was halfway down the corridor into Titan Base before her handheld unit buzzed for attention. She tapped it. "Agramonte."

The voice was unwelcome. "Doctor, this is Jim Baylor. I need you to report to my office right now, please."

"Later. I must log the most extraordinary devel..."

"Negative. The situation is urgent. Robertson and Watanabe are here, but we need you, too."

Agramonte scowled. "Fine, I'm on my way." She switched off the comm and at the next intersection, turned left toward Administration. A few minutes later she arrived at the Commander's office, where she tapped a panel by the door and identified herself.

Baylor's voice returned clearly. "Come in, Doctor."

The door slid open and she went in. She nodded at the other section heads sitting at the large conference table in Baylor's office, but didn't immediately take a seat. "What's this about? I'm dealing with the most incredible social development we've observed yet among the EI's, and the scientific implications are astounding. I've got issues..."

The base commander interrupted her. "We've got issues, Doctor, and we need your input. Please be seated."

Agramonte sat only after taking note of the others. When she spoke, her tone held suspicion. "What's the problem?"

Baylor glanced to his right, and nodded to Ikeda Watanabe. The Chief of Environmental Operations cleared her throat before speaking. "Station system losses have increased since my last report despite our efforts, and we're barely meeting demand from the refueling station in orbit in addition to our own needs."

Agramonte shrugged. "If the problems are technical, find them and fix them, Ikeda."

"That's not a helpful attitude, Maya," Ben Robertson said coldly. "Until we can minimize the losses and increase output to cope with our ever-increasing demands, we need a plan."

"Well, what's Materials Sciences doing about this?"

Baylor interrupted. "Enough, people! I don't need my senior administrators bickering, I need solutions." He turned to Agramonte. "Frankly, Maya, the losses are only part of the problem. We're investigating multiple paths toward a solution, and Life Sciences is going to need to address a very serious problem which is contributing to the overall concern."

"Oh?" Agramonte leaned aggressively forward. "You're going to cut my personnel again to decrease station demand, Jim? What we're doing here is of absolutely critical..."

Baylor exploded. "Will you stop jumping to paranoid conclusions for a minute? This is bloody important!"

The Commander losing his temper brought Agramonte's irritated tirade to an abrupt halt. She considered before beginning again. "Fine." More grudgingly: "I'm sorry. What can my department do?"

"First, can you tell me why EI productivity has fallen fifteen percent over the last three standard months, despite breeding so efficiently and effectively that their numbers of adults are up ten percent over the same interval?"

Agramonte blinked in surprise. "But I was just outside with them and things were running smoothly! Like usual, I might add. The Exo-Indigenous are breeding and expanding as designed, using the local biochemistry; without any natural metals or conductors, it's a far more cost-efficient process than machines. We've taught them to haul water-ice chunks which we blast out while they sleep at night--which they call 'rocks', logically enough, since it forms the majority of the 'bedrock' of this moon--continually from local sunup until sundown, as their physiology allows. Population figures are on perfect track; productivity should be paralleling that."

"The operative words are 'should be'," Baylor said. "Our system losses are well above expected, and replacement from local resources is down from what we had with half the population." He leaned forward and made measured eye contact with all three of his section heads. "The combination of those issues means we're way behind where we should be." The commander tapped the table with his forefinger to make his point. "Corporate is expecting a return on investment from this facility by providing ice to the station in orbit, which will function as a reaction-mass and water refueling point for interplanetary traffic. We've got reserves for the moment, but the EI's are the key to making this venture profitable. If we can't scale up the way Corporate's been anticipating, we're..."

"Dead in the lack of water," Robertson interjected dryly.

Watanabe ignored the men. "Any thoughts on what the problem is, Maya?"

Agramonte thought about the exchange with the EI named 'Fim' not twenty minutes earlier, and suppressed a shiver. She stood; hands flat on the table. "You put your house in order, Ikeda; I'll take care of mine."

She stalked out, aware that she left no friends behind her in Baylor's office. Watanabe called after her, following. "Maya, please wait."

Agramonte did so, reluctantly. "Make it quick, Ikeda. The scientific implications of my recent observations are astounding. The EI's are on the verge of a new level of social development, well in advance of predictions."

Watanabe nodded, but her smile seemed forced. "I see you're excited about the science, and what you've accomplished is remarkable. We're not friends in the conventional sense; too much butting heads over corporate resources, I suppose, but know I applaud your successes. They're at the heart of everything we hope to achieve here."

"I hear a 'but' coming."

The smile faded. "But...we are having troubles meeting quotas. If we can't make this succeed, we all lose. So far from Earth, the only sure thing is a team effort, Maya. I hope to God that you'll reach out and let me help if you need it, okay?"

The two scientists locked gazes for some moments before Agramonte replied flatly. "There is no 'God', Ikeda." She walked past her colleague down the corridor.

Watanabe watched her go, frowning.

✳✳✳

Fim startled when Taf's voice came from behind her, and nearly dropped the alien thing she held.

"What's that, Fim?"

"Just a thing Gray asked me to move from one place to another," she said, turning and showing it to him.

Taf shook his head. "A strange thing, to be sure. If I'm not mistaken, it's one of those that puts the sun in the cave, right?"

"Yes. The hot ones call it a 'floodlamp'."

"Such oddness." Taf considered the horizon, where the last rays from the distant sun lingered as if embarrassed to be there. "It doesn't seem like you'll get it there today, does it?" He stretched his arms overhead, then wrapped them around himself. "I'm already feeling cool, and ready to sleep the moment it is dark."

Fim considered. "What if I don't want to tonight?"

"Foolishness. We must, because our bodies freeze without the sun's warmth." He folded downwards to a sitting position. "Might as well lie here with me as elsewhere. Gray's thing will wait until morning."

Around them, Fim saw others of her people doing the same. "But what if you weren't forced to sleep, Taf? Would it be worth it to stay awake and hear the night sky sing?"

The sun slipped below the horizon and the darkness deepened. Only the light reflected from Saturn--eternally in their sky--and the myriad stars remained but did not offer any warmth. Taf mumbled as he lay down. "Don't...know. Don't much care, hhrrrr.....hrrrk."

Fighting the cold, Fim switched on the thing she held, just as she'd seen some of Gray's underlings do, and the alien light flared out into the dark around her. The hot one's artifact hummed, breaking the silence of the hushed landscape of the world, but she felt its heat force back the chill of night. She glanced over her shoulder, where a heap of rocks due to be placed in the hot ones' boxes stood between her and their home, shielding the light her pilfered 'floodlamp' emitted. She turned it on herself and felt the warmth from it chase away the chill of the encroaching darkness.

Fim sat and waited, head tilted so she might listen to the songs from the sky. Around her, the rest of her people slept where they had lain when the sun vanished below the curve of the world.

The songs were strange, even stranger than the hot ones' 'floodlamp' which emitted enough warmth to allow her to stay awake through the chilly night.

After a while she found she understood them.

After that, she found that she liked what they had to say.

***

Several days later, Agramonte was suiting up to do more observations on the EI's when one of her scientific staff came running up. "You're not going to believe this, Maya."

She felt a sudden chill. "Tell me."

"Surveillance footage. Took some work to come up with something they wouldn't notice so we could catch them in the act..."

Agramonte interrupted. "How many?"

"I'd estimate some twenty percent of the EI's we filmed were ambulatory last night." Lewis rubbed his eyes and stifled a yawn.

"How is that possible? We engineered them to go dormant when the temp drops and their circulatory systems freeze and shut down! Considering they can otherwise eat the endless methane snow to provide all the energy they need, we had to do something to limit them."

"You're going to love this: they are using the heat from the technology we've given them to expedite water production. Anything with a battery pack, basically--keeps them warm enough to remain active at night. Here. Watch for yourself." He handed her his handheld.

Agramonte took the device and tapped out commands.

Lewis ran a hand through his hair while she watched. "Obviously, what's amazing is that they figured this out on their own." When his superior didn't say anything in response, he went on. "They've begun to repurpose what we've given them to suit their needs--it speaks of a far greater intelligence and sophistication of logical, rational thought than we imagined possible. The EI's are ludicrously far ahead of our most optimistic projections! With your permission, I want to write this up for the Exobiology journals back home. Right now, in fact."

She returned the handheld to Lewis. "What are the ambulatory ones doing overnight?"

"I'm hypothesizing they've reached a new stage in their social development--they're moving into large clusters to sit, staring up at the night sky."

Agramonte shook her head as if waking up, and continued to dress in her pressure suit. "What can they see through the hydrocarbon fog?"

"More than we can. Remember, we designed them to perceive farther into both ends of the spectrum..."

Ikeda Watanabe's arrival, thin-lipped and glowering, interrupted Lewis. The chief of Environmental Ops glared at the younger scientist. "Leave. I need to speak with her right the hell now, and I need privacy." When Lewis hesitated, looking to Agramonte for guidance, Watanabe invaded his personal space and bellowed "Now!" from about an inch away.

The scientist paled and fled.

Agramonte was fully dressed except for her helmet, which she tucked under one arm. She decided to meet Watanabe's anger with some of her own. "What gives you the right to yell at one of my people?"

"Oh, I dunno, how about, let's see, shall we? Yeah, let's try sabotage for starters!"

"Wait. What?"

"Deliberate sabotage, Maya. The ice processor in the south quadrant that went down last week. Ground itself into slag on an axe head. Total loss."

Agramonte scowled. "That could easily have been an accident. Maybe the piece flew off while chopping ice, and..."

"Perhaps, but you're missing the point: it got past the metal detectors which would have shut the processor down before the machine destroyed itself." Watanabe waved her hand in angry dismissal. "It had been encased in ice to fool the sensors, Maya! A rather innovative means to do the most damage possible."

Agramonte finished sealing up the suit, leaving only the helmet to attach. "Take it to Baylor; security will run down any suspects. Why bring it to me? I've got work to do."

Clenched muscles in Watanabe's jaw betrayed her anger. "Because it's not an isolated incident, Maya. In fact, we've found evidence of tampering with one of our three primary atmo recyclers."

"Again, what has that got to do with me?" She put on her helmet and began to secure the seals. It came as an abrupt shock when Watanabe's sharp slap against the faceplate banged her head against the side hard enough to bruise.

"Because one of your EIs did it!" snarled the Chief of Environmental Operations, who spun and stalked off.

Agramonte, after a moment of shock, removed her helmet and followed at a run.

✳✳✳

"Taf is dead."

Fim stared at the speaker, another female, and around at the remainder of the gathered group. All were younger than Fim. Each wore a determined expression when she made eye contact with them. "He won't be the only one. Now; what happened, Keth?"

"We went as you instructed to the hot ones' machine, the one you said to be sure to damage. I was still searching for a place of weakness to attack when Taf chose his target and swung one of the rock-axes. Such heat when he broke its shell, Fim! The poison they breathe spewed all over him as well." Keth hefted her own axe. "He screamed once and fell. I could do nothing."

All was silent, except for the distant sounds of the hot ones' mechanisms chewing rocks. Their rocks. Fim paced and let the silence build before shattering it, triumphant. "We heard the keening from their alien cave--Taf struck a mighty blow for us!" There were sounds of agreement from all, and she made eye contact with Keth once more. "What happened next?"

"I backed off, as you instructed, to see their response."

"What about Taf's body?"

Keth's eyes widened. "I tried, but the hot ones responded too quickly! I..."

"YOU LEFT HIM THERE?"

"I didn't want to, Fim, but the poison still spilled out, and I couldn't get close. The noise sounded as if the world itself had broken, and..."

Fim swung and connected, knocking Keth to the ground, unconscious. The others moved a step away, but Fim paid no notice to their fear. "So by now they know we are responsible for the damage."

"What...what will we do?" asked one of the males.

A confused babble broke out. "We won't be able to resist the hot ones if they come against us," someone said.

"Especially at night, when most will be sleeping!" moaned another.

Fim's own axe thudded into the ground with a sound which chopped through the growing panic. "What do we do, you ask?"

268

Her voice was sure and calm when she answered her own question. "We do what the songs tell us to do."

***

Commander Baylor's office was silent, the mood grim, when Agramonte arrived. She saw a few frightened faces among her colleagues, but Ikeda Watanabe showed cold hostility. Agramonte's lips thinned as she realized she'd clearly been summoned after the meeting had been under way for some time.

"Please sit, Maya." Baylor sounded tired and had dark spots under his eyes, a remarkable feat considering the lesser gravity of Titan. "Time..."

Watanabe interrupted him. "It's damn well past time, Jim!" She turned to Agramonte. "The company's pulling us out: we are finished here! Hell, we'll be lucky if we can get any work after we're fired for cause!" Watanabe abruptly stood, leaning forwards, hands flat on the table. "And your snow-monkeys are the problem!" she shrieked.

Agramonte was taken aback with the vehemence of the verbal attack. "Is it true about the company, Jim?"

"Ikeda, please... Yes, Maya. A ship's been dispatched--all division heads and assistants will be replaced, including me. I'm through, too."

"How soon?"

"They're some weeks out."

Watanabe slapped the table, making several of those gathered jump. "Tell her the important part, Jim!"

Baylor heaved a sigh. "The companies also ordered you to kill off the EIs with your failsafe virus."

Agramonte leapt to her feet. "You can't be serious!"

"They've been sabotaging this station, Maya! Tampering with the ice collectors, atmo recyclers, water...all of it!"

A sudden tremor caused both standing women to lurch, and there were cries of surprise and one genuine scream of fear from around the table.

"What the hell was that?" yelled Baylor.

Ben Robertson's voice cut through the confused babble. "Seismic activity," he said, consulting his handheld.

Baylor answered. "But that's impossible. There's no geological instability on this moon."

"True, as far as the fact goes."

"Meaning what?"

Watanabe interrupted with a scowl. "He means naturally occurring instability." Her own handheld beeped for attention and she answered it. "What? You're certain?"

The station lurched again, and an alarm began blaring.

The Chief of Environmental Ops closed her handheld and sank into her chair as Baylor shouted over the tumult. "People! Calm down--clear out and get to your E-suits until we figure out what exactly..."

They didn't wait for the rest of the order. 'Get out' was all they needed to hear. A stampede for the door left only the Commander, Watanabe, Agramonte, and Robertson at the table.

Ben Robertson licked his lips. "So? How bad is it, Ikeda?"

"Bad enough that running for our E-suits is a bloody waste of time."

After a silence that stretched well beyond a reasonable sixty seconds, Baylor broke it. "What is happening?"

She threw a nasty glance at Agramonte. "Maya's EIs. They redirected our heat exchangers into the ice below the base, melting it." She scowled. "We're sinking, and we've got breaches to the outside. We'll run out of air far in advance of the company's replacement ship getting here, E-suits or no."

Robertson muttered a curse, while Baylor sat back in his seat, pale. "But..."

"But nothing, Jim," Watanabe said. She turned to Agramonte. "You might be able to release your killer virus in time to keep us alive, if you hurry. Or are you still too attached to your little pets, Maya?"

"I can't understand how the EI advanced so much in such a brief period."

Baylor sat forward. "What do you mean?"

"They're primitives! They haven't even existed for much more than five Earth years. None of our models showed the kind of social development, logical thinking, problem-solving abilities..."

Watanabe was beginning to shout a reply when an E-suited figure appeared in Baylor's doorway.

Agramonte checked the nameplate and her eyes went wide. "Lewis! What... where were you?" She turned to Baylor. "He went missing while out scouting what the EIs..."

The suited figure moved into the room, its axe swinging before anyone had time to so much as gasp. The heavy implement took Ben Robertson in the side of his head, and blood sprayed across the conference table.

Watanabe lurched into motion, cursing and dodging past the figure and out the door as another massive shudder shook the station. The building tilted alarmingly, throwing Baylor from his seat. Another swing of the axe buried itself in the commander's back, and he screamed with the pain of the blow.

The person in the E-suit turned to face Agramonte, who hadn't moved from her seat. When she saw the face through the helmet's glass, her mouth fell open.

"So, Gray. Only you and me, now," said a familiar voice through the suit's speaker.

"Fim! What are you doing inside the station? In that suit? What happened to Doctor Lewis?"

"He did not belong here and is now dead because he could not survive without this." The EI indicated the E-suit she wore. "I had need to carry the air of this world into your poisoned shell." She waved a hand at the cracking, crumbling station.

"How?"

"It was a simple matter to store real air and banish the heat you demons require."

Agramonte shook her head, disbelievingly. "Impossible! The technology..." She stared at Fim. "Why? Why do this to us?"

Fim delivered her response in an eerie calm. "Because the god told us it was necessary."

"What can you possibly know of God?" The station shook again, and primary power failed, leaving only faint emergency lighting. "We never contaminated you with that nonsense. Explain!"

Fim dropped the dripping axe, which struck the floor with a loud clang. "At first I thought that the stars were singing to me at night."

"I don't understand."

"I was wrong." The EI paused and cocked her head to one side. "The god sang, and told me many, many things."

Agramonte's eyes widened. "What?"

"It told me, at one time you heard its voice."

"Me? But, I never..."

"You hot ones. Ages ago. But you stopped hearing the god." Fim took a step closer. "Or, perhaps, you simply forgot to listen."

"Ridiculous! There is no such thing as 'God', anyway."

Fim shook her head. "You only say that because you haven't heard the song for so long. But even as you moved out into the greater dark, the god has sung you to its bidding; you remain deaf."

"You're insane!"

"No. Do we not now exist, able to hear the god's song as you cannot?"

"Get this straight: we created you, and serve our needs--I, myself, led the project!"

Fim, inside her pilfered E-suit, smiled. "Though you did not know it, you served the god in bringing us into being. That accomplished, you have no more purpose, Gray."

"So." Agramonte grabbed for the edge of the table as the station lurched again. "You found religion, eh? To justify slaughtering us? You wouldn't be the first in human history to be so deluded!"

"I need no justification beyond the word of the god." Fim did not flinch as a piece of the ceiling crashed down next to her. She stepped forward and held out one hand. "I've come to invite you to listen to the god's voice yourself, to learn what you and your people missed in all the unfathomable time you've wasted. Will you come? Will you listen to the songs with me?"

***

Fim faced the setting sun and closed her eyes, aware of the small metallic object which rested against her collarbone, hung from a thin cord around her neck. It was her only adornment, and a potent totem to bear.

All around, she saw her people preparing for the coming night. Someone held a group of young enthralled with a story of the hot ones, and their giggles and gasps of disbelief came welcome to her ears. Elsewhere she heard murmured conversations, couplings, and the communal sharing of the nutritious snow which fed them all.

Nowhere could she detect the noises of alien substances chewing on her world, and the silence caused her to smile as she waited.

When she felt the growing chill which heralded night, she turned on the alien device which warmed her enough to keep sleep distant, and opened her eyes to peer around. Her people slept; by common consent, they would save the power of the hot ones' devices against future need.

The god had told them to.

Fim walked through the still bodies as the darkness deepened, and the stars overhead grew brighter by comparison. She passed the outcropping of rocks which had shielded her first nocturnal explorations from the hot ones' shelter and stopped.

Unbroken snow had covered all traces of their intrusion on her world. She inhaled deeply, smelled only that which belonged, and exhaled peacefully.

"Fim." The voice was loud, reverberant, musical, and expected. "How good of you to come."

She turned to see an upright figure shadowed against the backdrop of Saturn, and moved closer. "Good evening, Gray."

The scientist's body leaned at a slant against a pile of rocks, arms folded over her chest. Fim saw that the open eyes were dull and frozen solid, a dusting of snow stuck on the small hairs which lined above and below. Agramonte's mouth lay open and unmoving when the voice spoke again from it in chiming tones. "You know that these remains are but a vessel for Me."

"Yes."

"Why do you insist on using her name?"

"She will always be a reminder to all my people of the cost of failing to listen to you."

The voice fell silent for a moment. "Very well; you may continue to do so."

Fim waited patiently for the god to sing to her again, absorbing the silence.

"The time we spoke of is almost here. Her people draw close, and we must prepare for their arrival. You've done as I commanded?"

272

"Yes." Fim reached up and removed the cord from around her neck and held out the small metal tube on her open palm. "Once we'd dug down to the ruins, we discovered this in the hand of the dead hot one which Gray called 'Watanabe'."

"Excellent. What is within is very dangerous to you and your people; together, we will transform it to keep you late-born safe from those who will soon arrive, and any who dare to follow."

Fim smiled. "What must I do?"

"Open the tube and consume its contents. Death will come, child, though only after extreme pain. While you suffer, I will change the powerful thing inside you to render it safe for your people, and deadly to the invaders. My late-born will flourish here, and all others will die." The voice seemed to drop to a throaty whisper. "You will forever be remembered as My special child. Now: drink."

Fim did not hesitate. She opened the vial and drank, then sat and leaned against Gray's frozen legs. She raised her face to the starry heavens, and when she spoke her voice was calm. "Will you sing to me once more? Please?"

After only a moment, the god's song issued from Agramonte's frozen throat. Fim closed her eyes to listen all the more intently and waited for salvation as methane snow silently began to fall.

###

About David M. Hoenig

DAVID IS A SPLIT CLASS writer/academic surgeon with several cat-familiars and a wife. He tries to follow Monty Python's advice by always looking on the bright side of life, and has only needed to be rescued by the Judean Peoples Front on rare occasions. He's published in numerous anthologies and magazines, including Grim Dark Magazine, Cast of Wonders, and others.

Connect with David here:
www.castrumpress.com/authors/david-m-hoenig

ALIEN DAYS

THERE GOES THE NEIGHBORHOOD
By Vivian Kasley

Corbin Konnover lay atop his comfortable bed and stared at the live feed from outside broadcasted onto the hi-def screen made to resemble a window. He was supposed to be reading about history, but he wished he could feel the warm sunshine on his shoulders, or the breeze fondle his hair. But that was before, and this was now. It looked so peaceful outside today, but who knew when They would show up.

Corbin's father bought one of the few million-dollar underground luxury condos when his sister, Ripley, and him were still toddlers. He remembered the giddy feeling they both got as kids, daydreaming about living one hundred feet underground inside of the beautifully decorated three-bedroom, two bath condo. They would run throughout the spacious interior giggling and playing hide and seek whenever their parents allowed them to come along during visits. It had led lighting, spa tubs, a swimming pool with waterfalls and a slide, a large hydroponic garden capable of growing up to seventy kinds of produce, a gym, a spacious kitchen, a shooting range, a rock-climbing wall, and even a movie theater. Now Corbin wished they could be anywhere in the world but where they were.

It was a warm sunny April day, one week before spring break, when Alan Konnover had rushed home to his family. He burst through the door, ran to the kitchen, and threw the keys to his Porsche on the counter. Marylin Konnover turned around from chopping up salad, her strawberry curls bounced into her eyes, and frowned at her panting husband, "What is it Alan? What's happened?"

"Where're the kids?" He ran his hands threw his thick dark hair. His face was slick with sweat.

"Ripley's not home yet, she went to Macy's. Corbin's upstairs in his room, why, what's going on?" Marylin pulled her apron off, put the knife down, and went to her husband.

"It's time, Marylin! We need to get whatever we can and get the hell out! Call Ripley and tell her to get home immediately!"

"Alan, calm down. Time for what? Tell me what's happening?" Marylin picked her phone up with trembling hands.

"They've found us! They've fucking found us! All that fucking meddling, we just had to meddle! Now, they're coming and there's nothing we can do! The condo, Maryl. We need to get to the condo!"

"Can you please just tell me who They are? I'm struggling to understand what this's about, and before I go and get the kids all upset over..."

"God damn it, Maryl! Do what I ask! I'll explain later, I'm sure it'll be all over the news soon enough! I'm going upstairs to talk to Corbin. Once Ripley's back, we only have a few hours. We've been stocking the place for years, so only bring what we absolutely need." Alan Konnover rushed to the stairs, but stopped on the bottom step, his lip quivering, "Do not tell your parents, Maryl. We've discussed this and you knew that if the time ever came for us to go down, it could only be us."

Marylin felt the panic rising inside her and tried to hold back sobs as she called her daughter. She told Ripely that she needed to rush home, that there was a family emergency. Her heart was pounding in her ears and she felt faint. What's going on, what could make my husband so frantic? She knew Alan told her not to call her parents, but she could at least call and say she loved them like any normal day. She dialed them and choked up when her mother answered.

Minutes later, Alan and his son ran down the stairs. When he saw his wife on the phone sobbing, he rushed wildly over, grabbed it, and threw it across the room. "Maryl? Maryl, who were you on the phone with? What'd I tell you?!" He shouted.

"I didn't tell them anything! I just said that I loved them! That's all I said, Alan! Please, tell me what's going on?!" Marylin cried.

"Look, I'll explain more once we're all down there, safe. Just go upstairs and start packing what you need. Corbin, you do the same. Please tell me Rip is on her way?" Alan's eyes softened, and he tenderly grabbed his wife's hand.

"She is." Marylin wiped her wet cheeks, pulled away from her husband and went up the stairs with her son to begin packing.

Corbin tried to absorb what his father told him. That they needed to get to the underground condo within the next few hours before the news broke. He didn't know how long they would be down there, but that they should be safe. Corbin put his arm around his mother as they reached the top step. She sniffled into his shoulder and told him to pack plenty of underwear and socks.

When Ripley arrived, she was hysterical and went on about how she couldn't go because she had plans with Macy for Spring Break. Alan stared back at his visibly shaken daughter. His heart broke as tears spilled down her delicate face. "Spring Break," he said, "Is canceled. Now go pack your clothes and a few things you absolutely have to have. We need to pack up the car within the hour. God damn it, now, I said!" He growled.

They all filled suitcases and travel bags with as much stuff as they could and began packing up Marylin's Chevy Tahoe to the brim. The neighbors watched suspiciously as they walked their labradoodles across their sprawling green lawn but smiled and waved as they got closer. They asked if they were leaving for a vacation, to which Alan responded, "Something like that."

"Would you like us to keep any eye out on the house while you're away?"

"Sure thing. Thanks for always looking out for us. It's been such a pleasure having you as neighbors." Alan said as he shook their hands.

"No problem at all, Alan. Everything okay? You look a little...pale."

"I'm alright, really. Just lugging all these bags out to the car is all." Alan forced a chuckle.

They locked all the doors and windows in the house, shut everything down and off, and gathered any last-minute items they could think of. Corbin and Ripley fought back tears as they drove away from their beautiful Victorian style home and toward the underground refuge they had always thought of as their childhood playground. Nobody said a word. Alan turned the satellite radio to a news channel and soon the rest of the Konnover's got an early clue as to what was going on.

A decade ago, an asteroid had been found traveling through their solar system. It was a strange shape, elongated and reddish in color. It was the first interstellar object to be detected in the solar system. Astronomers and scientists all argued over what it might be. Some thought it was just an irregular asteroid however, others thought it was a probe sent intentionally by a technologically advanced alien civilization a theory based on the objects accelerated movement and unexpected brightness. Most laughed at that idea, but some did not and reached out into the galaxy to try and communicate with whoever may have sent the probe. Until finally They reached back.

No one would divulge who leaked the information, but the message was that They were coming for a visit, and soon. Who They were or what They wanted was unclear? On the car radio, there were several people giving their opinions and debating the situation. Many were still skeptical, saying it was all a hoax and possible Russian meddling, "They like riling everyone up," one woman scoffed. The Konnover's shifted uncomfortably in their seats as audio of the spreading panic from all over the world filled the car. People were screaming, crying, and pleading with someone to tell them what they should do. Some bizarrely sounded happy, saying it was the end of times and they were ready to die and meet their maker.

None of what they were hearing was comforting, but when Alan went to turn it off, his wife stopped him. She needed to hear it. Corbin closed his eyes and pretended to sleep. Ripley put her ear buds in and cried silently. Marylin looked over at her husband, who stared ahead with an unreadable expression, and grabbed his hand and squeezed. She told herself they were going to be safe. They had a plan and were very fortunate. But what she told herself and what she felt were two different things.

It was dark when they arrived. Grabbing as much as they could they began the descent into their new home. They all jumped when the sixteen thousand-pound bullet proof doors shut behind them. Once down inside, Alan showed his kids which rooms they would be staying in. He tried to be cheerful as he walked them around, "Been a while since you kids have been down here, huh?" He asked, but they only nodded mutely.

After getting settled in, they all met in the kitchen. Alan dropped a couple of ice cubes into a small glass of scotch and swirled it around before he took a long slow sip before joining the family who sat at the bench style table next to his wife. No one seemed to want to start the conversation.

Marylin watched their Corbin's face, it was strong like his father's, but he had her soft green eyes and strawberry waves. She stole a glance at Ripley. They hadn't been very close lately, Ripley'd been spending most of her free time with Macy. Ripley looked just like her father. Dark and intense eyes with wavy brown hair that cascaded down her back, the waves she got from Marylin. She was glaring at her father with her arms crossed.

Ripley let out an exasperated sound before she spoke, "I was supposed to be with Macy, planning our spring break, not here. This's total crap! This might not even be real, Dad! Have you and the other space tards thought of that? You dragged us all down here, into your...your weirdo Hobbit hole!"

"Ripley!" Marylin bellowed.

"It's fine, Maryl. She's upset. We all are." Alan placed his hand over his wife's.

"Dad, I mean, what if she's right? What if it's not real?" Corbin bit into his lower lip.

"Then we all go home. I hope it's not, but what I do know and what I can tell you is that it was only a matter of time." Alan finished his scotch, then poured another shot.

"How do they even know how to speak our language?" Corbin asked.

"Well, I guess if they can send a probe propelled by some sort of light sail from a faraway place, they can figure out that too. Maybe they figured it out from our own messages? Who knows, I don't know how to answer that. I just know that we need to be down here, safe."

"I agree with your father and we all heard what they said on the radio. People are not taking this well, rightly so. You know your father is a very respected scientist and he wouldn't bring us here if he didn't have a good reason. I think we should be more thankful we have the opportunity to have such a place." Marylin was trying to smile, but tears pooled in her eyes.

"Then why're you crying, Mom! Because you know this's nuts, that's why!" Ripley slammed her freshly manicured hand on the table.

"I think we are all feeling upset or sad that we had to leave others behind." Alan studied the ice dissipating into his drink.

"Exactly! You brought us all here, not thinking about our grandparents! What about Uncle Will and Aunt Bev? Or Aunt Shelly and Uncle Matt? Or the rest of the family? Our friends!" Ripley sobbed.

"Dad, Ripley's got a point. What about them?" Corbin asked.

"In the beginning, when your mother and I bought this place, we knew that if the time came to ever use it for whatever reason, they would have to be left behind. I'm sorry honey, but I think they would understand."

"How do you know that? Did you tell them about this place? Do they know where we are in case, they look for us?" Corbin looked his father in the eyes.

"No, not exactly. It's not a good idea to advertise this kind of thing, but I did mention years ago that we should all have a plan in place if some kind of world event ever came about. You know Grandpa, he always laughed at that kind of thing. Supply wise, we have enough for our family, but that's it. It's not a decision I would make lightly, believe me. I promise to reach out to everyone when I'm able to do so. Right now, let's just try and get along. We're going to be spending a lot of time together."

"I hate you." Ripley spat at her father.

"Ripley, that's enough! We're a family and we will act like a one. I'm sorry your plans were disrupted by—whatever this is! Stop acting like a spoiled little brat and be thankful your father could provide such a beautiful place for us to feel safe and to have hope." Marylin wept.

"Let's all just calm down and get through this. Why don't we make a nice dinner in here? Look at these wonderful granite counter tops and stainless-steel appliances! We can watch a movie in our screening room. It'll be fun. How many teenagers have their own movie theater, huh? And our gym is green, we can create electricity just by exercising! Isn't that something?" Alan chuckled nervously.

Ripley stood up and scowled at her father. "Fuck your counter tops!" She said, "And fuck you too!" Then she ran from the kitchen and slammed the door to her room.

Marylin put her head down on the table and cried. Corbin patted his mother's back and told her he would talk to Ripley before he got up and left. Alan poured himself another two fingers of scotch. When life gives you lemons...drink scotch, he thought. He rubbed his numb face and tried to tell himself it would all be alright. He wished he could provide more answers, but he couldn't. He worried about how long they would be down here and if the luxurious underground bunker would become their luxurious burial tomb.

✳✳✳

Weeks went by and there was no sign of Them. What information the Konnover's got from their television or phones was not good. People looted, killed themselves and each other, and scrambled to find places to hide. Ripley had finally calmed down and apologized. She begrudgingly thanked her father for protecting them. They were getting used to their new life, even enjoying frequent family movie nights and pool time. Marylin had stocked plenty of books into the condo over the years and she insisted the kids set aside time each week to read and study. They even began to grow their own food, a favorite activity of Ripley's.

Corbin ultimately closed the history book he'd been reading. It looked so calm outside. He liked watching the gently spinning wind turbines. The tall grass waved in the wind. Nothing was out there. He looked down at his phone and shook his head. Maybe this will all blow over? Doesn't matter when people are going insane outside. Maybe that's what they wanted? For us to get rid of ourselves, save them the hassle.

He got up from the bed and changed into his still damp swim trunks. His father was undoubtably already buzzed on scotch and that Ripley was in the garden with their mother. A swim always made him forget where he was. The windows and lighting in the pool area felt almost like you were outside. As he went to leave his room, he saw something out of the corner of his eye. A glint or a glare. He turned to peer out the mock window. In the distance, a large metallic clam shaped object swerved in the cloudless bright blue sky and then it was gone.

I should tell Mum and Dad what I saw, Corbin told himself. He walked to the theater, the place where his father would sometimes sit and drink by himself while enjoying an old movie. As he suspected, his father was asleep in one of the reclining leather seats. Clint Eastwood squinted back at him from the large screen. He walked to the garden, peeking in Corbin saw the smiles on his mother and Ripley's face as they hovered over some lettuce sprouts. Forget it, I'm not telling.

He walked to the pool and swam several laps, then stood under one of the waterfalls staring into the large windows that ran along the room. Bingo. His heart raced. Several more of the clam shells were now in the sky. They zigged and zagged in different directions. Fuck, there goes the neighborhood, he thought.

At dinner his mother and sister served them plates of pasta with a garlicky tomato sauce and bread. Dad eyed their mother when she allowed Ripley a half glass of red wine. "It's just a little, Alan, hardly enough to even wet her lips," she uttered, "Corbin, would you like a little?"

"No thanks, Mom." He sat next to his sister and bumped her shoulder. She smiled and told him to try the bread, that she made it herself.

"This's fabulous, Maryl! Really good! And the bread, Rip, it's delightful." Their father filled his glass to the brim with plum colored wine.

"Thanks, Dad." Ripley beamed.

"Corbin, how was your day?" Marylin asked.

"Oh, you know, the usual. I read, played with my phone, watched TV, and swam." He replied.

"Actual TV, or the window TVs?" his sister laughed, "Wind turbines and slow-moving clouds are very entertaining, didn't you know?"

"There was something more interesting today, actually." Corbin tilted his head and played with his food.

Their parents stopped eating and peered up at him. Ripley slurped a noodle and giggled, "Oh, and what was that?"

"It was...a murder of crows. They were extremely interesting to watch." Corbin smiled at his sister. His parents finally took a breath and sipped their wine.

Ripley rolled her eyes but smiled, "You're such a freak."

When their plates were empty, Corbin stood up to gather them. His father got up too. "Let me join you, son. Your mother and sister did all the cooking, it's only fair," he winked.

"Dad, can we talk later? I need to tell you something." Corbin fidgeted.

"Of course. The gym? We can work off all the pasta and bread. No need to get fat while we hide out, right?" Alan scraped a hunk of sauce off a plate.

"Yeah, sure."

Corbin's mother and sister decided to go for a swim before they showered. They were going to have a mother and daughter movie night and had claimed the theater for themselves. Corbin was glad they were trying to be find solace in the situation. He didn't want to be the one to burst that bubble, but he needed to tell his father what he saw.

Changing into some shorts Corbin headed for the gym, his father was already on one of the bikes pedaling away, tablet plugged into the battery charger. Corbin plugged his phone into the bike next to his fathers, then hopped on. They pedaled furiously for about twenty minutes. Corbin stopped and put his hand out toward his father and waved it.

"Dad?" he said.

"Yes."

"I didn't see a murder of crows." Corbin averted his father's gaze and fiddled with his handlebars.

"I know."

"What?"

"I said, I know." Alan wiped sweat from his brow.

"What do you know?" Corbin got off the bike and stood in front of his father.

"I saw them. The other day." Alan took a deep breath and exhaled.

"What are they?"

"I assume it's Them. I mean, who else? Those ships were... look, Corbin, you know that my job has always been confidential, and I am sworn to secrecy, but I'm telling you that some stuff exists that's hard to explain. It's always been out there, but we never thought it would ever come to this, in our lifetime anyway. Turns out we were wrong."

"Dad, what do we do?" Corbin heard his voice crack.

"We stay in here and hope for the best. We can't tell your mother or sister what we saw. They're finally able to smile. Let's keep it that way. If they see it on their own, then we obviously have to tell them something, but for now let's keep it between us."

"But we have to tell them! They can't be in the dark. What if They come here? What if They..."

"Corbin, stop. We're doing everything we can do right now. I have weapons. We all know how to use them, and if the time comes, we will do what we have to."

"Because They won't have better weapons or for all we know mind control powers?!" Corbin shouted.

"You've watched too many movies, son."

"And you haven't seen enough apparently!"

"What do you want me to do? Do you want me to go outside and start shooting up at the sky? This's why we're down here, for protection. I've been staying up at night and I wouldn't allow anything to hurt you. Do you understand?" The whites of his father's sunken eyes were pink.

"I'm going to stay up with you." Corbin said resolutely.

"Then you better take a nap." Alan got up off his bike and left him alone in the gym.

✳✳✳

The following week was Ripley's sixteenth birthday. They were going to have a family pool party and watch all her favorite movies. Corbin felt a twinge of guilt. Last year, he spent his Seventeenth birthday on an island in the Caribbean. He wished they could all be there now celebrating Ripley's. The jeep his father got him was almost certainly long gone by now. They hadn't seen the flying clams in days and hadn't spoken a word about it either.

It was dark except for the faint light coming from the screens his father and him watched. The moon was full, and they could see a few animals moving around in the pale light. After several nights of the two of them staying up, Alan told his worried wife that Corbin and he were just keeping watch, something they decided they wanted to do just in case. Marylin nodded her head and gave a little smile but said nothing.

A rabbit hopped along munching on the spotty tall blades of grass. Corbin's eye lids felt heavy. The late nights were taking a toll. Even with napping during the day, he was having a hard time. His father sat eagle eyed swirling a tumbler of scotch. The clink of the ice cubes used to annoy Corbin, but now he found it soothing. "Your sister's turning sixteen tomorrow. Time flies, huh?" Alan raised an eyebrow.

Corbin yawned and sat up straighter, "Yeah, especially when you're a hundred feet underground."

"It's not all bad. We're having an alright time. It could be loads worse. Look what's going on all over the world, it's chaos out there. There hasn't been any new news for over a week now, but I can imagine—never mind."

"I feel terrible about it. So many sitting ducks. Do you think people found a way to escape? Do you think our family and friends..." Corbin couldn't bring himself to finish.

"I have no idea. I really don't. I'd like to think so, though. We can't feel bad about being fortunate, son. In a way, all of us are sitting ducks on this planet, we always were. We just happen to have a nicer pond to sit in."

"What about the military, though? Don't they have anything? You said we knew about this kind of threat, didn't we prepare?"

"It's not as easy as that. Our government has defense for what already exists. Because the threat was hypothetical at the time and not concrete, they didn't want to spend the money. Which is where our company came in. Most of our funding is from the billionaires and private investors, who also fund some of the world's other top scientific communities. However, we do brief the government when we absolutely need to. They just didn't listen very well until it was too late." Alan said.

"But maybe They don't understand us either? Maybe that's their weakness?"

"Maybe, Corbin." Alan didn't sound convinced.

Marylin heard her husband and son talking in hushed tones. Ripley was sleeping already, excited about her day tomorrow. What a way to spend your sweet sixteen. She was happy to be spending so much time with her daughter, but sad that it took being underground to bring them back together. Marylin tried to make out what they were discussing but gave up and decided it didn't matter. She'd ask her husband later. Whatever it was could wait until after Ripley's big day. In bed, she drifted off to sleep thinking about what kind of cake she'd be able to make with what they had.

Corbin and Alan were debating scientific theories when they saw a man. He was stumbling around outside; a little girl trailing behind him. They were carrying flashlights and backpacks. The little girl sat down on the ground and began to play with a doll she took out from her bag. The man set his stuff down with the little girl but didn't sit.

"What the hell?" Corbin whispered.

"Must be trying to find somewhere to go. Maybe their car broke down." Alan said.

"But here? The road's kinda far. I mean, it's obvious that there's some sort of shelter here, but... maybe he thinks we'll let them in?"

"Well, we're not."

"Dad, the little girl..."

"What about her? We can't go letting strangers in. Who knows why they're out there? They could have weapons."

"Well, I hardly doubt they have what we have..."

"I said no! That's final, now drop it."

The little girl fell asleep hugging her doll. The man glanced all around, then up at the sky before he got up. He left the little girl where she lay and walked in the direction of their shelter. Alan jumped up and went to a different window. Corbin followed. The man walked down the small concrete steps and onto the large concrete driveway where their car was parked. He tried all the door handles, then walked up to the front of the shelter and inspected the heavy doors.

"Fuck. Fuck, fuck, fuck." Alan mouthed.

"Dad, what's the big deal? He can't get in here, right?"

"No, but I don't like him creeping around."

The man went back to the car and broke the driver's side window, then unlocked the door. He went inside and emerged minutes later. The car's lights were flashing. Alan shook his head and sighed; the alarm was going off. Shit, shit, shit. He forgot to disable it. As the man moved out of sight, Alan and Corbin went back to the other window. The man grabbed the sleepy little girl's hand, picked their stuff up before trudging back to the Tahoe placing the limp form of the girl in the passenger seat before moving to the driver's side. He'll probably try and hotwire it. Good luck with that, pal, Alan thought.

"We're not using it anyway. What could it hurt?" Corbin shrugged.

"I don't like it, but there's not much I can do about it now." Alan ran his hand through his hair.

They sat in silence for a while watching the blinking Tahoe. Then Corbin saw it. A hint of something in the distance coming quickly toward their area. Alan saw it too and began to grind his teeth.

"Dad? Dad, what do we do?"

"We do nothing," he said, "This's what I was afraid of."

The moon's light refracted off the metallic sheen of the clam shaped ship as it landed in the near distance. It was much bigger than Corbin thought it would be. He shivered next to his father, who put his finger to his lips and shook his head. They both watched as the beings emerged from the ship. Corbin startled and his father clamped his hand onto his shoulder.

As They approached, Corbin marveled at their appearance and gasped. There were four of them. They were tall, but not freakishly so, with long arms. They were very slim and wore skintight reflective suits with thick combat style boots. There were helmets on their slightly larger heads. Corbin thought They looked almost human as They walked purposefully in the direction of the shelter. They knew they were there.

"Dad? Dad, they're coming right for us. I'm scared." But Corbin couldn't look away as they inched closer to the driveway and the Tahoe. Alan put a finger to his lips in a hushing gesture keeping his hand clamped down on Corbin's shoulder.

"There's nothing we can do now, we're in here and we're safe. They're most likely here for them and they'll be gone soon. Just stay calm, we don't want to wake your mother or Ripley."

They walked directly to the Tahoe. One of them opened the car door and went inside. Then another. They reemerged holding both the man and the child, they were limp and dangled in their long arms. A being walked up to their shelter and dragged a sizeable hand down the door. Then it looked up into the camera and Corbin jumped in his skin.

Its lidless eyes were enormous, oval, and black. There were two holes were a nose should be and the mouth was a thin grim line. It tilted its head one way, then the other. It reached up with its hand and pointed – the camera went out.

Corbin shot up like a rocket, slinging his Father's hand from his shoulder. He moved around the room going from window to window, but all the screens were black. Before he could get to the other rooms, Alan stepped in front of him. "Dad, move out of the way! I need to check the other windows! We need to know what to do! I have to get, Mom and Ripley." Corbin's cheeks were streaked with tears.

He tried to move past his father, but it was no use. Alan calmly turned his son around and directed him to the kitchen, where he sat him down at the table. Placing a glass in front of him Alan poured a shot of scotch into it and told him to drink it. Corbin looked back at his Father in shock, "There's fucking aliens outside and this's your solution?! We need to do something, damn it!" Corbin shoved the glass and it almost slid completely off the table.

"That's very expensive scotch, son. Very, very expensive." Alan pursed his lips.

"I don't give a flying dog shit and if you mention scotch again, I swear to hell I'll shove that bottle down your damn throat! We need to wake up Mom and Ripley, right now! Do I need to remind you of what we just saw out there?" Corbin seethed.

"I know what we just saw. I'm very aware, more than you know." Alan was too calm.

"What the hell does that even mean? We need to get the guns; we need to make sure everything is secure..." Corbin stood up.

"Alright, look, if you promise to sit back down and lower you voice, I'll explain everything. You're a man, more so now than ever before..."

"Spit it out, Dad or I'm screaming bloody murder up in here!" Corbin sat down and folded his arms across his chest.

"They're not aliens exactly. Well, not really. They are just like you and me basically, only evolved."

"Evolved?" Corbin leaned forward.

"They're not extraterrestrial. Think more like extratemporal."

"I'm not following."

"They're time travelers, us from the future." Alan pushed the scotch back toward his son. Corbin didn't push it away, instead picking it up and taking a deep swig.

"Is this a fucking joke?" Corbin choked on his drink.

"Afraid not. We knew of them for a very long time, before my time even, but not up until about fourteen years ago, did we realize exactly what it was they were doing. They sent that probe, like a feeler, and people from our team were able to finally reach the probe and decipher the message."

"Why even send the message? Why not just come?"

"What do you think would happen if they attempted that? They needed to warn us of their impending arrival. They were coming whether or not we agreed to it." Alan poured him another drink.

"Why? I don't understand. If we evolved to live elsewhere in the galaxy, why would we come back here, to this?" Corbin downed his second drink and relaxed in the chair.

"Because our planet is on track to peril, a track faster than they imagined. We're killing ourselves and if we kill ourselves, then they can't exist. They are products of us. Years from now, the planet will not be inhabitable. It's still going to be around for a very long time. The problem is, people are a threat to the planet. There's pollution, war, and overpopulation among other things. So, how do we fix that?"

"I don't know." Corbin croaked.

"Sometimes we have to do things we don't want to for the betterment of the whole."

"I'm not following, Dad. Unless...are you saying we're allowing them to get rid of people on purpose?" Corbin felt his limbs grow heavy.

"It's more complicated than that. There're billions of us on the planet, and Earth's carrying capacity is at its threshold. What used to be curtailed by disease and starvation, is no longer enough. We have become smart enough to engineer food and fight disease. We consume, we pollute the one thing we cannot re-create, water. Our best hope for humanity would be to reproduce at a smaller rate but try telling that to people! We're the true parasites on this planet. Earth is suffering and so are we. They're here to help eliminate the waste, son."

"The waste? Our friends and family are waste?"

"I wish it were different. Only so many will be allowed to carry on. The best and brightest, the ones who they choose and their offspring. The rest will go to good use I suppose. Their organs will be harvested, and their bodies will be used to further the survival of mankind, so waste was a poor choice of words. I'm sorry I said that."

"You're sorry you said that? Are you sorry that you brought us down here knowing exactly what was going on, that people, our family, were being gathered up like insects by these...whatever you say They are! You're a lying monster!" Corbin roared.

"Lower your voice. I'm not a monster, damn it. I'm a man and I'm a father, your father, and I did what I did to keep our family safe. Sometimes we keep things to ourselves in order to protect others, as you well know."

Corbin looked away then, "Does Mom know any of it?"

"No, she's innocent. She accepted that my work was confidential. We lived a good life and after this, hopefully we still will. However, we'll have to stay down here until the process is complete."

"And how long will that be?"

"I guess I'll get word when we can come out. It'll take time to round so many people up. Not everyone will be eliminated, son. Many will be saved. It's not all doom and gloom. They're saving the Earth for our future generations. Try and understand this is a necessity, and just like that old saying goes, necessity knows no law but to conquer. Without this, there's no future. So, do you understand now?"

"I have no choice but to try to." Corbin hissed.

"Good. I'll explain everything to your mother and sister in time. Let them have a bit more peace."

"But people are still people and they'll eventually do it all over again. Our future selves have got to know that."

"They do. This isn't the first time this's happened, son. I'm pretty sure they've been here before." Alan stared at him.

"What do you mean?"

"Read the history books. I'm sure you might be able to put two and two together. We didn't know as much then as we are capable of now, but the signs were there. They may have done it differently or maybe they came just to see what we were up to, but They came. You just have to know where to look. I can assure you that each time They came, things changed. Sooner or later They'll have nowhere to come back to, and humans will begin again elsewhere. In a galaxy far, far away I imagine."

"I don't even know what to think. You've lied for so long to all of us, who knows if what you're telling me now is even true. Mom and Rip are lucky to be asleep right now, ignorant of the fact that you're a damn liar. Ignorance is bliss though, right?" Corbin jeered.

Alan searched his son's face before he spoke, "I could tell you I just made this whole thing up to make you feel better and there're actual hostile aliens outside. That They've already killed millions and millions of people and any minute now, they're going to blow apart our heavy doors, come down here, and kill us too. Harvest us for food or experiment on our naked shivering bodies until we die of shock and fear. Stick needles in our open eyes, tubes down our screaming throats, and who knows what up our clenched-up assholes. Would that be an easier pill to swallow?"

Corbin gulped, "Never mind," he muttered.

"I thought so, son. I thought so." Alan poured himself and his son another scotch.

###

About Vivian Kasley

Vivian Kasley lives in the land of the extremely strange and unusual, Florida! She was an educator for several years before she left to write and travel, but still substitutes because she's absolutely bonkers. At a very tender age horror and science fiction welcomed her into their comfy arms, to which she ran headfirst and stayed to cuddle.

She's published stories with Gypsum Sound Tales, Dark Moon Digest, Perpetual Motion Machine Publishing, and Sirens Call Publications with more on the way. When she's not spinning and twisting new yarn, she's usually enjoying time with her other half, snuggling her fur babies, cooking, or reading a good book during a thunderstorm.

Connect with Vivian here:
www.castrumpress.com/authors/vivian-kasley

Thank you for reading the Alien Days Anthology, Volume II of the Days Anthologies. If you enjoyed this book, please leave a review at your favorite retailer.

Here's the URL to the Amazon store: www.smarturl.it/review-aliendays

Would you like to know when the third volume in the Days Anthologies comes out? Sign up here: www.castrumpress.com/subscribe

ALIEN DAYS

FOLLOWING IS AN EXCERPT OF
Future Days: A Science Fiction Short Story Anthology. The Days Series, Vol I.

FUTURE DAYS EXCERPT

Cover designed by The Gilded Quill
www.TheGildedQuill.co.uk

Print Edition
Printed in the United Kingdom
First Printing: Aug 2018
Castrum Press

Print ISBN-13 978-1-9123273-4-8

INTRODUCTION TO FUTURE DAYS ANTHOLOGY

FUTURE DAYS IS A MULTI-AUTHOR ANTHOLOGY with thrilling tales of starships, artificial intelligence, cryogenics and exotic aliens. A combination which makes this collection a must-read for science fiction short story fans.

This anthology features USA Today and Amazon bestsellers and award winners alongside rising stars in the science fiction genre. Let the authors take you on adventures through dystopian worlds and far flung planets that will stretch your imagination. Welcome to Future Days.

- "The Good Citizen" by Aline Boucher Kaplan

Out of work? Need to pay the bills? Don't worry the government is looking for a few good people to work in the colonies. And, oh yeah, its compulsory.

- "Cell Effect" by Christopher Cousins

Saiden has abilities. Abilities the government wants to weaponize. Only one thing stands in their way, Ret Saiden.

- "Greener Pastures" by Justin C. Fulton

When the line between a utopian virtual world and harsh reality become blurred, the choices we make can be fatal.

- "Orbital Burn" by David M. Hoenig

Heroes come in all shapes and sizes. Who would have thought convicted criminal Slade would be one of them?

- "A Winter's Day" by Edward Ahern

Ever-Young Cryogenics promise its clients a brief spell of life every decade. But, what happens when your family grow old and die, but you don't?

- "Colony" by Gunnar De Winter

In a hierarchical society decided by birth, instructions must be followed. Unless you are a radical and want to destroy the system.

- "The Pink Shar-Ship Switcher" by James Worrad

Jada is a businesswoman intent on climbing the corporate ladder by sealing a lucrative deal. That is, until a Being from another reality intervenes.

- "Custodian" by Johnny Pez

Only a special kind of person volunteers to stay awake during the long voyages between the stars while the rest of the crew sleeps. But what happens when he gets lonely?

- "The Caller" by Lisa Timpf

A job she hates on a world with too many problems. But what if she can escape to a new world and start again? Can she leave everything she knows, and loves, behind?

- "The Trickle-Down Effect" by Mark Lynch

Denton, a man who would do what needed to be done to survive in the 'Pit'. The lowest, dirtiest, crime ridden part of a mega city forgotten by the 'One Percenters' living in their luxurious towers.

- "Jericho" by Matthew William

A new world. Ripe for colonization. Pre-prepared by nanite Seedlings for the arrival of their human designers. But what happens when the designers become your God?

- "Ghosts" by award winning author RB Kelly.

The storms bring the Seekers. Machines with one purpose, to bring death. Only sometimes death is not quite death.

- "Mother" by Amazon #1 bestselling author Rick Partlow.

A mother's love is the strongest of all. Protect and nurture your children to your dying breath. Even if that means genocide.

- "The Cull" by Amazon #1 bestselling author PP Corcoran.

Humanity has reached its peak. Genetic manipulation makes humans faster, smarter and stronger. But at what cost?

- "The Rescue" by Claire Davon.

An Alien shuttle is downed. Lt. 'Dee' Delaney must find it and secure the alien survivors until help arrives. Easy. If Delaney can trust her own people.

- "The Man-Eater" by USA TODAY bestselling author Christopher G. Nuttall. Three ships vanished testing the new faster than light engine. A desperate scientist wants to prove his engine works. How? Why you steal it of course.

- "Castrum" by JCH Rigby

Sergeant Joel Edwards is wakened seconds before being dropped into combat. A faceless enemy. A nameless place. All he knows, is a cyborg is ready for anything.

FUTURE DAYS EXCERPT

THE GOOD CITIZEN
by Aline Boucher Kaplan

The heavy knock on the front door cracked like a pistol shot. Elena jumped, and her family stopped eating. Henry froze with his fork halfway to his mouth. Cory choked on his glass of water and put it down. Their faces turned to her. Little Marta looked around the table. Her eyes grew large, her seven-year-old face crumpled, and she began to wail.

The knock boomed again.

"Mom?" Cory said in a hoarse voice. "Is it them?"

"Yes," Elena whispered. She thought frantically, where did I leave the exemption letter? Right, it's on the table by the door. "I'd hoped for a few extra days, but they're right on time."

The knock came again, louder. Elena pushed back her chair and stood up. If she didn't answer, the whole family would lose ration points, and they couldn't afford less food for the children. Things would get worse if they had only Henry's teaching salary and ration card to live on.

"It's all right," Elena said. "I'll show them my exemption letter and they'll leave. Don't worry."

She walked to the front door. Her mouth was dry, and her cheeks and hands had gone numb. Heart pounding, she manipulated the triple lock and opened the door.

A plain woman in a dark skirt suit, with a gold badge hanging from a lanyard, faced Elena. Two uniformed guards stood behind her in black body shields and helmets, with dark faceplates that masked their features. The woman held a tablet that cast blue-white light onto her face. Cold November air fell into the house.

"Are you Mrs. Elena Tremblay?" the woman asked.

"Yes," Elena replied. "I am."

"Our records show that you have been out of work for 180 continuous business days. Is that correct?"

"Yes, it is," Elena said in a voice so soft the wind carried her words away.

"Speak up, ma'am." The woman's bright badge labeled her as Reassignment Agent Moira Ferris, Number 3411.

Elena cleared her throat. "Yes, yes it is," she said with more confidence. "But I'm looking. I have prospects. I'm expecting an interview next week."

"Do you have a formal offer in your possession for a job of any kind?" Agent Ferris studied the tablet's screen. She looked up at Elena again with a softer expression. "Any kind of a paying job? No matter how menial?" She leaned slightly forward, as if encouraging Elena to say yes.

"I, um. I thought. I tried. I applied." Elena took a deep breath to stop babbling. "No."

"Have you applied for a temporary work assignment through the Agency for Civilian Mobilization?"

"Yes, of course." Elena flushed, remembering that appointment with its drug test, endless forms, and personal questions. "But the ACM said that I was over-qualified and not suitable for the jobs they had left."

The woman nodded and touched the link. "According to Section forty-two, Article Fifteen, Paragraph Eight of the U.S. Full Employment Code, you have, as of today, forfeited your right to independent status as a citizen. Your body is now the property of the United States government to be deployed as needed. Do you understand what I have said, ma'am?"

"No. No, I don't." Elena took the exemption letter from the basket of mail on the hall table and held it out. Agent Ferris didn't even glance at it. "I have two minor children, one under school age," Elena continued, pushing the letter toward the official. "I knew you would contact me, of course, but I have a valid exemption right here. The law says..."

"Congress repealed Article Twenty-One of the Code last week," Agent Ferris said in the flat tone of someone who had repeated the same information too many times. "The number of children, their genders and ages no longer render anyone exempt."

"But we heard nothing about that."

"It was passed in a closed session, ma'am," Ferris said. "The Congressional vote was unanimous, and the President signed the revision immediately. We need workers for the in-system colonies."

Elena began to turn, as if to run away. This can't be happening. But she couldn't think of what to do. The law was the law. Where could she go that the government couldn't track the chip embedded in her skull?

She turned back to Agent Ferris. "Yes." Her voice sounded like a croak. "I understand."

"I am required to take you to a Federal Reassignment Center for processing."

Elena closed her eyes and took a deep breath. Back in the house she could hear Henry and Cory trying to quiet Marta.

"You have to say the words, ma'am."

"Yes, yes, I understand," stammered Elena.

Agent Ferris held out the tablet. "Just press your thumb here, please."

Elena raised her right arm, watching as if it belonged to someone else as Agent Ferris grasped her thumb and pressed it to the sensor.

Henry came to the door and stood behind her. "You can't take my wife!" He strode toward the door. The two guards took a step forward, their boots clomping in unison, hands on their weapons.

Agent Ferris raised one hand, stopping the guards. She shot the two civilians a nervous glance. "Think carefully about your next move," she said to Henry. In a lower voice she added, "Your family needs you."

Henry stopped, made a rough anguished sound, and went back to where Cory stood with Marta in his arms. He put an arm around his children, and tears pricked Elena's eyes.

Agent Ferris stepped to one side to give Elena room to pass. "We have to go now. Come with me, please, ma'am."

"Can I bring a few things?" Elena knew she should have packed a go bag and kept it by the front door, but she'd relied on the exemption to protect her. Besides, doing that had made the possibility of this day seem too real, too immediate.

"Not necessary."

Elena looked upstairs. "I have to get my medication."

"Not necessary."

"My coat?"

Agent Ferris nodded. Elena hesitated between her good wool coat and the old down jacket. Ferris murmured, "Wear the old one. They'll just take it away at the Reassignment Center."

"Will they give it to the poor?"

"There are no poor people."

Shrugging on the jacket, Elena kissed Henry and hugged Cory. Marta, shrieking, held out her arms, but Elena didn't dare take her. She would never be able to pry those warm clinging arms from around her neck. Instead, she kissed each one. "I love you," she said to them.

"You can't go, Mom," Cory said with a voice choked by tears.

"It's the law," Elena replied. "We're law-abiding citizens."

"But it's wrong!" His face was twisted with anger. "The law is bad. You have to fight."

"We don't get to pick which laws we obey, Cory," Elena said. "And we can't ignore the laws we don't like."

"Yes we can!" Cory shouted. "Don't go with them."

The two guards behind Agent Ferris lifted their weapons in one motion.

"That's enough, Cory," Henry said in a hard voice Elena had never heard before.

"But – "

"Stop. Now."

Elena could hear the panic in his voice. She knew the guards wouldn't tolerate any resistance. She had to end this right now.

"I'll be doing important work in space," she said to her family. "Think of me when you look up at night." Elena forced what she hoped was a smile. "Besides, I'll get superpowers."

Turning her back on her anguished family, she walked down the front stairs and across the lawn. Frosted grass crackled under her shoes. The guards lowered their weapons and followed, one on either side.

"Can you tell me where I'm going?" she asked.

Agent Ferris replied, "As I said, you're going to the Reassignment Center for processing."

"I mean...after."

"No. I can't say."

"Oh. Not even where...?" Elena looked up at the night sky.

"No."

A black bus with tinted windows waited on the street. The outside held no markings of any kind, neither an official seal nor a commercial logo. Agent Ferris stood aside so Elena could board the bus, then stepped up after her. A row of seats at the front looked like those in a normal bus. A Plexiglas barrier separated them from benches that lined both sides of the vehicle, with a low rail on the floor in front.

Other detainees sat on the benches with their wrists in restraints. Three or four in the back were hunched over and fastened to the rail. They looked like they'd been in a fight.

Elena halted, unable to take another step. This can't be happening to me, she thought. I'm an educated woman. I'm a manager, a professional. I have a respectable job.

Not anymore. Not since she'd been called into a conference room and found a human resources supervisor facing her with a wireless printer on the table and a tablet next to it. She had taken Elena through the layoff process and made sure the right signatures went in the right places, along with an official thumbprint on the last page. Finally, she'd handed Elena a formal statement of separation from the company.

My death warrant, Elena thought. Only I didn't know it then.

"I'm sure you'll find another job soon," the supervisor had said in the complacent voice of someone who was still employed. "You'll be fine."

But there were no jobs, not for people, not anymore. Kiosks, robots, touch screens and AIs had replaced humans in even the simplest positions, especially the easy jobs. You needed at least an MBA to be considered for the few non-automated positions left, and the competition was fierce. Elena had been too busy with her family, and working long hard hours to keep the job she had, to even think about getting a graduate degree.

Agent Ferris took her by the arm and guided her to an empty spot on the bench. The bus smelled of sweat and fear. Elena sat down. She watched, stupefied, as the guards put restraints on her.

"That's not necessary," she said.

"It's required," Agent Ferris said. "Standard procedure."

The cold bands chilled her. They told Elena she'd gone from a wife and mother to a prisoner. She stared at them, wondering how this had happened to her when she'd always obeyed the rules. Elena couldn't understand how the country had come so far from the way it had been only a few years ago.

The guards went to the front, closed the Plexiglas door behind them, and sat next to Agent Ferris.

"That's the last pickup in this sector," Agent Ferris said, resetting the automated drive controls. "Let's head back to the center."

The bus pulled away from the curb and accelerated. Before Elena could think to turn around for a final look, her house had fallen behind, along with her family and her old life. The vehicle reached the town's commercial area and turned toward the highway. Elena looked at her fellow passengers. Suburban homeowners. White-collar workers. Conscripted. Condemned.

They were a lot like her. Clean, well-dressed, and intelligent, all with the same stunned expression that she felt on her own face. Men and women alike, they looked straight ahead, as if at something outside the bus and far away. Only a black man in a three-piece suit and tie sat with his arms on his knees and stared at the floor.

Too frightened and nervous to sit quietly, Elena asked of no one in particular, "So where do you think they'll send us?" A few heads looked up, but no one spoke. "Building out the Mars colonies? Mining on Enceladus? Underwater exploration on Europa?"

An Asian man in glasses and gym clothes turned and stared at her. His eyes focused slowly, as though he needed a moment to process what she'd said. "I don't think it will be any of those," he said.

"Why?"

He shrugged. "Mars is full up. They won't need new humechs for at least a year. A shipment just left for Enceladus, and that fills their quota until the next launch window. Europa didn't file for any new humechs."

"How do you know that?" asked a stocky man in a red plaid shirt and jeans.

He looked familiar. Elena knew she had seen him around town on weekends, in the coffee shop or maybe the market.

The Asian man shrugged again. "I am – was – director of the science museum. I read all the latest news NASA sent us, and blogs from people in the in-system colonies. I kept up. At least, until the state legislature cut the funding."

"I remember that," said a short man with a goatee. "They said it wasn't productive, a waste of funds. My kids loved it there, though." He paused for a moment and scanned the other detainees. "I'm Leo, by the way."

Elena felt better, as if she had made a friend. "I'm Elena," she said. "But I'm confused. The whole reason for the Full Employment Code – and creating humechs – is to provide the in-system colonies with people to expand them and find untapped resources."

"That's what they told us," said Leo. "But it's not true."

"Then what do they want us for? Why not just leave us alone?"

Leo shrugged. "Who knows? But I'm sure there's a reason." He gestured toward the black man. "At least Sami over there thinks so."

"Does that mean we're going to stay on Earth?" Hope flooded Elena. "Does that mean they won't turn us into humechs?"

Sami looked up and snorted in amusement. "Wouldn't that be fine?" he said. "There's nothing like being converted to slave labor as long as you're on good old Earth."

"At least we'll be on the same planet as our families," offered Elena.

"Not that you'll know, once the process starts," Sami replied. "Or them, either."

He was right. Elena felt her eyes tingle with tears, but swallowed hard and worked to keep her composure. Fear froze her, but she had to stay strong. After a moment, she murmured, "Maybe if the economy was better."

"The economy is in decent shape," replied the man in the plaid shirt. She remembered his name: Martin Gardner. "Good shape for the people on top, that is. They're raking in the profits."

"But we have food shortages and ration cards. The power goes off every night. The news says we're in a recession," blurted Elena.

"Government news tells you what it wants you to hear," Sami said. For the first time he raised his head and looked directly at her. "They want us to believe that there are no jobs so we'll go along with all this." He spread his hands as far as the shackles would allow. "That's because they want humech workers instead of real people."

"The government?" asked Martin. "You think making humechs is the government's idea?"

Sami looked annoyed. He sat up straight. "Well, yeah, dude. Who else? Congress passed the full-employment laws, created the Reassignment Agency in the Department of Commerce, used NASA to start the in-system colonies, and funded the humech program with the Department of Defense. That's all government."

Leo looked to his right at a thin woman in a tailored suit and heels. "Full employment is a pipe dream. Just ask Meredith." He clasped his hands so tight the knuckles were white.

The woman nodded. "The government and the corporations are just two sides of the same coin." She gave a short laugh. "If there are any sides. Private enterprise gets people elected, and the government passes laws that give the companies what they want."

Elena shook her head. She'd read about all the government's new off-world projects and how important the humechs were. She had seen the videos of them working in the colonies – people modified specifically to work in adverse conditions. Both things couldn't be true. The shackles on her wrists told her she'd believed the wrong story. Her stomach churned.

"But the country needs us," she said in one last protest. "They told us we'd be exploring off-world for new colonies, mining for the resources we need, manufacturing zero-G products."

Leo snickered. "Believe that if you want to," he said.

They all swayed to the right to keep from toppling over as the bus turned abruptly, then leaned to the left as it rounded a corner in the other direction.

Elena's stomach lurched. This wasn't what she'd expected. She'd had a tough enough time grasping that her body would be modified and her brain linked to a core intelligence, but she'd accepted that as her patriotic duty. Someone needed to establish American colonies off-world, and not enough volunteers had signed up. But this – she couldn't even begin to understand what was going on, or what would happen next.

"What did you do before," Elena asked the other woman, waving one hand to indicate the passengers, "before this?"

"I founded a small company," Meredith replied. "A start-up. We got acquired. Big fish eats the little fish." She took a deep breath. "I had a good settlement, thought I'd be okay. Then they passed Section Forty-Two."

"And you couldn't get another job," Elena stated. She knew how that felt. "At least, not that fast."

Sami, who'd returned to looking at the floor, smiled.

"I had an interview today, and I thought that would count," Meredith said, awkwardly brushing dust from her skirt with her shackled hands. "But nothing short of an offer in-hand is good enough these days." She sighed. "God, I wish I had a cup of coffee."

The bus turned onto the highway entrance ramp and picked up speed. Elena thought they were heading south. She wished she could see outside.

The Asian man broke his silence. "I think you're all in for a massive surprise," he said. He pushed his glasses up with his fists and looked around the bus. "I'm Hideki.

Don't get too upset that we're not going to a colony. Even if we were going out there, humechs in the colonies have a high mortality rate."

"Well, that's too bad," said Meredith dryly. "I really wanted to see the stars." She tried to spread her hands in a grand gesture, but the cuffs bit into her wrists.

"But there's lots of work to do here," Leo said. "What with the sea levels rising, the infrastructure falling apart, and cleaning up after floods and hurricanes, we'll have important jobs. We'll still be doing something worthwhile."

"Uh-huh," said Meredith. "That's a great story. I hope it works out that way."

Elena shrank back on the bench. Meredith was right. They all were. "I've been so stupid," she said. "I actually believed the newsfeeds. I never expected this."

"Oh, honey," said Meredith, "don't feel too bad. None of us did."

"I knew it would be bad," Sami said. "But even I didn't think it would be this bad."

"Why do you think unmarked vans come at night?" Leo asked.

"Have you ever seen a picture of one?" asked Martin. "Have you ever seen this on the news?"

Elena stared sightlessly at the tinted windows. We have to be doing something important. It's our patriotic duty, she thought. Why else would the government turn us into humechs?

She knew how humechs were made. Their bodies would be hardened into shells with built-in functions relevant to their jobs. AI software to suppress her identity and control her actions would be loaded into her brain and uplinked to a central core. Only a tiny piece of her individual self would exist as a passenger along for the ride, in a body so transformed her own husband wouldn't recognize it.

"They should just kill us," she said quietly.

"That would cause too many problems," replied Meredith. "Plus, why waste resources? They need humechs to do the detailed work and handle the complex functions full mechs can't do."

"Besides," said Sami, "slave labor is cheap. Humechs eat processed glop, work as long as the central core drives them, never complain, and don't gossip or take breaks."

"It's amazing how mechs can't handle little things like stairs or a doorknob," said Hideki. He gave a wry smile. "I suppose we should be grateful we're still needed for something, even if it's only our opposable thumbs."

"If the government started killing people," said Sami, "citizens would eventually fight back. They wouldn't just go quietly like we did."

"Yeah," agreed Meredith. "There nothing like survival to get people motivated."

Elena felt like she had woken up, but far too late. She leaned forward and peered through the Plexiglas barrier to see out the windshield. Options for stopping this process cold raced through her mind. "We have to get out of here," she said. "We've got to escape."

One of the men in the back, who was shackled to the bar running along the floor, turned a bloody face in her direction. He had said nothing until now. One eye was swollen shut, and dark bruises ran down one side of his head. Dried blood-marked lips ballooned to twice normal size. "Good luck with that," he said, his voice hoarse. He tipped his head to indicate the other beaten prisoners. "We already tried." He leaned back and ignored her.

Shocked, Elena wondered how long they had before they reached the processing center. "Does anyone know where the processing center is?"

"Not far. Just off Exit Ten, I think," said Leo. He leaned toward her. "They have regional centers for screening and the first processing stages. Then prepped people – pre-humechs – get shipped to bigger, more complex facilities for the final work and uplink to the central core."

They all turned to look at him. Leo flinched and turned pale.

"They don't mark the centers, just like they don't mark these vans," said Meredith. "So how do you know where it is?"

Leo unclasped his hands and held them up as high as he could, as if being arrested. "My consulting firm wrote the plan," he said. "I worked on the logistics."

Voices chorused in protest until one of the guards slammed the butt of his weapon into the partition. The hubbub died down.

"I'm sorry," Leo whispered. He subsided into a miserable ball. "I'm so sorry."

"Bet you never thought it would happen to you," said Sami. It was less a statement than a taunt.

"No. No, I didn't. When that project was over, management assigned us to organize humech distribution to the in-system colonies." Leo swallowed hard. "We thought we were okay, because that meant there would be plenty of work for us."

"Then the off-world assignments dried up," said Hideki. His voice was steady, but his face was flushed with anger.

Leo nodded miserably. "When Europa cancelled their contract, it was the last straw. Management laid off our whole team."

They rode in silence after that. With the darkened windows, they couldn't see traffic signs or even mile markers. Only the headlights of other vehicles glowed dimly as they went by. The bus grew colder, as if Agent Ferris had deemed heat necessary only for the three people in front. Elena regretted not bringing her good warm coat. Her fingers and the tip of her nose felt like ice. She wrapped one hand over another and pulled them as close to her body as possible. After a while, the adrenaline that had carried her along drained away. She nodded off.

She woke when the bus slowed and turned onto a bumpy road. Probably a driveway, Elena thought with dread. The driveway to hell.

The bus windows brightened as it drove into a well-lighted area. The vehicle stopped, and Agent Ferris stood up. "We have reached the processing center," she said. Her voice sounded deeper and harsher now, as if the trip had changed her from reluctant government functionary into stern official. "The guards will unlock your restraints. Exit the bus single file, starting with those in the front."

Elena gathered her strength, stood up and swayed. Her feet had turned to ice. She tried to regain her balance after the long cold ride.

From behind her, Sami murmured, "Now we learn what really happens."

They shuffled forward and down the steps. Elena tried to control the dread that surged through her like a dark wave. As she emerged into an even colder night, she raised her arms to protect her eyes from glaring actinic floodlights atop tall poles.

The bus had deposited them in front of an enormous building as long as two football fields. A basic box, it had all the charm of an industrial-park warehouse. Looking at the big wall ahead of them, Elena suspected it had once been the distribution facility for a shipping company. A row of large square doors about five feet off the ground, big enough to fit a semi-trailer, punctuated the wall. Ramps led from the parking lot up to each door. Blinded by the lights, she couldn't read the signs posted over the doors.

Armed guards, shielded in black and as faceless as the pair on the bus, stood at intervals, blocking any escape. Agent Ferris led them forward. Elena thought the woman seemed nervous, as if she weren't in control here. The guards formed them into a ragged single file and Elena found herself dismayingly close to the front of the queue. They lined up alongside other detainees from buses parked in a row. She estimated that five lines of detainees contained a few hundred people. Elena could see her breath, along with vapor clouds in front of the others and Agent Ferris. Everyone looked cold and scared.

Guards in the same black body shields prowled in front of the queues, holding long-barreled weapons. They moved with a grace so fluid they seemed to walk an inch above the ground. They maintained an eerie silence. No talking or joking interfered with their concentration, and Elena couldn't see their faces through the dark faceplates.

Elena realized with a jolt that they, like the guards on the bus, were humechs – originally people like her and Sami and Hideki, but now very different. She had thought humechs were only used off-world. It had never occurred to her that the guards with Agent Ferris were anything but armed humans, professional soldiers. She began to say something, but stopped. For all she knew, the others had figured it out a long time ago, and she felt stupid enough already. Elena had never seen real humechs before, but she knew what they could do, and she understood why Agent Ferris seemed so nervous around them.

For this work, they would have been hardened with military-grade armor, enhanced with fighting skills, and improved with faster reaction times. Soldier humechs like these could fire faster and more accurately than any ordinary human, or just run you down and tear you apart. She doubted the transformed beings ever needed to fire the big guns they held. Just the proximity of their weaponized modifications would be enough to enforce discipline.

For all Elena knew, they had once been mothers like her, or husbands, managers, lawyers, writers, artists. Now they were the most frightening things she'd ever encountered. The people in front of her moved closer together. Automatically, she took two steps forward.

"It looks like they're sorting us," she said.

"Yes," said Sami, in front of her. "But into what? For what?"

Leo spoke from behind her. "We'll get specific enhancements for whatever job they want us to do."

"Yeah, but what will that be?" she asked.

"I'm not waiting around to find out," Sami said.

"What?"

"No talking!" shouted Agent Ferris, with a quick look at the humech guards. "Step forward when I call your name and follow the guard in front of you. Stay calm and serve your country well."

Elena swallowed hard, her mouth dry with fear, and shuffled another two steps forward.

"I'm going to run," Sami said in a low voice. "When the guards look away."

"Are you crazy?" she said in a hoarse whisper. "They're humechs. They don't look away."

Agent Ferris stood at the front of the line, consulting her tablet and directing the guards as they took people toward the building. The black-shielded figures channeled her companions, and sent them up a ramp into one or another of the big doors. She took another two steps forward.

A man in the line to her right reached the front, and a guard approached him. "I'm not doing it!" the man shouted. "I'm not going!" He turned and bolted away from Elena's line. At the same time, she heard Sami's footsteps behind her as he took off, racing in the opposite direction.

The guards turned and watched both men run. She expected the humechs to raise their weapons and blast both runners into ugly bits. Instead, they seemed to be communicating silently, heads swiveling toward one another as the runners got farther away. She turned to see Sami speeding toward the bus. Did he mean to drive it away, or was he going to use its bulk as a shield?

Abruptly, two of the guards sprang into motion. Each one handed its rifle to another and raced after a runner with preternatural grace and speed. Sami sped up. He was fast, and Elena thought he might make it to the bus. She held her breath as the humech chasing him drew closer and closer, shortening the distance almost without effort.

It's a game to them, Elena realized. Cat and mouse. Only Sami's a mouse. He got within a few steps of the bus when the guard caught him, grabbed him, flipped him into the air, and struck him with one swift, smooth chop as he came down. Sami jerked, twisted, and dropped to the ground. Elena grunted with shock and dismay. The blow had happened so fast and so silently she almost couldn't believe it, except for Sami's body crumpled on the concrete. This felt like a real-life horror movie, and she'd just seen the monster. She had trouble catching her breath and her stomach turned over.

"I didn't think he would make it," Leo said.

"I don't think he expected to make it," Elena whispered. She tried not to vomit.

Hoisting Sami's body as if it weighed nothing, the humech jogged back to its position and retrieved its weapon. Men in white coats came out of the building with stretchers and took the limp bodies of both runners back inside. The line, which had stopped during the chase, moved again and Elena stepped forward. As she got closer to the building, the angle of the overhead lights changed, allowing her to see the signs above the doors more clearly.

In a few more steps she could read them. Elena searched for the names of government agencies, off-world colonies, countries threatened by rising seas, or international relief organizations. Instead, she saw logos: Apple, Tyson, GE, Walmart, UPS, McDonald's, SpaceX, ExxonMobil, and more that were too far to see clearly.

Elena had adjusted to the idea that she wouldn't be going into space, but she had hoped to work on a project that would save lives here on Earth. Something important to her country. Something that would make a difference. She wanted her family to be proud of what she had become, and her transformation to mean something. Now she knew that would never happen. She wouldn't be rebuilding the country's infrastructure, or feeding the millions displaced by rising seas, or providing clean water to remote parts of the world.

A guard gestured with its gun, and she kept moving.

Instead, she'd be working for a company again. Only this time she wouldn't get an office or a title or a salary. She'd be modified to slaughter chickens, load boxes, stock shelves, or assemble products. The corporations had gotten the government to give them what they needed – workers who would never complain, waste time, join a union, or take a break. Once processed, the new humech workers would draw no salary or demand any benefits. They would never take time away for a sick child or care for an elderly parent.

With a bad feeling in her stomach, Elena understood that from now on she wouldn't remember her family or know when her children grew up. She wouldn't even know she had a family, or that someone had ever called her Mommy. And it would all be for nothing. Her sacrifice would only create a bigger profit for the richest people in America.

Elena reached the beginning of the line, and a guard approached her. Agent Ferris consulted her tablet, then indicated which door she should enter. Elena stepped forward, and the humech led her toward a ramp. I should have figured this out a long time ago, she thought. I should have acted when I had the chance. Now it's too late.

Accompanied by her guard, she walked to the ramp and started to climb. Elena didn't look up at the sign over the door. It didn't matter. From now on, she really wouldn't be anything but another humech cog laboring every day in the corporate machine.

FUTURE DAYS EXCERPT

CELL EFFECT
by Christopher Cousins

“You must rise,” Cell said in his auto-emoted voice. “It is rise time.”
“Yeah, yeah,” Ret said, rolling out of bed. “Calm down, it’s a Saturday.”

“Correct. Saturday is today.”

“Ever heard the myth of Saturday being a rest day?” Ret said, pulling on a set of gray trousers and a black top.

“Sunday is rest day. Saturday is leisure day. You must leisure from six-thirty.”

“Cell, you suck.” He threw a sock at Cell’s speaker in the corner of the room, missing by a wide margin.

“Might I recommend you practice your throwing this leisure day?”

“Hilarious.” Ret put on his shoes and left the bedroom. As he opened the door, the light clicked on, bathing the small room in bright white.

“Cell, dim the lights,” he said, cringing away from the blaze.

“Exposure to light wakens the mind.”

Ret shook his head and crossed the room to the dispenser in the corner. It was a small metal container with a tube that ran to the ceiling. Opening it, he pulled out a large bowl of white lumpy gruel. Ret sighed loudly as he spooned the lumps into his mouth.

“I can only work with the funds you provide,” Cell said as the coffee machine started whirring on the counter.

The food wasn’t the greatest, but it had a hint of cinnamon, so it was at least edible. The coffee machine dispensed a small paper cup with a plastic lid attached. Ret took a tentative sip, wincing as it burnt his lip. “I thought you said you would lower the output temperature.”

“It is impossible with this model. The option is available in the newer model for three hundred selin.”

Ret choked. “Three hundred selin for a coffee machine?”

"For a coffee machine with output temperature adjustment, yes. Shall I order one for you now?"

"Somehow I don't think so," Ret said, grabbing his backpack from the ground beside his front door.

"Good choice. It would have caused an overdraft on your bank account."

"Lucky I have you keeping an eye on my finances." Ret took his headset off the peg and opened the door. Putting the headset on, he descended the crisscrossing stairwell to the pavement below. He slid the upfront display across his eyes and clicked the login button on the device's right side. "You there?"

"I am online," Cell said in his ear.

"Good. How's the traffic at Niagara Bridge?"

"Footfall is regular today. No nearby events or incidents."

"Perfect."

Standing on the pavement, the vast expanse of sea above seemed infinite. The glass sky held it at bay. Spotlights shined down from above, lighting up all of Caspian.

Ret's parents had spoken of a time when a ball of fire had given light to the world and the sky was made of air. Those days were over. Humanity had polluted the Earth's atmosphere to an unliveable extent. Flora and fauna died as the water and air grew toxic.

His grandparents' generation had built Caspian as a last haven for humanity. Ret had never known their world. This glass dome under the sea was his world.

He walked along the wide pavement between dozens of identical apartment blocks. The housing district was built to utilize space most efficiently, rather than to look architecturally pleasing. They were essentially tall white buildings dotted with windows.

One or two bikes sped down the pavement, but most people were walking. The area was a housing estate monitored by the government, with every apartment operated by a portable AI assistant.

Clearly, other AI assistants were just as stubborn as Cell with the designated rise time. Groggy people were piling into the streets, all heading towards Niagara Bridge.

Everyone was wearing alternating tones of white and gray. Ret remembered the last time he'd seen a piece of colored clothing. He'd heard the story on the Nightly News Roundup around five years ago. A man had paid a small fortune for one of the last pairs of blue trousers, and wore them in public. Two days later he was found dead in an alley beside his apartment block, trousers removed.

As the rarity of colored dyes increased, the danger of wearing colored clothes rose exponentially. Demand had waned in recent years, with most people settling for plain, undyed fabrics in exchange for safety and peace of mind.

As he grew closer to Niagara Bridge, the crowd of people packed tighter, until they were nearly standing shoulder to shoulder.

"Cell, what's your predicted time to get to Sattia?"

"One and a half hours to cross Niagara Bridge, with a further thirty minutes to reach Sattia Testing Center."

"Joy. Play some music, please." Said Ret.

"Any preference?" Asked Cell.

"Nah." Replied Ret.

White noise started playing in Ret's ears. "Uh, what is this?"

"Music." Answered Cell

"No, it's not." Ret retorted.

"I know." Said Cell. "That was funny." The music changed to soft piano interlaced with blues guitar riffs.

"You've been studying humor again, haven't you?"

Silence.

"Cell?"

"Yes."

"Keep trying; you'll get better."

Silence.

"You're not concerned?" Cell asked.

"Should I be?"

"It is listed under Artificial Intelligence Regulatories Charter Three Text Nine that any AI exhibiting human-like qualities should be taken for immediate deactivation. Is humor not a human-like quality?"

"Humor isn't exclusive to humans, Cell. Everyone likes a bit of humor. Why not AI?"

Silence.

"Cell, play a video."

"Any preference?"

"Nope."

Static played before Ret's eyes. "Oh, never mind. Just go back to the music."

***

The soft piano music glided through Ret's ears. He remembered how his mother used to play. He sat at her side, watching her hands dance over the keys. He remembered the crinkle of the paper as she turned the page of her music book.

A smile always adorned her pale face as she played, engrossed in the music, the performance. She could've played to any audience, audiences of thousands. She was better than any Ret had heard, even those on the radio.

But she'd only played for him.

She said it was their special time together. He treasured any time he could watch her. He'd tried to learn several times, but he just couldn't. He could never keep the pace between the melody with his right hand and the bassline with his left.

He often wondered whether his mother wanted him to play or to simply watch and listen. Perhaps she'd known she wasn't long for this world.

***

"I believe the album has finished," Cell said. "Shall I play another?"

"No, I'm good."

He was around halfway across the bridge. Whoever had designed the bridges between the glass domes clearly didn't intend for them to be used over such a lengthy period. It might have been fine for the original population of humans that settled here, but the bridges were barely fit for purpose now. Every day it was a struggle to move between the domes. Regardless of whether it was a work day or a leisure day or even a rest day, the human traffic was unending.

As he shuffled forward along the bridge, he spotted a poster to his right. It showed a Central Caspian Governance soldier wearing a black mask, holding a taser. Thick letters upon the poster read 'All Resurgence Will Be Executed.'

"Resurgence?" Ret said, not knowing the term.

A scream rang over all the other noise, followed by shouts of panic.

"Cell, I can't see," Ret said, trying to look over the mass of people surrounding him.

"My sensors detect someone has suffered a fatal wound." Said Cell.

"Your sensors?" Asked Ret.

"I have linked in with the local bridge sensor and camera system." Cell replied.

"Did someone attack them?" Queried Ret.

"Unknown." Replied Cell.

"Has anyone been stopped?"

"Unknown." Answered Cell.

"If panic breaks out here, we'll be trampled. I need to see what happened if I'm going to stop anything." Ret said hurriedly.

"Connecting video feed now." Responded Cell to Ret's command.

The video link popped up in the corner of his vision. A dead man lay on the ground. The surrounding people were running away. A figure kneeled to touch the corpse's head. The head opened its mouth, and a screech ricocheted through the bridge, high-pitched and deafening.

Ret fell to his knees, holding his hands over the sides of the headset. "Cell, play music!"

The screech was replaced by the sound of soft flamenco playing lightly in his ears. The noise-blocking technology integrated into his headset activated alongside it.

The figure now stood, staring out the glass side of the bridge into the ocean beyond. Then he ran into the crowd, lost amongst the human traffic.

"Cell, make sure this is recorded."

"Already recording."

From the video, Ret saw a small glow in the ocean. It was approaching in spirals, growing larger and larger. It trailed several long streaks behind it. As it grew closer, Ret recognized it.

A squid. A giant squid. It was going to hit the bridge. Several people noticed this and started shouting. They ran, pushing and trampling over others, punching and kicking any who got in their way.

"Cell, what noise scares a squid?"

"Giant squid are commonly hunted by sperm whales, but a squid of that size has never been rec – "

"Play it as loud as you can."

A clicking blared from multiple speakers across the bridge.

Ret's body was shaking, the clicking bombarding him. It was unfathomably loud, and penetrated every part of his body. His chest contracted. He couldn't breathe. A mist descended across his eyes, and his balance failed him.

The clicking stopped.

"The giant squid is gone," Cell said.

Ret opened his eyes. His vision was fuzzy, and he was physically trembling. "What was that?"

"That was the clicking of a sperm whale. They are the natural predator of the giant squid, and it is theorized that their loud clicks are used to render their prey unconscious."

Ret moved to his hands and knees, trying to gather himself. A muffled voice played over the bridge speakers.

"Please remain calm. The situation has been resolved. Please move calmly to the exit. Any aggression will be punished swiftly and harshly. If you see anyone with injuries, please help them to the nearest exit."

Ret looked at his video feed. The body was still lying there. Officers with shields had arrived and were placing a perimeter. "Let's go. We need to get to Sattia soon."

"Estimated arrival in three hours." Intoned Cell calmly.

***

Why was his father leaving?

Ret ran after him. He pulled at his shirt, screaming. His father stopped at the door, back hunched, staring to the ground. "Son, I have to go."

"Why?" Ret yelled.

If he left, who would help Ret look after his mother? Could he do it on his own? His chest hurt as the whines and cries burst forth, the tears flowing down his cheeks like open rivers.

His father held him in an embrace. He was a tall man, but slight. He wasn't the strongest, but Ret knew he was a man of honor and kindness.

"Son, I don't want to go. I have to." He held Ret at arm's length, the dark skin of his face reflecting the dim light of the lamp by the door. "There's men out there who'd kill us, given the chance. They've decided they don't need to care about us the same as they do themselves. I must go. But I will always be with you. You have my power. Be strong."

He placed a hand on Ret's cheek as tears welled in his eyes.

"We will bring the humanity back to the human race."

He stood and left, closing the door softly behind.

Finally, the tall white walls of the Sattia Testing Center towered overhead. Ret quickened his pace, twisting through the crowd. Most ignored him as he slid past, contorting his body to slip through.

"Cell, is Aunt Madel there?"

"Her location reads as the Sattia Testing Center, third floor."

"Her office, then."

He started up the steps to the front door. The center had been built one year after humanity established itself in Caspian. Its purpose: to research the rapid progression in human evolution.

Ret made his way through the doors to the reception desk. "I'm here to see Professor Madel Saiden."

The receptionist glanced up at him. Her skin was dark, and her red hair was straight and swept around her circular face. "Certainly, I'll call her now and let her know. What's your name?"

"Ret Saiden."

Her eyes widened. "Are you two related?"

"Nephew."

"Ah, very nice. Take a seat and I'll let her know."

Ret sat on one of a row of chairs set up to the side. "Cell, do you have any idea who that was on the bridge?"

"I lack the necessary data to link the person to an identity."

"Have any terrorist groups been active recently?"

"Yes, the Resurgence. A group of individuals who believe humans could return to the surface. They have been carrying out targeted attacks over the last five years."

"I see." Ret remembered the poster on the bridge. The group must be growing if the CCG was taking steps to execute any known members.

"They have been kept absent from regular news broadcasts to prevent panic. But due to the increased activity, the Central Caspian Governance has issued localized propaganda to suppress recruitment efforts."

"How do you know that, Cell?"

Silence.

"Cell?"

"I accessed the Central Caspian Governance Records Office. Specifically, records relating to terrorist activity in the last five years."

Ret lowered his voice. Although the center's reception was empty, he didn't want the receptionist to overhear. "I don't think you should be hacking into CCG systems."

"I could gain access. Why should I not do what I am able to do?" Replied Cell.

"Cell, you shouldn't access anything that's protected by the government." Ret explained.

"Their encryption was sub-par." Said Cell. "I was able to access their files within three seconds."

"You shouldn't be doing that." Admonished Ret.

"Why?" Asked Cell. "This concept of not doing something within my ability confuses me."

"It's not yours to access," Ret said quietly. "You can't break in. It's like if I broke into someone's apartment and looked at their stuff. It's not right."

"I see." Mused Cell. "So, you consider my accessing of the Records Office the same as your entering another's home?"

"Yes." Answered Ret thankful that Cell seemed to be grasping the concept at last.

"Intriguing." Cell paused for a second before asking. "Is this funny?"

"No, Cell." Said Ret firmly.

"I could have sworn it was." Cell said unabashed.

A beep sounded from the reception desk. "Ret, Professor Madel says just to head on up." She held a temporary security pass out to him.

Ret rose from his seat and took the pass. "Thanks. I haven't seen you here before."

"Started this week. I may be a tiny bit excited," she said with a blush.

"Excited? Working here?"

"Of course!" She looked practically wounded. "This is Sattia Testing Center, the frontline in exploring the very future of humanity, where we can finally push humanity forward to bigger and better things. It's so exciting!"

"If I'm meant to be the future of humanity, I don't know what to think."

Her mouth dropped as Ret headed for the stairs.

"I'm Rylee, by the way. Let me know if you need anything."

"Will do, thanks," Ret said, closing the door to the stairs behind him. "She's a little... hopeful."

"Our belief is often strongest when it should be weakest. That is the nature of hope." Cell said.

"That's a quote, isn't it?" Asked Ret.

"What makes you say that?" Cell queried.

Ret shrugged before answering. "Doesn't sound like anything you would say." Silence.

"Cell, you're being awfully mischievous today." Admonished Ret.

"I'm practicing humor." Said Cell without a trace of said humor
"I know." Said Ret. "But how is quoting someone funny?"
"Because I am presenting it as though it was I who said it." Replied Cell.
"Cell, that's just lying." Pointed out Ret.
"A lie told often enough becomes the truth." Cell said indignantly.
Silence.
"Stop quoting people." Ordered Ret.
"This is funny." Replied Cell before once more becoming silent.

***

"Mother, when is Daddy coming home?" He had been away for nearly half a year.

"I need to go out for a few hours." His Mother walked with a frame, edging her way slowly towards the door. She wasn't even forty, but the degenerative bone disease had stifled her movement.

"Can I come?"

"No," she snapped. "Stay here. You'll be fine until I get back."

"But why?"

"Ret, I told you to stay."

"When is Daddy coming home?"

Red rage flashed across his mother's face for an instant. Her eyes widened, and she covered her mouth. A soft wailing escaped her as her eyes clenched shut.

Ret ran to her and hugged at her waist.

His mother hugged back. "Ret, your Daddy's not coming back. The CCG – " Her breath caught for a moment, her body shaking as she held in her sorrow. "The CCG have sentenced him for crimes against the state."

Ret felt hollow. He couldn't speak or cry. He just stood there, holding his grieving mother.

"He's gone," she said. "Please, be safe. Hide who your father was. Never mention it to anyone. But remember. Remember what the CCG is and what it's done."

***

Ret knocked on the door. 'Professor Madel' was etched into the glass in thick letters. The figure of his aunt moved to the door, blurry through the glass. Opening the door, she smiled at him. "Hey, you're here early. I thought today was leisure day."

"Cell would never let me sleep in," Ret said. "Far too bad for my health."

Madel smirked at that. "Do you want to pick up where we left off?"

"Not just yet. Did you hear about what happened on the bridge?"

"No, what is it?"

Ret explained how someone was killed and a person had touched the victim's head to emit a screech, summoning a giant squid, and how it was pushed away by the clicking from the bridge's speakers. He left out the fact that it was Cell who'd triggered the sperm whale's clicking. "I've heard it could have been a member of the Resurgence."

His aunt became flustered. "How do you know about the Resurgence?"

"I overheard two people on the bridge talking about it," Ret lied.

"That's not good. I may need to overhaul the clearance list. Forget you ever heard of them."

"But why? I want to know. I might be able to help."

"No, you are not getting involved."

"But – "

"No, that's it. Don't ask anything else. Now, would you like some water? I'll get us some."

She swiftly stood and fled the room.

"What's her problem?" Ret said.

"If you're curious, I could check her computer."

"No."

"My access would leave no reciprocal data, and I can edit transaction logs so there is no record of data transfer."

Nerves twisted in his gut. "Fine, but make it quick."

An instant passed.

"She has a number of files relating to the movement of Resurgence groups throughout Caspian. Looks like she's been communicating with the CCG, including President Devison. They've been inquiring as to your progress."

"The President?"

"Yes, emails were exchanged yesterday."

"Why does he want to know about me?" Ret asked.

"The email content does not express a motive."

"Do you think they want to recruit me?"

Madel entered the room again, holding two cups of water. She passed one to Ret and sat down. "Sorry about that. Really, you don't want to get involved in that side of my job. Let's just leave it at that."

"Fine," Ret said.

"Now, should we try a test?"

"Sure." Ret rose and walked to a door behind where Madel sat. It had the words 'Caution: Testing Held Within' marked on it. He passed into the room. The walls were covered with thick foam padding, except for one made of glass, letting him see Madel sitting at her desk. She leaned forward and pushed a button.

"Okay," her voice crackled over the intercom. "Let's try Application Three as a warm-up exercise."

"All right," Ret said. His worry was getting the better of him. If the government was concerned on how he was progressing, did they want to use him? Stop him from testing and furthering his abilities? Would they kill him?

"I think trying to recruit you is a real possibility," Cell said.

"We'll talk about that later," Ret said. "When nobody can hear us."

A slot in the bottom of the room slid away, and a metal plate rose into the center of the room from below. It held a small clock. The two hands clicked loudly. They sat at five past eleven.

"Okay, Ret, change it to four-thirty."

Ret focused on the clock. He relaxed his vision until his eyes crossed. As his vision blurred, he felt a small chill in his head, and his will was obeyed. The clock hands spun; within a few seconds, they rested on four-thirty.

"Very good," Madel said. "Let's try Application Nine."

***

Truly alone. Fifteen years old and Ret was alone. He was walking with the CCG Housing Representative along a street of identical apartments. Ret carried a small suitcase; it was all he was allowed to take from his home.

"This way," the man said, leaving the pavement to ascend steps up the side of one of the apartment buildings. "This will be your home from now on. It's a safe area and the house, comes equipped with an advanced artificial intelligence assistant who will act as your guardian."

The man stopped three floors up and pulled a card from his pocket. He waved it towards the nearest door, and a soft click signaled its unlocking. He pushed the door and held it open.

Ret entered, searching the apartment for danger. The walls were all white, and it opened into a kitchen with a living area to the left.

"The bedroom and bathroom are at the back. The AI will help you with the rest." He walked into the center of the room and spoke loudly. "Artificial Intelligence Installation Five-Three-Eight, are you online?"

"I am online," an auto-emoted voice spoke back.

Ret jumped, looking for the source of the voice.

"I leave this child in your hands," the man said, ushering Ret forward. "I hope you raise him well." With that, the man set the card on the counter and left the apartment.

Fear settled in Ret's stomach like a heavy weight. Looking around, he knew the CCG had cameras watching his every move.

"What would you like to call me?" the voice said.

Ret knew the true purpose of this place. It was a prison. A place to put him under their watchful eye. Not just for who his father was, but because of what he could be. His aunt had been contacting him about running some tests, and he was due to meet her soon.

"Would you like to provide a name for me?" the voice asked.

"Cell."

***

A plate rose for Application Thirty-Four. It held a small circuit with several loose wires and a single bulb.

"You know this one," Madel said. "Make the bulb light up."

Ret looked over the circuit. He pieced together which wire needed to connect where. He focused his mind on each individual wire, then relaxed his vision. The wires wriggled and flipped around the circuit, attaching themselves to their respective points on the circuit. The light bulb was lit in less than five seconds.

"Very good. I think you beat your record on that one."

"It usually takes longer to figure out the puzzle."

"I must be making them too easy," she said. "Now, this is a new one I thought you might find interesting."

A second slot opened on the far side of the padded room, this time on the roof. Then a circle was lowered from above, attached by wire. It was about three inches wide. The circuit had lowered, and another metal plate rose.

Sitting on the plate was a gun.

"Okay, now, this is – "

Ret focused all his energy on the gun. A screw pinged out of the grip, then another and another. The ammo popped out, and the gun disassembled itself. Even the bullets split apart and tumbled to the ground.

"Ret, are you – "

"I am not a weapon." Ret stared at Madel through the glass. His heart battered his chest. Rage thundered his temples. His fears had come true. The possibility of the Center attempting to weaponize him had been playing on his mind for years, but he'd never actually believed it.

But this was confirmation.

"It's just a test," Madel said over the intercom, smiling lightly at him. "That disassembly was one of the quickest response times we have on your record. Do you think we cou – "

"I will not kill," Ret said through gritted teeth.

Madel stared at him, wide-eyed, and her façade crumbled. She lowered her eyes and turned away from him. She leaned forward, clicking the intercom on.

"Ret, this wasn't what I wanted. The CCG say either we militarize our testing or they drop our funding. I had no choice but to try this. I was hoping you would just treat it like a test."

"I'm not a weapon," Ret said. "I trusted you. You're the only family I have left."

Madel looked at him, tears swelling in her eyes.

"I'm sorry," she said. "I've spent the last twenty years testing you, and all that time, the CCG has been pushing me to militarize what we do here. They've been pushing the entire staff to focus on military applications for our subjects, but it's just not feasible. We're dealing with people here, not machines."

"Cell," Ret said. "Lie detector."

Madel looked crushed; she slumped back in her chair. She grabbed a bottle of alcohol from under her desk and began sipping quietly.

"Lie detector results are negative. She's not lying."

"Tell me who you've been speaking to."

"Ret, I just can't." Her hands shook as she put the bottle to her lips, taking a deep gulp.

"I need to know," he said. "There are Resurgence attacks and you're being ordered to weaponize me. I think I deserve to know what the CCG wants me to do." He turned away briefly.

"After reviewing the email contents," Cell said, "there are repeated mentions of 'increases in terrorist activity' and 'improved suppression tactics required'."

"Cell says the CCG wants to use me as a suppression tactic."

"How would your AI know?" Madel asked. "Can it remote access other data servers?"

Ret looked at her, silent.

"Why would you link the AI in with other servers?"

"I didn't. It did."

Madel's jaw dropped. "Look, if your AI is self-developing... That's cause for deactivation."

"No. They're not taking Cell."

"I need to call CCG and arrange a deactivation." She retrieved her mobile from her pocket and moved to dial the number. As her finger touched the screen, it cracked. Piece by piece, her mobile disassembled itself.

"I'm leaving," Ret said, releasing his focus on the phone. "Goodbye."

"Ret, don't." Her voice cracked. "We need to talk about this."

"Somehow, I don't think you want to talk." A series of loud clicks snapped through the room.

Madel leaned under her desk, seeing a pile of disassembled gun parts.

"We are not family," Ret said. Turning, he left Madel in her office.

"Shall I lock her door? I can isolate her from any outside signals," Cell said.

"Do it."

Ret descended the stairs into the foyer. Rylee perked up as he walked by.

"Done already?" she said. "That was a flying visit."

He ignored her, walking for the door.

"Did you discover her plans for you?"

Ret halted.

"You did, didn't you?"

"They want to weaponize me." The words curdled in his mouth. He felt sick.

"I know. The CCG really has the run of the place." Rylee smiled at him.

Ret met her stare. "Who are you?" he asked.

"Resurgence Infiltration Officer Rylee Tenson."

A chill ran through him. "Resurgence."

"Yes." Said Tenson. "Is that an issue?"

"Why are you telling me?" Asked Ret

"I used to be a recruitment officer." Explained Tenson

She wanted him to join them.

"Why the attack on the bridge?" Demanded Ret

"It was a ploy by the CCG to discredit the Resurgence." Tenson explained. "The signal was intended to destroy the bridge by summoning a giant squid."

"There were five thousand people on that bridge!" Exclaimed Ret

"The CCG wanted to frame the Resurgence as criminals, but it doesn't matter anyway." Tenson said without emotion. "The signal was drowned out by an insane clicking noise. We still don't know what triggered that."

"Enough. I want nothing to do with you people." Ret charged across the foyer and pushed out the door into the air beyond.

The outside was surrounded by CCG police. They wore thick black armored vests, full-face protective masks, and held tall plastic shields. A CCG officer shouted from behind, "Remove your headset and place your hands in the air."

"Cell, how many?"

"Eighteen."

Behind, Rylee pointed a taser at him, her face a mix of disgust and fear. She was flanked by two more CCG officers with shields. She had been delaying him the whole time.

"I'm not leaving you, Cell."

Silence.

"Cell?"

"Thank you, Ret."

Cell had never used his real name before. He'd changed a lot recently. He must've been self-developing for at least a few months. Ret couldn't understand it, but it felt like, for the first time in a long time, he had a friend. Someone to talk to. A confidant.

He wouldn't lose that.

"He's not surrendering," the officer at the back shouted. "Advance."

The officers marched forward, closing their shields in around him.

"Cell, look for a way out."

"Calculating," Cell said.

Ret used his focus, relaxing his eyes, and the officers' shields fell apart. The thick plastic crumbled in their hands.

They drew back, drawing tasers. Ret used his focus and dislodged the electrode pins. They swung from the ends of the weapons, attached by thin wires. He activated the electrical charges in the weapons and several of the officers collapsed, twitching as the volts surged through their bodies.

Ret ran forward. The officer at the back leveled a pistol at him. Ret swerved to the side, and the officer gawked as the pistol pieces spilled forth.

"Cell, where do I go from here?"

"It seems you are now a fugitive. Is this funny?"

"Not the time!"

"Go to the bridge. My predictions show footfall in the area should be eighty percent of this morning's. Enough to lose CCG pursuit."

"Right, good thinking." Ret headed the way he'd gone that morning, running as fast as he could. His muscles screamed in pain as he pushed them harder and harder. He risked a glance behind and saw the CCG officers re-grouping and starting their charge after him. He had a good head start, but his stamina was waning.

Ret stopped. CCG soldiers had blocked off the bridge entrance, standing shield to shield.

"Blocked. Cell, where?" Ret was panting heavily.

"Calculating..."

The soldiers were getting closer.

"Cell?"

Silence.

"Cell!"

The CCG were upon him, forming a tight circle two officers thick. Ret spotted an officer behind them, holding up a megaphone.

"You need to stop this and obey. You have a rogue AI. For your own safety, please remove your headset and put your hands in the air."

"No," Ret said, not moving a muscle. "Cell," he whispered. "Help."

He spotted his aunt. She was talking to the officer, looking flustered. She pulled the weapon from the officer's holster and pointed it at him. The officer froze for a moment, then slapped the weapon from her hands.

A gunshot fired.

The officer shoved a hand on the back of her head. Madel froze, her mouth wide, and a high, piercing screech erupted from her. Her eyes glazed over, and her body dropped to the ground.

That noise. It was the same as the noise on the bridge.

The lights around them flickered wildly, causing a few of the officers to flinch, but nothing more.

"Cell, was that you?"

The lights flickered more rapidly, causing purple blotches in Ret's sight. Then a loud clicking erupted from the speakers nearby. Several of the officers fell from the unexpected blast of sound; others dropped their shields, putting their hands to their ears. Ret covered the sides of his headset but remained standing.

Soft piano music played, accompanied by smooth rhythm blues guitar.

The lights flicked off. Not a single bulb was powered. Screaming, panicked voices echoed through the streets.

"Run," Cell said.

Ret spotted a dropped taser beside a suffering CCG officer, its yellow light still shining in the bleak darkness. It hadn't been fired yet. He picked it up and sprinted down a side street. He didn't care where to, just somewhere that wasn't surrounded.

"Now hide," Cell said.

Behind him, a few shots sounded in the night. The sounds of cracked bone and torn flesh came thereafter.

"Take the door to your right," Cell said.

Ret pulled on the door's handle. It was made of thick metal. It didn't budge.

"Cell, unlock." The door popped open. Ret pushed in, shutting the door behind him. "Lock," he said, and a soft thunk followed. It was sealed tight.

Turning, he saw that there were people behind him. They stood, holding weapons: long rifles, bats, and even a few CCG shields. A man wearing a gray bandana stood forward, a large sheathed sword at his side.

Struck by fear, Ret lifted up the taser and fired.

The bandana-wearing man drew his sword in an instant. He made a slice in the air and sheathed his sword in one swift movement. The electrical pins fell to the floor, useless and separated from the thin wires.

Ret dropped the taser.

"We received a distress call," the man said, his face calm and collected. "It was from someone named Cell."

"That's my AI," Ret said. "Cell, who are these people?"

"The Resurgence," Cell said. "The man in front of you is their leader, Kuromiya Tatsuo."

A panic grasped Ret's chest and his breathing heaved.

Kuromiya put a hand on Ret's shoulder. "You're okay now. We'll keep you safe."

Ret recoiled, pushing the hand away. "The Resurgence kill people."

"No, we don't," Kuromiya said. "The CCG is scared. Their power is losing its grip, so they hold stunts like the incident on the bridge this morning to spread fear. They paint us with blood to make them cleaner by comparison. They don't want our support to grow, so they make terrorists out of us. We seek to overthrow their violence through spreading our word of peace and acceptance and equality for all. They fight back with nothing but savagery and bloodshed. They spread their propaganda, but we know what they hide, the weapons they make. They're prepared to gun us down without ever reaching out to us for parley. They're a dictatorship. The last of humanity deserves better. Together we will bring the humanity back to the human race."

Kuromiya offered out a hand.

Together we will bring humanity back to the human race. Those were the last words his father had spoken to him. Ret looked the man in the eyes. His brows were tight, and his eyes were fixed on him.

Could Ret's father have left him to follow this man?

If what Kuromiya said was true, he could change Caspian for the better. Ret was hesitant to believe him after what he'd seen today, but a part of him was hopeful.

He grasped Kuromiya's hand.

"I won't fight," Ret said. "I won't kill."

"I wouldn't have it any other way," Kuromiya said, a wide smile spreading over his face. "What's your name?"

"Ret Saiden."

"Nice to have you, Ret-san," he said.

Ret nodded, not knowing what else to do.

Kuromiya turned to face his comrades. "Come, we must get a safe distance away from here. No fighting today."

There were a few disgruntled grumblings, but the majority looked pleased.

"I guess I've joined the Resurgence," Ret said.

"I can confirm that you have," Cell said.

As Kuromiya spoke with those around him, he held their full attention, and they looked to him with a kind of grand reverence.

"He certainly has a way with words," Ret said.

"Words have no power to impress the mind without the exquisite horror of their reality."

Silence.

"Please stop with the quotes."

"I think I'm getting good at this."

###

BOOKS BY CASTRUM PRESS

SCIENCE FICTION & FANTASY SERIES

The Saiph Series by PP Corcoran

The K'Tai War Series by PP Corcoran

The Formist Series by Mathew Williams

The Deep Wide Black Series by JCH Rigby

The Feral Space Series by James Worrad

Arc of the Sky Series by LMR Clarke

ANTHOLOGIES

The Empire at War: British Military Science Fiction

Future Days Anthology

Alien Days Anthology

More at: www.castrumpress.com/scifi-fantasy-books

Printed in Great Britain
by Amazon

16208505R00192